Milly Johnson is a joke-writer, greetings card creator, newspaper columnist, after-dinner speaker, poet, winner of *Come Dine with Me*, *Sunday Times* Top Ten author and recipient of the RNA's Romantic Comedy Award of 2014.

She is half-Yorkshire, half-Glaswegian and is proud patron of two fabulous charities: www.yorkshirecatrescue.org and thewellatthecore.co.uk, which is a complementary therapy centre for cancer patients.

She likes cruising on big ships, Sciolti chocolates and Peller's Cuvée Ice Wine. She does not like marzipan or lamb chops.

She lives happily in Barnsley with her two massive lads, Teddy the dog and two very spoilt cats. Her mam and dad live in t'next street.

The Teashop on the Corner is her tenth book.

Find out more at www.millyjohnson.co.uk or follow Milly on Twitter @millyjohnson

Also by Milly Johnson

The Yorkshire Pudding Club
The Birds & the Bees
A Spring Affair
A Summer Fling
Here Come the Girls
An Autumn Crush
White Wedding
A Winter Flame
It's Raining Men

The Teashop on the Corner

milly johnson

**SIMON &
SCHUSTER**

London · New York · Sydney · Toronto · New Delhi

A CBS COMPANY

First published by Simon & Schuster UK Ltd 2014
A CBS COMPANY

1 3 5 7 9 10 8 6 4 2

Simon & Schuster UK Ltd
1st Floor
222 Gray's Inn Road
London WC1X 8HB

www.simonandschuster.co.uk

Simon & Schuster Australia, Sydney
Simon & Schuster India, New Delhi

A CIP catalogue record for this book
is available from the British Library

Export TPB ISBN: 978-1-47111-463-2
PB ISBN: 978-1-47111-464-9
EBOOK ISBN: 978-1-47111-465-6

Typeset by M Rules
Printed and bound by CPI Group (UK) Ltd, Croydon, CR0 4YY

This book is dedicated to the lovely Molly Clemit
who died 15 March 2014.
May she find heaven full of books,
friendly cats and teashops xxx

The Teashop on the Corner

Things will always get better.
After all, when you've hit rock bottom,
there's nowhere to go but up.

ANON

Chapter 1

'Man, cl-that is born of a woman, hath-cl but a short time to live, and is-cl full of misery. He cometh up, and is cl-cut down, like a flower; he fleeth-cl as it were a cl-shadow, and never continueth in one cl-stay.' The Reverend Duckworth relished the grave drama of his monologue as he sprayed the principal mourners on the front row with a light shower of saliva.

Behind Carla, her eighty-three-year-old neighbour Mavis Marple muttered under her breath to whoever was sitting next to her. 'He sounds like Louie Spence.'

Mavis Marple didn't do discreet very well. Still, she did love a good funeral, and a wedding. She'd attend anyone's in the hope of getting invited to the post-event buffet.

'They should have umbrellas on the front row.'

'Shhh,' someone else attempted to whisper, although the angry-python hiss echoed just as loudly around the church.

'Well he does,' went on Mavis. 'All those *cl-sth* sounds.'

'Thou knowest-cl, Lord, the cl-secrets of our hearts-cl,' the Reverend Duckworth went on, raising his left hand heavenward in a grand sweep. In his own head he was Laurence Olivier holding up Yorick's skull.

But the words were mere white noise to Carla, whose sad

dark brown eyes were fixed on the coffin behind him. She couldn't believe that Martin, her husband of ten years, was in there. In a wide wooden box. She had the mad urge to run up to it and prise off the lid with her fingernails to see him again, just one last time, to touch his face and tell him that she loved him. He had been torn from her too quickly. One minute he was eating a pork pie and mint sauce in the kitchen, the next he was dead on the garage floor. She wanted to see in his eyes that he knew how much she loved him and how much of a hole he had left in her heart.

'Arshes to arshes, dust to dust.'

'Did he just say "arses to arses"?' Mavis Marple asked no one in particular and set off a ripple of involuntary giggling. Carla wasn't angry though. Funerals were a powder keg of pressure. Had she been watching all this on a sitcom, she would probably have giggled too. The pantomime effect wasn't lost on her: old Reverend Duckworth in his thick brown wig attempting a National Theatre delivery, doing his best to enunciate all those elusive pure 's' sounds. But this wasn't a sitcom, it was real life. This time last week she had been a loving wife to Martin, washing his socks, waiting for him to come home to her on Friday nights after a hard week working all around the country; and now she was a widow, holding a fat red rose that she would place on his coffin which would soon be incinerated with him in a giant oven.

Someone's stomach made a loud gurgling noise as if water was rushing down a plughole.

'Sorry,' said the stomach's owner.

At the back of the church the huge heavy door creaked open and banged shut again, making a sound that wouldn't have been out of place on a Hammer Horror film. Pronounced tappy footsteps followed. Carla sensed people shifting in their seats to turn and see who the latecomer was, but she didn't join them. It couldn't be anyone important. There was no one here who meant anything much to Martin. There were a few neighbours, including Mavis Marple, who might have been inappropriately loud, but was also a good woman and kindness itself. There was Martin's cousin Andrew over from Bridlington, whom they hadn't set eyes on since their wedding; a few people that Carla didn't recognise, some probably men from the local club where Martin used periodically to play darts; and someone who looked suspiciously like a tramp who had come in for the warmth. Martin didn't have friends and there was no one from his workplace, at which Carla's disappointment edged towards disgust. Her husband had given Suggs Office Equipment a lot of hard-working years and yet when Carla rang them up to inform them of his passing, the woman on the switchboard didn't even seem to have recognised his name. She'd said she'd email the head of sales, and took Carla's number, but no one rang her back.

Carla mouthed a silent message to her friend Theresa. *Oh, I wish you were here.* Theresa was in New Zealand with her husband Jonty, visiting their son. How could she have rung them with her news and spoilt their holiday? Even though a little part of her wanted to spoil it, wanted to smash up their holiday with a hammer because she suspected they were going on a fact-finding mission, to learn if they could live over there. Their daughter-in-law was pregnant with her first child, in a part of the country that had all-year sunshine, so who could blame them? Selfish as it made her, Carla wished she could teleport her friend over to sit at her side today, instead of Andrew and his overpowering odour of sweaty feet.

Forty-eight was no age at all to die. Carla and Martin had been robbed of many happy years together. Carla had been saving up to take him on a cruise for his fiftieth birthday, at least until she'd been made redundant last month. It was so unfair. Martin had worked too hard – all that driving every day, constant stress to sell to clients and meet targets – no wonder he'd had a massive heart attack. Carla dabbed at her tears with her black gloves. Her foundation stained the material. She didn't care. She didn't care about the swish of whispers that was rising behind her like a tidal wave. She didn't care about anything at that moment in time. Martin had gone out to the garage alive and well to carry in the dressing table which Carla had finished stripping down and hand-painting. *Wait for me, it's too heavy,* Carla had called after him. *Just let me finish basting this chicken.* But he hadn't waited. He had lifted it single-handedly then collapsed and died on the spot. Their marriage, snuffed out, just like the candle on a birthday cake.

'The Lord bless-cl Martin Pride, the Lord maketh-cl his face to cl-shine upon him and give him peace-cl. Amen.'

There was an echoed chorus of Amens.

'I now invite Carla to lead you to cl-say your goodbyes-cl to Martin before he leaves-cl us to join his Lord in eternal peace-cl,' said the Reverend Duckworth, holding out his arm towards her to head up the final acknowledgement.

Carla pulled herself wearily up from the pew. She was totally distraught and felt twice as old as her thirty-four years. She was clinging on to her long-stemmed red rose as if it was the only thing keeping her on her feet. She walked slowly over to the coffin and laid the rose gently on top of it.

'Goodbye, Martin. Goodbye, my love.'

Then it all happened so quickly. Before anyone else could stand, a tall, grim-faced woman in a black coat and high red heels flounced forwards, picked up Carla's rose, threw it on the floor and placed her own red rose on the coffin instead. It had a head the size of a football. There was a churchful of gasps as Carla turned to her with shocked confusion and both women locked eyes.

'What do you think you're doing? Who are you?' Carla asked.

'I'm Martin's wife,' the woman in the red shoes replied. 'Or should I say "widow" now.'

Chapter 2

'Mrs Williams, I am on my knees. Just one more week, please. I am begging you.'

Will Linton was indeed on his knees as he pleaded with Mrs Cecilia Williams from the West Yorkshire Bank. He was desperately playing for time, even though he suspected an extra week wouldn't make a blind bit of difference. He had exhausted every avenue which might have saved his company from closing and his workforce from the dole. The bank had been more than fair, really. They'd given him two extensions already and no miracle had occurred to save him, however hard he had prayed for one. His accountant had warned him that they wouldn't listen and it was time to give up and throw in the towel, but Will felt duty-bound to try to give it everything he had.

'I'm sorry, Mr Linton,' said Mrs Williams, her voice firm but not unkind. 'We can't.'

She was probably a good woman who was nice to animals, a mother, a wife, a convivial host at dinner parties, but at work her job was to know when to say, 'No. It's the end.'

Will opened his mouth to remonstrate, but he knew it was over. He could hear faint strains of Simon and Garfunkel in the back of his mind. *Cecilia, you're breaking my heart*. This Cecilia had also broken his balls. But he didn't blame her – the fault was entirely his.

The massive Phillips and Son Developments had gone into receivership and in turn had taken down Yorkshire Stone Homes who, in turn, had taken down Linton Roofing, whose director had been idiot enough to put all his eggs in the Yorkshire Stone Homes basket. A chain of businesses had toppled like dominos, but this was no innocent child's game. Men were going to be out of work – good men with families and mortgages. He'd intended to retire in ten years max, when he was forty-eight. Throwing his all in with Yorkshire Stone Homes should have set Will up for life. It was a no-brainer whether or not to trust them – they had been a rock solid and highly profitable business for over fifty years. Oh, the irony.

'Thank you, Mrs Williams, for all you've done. I appreciate it,' he said, his throat as dry as one of the bags of cement in his builders' yard.

'I'm sorry,' she said again, and sounded it. 'I'll send you a letter confirming our conversation and advising of the next steps to be taken.'

He didn't say any more before putting the phone back on the cradle. He didn't know what those next steps would consist of. He couldn't handle even thinking about them just yet. He had a big wall inside his head, holding back the questions, the fears, the confusion, the shame. It was going to crumble at any moment, but until it did, he would savour the blankness.

He heard the front door open and close and smelt his wife Nicole before he saw her as she swept in on a wave of her perfume, something sickly and sweet and reminiscent of chocolate limes, which she used as liberally as if she were crop-spraying. He hated that smell, not that he had ever told her that.

She had shopping bags in her hands, of course. He wouldn't have recognised her had she not had bags in her hands. And all the bags had names on them: Biba, Karen Millen, Chanel. Actually, he didn't recognise her at all for a moment – the last time he had seen her she'd had short blonde hair, now she looked like bleedin' Rapunzel.

'So, what did they say?' she asked. There was no softness in her voice. 'I'm gathering by you kneeling on the floor that it isn't good news.'

Nicole had dropped the bags now and was standing with her arms crossed, her artificially inflated lips attempting to pucker.

'It's the end,' he said, turning his face towards her. He wanted her to stride up to him, put her arms around him, tell him that it was all right and they'd weather it. Instead she said, 'Fuck.' And looked furious.

'We've lost the lot, love.' He shrugged and gave a humour-less dry chuckle.

Nicole's head jerked. 'Don't "love" me.'

She'd had hair extensions put in and had been in the hairdressers' all day. It was two hundred pounds a pop to have a squirt of shampoo at Mr Corleone's in Sheffield – especially as Nicole always had the head stylist, the don himself: so with that in mind, what had those extensions cost? And God knows how much she'd spent shopping. Then again, daddy cleared her Visa bill every month. She was a married woman of thirty-two and yet daddy still gave her pocket money, although Nicole didn't know that Will knew that.

'I'll get it back. Everything,' said Will. 'I might have lost it now, but I'll bounce back stronger than ever. If I let them take the lot – the house, the car, the company, clear the accounts, I can avoid bankruptcy. I can start again.'

Nicole didn't say a thing in response. She just flicked her

new hair over her shoulder. The irony didn't bypass Will that at least one of them had been successful in getting some extensions today.

'You'll be living in a mansion this time next year,' he said, trying to coax a smile out of her. 'It'll make this place look like a pig-sty.'

Her expression didn't falter.

'It's the end of Linton Roofing. There's nothing I can do.'

'Don't be ridiculous. There has to be something.'

Ridiculous? She didn't know the meaning of the word. He couldn't remember the last time he had slept properly, without waking up in a sweat of panic. Or eaten a meal that he didn't want to throw up again. His anxiety levels were off the scale: he'd lost two stone in weight, he got dizzy if he climbed past the fifth rung of a ladder, and yet his darling missus was always out sitting under a dryer, shopping in House of bloody Fraser, having someone put false nails on the tips of her fingers or being wrapped in seaweed as if she hadn't a care in the world. That was ridiculous.

'I've tried everything, darling,' he said, which was a slight lie, as there was one thing he hadn't attempted and that was asking Nicole's father for a loan. But his pride was saved from going down that route because he knew that Barnaby Whitlaw would have burnt his money note by note in a barbecue before he lent it to a nouveau-riche vulgar type like his son-in-law.

'I'll get it all back, love, I promise,' he said again.

Nicole didn't gratify him with a reply. She merely snatched up her carrier bags and teetered upstairs to her dressing room on her red-soled Christian Louboutins.

Chapter 3

The Reverend Duckworth closed the vestry door behind him, leaving the two women in there as he went back into the church to ask the congregation to bear with them. In his forty years as a reverend, he had come across some bizarre things; but this was a first, even for him. He'd had ex-partners burst in on weddings intent on revenge, even a scrap at a christening over the alleged paternity of a child, but never a double wife showdown at a funeral.

Inside the vestry, Carla could only think: 'People will be waiting for the buffet.' Her mind could deal with that sort of problem. It couldn't deal with this woman standing in front of her with her big black buttoned-up swing coat and her enormous brimmed hat. She was older than Carla, she guessed, by about ten years, and her clothes would have cost Carla six months' wages at least; but they did little to disguise a brassiness that manifested itself in the woman's hard face and her fag-ravaged voice.

'I'm gathering you didn't know anything about me then,' the woman said, pulling off her black shiny gloves one long finger at a time, a ladylike, delicate gesture which contrasted with her aggressive cocky stance.

Carla opened her mouth to say that no, she hadn't a clue,

but nothing came out. She wanted to cry but her eyes were as dry as her throat, tears frozen by shock.

'Allow me to introduce myself then. I'm Julie. Julie Pride. And I have been for thirty years. Mrs Martin Pride, to be exact.'

Carla's legs started to tremble as if someone had replaced her usually sturdy pins with Bambi's new-born fawn ones. She let herself fall onto a chair next to the large rectangular wooden table that formed the centrepiece of the room. Could this day become any more of a pantomime? Was Widow Twanky going to turn up in a minute and join the two Widow Prides?

'I don't understand any of this,' said Carla. She wasn't so much gobsmacked as felled. 'You can't be married to Martin. I would have known. I've been married to him—' she stalled momentarily, to remember the church ceremony in which she had married him in a white dress in front of the very altar where his coffin now stood. A legal ceremony, with all the 'i's dotted and the 't's crossed: register signed, vows recited, no just impediments exposed . . . She took a deep breath and continued, '—married to him for ten years.'

'No you haven't,' snapped Julie, rolling up the gloves and stuffing them in the stiff black handbag she was carrying. It had a flashy gold double-C Chanel logo on the front. 'You only think you have. We split up soon after we were married; but we never divorced. Didn't have the money at the time, then I suppose we both just forgot.'

Forgot? thought Carla. You forgot to post a letter, you forgot to buy milk at the shop – you didn't *forget to divorce*.

'I know what you're thinking,' sniffed Julie, snapping the clasp shut on her bag. 'Forgetting to divorce is an odd one. I don't think either of us could be arsed, if I'm being honest. He slipped from my mind until I saw him a year ago in Leeds. Could have knocked me down with a feather. It was like a thunderbolt hitting us both from above. You read about these things happening in women's mags, but you never believe they could happen to you. Until it did. We went for a coffee and found the old spark reignited. Who would have thought?' And she laughed to herself as if the memory had tickled her.

Carla shook her head. Was she hearing all this correctly? Her husband had been carrying on with another woman . . . *his real wife* . . . for a year behind her back? When the hell did he have the time? Or the ability? He'd puffed when he got the milk out of the fridge.

'I don't understand,' said Carla, her head full of so many questions that were going to burst out of her eardrums any minute, fly across the room and shatter the stained glass window picture of Jesus having his feet washed. 'When did he see you?'

'He spent every weekday with me, of course,' said Julie, patting the back of her heavily lacquered yellow hair. 'I was frankly glad to have a rest at the weekends.'

'A rest?'

'From the sex.'

'The sex?'

Carla was totally bewildered now. They could not be talking about the same man. Martin was always too tired. She could count on the fingers of one hand, minus the thumb, the number of times that she and Martin had had sex in the last year or so.

'I'm not daft,' said Julie, inspecting her tart-red nail varnish. 'He promised me he wouldn't have sex with you after we became a couple again but I know what he was like. Very healthy appetite in that area, so I promised myself I wouldn't get upset about it. He was a bloke with needs after all.' She pulled her lips back from her teeth and Carla saw how white and perfect they were. Thousands of pounds worth of cosmetic dentistry of which any Osmond would have been proud.

'Are you sure you have the right Martin Pride?' said Carla. 'I don't recognise this man you're talking about.'

'Martin Ronald Pride. Birthday: thirteenth of January.'

'Works as a sales rep for—'

'He didn't work,' Julie interrupted. 'At least he didn't after the lottery win.'

Carla's brain went into spasm. 'Wha-at?'

Julie's black-tattooed eyebrows rose and a slow smirk spread across her lips. 'Oh, he didn't tell you about that either?'

Carla's head fell into her hands. She was surprised she had a head left as it felt in danger of exploding at any moment.

'Me and Martin won just short of a million on the lottery nine months ago,' said Julie with smarmy satisfaction. 'He told Suggs to stick their job up their arse on the same day.' Her eyes narrowed. 'Don't get any ideas. It's all in my name.'

Carla's head snapped up.

'But he went off to work every Monday and rang me every night from a hotel.'

Julie laughed. 'He might have left you on a Monday morning, love, but he certainly didn't ring you from any hotel.'

Carla covered her eyes with her hands to shut out the light, shut out everything around her whilst she tried to make sense of this. Martin wasn't that duplicitous. Living that sort of double life took a level of cunning and cleverness that Martin couldn't have aspired to: he was far too simple a creature. Every Monday morning, Martin had set off with his suitcase of cleaned and pressed clothes for the week. Every night he rang from Exeter or Aberdeen or wherever Suggs had sent him to sell paper. Every night he said the hotel was okay, nothing brilliant, but he was going to get something to eat and then have a good night's sleep. She'd never questioned it, she'd never had grounds to. And every Friday, when he got home, he'd given her a measly sum of housekeeping money. There was never anything left over to bank. There was a freeze on wage increases, he'd said. And all the time he'd been sitting on his share of a million pounds?

Naw. She didn't believe it. Martin would have gone out and bought himself the new iPhone if he'd had any money at all, that much she did know. She'd found his mobile in his pocket after his death and it was one which cost him ten pounds from Asda. There were few contacts on it when she'd checked it: Domino's Pizzas, The Happy Duck Chinese takeaway, Andrew, work, herself, but no record of Julie, nor any texts.

'Obviously, I'll give you some time to get your things together before you leave the house. You can have the furniture,' said Julie. 'A month okay with you?'

'What?' said Carla.

'The house. Obviously it's mine now.'

'My house is yours?' Now it was Carla's turn to laugh, but Julie wasn't smiling. Her granite features were set in a very serious expression.

'Martin's house. It's in his name, I do believe. My husband's name.'

Martin's house was indeed in his sole name. He had inherited it from his mother the year that Carla had met him and they'd never bothered to change the name on the deeds, or write wills. After all, they had no children and what was his was hers as a married couple ... except that she was now finding out that it wasn't.

Then Julie said a sentence that made Carla's stomach lurch.

'That house is our son's rightful inheritance.'

Son. Our son.

'Do you have a child?' Carla stammered. 'With Martin?'

'What do you think this is – wind?' said Julie, flicking open the two buttons on her coat and sticking out a surprisingly prominent stomach. 'I'm five months gone. And yes he's Martin's. And they'll never see each other because of you and your fucking dressing table.'

Carla's Martin had said he didn't want children. And because she loved him, she had sacrificed her desire to be a parent for his wish not to be.

Through her tears, Carla could see that Julie was savouring each twist of the knife. It was sick, cruel.

'You're enjoying this aren't you? How can you? I didn't know any of it.'

Julie's small sharp eyes hardened.

'Because he should have died with me, not you. Because if he hadn't been heavy-lifting your tatty furniture, he wouldn't have had a fucking heart attack and left me. Because you arranged his funeral and not me. Because I had to find out about my husband's death from a story in yesterday's bleeding newspaper.' She opened her bag again, pulled out a page torn from the *Daily Trumpet* and proceeded to read it.

'"Paper salesman dies suddenly trying to shift wife's hand-painted furniture from garage into house". How's that for a snappy headline?'

Carla gasped. 'I didn't even know it was in the newspaper.'

'They reported the wrong funeral time and the wrong church. And they said that Martin was seventy-four. And that his grieving widow was called Karen. I've been ringing no end of churches and funeral parlours this morning trying to find out what's bloody happening.'

She wiped a tear that fell from the corner of her left eye and despite everything, Carla felt a too-kind surge of sympathy welling up within her for the older woman. If what she was saying was true then what a terrible shock she must have had too.

'Julie . . .'

Julie snarled at the pity in her voice and stabbed her finger at Carla. Her momentary lapse in composure was over. 'Don't you dare feel sorry for me. And don't you think you're going to take his ashes. They're mine. He was my husband and I fucking want them. Every single one of them.'

And with that, Julie Pride and her posh black handbag, her swingy coat and brazen red shoes clipped out of the vestry and boldly walked down the aisle. Carla listened to the sound diminishing, heard the heavy church door crash shut and then realised that her body didn't have a single clue how to react.

Chapter 4

As Shaun McCarthy drained the last of the coffee from his cup, he watched the woman with the spiky dark brown hair tip her watering can over the brightly coloured flowers sprouting from the boxes in front of the teashop windows and thought of the cover of an old Enid Blyton book he had once had, with an elf on it. That's what *she* reminded him of: a fragile little creature with wings hidden under her bright blue pinafore dress. He was too far away to hear, but he bet she was humming as she watered the plants. And smiling. She was always smiling, as if she had been born with a natural upturn to her lips. *Ms Leonora Merryman*. One of those infuriating people for whom life was filled with confetti, sparkles and fairies, no doubt. Her glass wasn't just constantly half-full but fizzed out coloured sprinkles as well. He suspected that despite being around the mid-thirties mark, she would have a collection of My Little Ponies in cabinets at home.

Still, it didn't matter. As long as she paid her rent for the shop on time, he'd be equally happy as she was, if not as outwardly smiley; and there was no reason other than business for their paths to cross. She was initially on a six month lease, although he had given her one month gratis in exchange for decorating the place, because she had wanted to do it herself and at her own expense. He suspected that she would terminate the lease at the end of the period rather than renew it. He'd hardly seen any customers in there since it opened a month ago and surely she needed footfall through the door to make a living? Any idiot knew that. Still, he'd been fair on the rent seeing as she was the first of the businesses in this quadrangle of shops to open up: Spring Hill Square. The second unit was finished – although the least said about that, the better – and they had now started on the third. The other four units weren't finished but there had been a few enquiries about them. He'd said no to the couple who wanted to open a sex shop. He was, after all, a good Irish Catholic boy with guilt and honour issues, as well as being a savvy businessman.

The Teashop on the Corner. 'It's a sort of literary café,' she had told him. No doubt Leonora (*'Oh do call me Leni'*) thought she was in Oxford or St Andrews, and the erudite and scholarly types would be queuing up at her door every morning demanding their skinny lattes. He wondered if he should be the one to inform her that they were actually in a small backwater outside Barnsley on land which had been a real shit tip until Shaun had bought it to turn into his empire. He'd had to demolish an old wire factory and level the ground, which had cost a small fortune; but he hoped it would be worth it, cashing in on the increased trade which passed by en route to Winterworld, a Christmas theme park only a few miles down the road.

Ms Merryman had had a lot of furniture delivered. He kept seeing the vans turning up and men carrying it in. He'd peered through the window a few times when she'd gone home. The walls were now delicate shades of cream and shell pink and around three edges of the room were runs of glass cabinets full, from what he could tell at first glance, of paper and pens and other items of stationery. The central space was taken up with six round tables, cream-painted iron-work, three with four heart-shaped-backed chairs around them. It was all very pretty and girly and French-chic. He gave it another two months before she did a moonlight flit and he turned up on site to find her and her fancy furniture all gone.

She was smiling. Again. He could see her lips curved upwards as she turned to one side. That sort of constant chirpiness irritated him. What the hell was there to be so cheerful about, anyway? Everyone he knew was complaining about it being the crappiest spring in history. Sub-zero temperatures without let-up ever since November, even snow on May Day Bank Holiday. Only now, in mid-May, was the sun attempting to blast through the clouds with its rays; but bright as its beams were, they were half chilly too.

Leni turned without warning and caught him staring at her. 'Mr McCarthy!' She waved. 'Hello there. Have you got a moment?'

Shaun cursed himself for not averting his eyes quickly enough. 'Sure,' he said, grumbling under his breath. He strode over to the pretty teashop and nodded a man-greet-ing.

'Good morning, Mr McCarthy. The square is really coming together now, isn't it?'

'Yes, it is,' he said, thinking, *Did she call me over just to ask me that*? He had neither the time nor the inclination for idle chit-chat.

'I hope you don't mind me mentioning that the tap in the teashop sink has a leak. It's just a small one but I don't want it to get any bigger.'

'I'll get my tool-bag and come back in a couple of minutes.'

'Thank you.'

The tearoom was invitingly warm and smelt delicious when he walked in.

'I've made a jug of vanilla hot chocolate. Would you like one?' Leni smiled at him.

Shaun hadn't had time to stop for lunch and was both hungry and thirsty in equal measures. 'Thank you,' he said.

'Cake?' She pointed to two glass domes on the counter. A dark brown cake sat under one, a lemon cake under the other. They looked good but he passed. He'd mend the leak and then get quickly off before she started talking girly things to him. Rainbows and teddy bears and how to make cupcakes.

She poured him a mug of chocolate with a swirl of cream on the top and stuck a flake in it.

'New recipe,' she said. 'For when all the crowds come.' Her eyes were sparkling with mirth.

He humphed inwardly.

'Do you think they will?'

'Of course,' she smiled. She had white, even teeth, he noticed. 'I've had someone in who has been back three times so far for lunch. A Sikh gentleman. He's bought two pens from me as well.'

Wow, you're just months away from retiring on the profits, thought Shaun, digging his wrench out of his bag whilst taking a swig of chocolate. The cup had a large ginger cat on it.

'*Miaow.*'

For a moment, Shaun thought the cup had made the noise.

'Now Mr Bingley, you get back to your bed and stop being nosey,' said Leni, bending down to a huge ginger cat who had wandered over and was sniffing around Shaun's bag. She lifted him up, turned him around and he toddled off to where he had come from.

'Are you allowed that thing in a café?' asked Shaun, wrinkling up his nose.

'I don't know,' said Leni. 'But he's staying. Chocolate okay?'

'Er, yeah,' said Shaun. Environmental health would be swooping down on her very soon, he reckoned. Surely cats and cafés didn't mix?

'Is it too thick? Does it need more milk in it, do you think?'

Dear God, thought Shaun. It was a cup of hot chocolate, not an entrant for *Masterchef*.

'It's fine,' he said, tinkering with the tap. He noticed her apron was patterned with covers of old Penguin books but the pocket at the front was an orange sleeping cat. *She's added that herself*, he thought. *And made a good job of it*. She looked the arts and crafty type. He could imagine her making her own rugs at night in a house full of shelves of books.

Shaun liked books and read a lot at home in the quiet evenings. He didn't like cats particularly, but then he had never had much contact with pets. He didn't do emotional ties.

'What happens to the cakes that you don't sell?' he asked, bending to check the cupboard underneath the sink for leaks.

'I drop them off at the homeless shelter,' replied Leni. 'But soon there won't be any left to take. I have every confidence this little place will be booming. Anyway, selling tea is just my folly. The shop is the real business of course.'

And that's just as heaving, Shaun muttered to himself.

'Most of my orders come from the internet,' Leni expanded, as if hearing his thoughts. 'I'm very busy ordering and packing up what I've sold during the day when the teashop is empty. So you don't need to worry about your rent, Mr McCarthy.'

And she laughed and he thought that the sound it made was like that of a tinkly bell.

'There, it's done,' he said, throwing the wrench back into his bag. He drained the cup of the last dregs of chocolate. It tasted like melted-down biscuits and would keep him going for another hour or so before he stopped for a sandwich. He could have done with another, if the truth be told. He had no doubt that if he asked for a fill-up, she would have obliged – with another smile – but that would mean more small talk and Shaun McCarthy wasn't in the mood.

'Thank you,' said Leni Merryman. 'Do I owe you any-thing?'

'No,' he said, waving the suggestion away. 'All in with the rent.'

'Well, you know where I am if you want to give me some custom,' Leni tilted her head as she spoke.

'I'm not a visiting-coffee-shops sort of person,' said Shaun. 'Too busy. I only build them.'

She chuckled as if his gruffness amused her. 'Well, thank you anyway.'

Shaun lifted up his bag and walked back through the teashop. It was a shame it was always empty of customers because she'd done it up really well. He dragged his eyes along the glass cabinets as he passed them. They were filled with gifts – quality gifts – cufflinks made from old type-writer keys, tiny silver charms in the shape of books, gift tags made from book pages: romantic books, he presumed, seeing as the word 'Darcy' was ringed in red. All quirky, fancy things that literary types would go gaga over – himself excepted, of course. He might enjoy reading books, but he had no use for a tie-pin silhouette of Edgar Allan Poe.

Between the last cabinet and the door was a long

pinboard studded with postcards sent from all over. He spotted one from Madrid, one from Kos and one from Lisbon.

'What's your online shop called?' he asked.

'Book Things. Nice and simple. You have a lovely accent, Mr McCarthy. Is it Northern or Southern Irish?'

'Northern,' said Shaun.

'My daughter Anne was born in Cork,' said Leni. 'She wasn't due for another two—'

Shaun's small-talk alarm went off. Time to go.

'Thanks for the chocolate,' he said, taking hold of the door handle. 'Must get on and earn a living.'

'Of course,' said Leni with an understanding nod. 'Busy lives.'

Busy lives indeed, thought Shaun. He liked his busy life. He liked filling his head with his work and his business and his books at the end of the day that stopped him thinking about his years in Belfast and his earlier days in Londonderry which still haunted him, thirty-four years on.

Leni bent down at the side of the ginger cat curled up in his basket.

'Oh Mr Bingley,' she said, giving him a rub behind his ear which set him off purring. 'I wish Anne were here to see this. She'd love it here, wouldn't she? She *will* love it, won't she?'

Chapter 5

After Julie had left, Carla had sat in the vestry like an animal which had been stunned before being slaughtered. She was shivering but it was only partly because of the cold, still air of the room. Her body was in shock down to the bones and was vibrating to drum up some heat and comfort. It wasn't working. She couldn't remember hearing the door open and the Reverend Duckworth entering. Not until he covered her shoulders with a throw did she become aware of his presence. It was heavy and velvet: maybe one of his vestments. She sat there for a few minutes, absorbing the warmth it afforded.

'Cl-Shall I direct people onwards?' he asked softly. 'The cl-Ship next door I do believe?'

'It's fine,' said Carla, surprising herself by standing because she didn't think she still had a spine. It felt as if it had been ripped out of her. 'I'll do it.'

The Reverend Duckworth squeezed her hand and she felt him willing her strength. He was a nice man. A kind man.

She pulled in a long lungful of the chilled vestry air, let go of the warm hand lending support to hers and pushed the material from her shoulders. She strolled out into the church, forcing a smile onto her lips, unstable as it was, and addressed the pews of mourners more slowly and calmly than she would have thought possible.

'I apologise for the disturbance to the ceremony. Please make your way to the Ship next door where refreshments will be waiting for you.' She focused her eyes on Andrew. 'I know some of you have travelled a long way so please, join me.'

People rose and started to file out, whispering to each other, the subject matter obvious. Carla couldn't blame them. She would have been the same had she been out there observing all this. She wondered how many of them would ask her what was going on, how many times she would have to tell the same story. She couldn't do it. She didn't want to be put on the spot.

'Wait!' she shouted on impulse. Everyone turned to her and she momentarily lost her nerve. She didn't so much forget what she was going to say, because she hadn't planned anything. She opened her mouth and let the words make their own exit in whatever order they happened to come out.

'You'll all be wondering what that was ... what happened. It appears that Martin had another wife. That is as much as I know, so please don't ask me for details because I don't have any.'

The church was filled with gasps.

'Please, today, let's just say goodbye to the Martin we all knew and ... loved.' She stumbled over the word. It had been true until half an hour ago.

She hoped that would stop any questions. Fat chance. Five seconds later, Andrew was at her side.

'What do you mean he had another wife?'

'Well, he had another wife,' said Carla, shrugging her shoulders. 'That woman in the red shoes apparently was

Julie. His first wife. The one he never divorced, as I found out today. That makes *me* the "other wife", I suppose.'

'That was Julie?' Andrew pointed towards the back of the church, as if she was still there, hiding behind the large arched door. 'Blimey, she's changed. She was a great big fat lass the last time I saw her. Long brown hair. Teeth like an abandoned graveyard.'

Carla suddenly felt full of anger and frustration which needed to be vented. In the absence of Martin she turned to the nearest thing she had to him – his cousin.

'Why did no one ever mention her to me? I didn't know he'd been married before,' she snapped, her voice carrying more wobble than aggression.

Andrew shook his head and his great jowls flapped.

'They were just kids. They were met, married and separated within a year. I'd forgotten all about her if I'm honest. Still, I would have thought Martin should have mentioned it.' He raked his fingers through the little hair he had left. 'And you say they never divorced?'

'No.'

'How does that leave you?'

Carla sighed. 'Up a certain brown smelly creek without a paddle, I imagine.'

'I can't believe it,' he said. 'I honestly didn't know he hadn't divorced her. Who gets married to a second woman when you're not divorced from the first one?'

I can't blame Andrew, thought Carla. It wasn't a subject that would normally have raised its head when you mainly kept in touch via the medium of Christmas cards. Martin hadn't really liked Andrew all that much. Then again, Martin hadn't really liked anyone that much. He'd taken being anti-social to an art form.

'I need a large drink,' Andrew said, taking hold of Carla's arm. 'I suspect you do as well.'

And he led her out to the Ship, where Carla endured all the 'sorry for your losses' she was offered, attempted to ignore all the gossip happening around her and tried her best to get through the next hour without throwing herself on the carpet and screaming out her pain.

Chapter 6

'Honestly, Molly, this house is far too big for you to manage. Gram and I do worry about you.'

Molly's daughter-in-law, blonde, buxom Sherry Beardsall, angled the teapot over Molly's cup, topping it up to full, whilst launching into what had become, over the past weeks, an all-too-familiar speech. 'I mean, what do you really need with three bedrooms?'

And Molly answered as she always did, with a timid smile. 'Well, it's not really all that big.'

Molly wasn't half as daft as Sherry thought she was. She wasn't taken in by the mask of concern that Sherry wore over her heavily powdered face because this conversation *always* steered towards the words 'Autumn Grange', just as surely as if it had been a destination programmed into a sat-nav.

The house *was* too big for Molly, although it wasn't a fraction as large as her sister's next door. Margaret lived in a very old, grand house with six bedrooms and a small lake in the grounds. Her husband Bernard had inherited The Lakehouse from his parents and it was he who'd had Willowfell built for Molly on their land many years ago. Houses in the village of Higher Hoppleton commanded a greater price with every passing year. Molly's house, with no mortgage on it, was worth a ridiculously pretty penny and her son Graham and his wife Sherry were in an unobstructed line to inherit it.

'Here, have a slice of cake.' Sherry cut them both a piece of sponge. 'I won't give you too much to start with,' she simpered, handing Molly a slice which was half the size of her own. Sherry shoved the cake into her mouth and devoured it in two bites. Cream and icing sugar stuck to her red lipstick and when she dabbed it away with her serviette, the colour strayed over her lip-line. She looked like she had blood, rather than make-up, on her mouth.

Molly nibbled delicately at hers, not really wanting to eat cake, and certainly not with Sherry, who had begun these Tuesday morning visits a few weeks ago out of the blue. The attention she paid to her mother-in-law had gone from nought to sixty and Molly knew there had to be a reason for it. She doubted it was money because Graham had his own business; he and his wife both had flash cars and a new-build double-fronted house painted monstrous pink and yellow. But whatever Sherry wanted from her, it hadn't raised its head properly yet; it remained shrouded in gifts of cake, small talk and subtle mentions of Autumn Grange.

Sherry usually started by alluding to how Molly was getting on a bit and how worried Gram and she were that she was coping okay.

Graham, although Sherry always called him Gram, obviously wasn't *that* concerned because he seldom visited; only when he had to, at Christmas, birthdays and Mother's Day – unless they happened to be on holiday in their Greek villa. He left all the social stuff to his wife, a woman named, by no coincidence, after a drink that was sickly-sweet and best encountered in small quantities once a year at Christmas.

'I mean you've still got a bedroom reserved for Gram and he isn't likely to sleep in there again,' chuckled Sherry.

'No,' replied Molly with a sigh of resignation. She didn't want him sleeping in it either, if the truth be told. She wanted her little Graham, her baby in there. The one she had had before his father had moulded him into his own mini-me. She wanted to reach back into the past and take her baby boy and run, run with him so that Edwin couldn't ever find them.

'It's far too big a house for one person. Gram and I do worry that the housework will get on top of you. And that you don't have a turn on the stairs . . .'

Sherry was still going on, still trying to convince Molly that she was an eighty-eight-year-old invalid reliant on incontinence pads and mashed foods instead of a sixty-eight-year-old competent woman. Why would she need sheltered housing at her age? She was perfectly capable of negotiating a staircase and pressing a button on a washing machine. Physically she was fine; mentally – well, her memory was starting to fail a little. She'd had a few incidents recently of forgetting where she had put things. She'd misplaced her silver compact which was usually in her handbag and an antique gold pen which she had bought herself as a fiftieth birthday present. And harder to explain, she had lost a small Royal Doulton figurine of a lady. It was a rare one too, an early one. She had thought it was safe on a shelf in the second bedroom with five other collectable figures. But it wasn't there any more. It had been a present from Harvey, her second husband. The man whose wedding ring she had ripped off her finger when she found out about his affair. And he'd had the cheek to take the ring with him when he left.

She hadn't mentioned to Margaret that Sherry had been visiting every week because her sister would have marched right up to her daughter-in-law and asked what her game was. Margaret didn't trust Sherry or Graham as far as she could have thrown them – and that wouldn't have been very far with their combined weight of over fifty stone. Margaret could smell a rat before its parents had even conceived it. And Margaret was fiercely protective of her sister.

In the womb, Margaret had taken the lion's share of any bravery on offer, leaving her twin with crumbs of it. Margaret didn't like Sherry and she liked her nephew even less and stuck in the middle, Molly didn't want to stoke any more fires of dislike between them. She loved Margaret and it hurt her that she had no time for Graham – and that the feeling was whole-heartedly reciprocated.

'Gram and I drove past a lovely house yesterday,' said Sherry, casually, sweetly. 'I said to Gram, "Isn't that a beautiful building?" An old mansion. I couldn't believe it when Gram said it was Autumn Grange. I never realised it was so beautiful. I'd love to show it to you.'

Here we go, today's mention of Autumn Grange, thought Molly. She sipped her tea with her eyes down. She didn't need to go and visit Autumn Grange – she knew it already. It was the old Woolstock mansion on the edge of Ketherwood which had been converted half into sheltered housing flats, half into an old people's home. Ketherwood was the least desirable location in the area, dominated by a sprawling depressed sink estate. Not even Alsatians ventured out alone in Ketherwood. Molly, Margaret and Bernard had visited an old friend in there a few months ago. It had been a grand old building in its time and though the façade remained impressive, inside it was shabby and tired, with a pervading air of school dinners that had lingered in their nostrils long after they had left.

'I don't think I'll bother,' said Molly, noticing Sherry's top lip tighten slightly. 'I'm not one for looking at old buildings.'

'I'll just go to the toilet, if I may,' said Sherry, taking two attempts to rock to her feet. She was a thick-waisted woman with an enormous bust that would have permanently tipped her forward had her backside not given her some ballast. Still, she had been a good wife to Gram . . . *Graham*, a great support to him. And, best of all, Graham seemed to love her, really adore her. Once upon a time, Molly had feared he wasn't capable of love. He had always found it so hard to form attachments. At school he had no real friends, and he'd been a loner at college. Molly had wanted to believe that it was because he was so very bright, and the super-intelligent sorts often had a problem socially, didn't they? But deep down, though she fought against admitting it to herself, she knew it was because Graham Edwin Beardsall was inherently unlikeable.

Molly heard the tell-tale creak of the third bedroom floor upstairs, the one where she kept her computer and all her paperwork locked away in her desk. She'd lived in the house long enough to recognise every groan and whisper the wood made. Was Sherry in there and if so what was she doing? She wished Margaret were here. Margaret had the effect of citronella on flies where Sherry was concerned.

As if by blessed magic, Margaret's head poked around the door. 'Only me, darling. Is the kettle on?'

'It's always on for you.' Molly leapt up from her seat to get out a cup for her twin sister. They had been identical in looks until their early teens when Molly lost weight and Margaret found it and suited it, so it stayed. Molly had remained dainty and thin – too thin, Margaret told her often, and bossed her into clearing her plate whenever they ate together. Personality-wise, Margaret had always been bossier, bolshier and more confident. Those qualities had propelled her career forwards to the top of the nursing tree, whilst Molly's gentler, less ambitious nature had served her well as a doctor's receptionist in the small local village practice.

The other way in which they differed was Margaret's secret *gift*. Although it had been more of a curse to her.

Margaret wafted the air in front of her nose. 'What is that smell?'

It was Sherry's perfume. Cloying and thick, it welded itself to the insides of nasal passages. The army could have used it as a replacement for CS gas.

Margaret noted the large, gaudy leopardskin handbag and paired it to the smell pervading the room. There was only one person she knew who might carry around a bag like that. Barnsley's answer to Bet Lynch with a thyroid problem.

'Not alone, I see.'

'Sherry's upstairs.'

On cue, the toilet flushed and Molly thought she must have been mistaken about the bedroom. Sherry was in the bathroom after all.

'Sounds like a herd of elephants,' said Margaret, as Sherry's leaden footsteps began to descend the staircase. 'I'm presuming the diet hasn't worked.'

Molly held a finger to her lips. 'Behave,' she warned.

'Fee fi fo fum . . .' said Margaret, mischievously, winking at her reproving sister.

'Oh, hello Margaret,' said Sherry, re-entering the room. 'What a pleasant surprise.'

I'll bet, thought the twins in mental unison.

'Hello, Sherry,' smiled Margaret. Molly knew it was her fake smile because she was baring her teeth and she never did that with her genuine smile. 'How nice to see you again. How's the family?'

'Very well, thank you. Gram is working hard as usual and Archie is in his second year at university now.'

'What's he studying?' *Crab-torturing? Genocide?*
'Sociology.'
Sociopathy more like, thought Margaret.

'He's a brain box. Just like his father,' said Sherry proudly.

'I've forgotten what they both look like,' said Margaret, holding on to that scary smile which looked as if it had been fixed by rigor mortis. 'I don't think Graham had started puberty the last time I saw him.' *And had it been up to me, I'd have drowned the little bugger before he got to it as well.*

'Ha ha,' laughed Sherry. 'I think our wedding came after puberty. He's very busy. He wishes he could spend more time with his mother, of course. *C'est la vie.* I hardly ever see my little Archie, either.'

'Lucky you,' whispered Margaret under her breath. Archie was as much a mini-me of Graham as Graham was of his father Edwin. A selfish blighter put on this earth to serve his own interests and sod everyone else. Archie made the hairs on the back of her neck stand up, not that she had ever admitted that to her sister. Even as a little boy, there was something about him that made his father look like St Francis of Assisi by comparison – and that was no mean feat.

'Well, I'd better get back home then and polish my brasses,' said Sherry, sliding her coat from the back of the chair. The coat looked expensive. It had a plush satin lining and a gold chain inside the collar to hang it up by. 'I'll see you very soon, dear.' She bent over her mother-in-law and kissed her cheek, leaving a red-lipsticked imprint. She blew a kiss towards Margaret. 'So nice to have seen you again, Margaret. You look well.'

'So do you,' smiled Margaret, teeth still exposed.

And with that, Sherry exited the room, leaving a fug of scent and hairspray hanging behind her in the air.

Margaret wafted the smell away from her before it contaminated her lungs.

'What is that perfume? Zoflora? She must have put a bucket on. And a full can of Silvrikin.'

'She'd just come from the beauticians.'

'Were they shut?'

'Naughty Margaret,' chuckled Molly.

Margaret reached for a biscuit. 'I suppose it's too much to ask why Graham hasn't been to visit you in months.'

Molly shrugged her shoulders. She hadn't seen her son since Mother's Day, and then it had been a rushed ten-minute visit. 'I sometimes wonder if he remembers I exist.'

Margaret bit her tongue on what she'd been going to say. She leaned over and put her arm around her sister instead. 'I'm sure he does. You raise them, teach them to flap their wings, then have to stand and watch when they fly off to their own lives. That's a mother's duty.' Except in Molly's case, she'd never really had the chance to raise him. Margaret doubted it would have made much difference though. Graham was intrinsically rotten, the way his father was. He wouldn't have turned out well if he'd been raised by an abbey-ful of Julie Andrews in a jolly singing nun ensemble. 'We ask them not to look back once they've left the nest and it breaks our hearts when they obey us.'

'That's not what Melinda is like.' Molly's reply was weighted with sadness.

'Boys are different, love.'

Margaret injected as much tenderness into her voice as she could, although she hated her nephew with a vengeance, ever since her six-year-old daughter had run in screaming that her twelve-year-old cousin was trying to hang their cat Claude with her skipping rope. Margaret had given him the spanking of his life and they'd loathed each other ever since. Claude had been so traumatised that Bernard was the only other male he would tolerate after-wards. Graham had only invited her to his wedding because his auntie Margaret had a few bob and he was banking on a big present, she was sure of it. He hadn't got one though.

'Darling. I've got something to tell you,' said Margaret, changing the subject. 'It's about our holiday this year. We're taking a cruise. We leave in just over a fortnight, on the first of June, and we're back on July the seventh. It's all very last minute. I'm sorry.'

Molly brightened up instantly. 'Oh are we? I've always wanted to . . .'

There was something about her sister's expression that made her words dry up.

'Ah,' she guessed at it. 'I'm not going, am I?'

'Oh love,' said Margaret, softly. 'Bernard has found a cancellation that we can't turn down and booked us on a leg of the world cruise for our Golden Wedding. Just the two of us, for once. Are you dreadfully upset?'

Molly shook her head wildly. 'Don't be silly, Margaret. I've been on holiday every year with you for a quarter of a century. I think you're overdue a little couple time. You *must* go, and of course I'm not upset.'

'Just for once. You will be all right, won't you?'

'I should think I'll manage,' smiled Molly, gulping back a throatful of tears. She had never been apart from her sister for anything like as long as that. Margaret was likely to come back and find her in Autumn Grange with her beloved Willowfell sold and the proceeds transferred to Graham's bank account, if that's what he and Sherry were after.

'Bernard was worried about how you'd take it,' said Margaret, squeezing Molly's hand. 'He says he'll make it up to you and we shall all go on a cruise together next year.'

'Ooh, now that is something to look forward to.' *Dear Bernard*, thought Molly. She had been looking for her own Bernard Brandywine all her life. Twice she thought she had found him and twice she found she hadn't.

'Come and have lunch with us,' said Margaret. 'Bernard is cooking coq au vin. And we've just had a case of ice wine delivered. I think we should test it to make sure it's a good year.'

'Oh well, that's convinced me,' said Molly. 'I'll be over soon then. I want to put some sheets through the wash.'

Margaret returned home and Molly went upstairs to strip her bed as today's warm breeze was too good to waste. The door to the third bedroom, which was always kept shut, was slightly ajar. She'd been right, then. Sherry Beardsall had been snooping around in there after all.

Chapter 7

Margaret's long drawn-out sigh as she walked through the back door into her kitchen answered her husband's question before he had even asked it. He put his broadsheet paper down on the table.

'She didn't take it well, I gather? Poor Molly.'

'Molly took it very well, actually,' said Margaret, sitting down with him. 'She gave us her absolute blessing to go.'

'Why the long face, then?' said Bernard, reaching across the table to put his hand on hers.

'Sherry Beardsall was there when I went in.'

'Sherry? What was she doing there?'

'I don't know, but I don't like it. I smell a rat.'

'Maybe, just maybe, she didn't have an ulterior motive. Maybe she called to see how Molly was,' Bernard suggested.

'And maybe I'm the Shah of Persia,' said Margaret. 'No, the Beardsalls don't do anything out of the goodness of their hearts. Sherry was up to something, you mark my words. '

Her lip pulled back over her teeth when she thought about the Beardsalls – past and present. She understood why the young twenty-year-old Molly had fallen for the tall, well-built charmer and older man Edwin Beardsall. She had wanted to find her own guardian angel, as Margaret had

found hers in Bernard. Edwin Beardsall had whisked pregnant Molly up the aisle before she had a chance to breathe;
and when Bernard had to step in and rescue her poor sister
from the violent brute a year later, Edwin had refused to
let her take the baby with her. He could prove Molly was
mentally unstable, he said. And even Bernard with his legal
connections couldn't win against Edwin and his family's
old-established masonic ones. Molly always maintained
that growing up with Edwin and Thelma, his old bat of
a mother, had ruined young Graham. Margaret was more
inclined to think that young Graham was a bad lot from
the off, and her intuition had always been spookily accu-
rate. Even if he had been allowed to live with his lovely
sweet kind mother, Margaret doubted that Graham Beardsall
would have turned out any differently to the way he had.

'I wish Molly had found her Bernard Brandywine,' said
Margaret, savouring the warmth of her husband's hand on
top of her own.

'What a lovely thing to say,' replied Bernard, smiling at
her. He was still able to make her knees go a bit weak at the
thought that she was the sole recipient of that smile.

He had been her knight in shining armour from the
moment he laid eyes on her at the bus stop on her sixteenth
birthday. Her umbrella had blown across the road and into
Maltstone churchyard and he had chased it; a strapping
nineteen-year-old on his first term break from a law degree
at Oxford, climbing over the wall to retrieve it for her. She
had been in love with him within the first five minutes and
that love had only deepened over the years.

'I think she's been looking for someone like you her
whole life,' said Margaret, with a heavy sigh. 'She thought
she'd found you, both in that awful Edwin and in Harvey
Hoyland. I only wish she'd married someone who had been
kind to her. She deserved much better than either of them.

Good God, even Graham has found a soul-mate. If there is someone out there for him, there must be someone out there for everyone.'

'I always liked Harvey,' mused Bernard, shocking his wife.

'You what?'

'Harvey. I always thought he and Margaret made a good couple.'

'After what he did to her? Don't be ridic—'

Bernard held up his hands to quieten his wife. 'I often wonder if they talked. I wish I'd interfered at the time, you know, taken Harvey to one side.'

For once Margaret didn't have a comment to make. She had always presumed that Harvey *knew*. That's what made his walking out so extra cruel. She and her sister were close as twins could be, but there were some things that Molly would never talk about, not even to her.

'What Harvey did was wrong, of course, but I don't think we know the whole story. It was far too easy for us to bring down the protective curtain over Molly. I know it, and you know it, my love.'

Margaret swallowed hard. Over the past twenty-eight years she had discarded all the warm memories of Harvey Hoyland making her sister the happiest she had ever been. It would have been disloyal to Molly to admit, even to herself, that she had liked him enormously and had felt an honest, genuine vibe from him. It was much easier to admit that her intuition was wrong on this occasion. After all, how could he have been a decent man when he walked out on Molly for a floozy barmaid with hair like a haystack and breasts that announced her arrival five minutes before the rest of her appeared?

'We will all go somewhere warm for a week in October,' said Bernard, changing the subject. 'We will make it up to Molly with a lovely holiday. Wherever she wants to go, we will let her choose. Then next year we will take her cruising with us, as I said.'

'That will be lovely, darling,' said Margaret. She was such a lucky woman: she had her Bernard and their beautiful daughter Melinda, a vet working in a gorgeous part of the Dales. Molly had an unhealable broken heart and a son, daughter-in-law and grandson who made the Addams Family look like The Brady Bunch.

Poor Molly.

Chapter 8

When Carla opened the door to the house she had shared for ten years with Martin, it didn't feel like her home any more. It had been somehow transformed into a stranger's domain in which she was an interloper of the highest order. She had expected to return to rooms full of reminiscences, happy ones that might lessen the sadness of the funeral day, of her newly-widowed circumstances, but every thought of Martin sliced into her like a knife and her eyes couldn't bear to rest on anything. It was as if everything retained a poisoned memory. Even the kettle. He had made her a coffee the night before he died. What was going through his head as he waited for it to boil? How to tell her that he was leaving her? When to say the words? What words to say? She switched the kettle on and made herself a cup of tea. The mid-May sun was shining through the window, warming the kitchen, bathing it in a cheerful yellow cast as the light filtered through the lemon curtains, but Carla was frozen to the core and felt black and dead inside.

She sat at the table and tried to draw some comfort from the heat permeating the cup. They'd had sex on the

Friday before he died. He'd been really up for it, for a change. They'd eaten a delicious Chinese takeaway that she'd paid for as a treat, because he said he'd had a bad week sales-wise and wouldn't hit his target. Oh God, the lies. He'd opened two bottles of Peroni for them and they'd sat in companionable silence watching a *Poirot* which she had recorded on the TV. Then they'd gone to bed and she'd known he was in 'that mood' because he had slipped between the sheets without his pants on and had sprayed himself liberally with the Joop she had bought him for Christmas. Carla had welcomed his attentions – although he was hardly Mr Foreplay and those 'attentions' were short and perfunctory. But if he was happy, she was happy. Satisfied, he slid off her and directly into a snoring contented sleep and Carla had cuddled up to his plump, hairy back.

Until she heard the splash, she wasn't aware she was crying into her cup. How much of the past ten years with Martin had been a lie? He'd had an affair in the first year of their marriage, a brief stupid fling that she'd found out about because he hadn't been very good at covering it up. She had known without a doubt that if it ever happened again she would have seen it coming a mile off because he was rubbish at deception. But she hadn't, had she? Somewhere in their marriage he had acquired a master set of duplicitous skills. But why? He had to have been unhappy to have started up another extra-marital relationship, didn't he? What had she done wrong? She kept a clean house, cooked and washed for him, never gave him grief about being away from home so much with his job, always greeted him with affection when he came home on Fridays. She looked after herself, she was always clean, and nicely dressed. She might have been carrying a few extra pounds on her but she could still squeeze into a size fourteen and she was curvy rather than fat – her waist was ten inches smaller than her bust and hips, just as her Italian mother had been built. So why had he wanted to leave her for a woman he hadn't seen for thirty years? Her mind wanted to rip apart the last year and scour it for answers to the questions which were banked up in her head but she knew if she let them, she would be drowned by them, destroyed by the sheer weight of his dishonesty.

She felt as though she would never be able to sleep again. As soon as her brain was off its leash, it would begin its quest to dissect every single part of her life with Martin from the phone calls he made to her from 'hotels' when he was supposedly on the road to the ten days he spent 'team-building' playing golf in Scotland last October when he'd returned as brown as a berry and blamed a freak Indian summer up there. On Christmas Day, he had gone out for a lunchtime drink with 'an old friend' who had come over from Los Angeles and she hadn't batted an eyelid when he came in at four p.m. apologising that he hadn't been able to get away. And because she'd served up a very dried-out dinner, she hadn't blamed him when he hadn't eaten all that much. Had he had his Christmas dinner with *her*? Did the friend from Los Angeles even exist? He had never mentioned him before or after so what did that tell her?

She hadn't doubted a single thing he'd said to her. How stupid was she? He could have told her that he was late home because he'd been abducted by aliens and she would have believed him because she loved him and trusted him. She picked up her mug and then noticed it was one Martin had bought her. 'World's Best Wife'. He had given it to her on Mother's Day. He always bought her some trinket on Mother's Day because she didn't have a child's card to open.

Something like a mug was supposed to take that pain away. She'd thought he was kind to do that.

Carla launched the cup, still full of tea, at the wall with a primal scream. Then she watched the brown liquid roll down the pale-painted wall, which it would stain indelibly.

Chapter 9

'Ah, good morning, Mr Singh,' said Leni, as the bell above the door jangled and the handsome Sikh gentleman came into the shop as immaculate as ever in a suit and dark blue turban. Leni thought he must have been a very handsome man in his youth. He had a generous mouth, large, beautiful dark eyes and thick eyelashes that any young woman would kill for.

Pavitar Singh had just earned the title of her very first 'regular' and that thought made her smile inside. This was the fourth time he had been in the café now. They had both introduced themselves formally last week. He called her by her first name now, yet it didn't feel right to call him by his.

'Good morning, Leni. It's a nice bright one.'

'Rain forecast this afternoon, Mr Singh. So don't hang out your washing,' laughed Leni. 'Now, what can I get for you?'

'Tea. And what is the cake of the day please?'

'Carrot and orange or chocolate and brandy. The latter is quite naughty.'

'Oh,' said Mr Singh. 'That sounds very interesting. I think I will have to try the chocolate and brandy.'

'Cream?'

'No thank you. Now, what do you have new that I haven't seen yet?'

'The handbags,' said Leni. 'They're made out of actual classic books. A present for your good lady perhaps?'

'Alas, my beautiful Nanak is . . .' Mr Singh raised his hands heavenward by way of explanation.

'I'm sorry,' said Leni.

'No, no, don't be sorry, it was ten years ago.' Though it still hurt him, even after all that time, to say that she had gone. They should have been enjoying their retirement, seeing the world as they had planned, visiting their daughter in America. But Nanak's car had been rammed by a drunken driver who had been celebrating his release from prison – for drunk driving. 'My daughter loves handbags and she has always loved her books. That would be a perfect combination.'

'Not just handbags, the wallets are new. And those gift money wallets. What else? Oh yes and those rocking desk ink blotters with the refill paper. Walnut. They're from a retired craftsman in Maltstone who makes them himself.'

'Oh my,' said Mr Singh, hardly able to wait until Leni opened up the cabinet to show him. He handled the largest blotter with a reverence worthy of a rare religious artefact.

'Beautiful, aren't they? That one is the most expensive at fifty pounds. But you're in luck. I've decided to try and drum up some trade by having special offer Tuesdays. Ten per cent off.'

'I have to have it,' said Mr Singh, his large chocolate-coloured eyes shining. 'You understand of course.'

'Oh yes, I understand. I totally *get* the stationery thing,' nodded Leni. 'Ever since I was a young girl I always loved nice stationery: pads, pens – couldn't get enough of it. I thought I was the only one, until I read an article in a magazine about other people who love it too.'

'And so you started this wonderful business,' said Mr Singh, taking one of the handbags out of the cabinet. It was a large hardbacked book version of *Pride and Prejudice* converted into a proper purposeful handbag with handles and a red velvet lining inside.

'That's fifty pounds too,' said Leni, not sure if he had seen the price tag. 'Less ten per cent today of course.'

'It's very nice,' said Mr Singh. 'My little Siana would love this. Although she's not so little any more. She's a surgeon in an American hospital. Do you have a sturdy box, Leni? I think I would like to buy this for her birthday next month.'

'I am sure I can find you a box, Mr Singh,' replied Leni. 'Is this the book you want? I have *Wuthering Heights*, *The Hound of the Baskervilles*, *The Tenant*—'

Mr Singh held up his hand and stopped Leni talking. 'This is her favourite. If only I could get Mr Darcy to deliver it to her in person.'

Leni chuckled. 'I can't arrange that, but I can get you a box,' she said, taking the bag from him and locking up the cabinet. 'Come and have your tea and cake and tell me what you think. It's a new recipe.'

'I will indeed,' said Mr Singh, taking a place at a table and reaching in his pocket for his wallet. He was so glad that he had stumbled upon this teashop on the corner with its kind-eyed, cheerful owner a few weeks ago. It was such a relief to be lifted from his lonely existence, if only for an hour or so.

'This chocolate and brandon cake is divine,' chuckled Mr Singh with a look of rapture on his face. 'I mean brandy, forgive me. I am being taken over by Jane Austen.'

'No need to apologise, Mr Singh,' mused Leni. He had just given her a cracking idea.

Chapter 10

For Carla, the next week passed in a smog of confusion. Something deep within her did its best to help her survive. It drove her to take a shower, get dressed, try and eat something. She did so with the air of a zombie who had managed to retain a smidgeon of its humanity. Everything seemed a major effort – brushing her teeth, putting a slice of bread in the toaster. *Get a grip,* said the voice within her. *This is doing you no good at all. You need to start thinking about your next moves.* Seven days after Martin's funeral, Carla plugged in the vacuum and forced herself to run it over the carpet. Then she took the sheets off the bed and washed Martin from them and cried watching them tumble around in the machine.

She couldn't go on without answers, but she had to. But she couldn't. It was a never-ending circle which she couldn't break. She sat down with a bowl of soup and turned on the TV. An old black-and-white film was showing – *Séance on a Wet Afternoon.* She remembered seeing it years ago. It was the story of a medium who kidnaps a child in order to receive praise for finding her with her 'psychic' skills.

A medium.

The word landed in Carla's brain like a seed and immediately began to germinate. Of course. That's what she needed. A medium. A bridge between this world and the next. Theresa would have said she was mental even to entertain such an idea, but Theresa wasn't here, and it was the only place she had to go.

She put the soup down, glad to have an excuse not to eat it, and reached for her laptop, typing the words *clairvoyants, Barnsley, Sheffield, Leeds* into Google.

She found loads on the internet and a couple in particular stood out. The first had an incredibly slick website so Carla rang her and found that she could make her an appointment in fourteen months at the earliest. The second, in Rotherham, had a massive parade of testimonials, but couldn't see her until Christmas. The third, in Leeds, carried the profile pic of a friendly, down-to-earth lady sitting on a sofa and holding a crystal ball. She looked warm and genuine and Carla felt drawn to her for a reason she couldn't fathom. *Pat Morrison, Clarevoyent for forty years* – as her website title proclaimed – could fit her in the next day at two p.m.

Pat Morrison lived in an estate of well-looked-after 1960s semi-detached houses in Horcroft on the outskirts of Leeds. The gardens were neat without exception, with well-tended borders and lots of coloured flowers, wishing wells and gnomes with fishing rods. Pat Morrison's door was a striking shade of cyclamen and the nets that hung at her windows, a delicate hue of blush pink. Carla suspected it was a definite pointer to pink overload inside – and she wasn't wrong.

Pat Morrison herself was a vision in fuchsia. She opened the door in a floor-length kaftan that did nothing to hide her small bulky figure. Her lips were coated with a thick slick of neon pink that could have been seen from orbit.

'You must be Carla,' she said, her accent thick Leeds with a nasal twist. Vera Duckworth with a sinus problem. 'Come in, lovey, I'm just with a client at the moment.' She waddled down the hallway, her kaftan-clad girth rocking from side to side like a fishing boat in a force ten crosswind. She opened a door to the left which led into a small sitting room smelling strongly of berry pot-pourri and gestured that Carla take the dark pink-upholstered chair in the corner. From a dish on an oval coffee table at its side, Pat picked up a crystal sphere the size of a tennis ball and handed it to Carla.

'I want you to hold this in your hand for five minutes whilst I leave you here,' she instructed. 'The ball will absorb your energies which I will read and interpret. That's how I work. Now you just take this – that's it – and I'll be back for you. And whilst you're waiting, look through these and pick the one you are most drawn to. Okay?' She took a square plastic tub from the top of a display cabinet and put it on Carla's lap.

Carla nodded obediently. Pat wobbled off and shut the door behind her and Carla rolled the ball around in her hand, letting her eyes take in her surroundings. There were two framed pictures on the wall: one of Pat as a younger woman standing next to an old lady wearing a veil, in front of a tent with a large Petulengro sign behind them. The other featured Pat holding her crystal ball and sporting that bright pink lipstick. Carla wondered what the shade was called. Boiled crab? There were small bowls of cherry-pink pot pourri everywhere and a huge one on the display cabinet which housed a variety of topical items within its ornate glass doors: a rabbit's foot, models of black cats, crystals, sets of tarot cards, horseshoes, more photos in frames of Pat posing with people.

Carla poked around in the tub with her right hand whilst

holding on to the ball in her left. There were lots of different items: a brooch with the word 'Mother' on it, a pipe, a packet of needles, a souvenir pen from Blegthorpe-on-Sea, a ring, a small brass cat, a military medal, an enamel red heart, a lipstick. Carla plucked out that one, took off the top and twisted it out. It was the very same shade of pink that Pat wore. She turned it upside down to read the name on the bottom: *French Fanny*.

Blimey, are French ones really that pink, thought Carla with a sudden inner giggle. She squinted to read it again. The letters were slightly worn, hence the mistake. *French Fancy*. She covered her mouth to stop the laughter frothing up inside her from escaping. The harder she suppressed it, the more it bubbled up. *French Fanny*. It was too funny. The censoring silence of the room wasn't helping. She had a sudden vision of being sixteen and having a fit of giggles in her Maths GCSE when the exam invigilator sneezed and let out a giant fart at the same time. She'd thought she was going to burst from keeping that laugh in, it was seeping out of her eyes in tear form, so desperate was it to find its way to the outside. Just like now.

This was the first time the corners of her mouth had turned up since ages before Martin died, she suddenly realised. She chose the lipstick as her object, then her brain went into reverse thrust. *Am I only picking this because I was drawn in by the colour and the comical reading error?* she asked herself. She needed to think carefully – after all, the object she chose could have important repercussions. She dug into the tub again and examined the scraps of jewellery and charms but there was nothing that had captured her attention as much as the French Fanny lipstick.

She sat happily passing some vibes to her ball, zoning out in the process. Trying to empty her mind was impossible. She gave it her best shot, though it would have been easier to build a life-size model of the Taj Mahal in matchsticks. Blindfold. She closed her eyes and let the mellow sound of the clock on the wall fill her head. *Tick-tick, tick-tock, tick-tock.* She hadn't slept properly since Martin had died and found herself being lulled by the rhythm and drifting onto another plane.

The minutes passed and Carla was shaken out of a light doze by the sound of a door opening and voices outside.

A nasal Leeds accent. 'Now you remember what I said, lovey. Positive thinking.'

'Yes, thank you. Thank you so much.' A timid, relieved voice. A comforted one. That boded well. Carla couldn't wait to get started.

Pat Morrison entered the room and beckoned Carla towards her.

'Come on, lovey. We'll get started. Bring your ball and your object of choice.'

Carla picked up her French Fanny lippy and squeezed some last minute vibes into her ball as she followed Pat down the hallway into a larger sitting room with a huge dusty pink sofa and thick pile pink carpet. There were a lot of lit pink candles around the room – strawberry scented. Pat invited her to sit, and Carla obeyed. Pat dropped into a huge armchair opposite, also pink, a bank of cushions in various shades of pink at her back propping her forwards.

'Your object lovey, please.' Pat held out her hand. She had huge curved talons painted pink, surprisingly enough. Carla handed over the lipstick.

Pat nodded sagely. 'The lipstick. Your femininity is very important to you, isn't it, lovey?'

'Erm, yes, I suppose so,' said Carla. She had no desire to start drinking pints or wearing Brut anyway.

'You were drawn to this object because it signifies your womanhood,' Pat told her in no uncertain terms. 'You feel the need to accentuate your femininity because it has been threatened.'

Pat Morrison noticed Carla's back straighten to attention and she smiled. Yep, she had this one sussed. Not that she didn't have some psychic ability, but how much exactly she was unsure because she was a great expert at reading people – so much so that this talent alone would have made her appear like a mystic. Her dad had been a notorious con-man, Velvet Vernon, a genius charmer with a line in patter as smooth as whipped cream. He could have a woman's wage from her purse and her knickers round her ankles after a minute in his presence. She had been her father's daughter, though she had never used her skills in the illicit way he did.

She was quite content to parade herself publicly as a professional psychic; it was easy, lucrative and legal. Most people who came to see her wanted someone quickly on hand because they were in crisis. And that made them utterly transparent. Most of the time they did her work for her – *Can you see my mother in spirit, she's got white hair and a limp? Is she sending me her love? Has she met up with my dad and the dog?* Not that Pat wanted to exploit anyone mercilessly, like her father had done. Pat saw herself as an excellent giver of service and bringer of smiles. The people who came to see her didn't want an hour's intense forecast of the rest of their lives, they wanted a quick fix, a fifteen-minute injection of hope that would get them through the next few weeks. She had fitted thirty clients in on one day last week. At forty pounds a pop – cash mostly – Velvet Vernon would have been proud.

Pat could see that she was spot on with her lipstick deduction so she carried on down that path. It wasn't hard to figure out what had knocked this woman's confidence in herself.

'A man has made you feel less than worthy.' She sighed sympathetically as if she heard this so many times, which she had. Ninety per cent of the women who came to see her had a bloke in the background who had stamped all over their hearts wearing pit boots. 'But all is not lost,' Pat went on. 'The fact that you picked this item means you haven't given up. You are clinging on to your woman power.'

She said this with such gusto that Carla believed her for a split second before she remembered that she had absolutely no power at all – womanly or otherwise.

'Trust in pink. It's a lucky colour for you,' said Pat, tapping the side of her nose with a long talon, pierced with a small four-leafed clover charm, then she held out the same hand for the crystal ball. Receiving it, she closed her eyes and tilted her head backwards in concentration whilst taking in a slow deep breath.

'Oooh interesting,' she said, tantalisingly.

What, what? thought Carla.

'I can see a cat. A big black cat.'

Carla felt the anti-climax right down to her shoes.

'Have you got a cat, lovey?' Pat asked.

'No,' said Carla.

'Not *yet*.' Pat wagged her finger. 'You must look out for this lucky black cat. It will bring you luck.'

What else would a lucky black cat bring but luck? thought Carla, disappointed by that prediction. Fleas, perhaps – or dead mice. She didn't have a cat, never had had a cat and wouldn't be getting one, either.

'I sense a man,' said Pat. 'Deception. Past the point of no return.'

Carla's eyes widened.

'I see him clearly. You have to forget him and move on. He won't come back to you and if he does, you must say no, lovey.'

Pat noticed the small twitch Carla's head made. She'd cocked up slightly saying that. How? She slid into repair mode.

'I mean he may try to contact you and ask for forgiveness. Not necessarily in person.'

Carla gave a slow heavy nod. Ah, thought Pat. That struck a chord. He's dead.

'He has passed. You are full of questions that he cannot answer. You must let him go, lovey. The answers would only hurt you.'

Carla burst into tears.

'There is great loss here,' said Pat with her best nasal sympathetic voice. 'Far more than just the man. There are material things. You must let them all go. Start again.'

Carla was nodding like the Churchill dog. Pat had struck gold.

'Think of the lipstick. You have yourself and your woman power and that will carry you forward, lovey. You need fresh things. Leave the memories. They aren't good.'

Pat handed Carla a box of pink tissues from which Carla ripped two, blowing her nose on one, and wiping her eyes with the other.

'You think I should let it all go?' asked Carla.

'Yes, I do,' said Pat. 'I can feel no positivity in hanging on to your past life. I feel very strongly that you must go forwards. Even if you do feel as if you're going backwards for a while, getting away from your past life is most definitely moving forwards. Trust in pink, lovey. And look out for the lucky black cat.'

A black cat was always a good thing to say, Pat thought. Who didn't see a black cat occasionally? And when this poor cow saw the black cat, she would perk up and the positive energy would propel her up and on. What was wrong about telling someone that good things were around the corner – it was as good as magic, even if it was bollocks? She held out her hand for her forty pounds. Her client was wet-eyed but smiling. *Ker-ching.* Another satisfied customer.

Chapter 11

Will Linton opened the door to two men who looked as if they had just swaggered out of *Lock Stock and Two Smoking Barrels*. One, small and squat in a black leather jacket and a gold medallion around his neck that would have had Mr T turning green with envy; the other thin, haggard and hard-faced, with skin that told of cigarettes and too much alcohol, possibly a lasting legacy of drugs from his earlier days. It was the latter who spoke, in a surprisingly genteel voice.

'Mr Linton. Mr Will Linton?'

Parked on the road outside their house was a long truck. Will closed his eyes and shook his head slowly from side to side. *This couldn't be happening. Everything was moving too fast.* It was only a week and a half ago that Cecilia Williams had told him that the bank was giving up on him.

Mr T was holding a clipboard and a pen. He could tell from Will's expression that he knew why they were there.

'I'm here for your car sir, unless you can give me a cash amount of . . .' he referred to his paperwork '. . . two thousand, eight hundred and sixty two pounds exactly.'

Will sighed and moved his head slowly from side to side.

'I only wish I could.'

'Or I could put the car in our pound and you have twenty-four hours to claim it back.'

Will looked over at his pride and joy Jaguar sitting on the drive. He would be so sorry to see it go. But go it must.

Across the road in the seven-bedroomed detached with the stone lion sentries, he saw the lounge curtain twitch. Then Mr Roy 'Koi-Carp-Pond' Wright next door emerged from his house, briefcase in hand, just in time to witness some more of Will's humiliation.

'If not, could I have your car key, sir,' the man said with a *look, I feel for you mate so let's make this as simple and pain-free as we can* tone to his voice.

Will foraged in his pocket and took out the car key. He hadn't thought it would be repossessed quite so soon, but now the moment was here and he had no fight left to contest it.

Roy Wright was taking an age to get into his car. Will could see him over their adjoining low hedge, pretending to look through his briefcase but really eavesdropping on his poor unfortunate business-failure of a neighbour.

'Do you need anything out of the car, sir?'

'No thanks,' said Will. They could keep the windscreen sponge and the wine gums in the glove box.

'Do you have spare keys, sir?'

'Yeah, course.' Will stepped back inside the house and took the two spare car keys from the hook behind the door. They were still on a Linton Roofing promotional keyring. He handed them over with the MOT certificate and the service book.

'Thank you, sir.'

Nicole was sitting silently on the stairs, her head in her perfectly manicured hands and hostile vibes missiling out from her every pore. After he had finished his business with the repossession men, Will shut the door and hurried to comfort his wife. As soon as his arm fell around her shoulder, she erupted like a volcano. She pushed him violently away, lashing out at him, then jumped up, her forehead as creased with fury as the Botox would allow.

'Don't fucking touch me,' she said.

'It's just a car, love. A lump of metal . . .'

'I have never been so ashamed. The neighbours watching—'

'Sod them,' said Will. 'It doesn't matter. There are greater men than me who have found themselves in this position. I don't care what a few nosey neighbours think . . .'

'Well I do,' screamed Nicole, thumping herself in her three-thousand-pound boob job with her fist. 'I fucking do.'

'Nicole . . . darling,' he took one step towards her and she took a longer one back.

'It's the last straw, Will,' she said. 'The shame, the humiliation. I can't live with it any more.'

He caught her arm as she turned up the stairs. 'You can't live with the humiliation or you can't live with me?'

Her head swivelled slowly on a smooth arc to face him. He had the funniest feeling that if she had wanted to, she could have turned it through three hundred and sixty degrees. Like an owl. Or the possessed kid from *The Exorcist*.

'Okay then: you,' she said, fixing him with her cold eyes. 'You and the humiliation are one and the same. You're a failure, Will Linton. And I don't do failures.'

'For richer or poorer, remember those words?' he reminded her, calmly, although his heart was thumping inside. She couldn't abandon him as well. His life as he knew it was landsliding away from him. 'You married me, not my money, Nicole. Six years ago, you said your vows to William Benjamin Brian Linton, didn't you? Not William's bleedin' bank account.'

She didn't answer; and then he knew. He didn't want to let himself believe it because it would really hurt. She had never known him poor. He had owned a business, a big house and a flash car when they met. Being married to Will Linton was not the main attraction of being Mrs William Linton.

'I'm not made for being poor and struggling,' she said, removing his hand from her arm with careful pincered fingers, as if it were diseased.

'Nicole. I love you,' he said, unable to fully comprehend he was hearing this. She was going to turn around in a minute and say, 'ha ha, not really.' But in the seven years he had known her, he suddenly realised, he had never heard her once make a joke.

'You'll get over it,' she said in her elocution-lessoned voice. 'Don't try and stop me leaving. I'm going home to my parents. If you follow me, Dad will set the dogs on you; and when they've finished with you, if there is anything left to arrest, he'll call the police. My solicitor will be in touch. Let's make it quick and painless, shall we? It's over, Will. You can go down with your ship but don't expect me not to catch a lifeboat.'

He didn't follow her. He poured himself a scotch and sank onto the huge cream leather sofa, imagining her moving about, packing her suitcase, taking her jewellery out of her safe. There was no point in fighting for her. She wasn't doing this for effect, so that he would bounce upstairs and seduce her into staying. He knew her too well. Nicole's idea of roughing it was there being no lobster option on a business-class flight menu. She didn't even bother to say goodbye an hour later when he was half-wrecked on single malt, tears cutting down his cheeks. She just climbed into the sports car that daddy had bought her last year instead of an Easter egg and drove off, viciously spitting gravel in his direction.

Chapter 12

By some miracle the *Barnsley Chronicle* had not reported what had happened at Martin's funeral. There had been some armed robberies in the off-licence chain The Booze Brothers, which had grabbed the headlines for two weeks. The first report covered the actual robbery, the second the arrest of the culprits after one of the thieves had pasted his own *Crimestoppers* photo on Facebook, adding the caption 'Fame at Last'. Carla was only glad to know there were idiots like that in the world to keep what potential press interest there might have been in her fully occupied. By an even bigger miracle, it had also bypassed the *Daily Trumpet*, the sensationalist South Yorkshire newspaper and the most inept publication in the history of mankind. Carla had checked it every day for a week and a half after the debacle, by which time she would have qualified as being 'old news' and unworthy of column inches. Most of the *Daily Trumpet* was taken up with apologies for stories it had wrongly reported in the past few days. By rights, it shouldn't have made any money, but it had acquired a certain cult status with its readers who purchased it merely for the errors and pushed the privately-owned business into decent profit.

A letter had arrived from Julie's solicitor demanding that Carla vacate the property by the last day of June. Carla didn't know if she should see a solicitor as well. She felt numb and, for the first time, very hungry. She tipped three Weetabix into a bowl then realised that the two-pinter of milk in her fridge had the lumpy consistency of old yogurt. She walked to the shop down the road for some fresh and a loaf and a tub of butter. It was the first time she had done any shopping since before Martin had died. The Weetabix tasted bland and unappetising in her mouth, despite her ravenous hunger, but she forced it down. Before that, she couldn't remember when she had last eaten. Her jeans were hanging from her.

She didn't know what to do with herself. She didn't even know what day it was. How long was it until the end of June? Where would she go? How could she pack up and leave – she barely had enough energy to brush her teeth. She wished Theresa was home; then again she wished she wasn't. She didn't want Theresa to walk through the door all full of smiles and sunshine and for Carla to fall on her sobbing. She couldn't remember when Theresa was coming back. The last Monday in May was ringing a bell for some reason.

There was a knock at the back door and it was pushed open by whoever was on the outside and in walked Theresa, all smiles and sunshine.

'Coo-ee. Guess who?' Then the smile dropped from the tanned face. 'Jesus. Have you been on a diet?'

And despite her best intentions not to, Carla fell on her best friend sobbing.

Chapter 13

Molly was determined to find the Royal Doulton figurine. It had to be in this house somewhere because she wouldn't have thrown it out. Her compact and pen might have been mislaid or accidentally fallen out of her handbag, but a figurine was harder to lose and it was needling her that she couldn't find it. It wasn't in any of the obvious places, so she started to look in the more obscure ones, secretly hoping that she wouldn't find it at the back of a drawer or in a box of photographs – because what would that say about her mental state if she had put it in there and couldn't remember doing so?

There was nothing in the wardrobe or the large bedding chest. There was no trace of it in the beautiful old rolltop desk which used to belong to dear Mr Brandywine senior, which he always promised Molly she would have – and the family had honoured that promise. Molly could never think of Emma and George Brandywine without a fond smile. They were the kindest, most gentle couple she had ever met. She had loved them and grieved for them as a true daughter would when they died.

Molly kept a treasure box in the deep bottom left drawer of the old desk. If the figurine was anywhere other than on the shelf, the odds were that she had mistakenly put it in there – but when she took off the lid, it was clearly not inside. Top of the pile of contents was a card from Emma and George congratulating her on getting her first job as Dr Dodworth's receptionist. Inside, Emma's scrolling sentiment was written in her scratchy fine ink pen. *We are so proud of you, Molly. We know you will make a wonderful receptionist. With Lots of Love, 'Ma & Pa'.*

It had begun as a joke, Molly referring to them as Ma and Pa, but it stuck. She suspected the Brandywines knew how much she wanted someone to call parents and they accepted their titles willingly. Molly's eyes filled with unshed tears and she blinked hard to stop more rising. A thought of Ma and Pa Brandywine visited her every day without fail.

Underneath was a twenty-first birthday card to her from Bernard and Margaret. It had been scented, but the fragrance of roses was long gone. Molly couldn't even remember how she celebrated that birthday. She was married then, but her life was a sham, she was miserable and low and the youthful years that should have been filled with hope and a new beginning were worse than those of her earlier life of confusion and helplessness. There was no reference to Edwin Beardsall in her box. She had not carried one single good memory of her ex-husband forward.

Next in the pile was the Mother's Day card Graham had made at primary school. The front had a picture of a daffodil on it, a cup from an egg carton painted orange forming the flower's trumpet. It was the only hand-made card she had ever received, and that was because the kind teacher at school had posted it to her directly. She had been under strict instructions to send any Mother's Day cards he made to his paternal grandmother, not to Molly, and so she had helped Graham make another in secret at playtime. The glue was failing and the cup had almost fallen off entirely.

Molly's finger lightly traced the large heavily-looped letters: 'To My Mother'. He had never called her mum, only ever mother.

There was her school report card. It read:

```
Molly is quiet, unconfrontational and works
very hard. Her attention to detail should be
praised and her hand-writing is exemplary.
She would make an excellent secretary.
```

The 'unconfrontational' comment was an indirect reference to her sister, whom Miss Wolf had found very confrontational. Their teacher was a horrible old bat, Molly chuckled to herself. She hadn't liked any of her pupils very much, and Margaret least of all. She had been terribly unfair to ... what was her name ... Phyllis ... Phyllis Wood, that was it. Phyllis came from a very poor family: her clothes were often stained and tatty and she wore the same socks day after day. Miss Wolf had made Phyllis stand on a chair as an example of how *not* to dress for school and Phyllis had been crying until Margaret grabbed her hand and pulled her down from her pedestal of ridicule. Before Miss Wolf could get her words out, Margaret had told her that she was evil and that their uncle was a solicitor and Margaret was going to tell him what she had done to Phyllis and persuade Mr and Mrs Wood to press charges.

Miss Wolf had stuck her face in Molly's and demanded of her: 'Is your uncle a solicitor?' She had known that Molly wouldn't dare lie to her.

'Yes,' replied Molly, hoping Miss Wolf hadn't noticed the nervous gulp in her throat. 'Our mother's brother, Uncle Frederick. He works in Leeds, for the court.' Deception didn't come easy to Molly, but she would rather tell a lie than get Margaret into trouble.

Molly hadn't been able to sleep properly for weeks, thinking that Miss Wolf was going to ask their mother and father if Uncle Frederick really was a solicitor. They didn't even have an uncle. But Miss Wolf never did. And she never put Phyllis Wood on a chair again and mocked her either.

Molly shivered. Miss Wolf had turned out to be an angel compared to some people she had encountered in her life. She could have laughed when the next card in the pile came from *him*. A postcard, from Blackpool. Harvey Hoyland. The biggest devil of them all.

My dear Molly,
Wish you were here
H x

He always had such lovely handwriting. She had once looked up his wide-spaced, slanting style in a graphology book to see what it said about him: Trustworthy, loyal and well-adjusted. Enjoyed freedom and didn't like to be hemmed in. Well, the last part of that analysis was as true as the first part wasn't.

He had been gone three months when that postcard had arrived and she hadn't known what to make of it. Even now she could recall the quickening in her heart when she plucked it out of the letter-box. She analysed it for days: did it mean he wanted her to go up to Blackpool and find him? Did he really miss her? Why had he sent it if he didn't miss her? What would his fancy-piece think about him sending a postcard to his estranged wife? Did he mean he wished Molly was there as well as, or instead of, her? Was the front picture of a child on a donkey of any significance? Or was he rubbing it in by telling her that life was so good for him now that he wished she were here to witness it? She didn't know and never would.

He didn't write again. He slipped out of her life like a shadow runs from the sun, never asking for anything in the divorce settlement. She had hated him so much for the silence which was a torture. Why had she kept that damned postcard anyway? It held a ridiculous power to stir up settled waters within her where old feelings still subsisted in glorious technicolour, even now after twenty-eight years. Molly made to tear it in two, rip it in shreds the way that Harvey Hoyland had ripped up her heart. It wasn't the first time that she had tried to rid herself of it, but she had never managed to. This time was no exception. She hurriedly put the lid on the box and stuffed it back in the desk drawer. Out of sight, out of mind.

She wished she could have wiped the blackboard of her life clean and started again: been more like Margaret, stood up to Edwin, run away with her son and never let his father or grandmother see him again. *And what about Harvey Hoyland?* A voice in her head asked her. And she didn't know the answer. Half of her would never have said yes to agreeing to go to the pictures with him that frosty November night when she had slipped on a patch of ice in the town centre and he'd caught her. Half of her would have given him free rein to all the parts of her heart and her mind to which she had denied him entry.

Molly shook her head as if trying to purge it of the vision of her second ex-husband. There was no point in philosophising about him. She would never see him again. He could even be dead and buried. He smoked, he drank rough spirits, though he was more likely to have been murdered by some husband whose wife he had stolen or by a gambling-house owner to whom he owed money than to die peacefully alone in a bed.

Molly carried on with the business of searching for the figurine, but she didn't find it.

Chapter 14

Will went out at nine a.m. exactly to catch the train for a meeting with his accountant in Huddersfield, who sighed and shook his head a lot at him, and then he went to pick up his new vehicle – a battered Nissan white van which his regular car mechanic had bought at an auction and kindly offered him first refusal on after hearing about his troubles. Will was touched by his thoughtfulness and said yes on the spot. Cosmetically, it looked shot at, but it was still a snip at eight hundred pounds. A very short time ago, eight hundred pounds would have just about covered the cost of two wheels on his Jaguar, and he wouldn't have thought twice about the expense. Ironically, his first ever car had been an old Nissan and now he had gone full loop back to the beginning. Still, it would be a useful runaround with a sound engine and it would get him to where he wanted to go without haemorrhaging petrol and he would just have to get used to travelling from A to B without turning heads for the foreseeable future.

By the time he arrived back home, he opened the front door to find that Nicole had returned and gone through the house like a locust. It was stripped. He didn't mind that she had taken the dining table and ten upholstered chairs or the swanky Harrods dinner service that had been a wedding present to them *both* – or even the display cabinet that housed the swanky dinner service. He didn't even mind that the huge leather sofas were gone, or the baby grand piano that she had insisted she wanted for Christmas but couldn't even bang out Chopsticks on it. He even laughed that she had taken the Christmas tree from the garage – and the box of baubles and tinsel. Jesus – she must have had a team of joiners primed to disassemble their ornate four-poster and the huge French armoire wardrobes and transport them to waiting delivery vans.

She did have the decency to leave him the double bed in the spare room – and the bedding on it. One bath towel, one cup, one plate, one knife, one fork and one spoon. She also left the kettle and all the food in the cupboards and the built-in fridge, dishwasher and washing machine. But what he couldn't – and wouldn't – stomach was the sight of *his* open safe in their bedroom. When he checked it, it had been wiped clean of the Tag Heuer watch she bought him for Christmas – not surprisingly – but also of the small shell box in which he kept his mother's wedding and engagement rings, his dad's wedding band and his sister's twenty-first emerald ring, which their parents had bought her two months before she died of leukaemia.

Will hadn't been really angry for a long time. He'd been roused to a few expletives when Yorkshire Stone Homes said they were making an immediate bank transfer which would save his company, only to find that they'd reneged on the promise and the money never appeared in his account, driving the last nail into his financial coffin; but the anger bubbling through his blood now took fury to another level. He picked up the keys of his new old van and flounced out of the near-naked house, each stride of his long legs powered by pure unadultered rage.

Nicole's parents lived in one of the very grand houses at the back of Barnsley park. The Views had a long private drive flanked by romantic stone armless statues every ten yards. Will passed them in a blur of speed. He hoped that Barnaby Whitlaw wouldn't set the dogs on him – or, worse, his wife Penelope – before he got to Nicole. Then again, the way he felt, he could have taken them all on: wife, parents, Dobermanns, the lot.

Parked on the large paved circle outside the house were two delivery vans, and men were carrying Will's furniture out of them and into one of the outbuildings. He slammed on the brake which squealed like a terrified mouse. The blubbery-bodied Barnaby Whitlaw appeared as soon as he spotted his son-in-law springing out of the old white van. He opened his mouth to speak but Will got the first words in.

'Where is she?'

'If you mean Nicole, then she isn't in . . .'

Will had already noticed Nicole's sports car parked in the open garage. She didn't walk anywhere, so he knew the likelihood was that she was in the house.

'Unless you want an almighty show in front of the delivery men, Barnaby, I suggest you get her out here now.'

Penelope Whitlaw came striding out of the front door, smoothing her steel-grey hair away from her face as if she meant business.

'I'm calling the police,' she said flapping her long bony hands.

'Oh you do just that, Penelope,' said Will, pushing his sleeves up his arms, ready for a battle. 'But it won't be me they'll be taking away. It will be your darling daughter.'

Barnaby was aware that the delivery men could hear all this.

'Get inside,' he barked at Will. 'Penelope, go and fetch Nicole. Let's get this over and done with in private.'

'Thank you,' nodded Will and headed inside, where he stood in their spacious hallway at the bottom of their grand staircase, seeing as no one asked him to go into the lounge, sit down and take tea. Barnaby paced around impatiently, hands behind his back as Penelope trotted upstairs. There was no love lost between Will and his in-laws. The Whitlaws might have admired his bank balance, but never *him*. He wasn't 'their type'. He had a 'common accent reminiscent of that provincial Southern soap opera' and would never have been accepted into their social circle. Will hadn't inherited his money like the Whitlaws; he had worked his nuts off for it. He was a mere barrow boy made good and as such would never have class. He came from impoverished East End stock. His mother and father were kind, lovely people but struggled constantly for money after his dad developed a lung condition and couldn't work. Will wanted more for himself and his family, and worked as soon as he was old enough to get a job. He ran errands for neighbours, served on markets, laboured for Jimmy McKintosh, one of the famous local builders who quickly realised that his Saturday boy was as lithe as a monkey on roofs. Will was bright, but he hated school as much as he loved working with Jimmy, who took him on officially as an apprentice at sixteen. Will bought his mum and dad and sister a cottage by the sea before his twenty-first birthday. By twenty-five he was an orphan and had moved up north and opened his own roofing firm. But his money would never be clean enough for the Whitlaws senior. It was tainted with sweat and rough hands and labour.

Nicole still hadn't arrived after five minutes.

'You better tell her to hurry up,' growled Will. 'I'm losing patience.'

'Just wait,' snapped Barnaby, temporarily halting his rather annoying pacing.

'I've waited long enough,' replied Will, dodging past his father-in-law to take the steps two at a time, blocking out Barnaby's splutters of protestation. He presumed rightly that she would be in her old room. He burst in through the door, making her mother, who was in there with her, jump; but Nicole was totally composed as she sat at her dressing table straightening her new hair. She didn't turn around, merely looked at Will in the mirror and carried on smoothing some Russian girls' glued-in locks with her gold GHDs.

'I thought you might turn up,' she said.

'You thought right then,' he replied.

'Mum, leave us for a few minutes, would you?' asked Nicole.

'I'm not leaving you with this maniac,' snorted Penelope.

'Maniac?' Will's eyebrows shot up. 'I can assure you that I'll leave very quietly when I get what I came for, and I *will* get what I came for.'

'Which is?' asked Nicole, unplugging the straighteners and setting them down on the dressing table top.

'My family's jewellery, which you took from the safe. You can have the sofa, the bed, all the bleeding silver forks, the watch you bought me, but you're not having that.'

'I don't know where I've put it,' shrugged Nicole, at last turning around to him. 'I'll send it on . . .'

'No,' said Will adamantly, crossing his arms. 'I'm not leaving without it.'

As he stared at his soon-to-be-ex wife, he was almost fascinated to find that she looked like a stranger to him. He hadn't noticed before the small lines at the corners of her mouth, indicating that the natural set of her lips was a scowling downturn; or the fact that there was no light in her eyes; they were dull like a snake's. And had they always been so small? Temporarily devoid of her false eyelashes and smudged shadow, her irises were mean little circles of black.

He wasn't feeling any love, any attraction, not even a ghost of it for this woman who had only ended their marriage a few days ago. All he felt was anger at her self-serving greed, and yet he wasn't surprised by it. It was as if he had always known that the glue of their marriage was money rather than love.

'Nicole, are you all right?' asked Barnaby breathlessly from the doorway. Clearly the effort of clambering up the stairs instead of using his lift had totally knackered him.

'Come on, be on your way. Shoo,' said Penelope, talking to Will as if he were one of the dogs.

Nicole just scowled. She wasn't in control here and that was making her cross.

The air which hung between Will and Nicole was so icy he could have raised his fist and smashed it.

'Okay, I'll give you a choice,' said Will, enjoying the chaos he was causing, enjoying the feeling of having some power again. 'I'll go without the jewellery, but I'll make sure that when we divorce, I will chase you for alimony; and I will get it, because here you are living in a mansion and I've got sod all. And I'll also make a claim on your pension so we will be tied together forever. And I'll request half the furniture back – so please don't sell it. I'll be taking photographs on my way out. If you do sell it, then I'll take the monetary value, because I've still got the receipts for it in my files. And I'll send the creditors your way. I think they'll be very interested in your private stashes of off-shore money that you didn't think I knew about. The banks aren't stupid, Nicole. They see it all the time, couples pretending to split up so one of them can hide a load of money. I'll confess to them that was our master plan. Say goodbye to your assets, Nicole.'

Will turned to go and started to walk out slowly, because he knew he would be called back any moment. Three beats and Nicole yelled, 'Wait.'

She tore open the drawer of her dressing table, lifted out the shell box and thrust it in Will's direction.

He took it from her hand, opened it and checked everything was there – it was. He overrode his polite reflex to say thank you. He had nothing to thank Nicole for. His entire marriage flashed before his eyes as she pouted at him with her hard Restylane-filled mouth, oozing indignation at not having her own way for once. She had taken from him since day one and – to be fair – he'd been happy to give it, and never asked for anything back, which was lucky, because she never gave anything back. Only on one day had he truly needed something from her – a kind word, support, a hug on the day when Mrs Williams had closed down negotiations with him, and she hadn't even been able to manage that.

He turned towards the door again.

'That's us quits, then, yeah? You won't be claiming against me in court?' Nicole called to his back.

He didn't answer as he walked away from her and her parents and out to his van. He belted himself in as he watched the canopy of his four-poster bed being carried from the furniture van and he surprised himself with a laugh. He had the clothes in his wardrobe, the food in his cupboard, a couple of thousand quid in cash hidden in the bath panel and a van with old wind-down windows. But at that moment, with the box of his family's jewellery in his hand and with the certain knowledge that his ex-wife was stamping her feet on the family three-inch shag pile, he felt like the king of the jungle. No, it wasn't all over for Will Linton. There was still some fire left in the old dog yet.

Chapter 15

Carla had made seven tissues soggy by the time Theresa put the cup of coffee down on the table in front of her.

'Right, start from the beginning,' she said. 'I can't believe you didn't phone me.'

'And spoil your holiday? What sort of friend would that have made me?' sniffed Carla.

'I'm so cross with you,' said Theresa in her very posh accent, whilst fluttering her hand as if to waft away her annoyance. 'But I'm here now, so tell me. Everything. Don't leave a single detail out.'

Carla began at the beginning: Martin going out to the garage to carry in the dressing table, then Carla finding him flat out on the floor after checking why he was taking so long. The ambulance, the hospital, the doctor telling her that Martin had suffered a massive heart attack and would almost certainly have died instantly and not suffered. Then the funeral and Julie. Theresa's mouth dropped open by more and more degrees with every sentence.

'Have you checked this woman out?' she asked. 'You haven't just accepted that what she says is true?'

'Her solicitor has sent a letter.'

'Right.' Theresa slapped her hand down on the table. 'We

need to validate both her and this so-called solicitor then. That's the first thing we have to do. She might have composed that letter herself.' She took her smartphone out of her handbag and scribbled down reminder notes on the screen. 'You need your own solicitor. She might be a nutter. Have you given her Martin's ashes?'

'I haven't picked them up yet.'

'Jonty knows a solicitor. He'll come out to the house and see you if you aren't up to going into town. What about insurance policies?'

'I haven't looked at them yet.'

'Go and get them now,' commanded Theresa. 'Jonty and I will look at them and sort them out for you. Have you checked your bank account? If this woman is who she says she is, she may have access to Martin's cashpoint card. Don't tell me – you haven't checked.' She growled with upmarket frustration. 'Go get the policies.'

Dear Theresa had always been so wonderfully bossy, ever since Carla had met her eighteen years ago when they both worked in the regional office of the DIY chain Just The Job. Theresa, ten years Carla's senior, had been her section head in Purchasing and the two women had hit it off from day one. Theresa had been the poshest person Carla had ever met, but also the kindest. The friendship had long outlasted the job. Theresa was now a private elocution tutor. Carla fetched her box of paperwork from the cupboard in the dining room and Theresa began pulling documents out and separating them into relevant and irrelevant piles.

'Martin has a life insurance policy, that's good news. Ooh and it's rather a fat one. And you're the sole beneficiary, so we need to claim this asap. I presume you have a death certificate?'

'It's in the box,' nodded Carla.

'Where's the will?'

'He never made one.'

'Bloody marvellous. Joint savings account?'

'Yes, but there's not much in it. He took most of it out last year to pay for the new fence outside.'

'He used your savings when he was sitting on a fortune?' Theresa's lip lifted up in a sneer, then she mumbled a lot of four-letter expletives not very much under her breath. 'Okay. What about the house? Who owns it?'

'It's in Martin's name. We didn't transfer it to both names because I never asked him to, I didn't think we needed to. If I died first, he would get everything and if he died first . . .' Her voice trailed off.

'Jesus Christ,' muttered Theresa. 'Is there a mortgage on the house?'

'No. I don't want it though. I don't want to live here any more, Tez.'

'Well you can't just wave goodbye to your home and your security without a fight. Especially if this other woman is sitting on all that money. Greedy cow.'

'I could quite happily walk away from this house now, as I am, taking nothing.'

'Darling,' Theresa said, carefully but firmly. 'You haven't sustained a recent bang to the head, have you?'

'No. She can have everything. I just don't care. I really don't.'

'Well luckily for you, I do,' huffed Theresa. 'Now get that kettle on, please. My coffee has gone cold and I can't concentrate without a hot drink. I'll get Jonty on to this as soon as I get home.'

Jonty Pennant was an estate agent with an extensive database of contacts and a knowledge that far exceeded the boundaries of his job. He knew more about law than a lot of solicitors, more about numbers than most accountants and more about everything else than a whole seriesful of *University Challenge* contestants.

'How was New Zealand?' asked Carla as she waited for the kettle to boil.

'Good. We'll talk about it later,' said Theresa briskly.

'You're going to live out there, aren't you?' said Carla, trying to keep her voice steady.

'Don't know.'

'Liar.'

Theresa stopped rifling through the box of papers. 'I'm not going to leave you whilst you need me,' she said, swallowing down a lump of emotion in her throat. 'We haven't fully decided what we are doing yet.'

'I should think you were a pair of idiots if you stayed here when your son was having a baby.'

'Okay then,' said Theresa with gruff resignation. 'Yes, we are going out there. But it won't be for ages. Now get out any biscuits you have as well. I need carbs to concentrate.'

Theresa lifted her eyes and smiled at her friend who was reaching for the biscuit tin in the cupboard. How could Martin have done this to lovely Carla? He should have been counting his blessings, not playing away. Theresa had never really liked Martin that much. He wasn't a catch, lookswise, and had been very anti-social, barely able to grumble a 'hello' if Theresa ever called around at weekends. She'd always thought Carla far too good for him. *Carla would have thought the same had she seen herself through my eyes*, thought Theresa. Carla thought of herself as very ordinary and a bit plump and Theresa suspected that Martin encouraged her to think that way. She would never have thought of herself as a pretty woman with huge chocolate-brown eyes, a long thick mane of Italian-dark hair, a wide sensuous mouth and cheekbones that could have cut glass. As for her voice – smoky and soft – Theresa had told her on more than one occasion that she should be running a phone-sex line.

Carla made fresh coffee and tipped out some biscuits onto a plate. This Martin and Julie mess wasn't going to go away, but at least with Theresa and Jonty on her side she could see a prick of light at the end of the – albeit very long – tunnel ahead.

Chapter 16

Sherry made her Tuesday visit to Molly's house again, bringing two custard slices the size of house bricks this time. It would have taken Molly a year to digest hers had she eaten it all, and given her diabetes if she'd managed the half-inch-thick sticky sugar icing on top. She forced down a little piece, trying not to gag, and said that she would have the rest later for tea.

'Oh, you won't see me for a couple of weeks,' said Sherry as a shower of pastry crumbs shot from her mouth. 'Gram and I are going to our villa. Not sure when we will be back; we'll ring you, obviously.'

'Oh how lovely,' said Molly, adding 'for you', but meaning, *for me.*

'Yes. Gram wants a break. He's working far too hard. We both need some sunshine and stifado. Is there any more tea in that pot, dear? This pastry is making my throat very dry.'

Molly filled Sherry's cup up, whilst wishing she would go. She had already mentioned Autumn Grange twice since walking through the door. Apparently they were having an open day and afternoon tea next month and a local celebrity's aunt had just been admitted. Molly was tempted to tell Sherry that she had been totally won over and would like to move into Autumn Grange as soon as possible, but she was worried that Sherry would have her bags packed before she admitted it was a joke.

Molly noticed that when Sherry went to the toilet she had taken her cavernous handbag with her. Molly definitely heard the creak of the third bedroom floor whilst she was up there, but wouldn't have dared to confront her about it. She was scared to tell Margaret that Sherry was snooping around too because she knew her sister would launch straight into accusation and it would cause all sorts of trouble. She foresaw that Sherry would flounce out and persuade Graham never to see his mother again.

Finally, Sherry announced that she should be off. Apparently she needed a new suitcase from town and was heading off to Argos. The sight of her car backing down the drive was sweeter than the pastry sitting in her fridge, which Molly could now tip safely in the bin. As Molly was waving her off it came to her how strange it was for Sherry to admit she was off to Argos. Sherry had once told her that she only ever bought Louis Vuitton luggage.

Molly had things to do today. She wanted to take a trip out to Holmfirth to find a suitable wedding anniversary present for the Brandywines. There was a lovely shop there which sold cruisewear: tuxedos, long dresses, costume jewellery, stoles and the like. The summer was finally here at last. It had been a long winter, but the sun was making up for lost time by shining its best and the drive out there was very pleasant.

In the cruisewear shop, she found a beautiful peacock-blue shawl fringed with feathers for Margaret – her favourite colour – and a matching bow tie and cummerbund for Bernard. She had already arranged, via the travel agent, for there to be a basket of champagne and chocolate and flowers and other goodies delivered to their cabin on the actual day of their anniversary too. Molly wished she

was going with them. She had always wanted to take a
cruise, but the Brandywines hadn't fancied it until recently.
She would miss her sister terribly; not that she would admit
that and spoil it for them. She would send them off on their
way at the weekend with a delighted smile.

Holmfirth was rich with lovely shops: tearooms, old
bookshops, gift emporiums, antique shops and the gallery of
the watercolour artist Ashley Jackson. Margaret and Bernard
had an original Jackson in their sitting room: a moody view
of the moors, the sky full of anger, threatening a downpour
on a rugged landscape splashed with bright purple heather.
It was understated and very beautiful. She had liked it so
much, they had bought her a small print of it for her own
bedroom and the artist had personally signed it for her and
kindly written 'Happy 65th Birthday Molly' on it. Molly
took a walk up to the gallery to look at the pictures in the
window, then she crossed the road to Moores antique shop,
around which she had enjoyed many a potter. Inside was a
jumble of old typewriters, scythes, books and chairs,
although the glass cabinets against the wall housed finer and
more sophisticated pieces: china, vintage biscuit tins, glass
vases, collectable toys of yesteryear. Upstairs there was more
of the same. Nice to look at but nothing that she wanted to
buy. Molly was about to turn back to the staircase when she
spotted it on the bottom shelf of one of the cabinets, next
to a stuffed hare: the Royal Doulton figure she had been
searching for. She blinked hard. It had a nine-hundred and
fifty pound ticket on it.

Molly went back downstairs to ask the shopkeeper if she
could take a look at it. The shopkeeper unlocked the cabinet door then placed the figurine gently into her hands.
Molly turned it over, hunting for a sign that it wasn't hers –
a mark, a chip, but just as her own was, this was in perfect
condition.

'I've never seen that one before. It's very rare,' said the shopkeeper. 'And especially in as good a nick as that.'

'Where did you get it?' asked Molly, her throat dry enough to crack.

'Someone brought it in and asked us if we were interested in buying it.'

'Can you remember what they looked like? Was it a man or a woman? When was it?' The shopkeeper shrugged. 'Sorry, I can't remember, we see so many people. I think it was about a month ago.' He scratched his head. 'It might have been longer though. Or was it a couple of weeks ago?'

'Thank you,' said Molly, handing it back. 'I had the same piece but I lost it.'

The shopkeeper pulled in a sharp intake of breath. 'Expensive loss that one. I'd have a good look around for it if I were you.'

'Yes, yes, I will,' said Molly. She couldn't afford to buy it. She couldn't prove it was hers and if it was, how on earth had it ended up in a shop in Holmfirth? The daft thing was, she knew it *was* hers. But she couldn't explain it at all, and that frightened her.

Chapter 17

Today in the tearoom, it was Charles Dickens Tuesday. The last time he had visited, Mr Singh had called her chocolate and brandy cake 'chocolate and *Brandon* cake' following a conversation about Jane Austen, and it had given Leni the idea to have her ten-per-cent-off Tuesdays themed. Any object in the cabinets which had anything to do with the author was discounted today and she had special cakes – Oliver Twist strawberries and cream cake and Great Expectations violet and dark chocolate cake. She had just finished sticking a poster on the wall advertising her author-themed days when the bell on the door jangled, announcing a customer. She twisted around to find a small elderly lady, slim as a reed but very smartly dressed, with beautiful snow-white hair pinned into a pleat at the back. She looked slightly disorientated.

'Can I help you?' asked Leni.

'Are you open?' said Molly.

'Absolutely,' smiled Leni. 'Take a seat. The menu is on the table.'

'Thank you.' Molly sat down on the nearest heart-backed chair and reached for the menu, propped between ceramic book-shaped salt and pepper pots. There was a small selection of dishes: choices of sandwiches – on granary, white, cold or toasted, a warm chicken and mushroom pastry, scones and cakes of the day (with a note saying, *please ask for flavours*). Molly chose a scone and a pot of tea and whilst Leni was preparing it, Molly pressed her head in her hands and hoped her fast-developing headache would subside. It had been coming on since she left the antique shop in Holmfirth. She had felt so shaky up the road that she knew she had to stop for a few moments or she would have crashed the car. Questions had been flying around in her head: how could that figurine be hers? But she knew it was. So how had it ended up there then? It didn't make sense. It obviously wasn't hers. *But then where is yours?* She racked her brains, trying to think if she had put out any bags for charity recently and might inadvertently have put her figurine in there; but she knew she hadn't. She'd had a big clear-out before Christmas and had nothing left to donate, and the figurine had definitely still been in her house then, she remembered – or did she? Was her mental state slipping and she was the last to be aware of it? Is that why Sherry kept mentioning Autumn Grange?

She was going to pull in at Maltstone garden centre and take a driving break, and then she spotted the much nearer new development at Spring Hill, with a sign reading 'The Teashop on the Corner'.

She let her eyes wander around. It was a pretty little place. The cabinets against the walls were filled with wonderful things that appealed to her love of both books and nice stationery. Molly got up to take a closer look. There was a beautiful set of notecards decorated with all the books the Brontës had written. No one wrote letters any more, she thought sadly. It was all email and texting. History was going to be robbed of detail if people weren't careful. And poor lovers – how could an email replace a hand-written letter on heavyweight paper? She thought of all the letters she had in the bottom of her treasure box, tied together by a ribbon. Letters she had written and never sent. Letters that held all the secrets of her heart. *All of them.*

Harvey Hoyland. Why was he on her mind so much of late?

'Here you go,' said Leni, setting a tray down on the table. There was a plump cherry scone, curls of butter, a pot with clotted cream and one with jam. The teapot was a china one covered in roses. It didn't match the delicate cup with bluebells on it, which didn't match the gold-rimmed saucer yet the effect was all the more charming for it.

'You have such lovely things in your shop,' said Molly. 'I didn't know this place existed.'

'I don't think anyone does,' laughed Leni. 'Not yet anyway. I did have an open day and put an advert in the *Daily Trumpet* but they printed that the shop was in Penistone.'

'That's a shame, though sadly too typical of the *Daily Trumpet*,' said Molly, sitting back down and slicing the scone in half. 'I shall tell my sister. She would love it here. She and I are both great readers. I've already spotted her Christmas present, I think. That stationery set with the Brontë books on it.'

'You should wait for Brontë Tuesday then,' smiled Leni. 'There will be ten per cent off. It's Charles Dickens day today.'

'I shall,' said Molly. 'Thank you for telling me. That was very kind of you.'

'Isn't it sad that hardly anyone writes letters any more?' said Leni, as if she had picked up Molly's thoughts. 'If we aren't careful, there will be no records left for future gener-ations.'

'I used to love getting letters,' mused Molly. 'I can't

remember the last time I had one, though. The post only brings me junk or bills or advertising.' She noticed there was a wall covered in postcards by the door. She thought of the postcard in her treasure box, the seaside donkey. *Wish you were here.*

As Leni busied herself behind her counter, Molly nibbled at her scone and drank her tea and felt her nerves settle as if the calm of the room had reached inside her. Fears about her mental state were steadying and were no longer fizzing and firing in her brain like unstable fireworks. She made a promise to herself that the moment she had another panic attack about her actions, she would book an appointment with the doctor.

Then the bell above the door tinkled, and another customer walked in. A woman with dark circles under her eyes; and Molly, just for a moment, wondered if this charming little teashop drew people with worries to it so that it could work its magic on them.

Chapter 18

Carla had done her shopping in the Tesco in Penistone. That way she was sure of not bumping into anyone she knew, because it was sod's law that when you weren't feeling or looking your best and were in no mood to chat, you instantly fell into an orbit of people who wanted to catch up. She didn't buy much because she wasn't hungry at all. She put some microwave meals, coffee, cheese and eggs, some headache tablets and a packet of multi-grain Ryvita in her trolley and added a hand of bananas to give her some energy, though she knew deep down that they'd go black and she'd end up throwing them out.

She headed back home a different way to the one she had come for some variety and noticed that there was a new building complex on the side of Spring Hill. The last time she had been up here, there had been a half-derelict old wire factory on the site. Now there was a stone quadrangle of half-built shops and a sign advertising the Teashop on the Corner. On a whim, she decided to indicate right and check it out. She was really starting to hate her marital home now. She didn't belong there; it felt cursed by Julie, so the less time she spent there the better. Having a coffee would kill an hour at least, and give her something to think about other than the mess she was in.

The teashop was indeed on the corner, the door flanked by pots of cheerful flowers. She could guess from the outside what the inside might be like and she was right – pretty and chic and very inviting. There was an old-fashioned counter at one end, with cakes under glass domes and – *my oh my* – the most gorgeous displays of book-related items in glass cabinets.

An old lady was the only other customer and smiled a hello. There was a spiky-haired small woman behind the counter. Carla thought she looked like an elf, with her cheerful face and almond-shaped eyes.

'Please take a seat. The menus are on the table,' she called.

It was the weirdest feeling, thought Carla as she reached for the menu. She felt the tension which had been gripping her shoulders like eagles' talons loosen off as if it was afraid of cake.

Molly poured out some more tea. She felt instantly better for a kind word and a few mouthfuls of scone. So much nicer than those monstrosities of confectionery that Sherry brought with her. She would come back to this place when Margaret was on her cruise and buy something from the cabinets to chase away some boredom. It had a lovely feel to it, and the shop owner was one of those people who had 'laughing eyes', as Ma Brandywine called them. You could fake a smile on the mouth, but never one in the eyes. Molly figured she must be in her mid-thirties, from the faint lines radiating from those eyes. With her spiky brown hair and her tiny, turned-up nose, she reminded Molly of an elf. A friendly elf. And the elf's scone and tea had worked wonders to lift her headache away.

'Warm today, isn't it?' she said to the dark-haired lady at

the next table. She expected her to answer with an Italian accent, but she was a townie.

'Very. We should be out sunbathing, not sitting in teashops.'

'Indeed we should.'

Carla ordered a latte from Leni and a slice of the chocolate cake.

'I've been to Holmfirth,' said Molly. 'I wouldn't have known this place existed if I hadn't passed it.'

'Same here,' said Carla. 'I've just come from Penistone.'

The door tinkled and in walked Mr Singh. He seemed delighted that Leni had customers.

'I think your discount Tuesday is working,' he said.

Leni had heard the ladies admit that they'd driven in on a whim when passing, but nevertheless she nodded.

'Today is Charles Dickens Tuesday,' she told him.

'I know. I have seen the poster in your window. I think I shall have some of that strawberry cake,' said Mr Singh, rubbing his hands together and grinning at the two ladies.

'It's not strawberry cake, it's Oliver Twist cake, I'll have you know,' Leni gently admonished him.

'Oh,' said Mr Singh. 'And what flavour is the Oliver Twist cake?'

'Strawberry,' smiled Leni and Mr Singh laughed and so infectious was the sound that Carla and Molly chuckled quietly too.

'Very good, very good,' said Mr Singh. 'Tea and Oliver Twist cake then please, Leni.' And he sat down on one of the vacant tables.

I'll definitely come back here, thought both Molly and Carla when they left. There was something about the little teashop and the friendly owner that took them away from dark places in their heads. It was a temporary magic, but it might just work again, they hoped.

Chapter 19

Theresa and Jonty arrived at Carla's house with a Chinese takeaway and two bottles of red wine. Dear Jonty, the tallest and cleverest man she knew, enfolded her in a huge bear hug. By the time he had released her, Theresa had taken out the plates which were warming in the oven.

'Come on, whilst it's hot. I'm absolutely famished, so we can talk whilst we eat. Jonty – pour the wine, darling.'

'Aye, dun't worry. I've got it soor-ted.'

Jonty's acccent was as broad Yorkshire as Theresa's was cut-glass.

'Don't give me a lot of food, I'm not hungry,' said Carla.

'You'll eat what you are given,' replied Theresa sternly. 'You're going to need all the strength you can get.'

'That sounds ominous,' replied Carla.

'We aren't going to dress it up,' said Theresa, ripping the top from a carton of egg fried rice. 'It could be better news. Jonty and I have dissected all your paperwork.'

'I've spoken to Freddy on your behalf. He's put you a formal letter in the post outlining everything,' said Jonty, screwing the top off the first bottle of red. 'Bloody good solicitor, I have to say. You're all right with me talking to him for you?' he checked.

'Of course,' replied Carla. 'I'm grateful for any help you can give me, and I know you've got my back, Jonty.'

Jonty pushed his gold-rimmed glasses further up his nose.

'Sit,' commanded Theresa, fitting a fork in Carla's hand as if she were a five-year-old.

'Julie *is* Martin's legal wife, that checks out,' began Jonty. 'But we might still have a case for claiming something from the estate under the 1975 Inheritance Act if you can prove you were dependent on him prior to his death. When were you made redundant?'

'About a month before Martin died.'

'Hmm . . .' replied Jonty, spearing a mushroom. 'Well, I am absolutely sure there is a way to secure this as your home, at least until any claim you make has been decided upon.'

'I don't want to,' replied Carla. Pat Morrison's words about starting afresh had never left the forefront of her mind. 'I want to leave this house. I'm going to lose anyway in the end. Julie Pride told me herself that their money was in her name, and I'm sure she could prove that Martin was going to leave me. She's pregnant with his child. I don't have the money or the energy to put up a fight. I don't want to end up in a newspaper as a sensationalist story, I just want to go quietly.'

'Don't be insane, darling,' replied Theresa, raking a hand through her short red curls. 'You contributed to the upkeep of this house. You have a case.'

'Julie said I can have all the contents. I'm going to sell them and start again somewhere. There's only two hundred pounds in our joint savings account, but I'll transfer it out and close it down. I have Martin's insurance policy and a couple of thousand pounds of my own so I'm sure I'll be able to rent something.'

'Have you had a look around for any of his bank books?' asked Jonty.

'Yes, but I can't find them. He always used to keep things like that in a shoe-box in his wardrobe. I presume he must have taken them to Julie's house so I couldn't see them.'

'Bastard,' snarled Theresa, pronouncing it 'bahhh-sted' and making it sound a classy, desirable thing to be.

'He is that,' agreed Jonty. 'What a chuffing nightmare for you, love. We'll get you sorted though, don't worry.'

'Are you absolutely sure you don't want to fight?' asked Theresa. As a red-head, she hated to think of battle not being raised.

'Yes,' said Carla. 'Really.'

Theresa heard the weariness in her friend's voice and she bit her lip to stop herself from trying to discourage her from walking away. She had to recognise that Carla was a very different animal to her and it wasn't fair to make her do what was not in her nature, especially as Jonty had more or less told her that the chances were that Carla would end up with very little and possibly, a large legal bill to boot. Any victory would more than likely be a Pyrrhic one.

'Then I'll help you pack up,' she said.

'Thank you but no, I'm going to do it alone,' replied Carla. 'I want to go through every single thing myself.' Theresa opened her mouth to insist, then shut it again when Jonty gave her a look of admonishment. 'You're very sweet, Tez, and thank you and I hope you understand.'

'Yes, of course I do,' nodded Theresa. And she did.

'Well, there is some good news,' began Jonty, forking up some noodles from a carton. 'Exquisite timing on Martin's part for dying and opening up this opportunity for you.'

'Jonty, please,' exclaimed Theresa.

'Shhh, my love. Now, Carla, one of my clients has to get rid of a property very quickly. Nice little house, albeit rather an odd design. Architect must have been pissed when he designed it. Could deffo do with a lick of paint and some cosmetic changes, mind. He converted one side of the house to a granny flat for his mother, who sadly never got the chance to live in it. It's cheap and if you bought it, you could rent out the separate flat and earn some revenue to live off.'

'A separate flat? It sounds expensive.'

'You'd be surprised.'

'Where is it?'

'Little Kipping. Maltstone way.'

'I know it. It's nice there.' It was near to that lovely little teashop she had been to today.

'Bit far out of town but he wants it sold quick. You, as a potential cash buyer, are all his dreams come true.'

'Cash buyer?' Carla laughed.

'Your insurance policy on Martin's life would more than cover the cost of buying this house. It would also leave you with, perhaps, ten thousand spare,' said Jonty. 'Sounds a lot, although that sort of money doesn't go far these days. But you would own a house outright.'

Carla's hand froze on a prawn toast. 'What?'

'It's true. I've checked all the figures through with Freddy. It would be far better for you in the long run than renting and you certainly won't get a mortgage being unemployed. The banks aren't loaning anything at the moment. The good old days of easy lending are well and truly gone.'

Carla sat in silent shock for a few moments, then rotated her finger in the air.

'I'm sorry, Jonty. Can you run that past me again?'

'In layman's terms,' said Jonty in his gruff but patient voice, 'you took out an insurance policy on Martin's life, and whoever sold it to you should have had a slap. Had Martin stayed alive until he was sixty-five, the policy would have ended and you'd have got nowt. And you've been paying far too much every month for it. Very badly advised. However,' he paused to make sure she was with him so far, 'Martin died whilst the policy was still in effect, which means that you are due a cheque for about two hundred thousand pounds.'

All Carla could manage by way of reply was 'Jesus Christ.'

'Now, I'm not telling you what to do with that money. What I am saying is that you can rent a house and throw your money away, or you can buy one and have some security. And I happen to have one on my books that is worth a lot more than the price tag says it is. And it will generate a revenue for you as well.'

Carla was gobsmacked. The thought of her owning a house outright was too much to take in in one single bite.

'And you do know that Jonty isn't just trying to offload any old house onto you,' said Theresa.

'Of course I know that, Theresa,' said Carla with a tut. The thought never even crossed her mind. She trusted Jonty implicitly.

'You must take everything of value out of the house and leave the rest for his wife to sort out.' Theresa could no longer say Martin's name.

'eBay is very good for a quick sale of the bigger items,' put in Jonty.

Carla gave a hoot of laughter. 'Have you seen our furniture, Jonty? Who'd buy it?' She waved her arm towards the sample which the room held. So many things had needed replacing for years: the cheapest-of-the-cheap dining table they were sitting at had been supposed to be a temporary make-do when she moved in; the kitchen dresser was something that Martin had inherited with the house. In the lounge the sofa sagged down in the middle and the TV was so old it had been invented before pixels. And Carla would definitely not be taking her bed with her. That was the first thing she would buy new when she moved.

'Well, before you start your escape plans, I'll pick you up at eight o'clock sharp in the morning and take you out to Little Kipping to see the house. If you like it, I can draft up a short rental agreement so you can move in whilst the buying procedure gets up and running – a month should do it. I'll sure I can twist my client's arm to agree to a pepper-corn rent.'

Carla blinked back the tears which were fast rising to her eyes. What would she have done without Jonty and Theresa's help? How would she cope when they were living on the other side of the world? Well, she would; she'd have to. She was being forced into a new chapter of her life and she could either kick against it or run with open arms towards it and embrace it. She had to take Pat Morrison's advice and leave everything behind and move forward. She lifted a spring roll to her lips and felt the spark of an appetite returning.

Chapter 20

Even now, after all these years, Shaun still awoke in the middle of the night imagining that he was back in *that* house, in bed, drawing warmth from a brother or sister – he couldn't remember which – snuggled up next to him, hearing the battering of someone's fist on the door outside. Shouting. Footsteps travelling up the bare wooden stairs, the light switching on. He felt the cold as he was ripped from the bed, arms around him that offered no comfort. Behind him he could hear one of his siblings protesting. 'Let me go.' The baby crying in the cot.

His mother swaying. 'Leave them be, you bastards.'

'You're drunk, you durty bitch.'

Neighbours were outside on their steps, alerted by the commotion.

'About time.'

'You should have looked after your children, then they wouldn't be takin' them away, you durty whore.'

'Not two of your wee ones has the same father.'

He was inside a car, being driven away from everything he knew, away from his yellow toy car, his teddy that smelt of tobacco, his books with the big letters. He would end up in a succession of bigger, cleaner foster homes with sober, cold people and then, at ten, a home for unwanted boys in which, so his memories led him to believe, he was constantly fighting. Fighting to get stolen possessions back, fighting against bullies, fighting the priest who battered him with a cane. They threw him out at sixteen without a backward glance and he vowed that he would never again be at the mercy of anyone else. He'd be his own boss, he wouldn't answer to anyone, he wouldn't be controlled by anyone or be hit again. He'd survive and he'd work to make sure that he would never have to fight for his food or his safety. Shaun McCarthy never saw his mother or his siblings again.

Chapter 21

'Well, what do you think from the outside?'

'It's nice.' Carla tried to inject some enthusiasm into her voice, even though she wasn't feeling it.

Jonty laughed as he reached up to fasten one fallen side of the 'Dundealin' sign back onto its hook. 'It's the weirdest house I've ever tried to sell, but I think it would suit you very well. It's structurally sound, it's cheap, and you could get a nice rent from the mini flat. No need to furnish it; let the tenant worry about that. Obviously needs a good clean. And a few air-fresheners to take that not-lived-in smell away. Come on, let's give it a proper once-over.'

He opened the door which was placed near one end of the long narrow house.

'Where's your client live now?' asked Carla, taking in the snug sitting room which was next to a much-bigger-than-expected kitchen-diner.

'Costa del Sol at the moment.' Jonty tapped the side of his great nose. 'Ask no questions. Let's just refer to him as *Mr Pink*.'

Three words whispered from one part of Carla's brain into another: *Trust in pink* . . .

'He made a right arse of converting it, to be honest, which hasn't helped him secure a buyer. But, as I say, it is structurally sound. I've had an architect pal of mine look at it to check it out.'

'Have a lot of people viewed it?' asked Carla.

'Hardly anyone,' replied Jonty. 'Someone put in a stupid bid and Mr Pink was so insulted by it that he wouldn't accept their revised offer. I'll not say what he told me to tell them to do with it.'

'I thought he wanted a quick sale?'

'He does,' Jonty sighed. 'He also wants to have his cake and eat it. I'm forbidden from letting Russians view it and anyone from the police or armed forces.'

Carla's eyebrows rose. 'Is that legal?'

'Mine is not to reason why,' replied Jonty, throwing his arms wide. 'But I'd be lying if I didn't say that it does make my job easier if I secure him a sale with a thirtysomething female from the town in return for a stress-free cash sale for his asking price. I can arrange for a rental agreement to be drawn up for your tenant when you find one. I wouldn't charge you, of course.'

'You're too kind, Jonty,' said Carla. 'I'm going to miss you when you emigrate. I want to get settled in a new place as quickly as possible, then Theresa can stop worrying about me. I don't want to spoil your excitement.'

'We're both worrying about you,' said Jonty, bumping his head on one of the beams in the sitting room. This house with its low ceilings wouldn't have suited someone of his six-foot-seven height. 'You could always come with us to New Zealand, Carla.'

Carla gave her dear friend a fond smile.

'I like the UK, Jonty. I like the history and shopping in Leeds and going down to London and seeing the Queen. I like the seasons. I like battening down the hatches in the winter and watching the snow through the window and moaning about the rubbish summers. New Zealand is your dream – not mine. And I know it'll be fabulous and I'm very probably mad, but I like living in Yorkshire. I'll be okay. I'm a big girl.'

Jonty nodded slowly. 'Well, the offer remains there. You'll have to come out for a holiday. Anyway, let's get back to business.'

The house was beyond weird. It was a double-fronted build that had been split into two. The bigger half had a downstairs loo and a small cellar below the kitchen/diner which was a generously sized square room. There was a built-in oven, a fridge freezer and a washing machine. Jonty said that the owner was leaving them in. They had all seen better days, but they'd do for a while. In between the kitchen and lounge was a handsome swirl of staircase with a solid mahogany balustrade. The carpet on it was rather worn and a revolting shade of brown, but that was cosmetic and could be changed. Upstairs was a bedroom with a cheap white built-in wardrobe and a bathroom with a burgundy suite like something out of a 1970s MFI catalogue. Next door was a small box-room under the eaves which would be okay for storage but nigh on impossible to use as a spare bedroom. There was a long length of landing and a door at the end which led to the mini flat. This consisted of a bedroom with a small en-suite shower room complete with an avocado toilet and sink. A spiral staircase twirled down to a small sitting room with floor-to-ceiling French doors leading to a small square of private paved garden. There was no separate kitchen: the renter would need to share those facilities with Carla. Dundealin was detached, surrounded by a garden that was in serious need of some TLC. There was an old shabby shed at the bottom of it and two posts with a sagging washing line strung between them. High walls on each side separated it from its neighbours. It seemed the owner – *Mr Pink* – valued his privacy.

'I think I can get him to stump up half the stamp duty an' all if you move fast,' said Jonty. 'He wants to release his capital as quickly as possible. And then disappear.'

Carla blew two large cheekfuls of air out. 'I've never owned a house in my life. I can't imagine even having the amount of money to do it, never mind handing it over to buy one.'

'Personally, Carla, and you know me well enough to know that this isn't bullshit, I think you'd be mad to turn it down. You can afford the house. My advice would be to buy it. It's the best investment you'll make in a lifetime, unless you count over-insuring a feckless husband.'

'I'd own the house outright?'

'Yup.'

Carla thought about having a lot of money in the bank and all the things she could buy with it. She could go on holiday to the Maldives, buy a whole wardrobe of clothes from Vivien Westwood. A brand new Mercedes. Then Sensible Carla gave her a sharp rap on the side of her head and reminded her that she needed a home.

Let's call him Mr Pink.

'Shall I tell him you're interested? ' asked Jonty, taking out his mobile phone.

Trust in pink.

The words bubbled out of Carla. 'Yes, Jonty. Please.'

'Excellent.' Jonty began to scroll through his contact page.

Carla tried to imagine herself living there but couldn't. She'd thought she and Martin would grow old and grey in his bungalow. She had been happy there, happy as Mrs Pride. At least she had thought she was. She got back into Jonty's car and prepared herself mentally to start the final separation from that married life that never was.

Chapter 22

There was no time like the present. Carla was back home by nine a.m. and, after a fortifying cup of strong coffee, she changed into some tracksuit bottoms and an old T-shirt and said to herself, *Let's get cracking.*

Except she didn't know where to start. The task in front of her took daunting to another level. She gave herself the hard word. *Look, Carla, it's simple. Divide everything into the stuff you are taking, the stuff you intend to sell on and then you leave the rest for Julie. Okay?* Then she clapped her hands and got stuck in.

She pushed all the furniture in the sitting room to one end, designating an area for things she was going to claim. There were some nice pieces of pottery and ornaments in the cabinet which had belonged to Martin's parents. She didn't want them but they might fetch a decent price on eBay and she was going to need all the money she could get. She felt down the sides of her grotty sofa to see if there were any treasures. She found Martin's old Zippo lighter and 20p amongst a lot of fluff. She turned the metal lighter around in her hand and thought of him puffing the life into a cigarette, sitting in the chair tapping ash into a saucer whilst she scurried around getting his tea on a tray, ready to pamper him after a hard week working away from home. She didn't know whether to cry or spit and decided she might want to do a mixture of both. What would Julie think of the furniture she was going to leave for her, she wondered? It wasn't even good enough for a skip. Julie and Martin probably had one of those curving leather suites that seated eight. She pictured him sitting on it, watching a sixty-inch 3D LED TV and drinking a glass of champagne, and a pain cut through her as if Martin had stubbed out one of his cigarettes on her heart.

Sod what Julie thinks. You can either cry or get on with it, so which is it to be, girl? That voice again.

Carla used her anger to fuel her strength and pushed the sofa to the end of the room designated for the rubbish. Martin's tatty reclining chair joined it. So did the chipped and scratched coffee table and all Martin's videos and DVDs and their cronky old TV set which was two foot deep and all the ancient media equipment and his stack of *Which* magazines. Then she went into the kitchen to start there.

Dundealin had an oven, which was good, because Carla didn't want to take Martin's ancient one with her, the oven in which she had cooked his meals. She packed a few plates and pans and utensils to see her on for a bit until she could afford new, because eventually she was going to rid herself of everything Martin had ever touched. She made a note on her hand to ring the scrap man whose number she had torn out of the *Chronicle*. He would give her peanuts for the metal appliances and the bed frame, she knew, but it was better in her purse than in Julie's.

Carla checked every pocket of every garment in Martin's wardrobe before putting them in bin liners. She found he had the latest iPhone, battery totally flattened, in a pair of trousers. Presumably that was the one on which he used to contact Julie. For a moment she considered charging it up and reading the messages, then countered that by slamming it down hard on the windowsill until it shattered. Then she immediately regretted doing that because maybe it held answers to some of the thousands of questions floating around her head. Still, it was done now and maybe she was better off not knowing.

She found a roll of twenty-pound notes in the inside pocket of a jacket – over a thousand pounds. Other pockets yielded another two hundred. She'd cried to him the week before he died because she couldn't get a job and he'd put his arm around her and told her not to worry, that they'd manage. He'd given her a tenner and told her to go and buy them a bottle of wine to have with their dinner. And she'd bought as cheap a one as she could find to give him back some change. Carla wanted to scream. She wished she had checked his pockets when he was alive. But they didn't have that sort of relationship – she trusted him. She hadn't seen the slightest sign that he was about to leave her for another woman, especially one that he had impregnated. How stupid she was.

She emptied his drawers and there, in a sock, she found a long case with the word 'Cartier' in sloping letters emblazoned on the lid. She clicked it open to find a gold ladies' watch, the face ringed with diamonds. Carla's fingers were trembling as she lifted it out and turned it over to see if it had been engraved: it had. 'To J with all my love M.'

Carla remembered the box of Thornton's chocolates and the cookery book he'd bought for her birthday in February, still with the half-price label stuck on the front. The receipt in the sock said that Martin had paid four thousand two hundred pounds for that watch. Carla had to stop herself from launching it at the wall and smashing its smug little glittery face. She'd take it to a dealer and sell it.

'You . . . you . . . bastard,' Carla growled upwards, but the word wasn't enough to carry all the hurt and anger she wanted to direct towards him. There wasn't a word in existence to describe what Martin Pride was. She huffed. That was another thing she'd have to do – change her bank book and passport and Visa and so much other stuff back into her maiden name – *her real name* – Carla Martelli. She had never minded being a Martelli, but she had enjoyed being a Mrs, a Mrs Pride. And now she was a Miss Martelli again – well, she always had been really. And she had been washing Mr Pride's grotty pants and cooking Mr Pride's meals for ten years under the illusion that she had been doing wifely duties.

She put Martin's underwear in a separate bin bag. The charity shop might have been able to make use of his suits but no one would want to wear his old XXL Y-fronts or his socks. His bedside cabinet contained nothing of interest: spare pair of glasses, driving licence, passport, a packet of condoms, an ancient wrap of Beecham's Powders and a toe-nail clipper. In his best shoe, Carla found another roll of money which she shoved in her pocket. That would buy her some new bedding because she wasn't going to take her old duvet and pillows and sheets with her. And she couldn't take the dressing table which she had so lovingly restored because it was too wrapped up with memories of causing his death. Then again, maybe that was a reason to take it. She was so angry. In the cold light of day, she could see so clearly how worn out this house was – not dirty, because Carla couldn't abide dust or mess – but tired, everything in it in dire need of being replaced. She hadn't noticed it before, living in such close proximity to it all, but then a huge beam of torchlight, in the form of Martin's deception, had been shone on her life and she would never see anything the same way again.

Carla opened up another bin bag. She still had a long way to go. And who knew how many other rolls of money she would find. She would make sure she bought the biggest bottle of bloody champagne out of it to christen her new life.

Chapter 23

On the following Tuesday, Carla attended her dentist in Maltstone for her sixth-monthly check-up. She had meant to cancel it but they didn't have another appointment for six weeks and so she felt that she should go. Luckily she needed no treatment, which was some good news. She'd half expected to be told she needed root canal surgery, five crowns, twelve fillings and some new gums; that seemed to be the way her luck was running.

The receptionist gave her a funny look when she asked for her record to be changed back to her maiden name when she informed them of Martin's death. Carla wanted to shout at her, 'I'm not rejecting his memory, he was married to another bloody woman.' But she didn't want to wash her dirty linen in public.

Carla didn't want to go home yet and sit in a house which she had already mentally left. This was to be her last full day there. The scrap metal man had been, the charity wagon had picked up Martin's suits and the house clearance people were coming that afternoon. She had picked up Martin's ashes at the weekend and resisted the urge to kick the urn around the garden. She would be glad to leave the bungalow, she didn't want to live in it any more, but if she was totally honest, she didn't particularly want to live in Dundealin either. She could break out in a cold sweat if she thought about spending all that money on the odd-looking house with the worst internal decor she had ever seen. She took a detour to Little Kipping and sat in the car for a few minutes gazing at her new home. It looked grim and unfamiliar and her heart sank. *What the hell have I done?* she asked herself. At that moment, staying in her old home and battling it out with Julie for a share of Martin's estate seemed like the slightly better option, but she rejected it almost at once. She could imagine Julie's side of the story appearing on the front page of the *Daily Trumpet*, Carla's worst nightmare. Nope, her only option was to move into Dundealin, a place that meant nothing to her. Carla felt suddenly adrift; she belonged nowhere, she had nothing, no one. Panic gave all her organs a squeeze simultaneously with its long bony claws.

Spring Hill was nearby and a cup of coffee in the lovely tearoom was a welcoming thought. She turned into the car park, waiting patiently for a digger to make a three-point turn. To the right, men were working on the unfinished units of the quadrangle. The teashop in the corner looked sweet and inviting with its brightly coloured pots of flowers outside it and hanging baskets. Carla loved to read. Most of the boxes she was taking from the bungalow were full of her books. They had entertained her for many an empty hour but, alas, not this week. She had tried but failed to lose herself in a good story.

There was a poster in the window informing would-be customers that today was Arthur Conan Doyle Tuesday. The tables in the centre of the shop were empty except for one, occupied by the elderly Asian man she had met the previous week. He nodded a greeting at Carla as she passed him and took a seat.

Behind the shop counter Leni was wrapping a parcel.

'Good morning,' she called, her brown eyes smiling as much as the curve of her mouth. 'The cakes today are Watson white chocolate and Holmes rum truffle. Just call me over when you're ready to order.'

'Thank you,' said Carla and slipped off her jacket. She picked up the menu then, but her eyes were anywhere but on it. There were some new things in the cabinets: a pretty magnifying glass on a necklace; a spectacle case which looked as if it had been made from one of the old Penguin classic covers; a pack of postcards reproduced to replicate old Victorian cards in their rich, heavy colours; the most darling old-fashioned library kit with a stamp and borrowing cards and pockets to stick in books; and a Home Sweet Home hanging made to look like a classic novel. She noticed that next to that cabinet was a wall full of postcards pinned at random angles. The top right corners had been removed. She guessed that the stamps had been cut off to save for guide dogs, because that's what Carla did with any stamped mail that she received. Not that she got that much these days that wasn't franked. She noticed one on the floor and picked it up. It had a picture of a Flamenco dancer on the front and she couldn't resist a sneaky peek on the back as she went to pin it back up.

Dear Mum
So *beautiful* here. Flooded with sunshine.
We are all having such a great time.
Wish you were here.
Anne XXX

It must be from the owner's daughter, thought Carla. She imagined a young student type having a ball in the sun with friends before life got serious. And full of crap.

There was a pinboard between the front windows with some cards on it – *Saturday Girl/Boy wanted*, she read. One had a window-cleaning service advertised, another was an offer to clear leaves out from guttering. That reminded her: she had some prepared cards in her bag advertising the Dundealin flat. She was going to call in at Maltstone post office and leave one there and in Morrison's and Tesco in town. They'd be a lot busier than this place, but the teashop had the advantage of being very close to Little Kipping. She was now the official sitting tenant on a month's lease but soon to be Dundealin's owner. The sale was well underway.

Carla turned her attention to the menu. She'd only intended to have a coffee but the Holmes cake sounded too good to miss. The old guy in the dark-blue turban was eating that, she noticed. He had crumbs on his clipped grey beard.

'Is it nice?' she asked him.

'Delicious,' he said with a wide friendly smile. 'I very much recommend it.'

'Okay, you've sold it,' smiled Carla and waved to Leni.

'I'd like a white filter coffee and a slice of the Holmes cake please.'

'Cream?'

'Oh, why not.' It wouldn't hurt her. She had lost so much weight since Martin died, she could do with putting some on before her skirt fell down in the supermarket and exposed her pants.

Carla heard her phone beep in her bag. Jonty had chased up the insurance company and was sending news that the monies would be in her bank account within twenty-four hours. She had just finished replying her thanks to him when the cake and coffee arrived.

'I wonder, could I put a card up on your noticeboard?' asked Carla. 'What are your rates?'

'A pound a month, payable in advance,' replied Leni. 'It goes in a charity tin for guide dogs.'

'Is that where the stamps on your postcards go too?'

'Yep,' said Leni.

What a lovely face she has, thought Carla. She wished she had a cute nose like a pixie too. She had her mum's nose – long, straight and narrow. Still, at least it wasn't like her old dad's – a proper Roman nose if ever there was one. She missed them both so much. Her dad had died a year before her wedding and her mum had joined him only a few months ago in November. They would have both been furious on her behalf about what had happened to her.

Carla reached in her bag for one of her cards and her purse.

'I have a room to rent. It's near to here.'

'Happy to put it up for you,' replied the smiley lady. 'I'll do it now. You enjoy your coffee and I'll bring the bill over in a moment.'

Chapter 24

Molly was missing Margaret and Bernard terribly and they'd only been gone three days. She'd had a phone call from them that morning from Venice and they sounded as if they were having a wonderful time.

She took herself off to the teashop on Spring Hill. A poster in the window told her that it was Arthur Conan Doyle day today. Molly was delighted to find the Asian gentleman and the Italian-looking lady there.

'How good to see you again,' Leni greeted her. She was pinning a card to one of the noticeboards, advertising for a tenant.

'You remembered me?' asked Molly.

'Indeed I do,' replied Leni. 'Tea and scones and you expressed an interest in the Brontë notecard set.'

'Is it a good thing or a bad thing that I'm so memorable?' replied Molly with a little laugh.

'I would have said nearly always a good thing,' butted in Mr Singh.

'I love that handbag you've got made out of a *Hound of the Baskervilles* book,' said Carla.

'You should buy it,' said Mr Singh. 'There is ten per cent off today.'

'Mr Singh, are you after a job as a salesman?' chuckled Leni.

Mr Singh's laughter joined hers. 'I think I would make a very good salesman, Leni,' he said.

Molly looked behind her to see which bag Carla meant.

'It's in this one,' said Mr Singh, pointing to the cabinet next to the wall of postcards.

Molly walked across to look at it and decided that would make an even nicer present for her sister than the notecards.

'I bought a bag for my daughter,' said Mr Singh, drinking the last of his tea. 'No one will have one quite like it in America. It was a Jane Austen one.'

'I love Jane Austen's books,' returned Molly. '*Persuasion* was always my favourite.'

'Ah, with the gallant Captain Wentworth,' sighed Mr Singh.

'You've read it, Mr Singh?' asked Leni.

'Of course,' he replied, taking his wallet out of his pocket to settle his bill. 'You sound surprised.'

'I confess, I am, Mr Singh,' replied Leni.

'I have read all the books by Dickens, Thomas Hardy, the Brontës, Jane Austen and many more. I fell in love with them all when I came over here to live. I have always been a great reader, ever since I was a small boy.'

'Me too,' nodded Molly. 'I can never understand people who don't like books. I derive so much pleasure from them. I can't tell you how many times I have read *Persuasion*, yet it remains such a fresh, wonderful story.'

'I agree totally,' said Carla. 'Everyone goes mad about Mr Darcy but I always thought Captain Wentworth would have made my heart flutter more.'

'It's the uniform,' smiled Molly. 'All the nice girls love a sailor.'

'Her last novel,' sighed Mr Singh, standing to go. 'And

her best, I think. The story of a woman who thinks she will never blossom and of the love of her life returning for another chance.'

'Yes indeed,' said Molly, giving her order for a pot of tea and a scone. But unlike Anne Elliott, Molly would never know what that felt like. It was far too late in the day.

'Pavitar Singh,' he said, holding out his hand to Molly.

'Oh, er, Molly. Molly Jones.'

'Nice to meet you, Molly.' He then held out his hand to Carla.

'Carla Pr ... sorry, Martelli,' she said.

Mr Singh chuckled. 'How could you forget such a beautiful name?'

'I'm recently ... divorced. I'm getting used to my maiden name again,' Carla said.

'I'm very sorry to hear that,' said Mr Singh, his voice now weighted with sympathy. 'Anyway, I hope I have the pleasure of seeing you ladies again.' Had he been wearing a hat instead of a turban, he would have tipped it towards them.

'What a gentleman,' said Carla when he had gone.

'Isn't he a darling?' said Leni. 'Oh and I'm Leni by the way, seeing as it seems to be introductions day.' She then presented Molly with a giant scone.

'I'll never eat all this,' Molly laughed. 'And if I do, you might have to widen the doorway.'

Carla thought the older lady could do with a bit of meat on her bones. She was very thin.

'I've put a pound on just looking at it,' she said. 'But then I have Italian blood. We are very good at putting weight on.'

'I thought you might be,' said Molly, then added quickly, 'Oh, Italian, I mean, not good at putting weight on. You have such beautiful colouring.'

Carla blew out her cheeks bashfully. 'Black hair shows the grey too quickly.'

She's putting herself down, thought Molly, sensing the very attractive woman didn't have much confidence.

'Have you any ideas what theme you're going to have next Tuesday?' asked Carla as Leni brought her bill over.

'I think we're due a Brontë Tuesday,' replied Leni with a cheery smile. 'I've got some gorgeous author pendants arriving next week with the sisters' heads on them. And some shopping bags.'

'Where do you find it all?' Carla asked. 'I've never seen any of this stuff in shops.'

'Oh everywhere,' replied Leni, 'I have to look all over the world. And I send it out all over the world too. The Japanese are mad for the Brontës.'

'*Jane Eyre* is one of my favourite books too,' Molly put in, as she buttered her scone.

Carla tried not to think that she had too much in common with Jane Eyre and Rochester's wife that he hadn't divorced. Oh how she wished she could stuff Julie Pride up in an attic. Then again, Martin was becoming less and less of her Mr Rochester with every passing day.

She checked her watch and realised she had better get home. The house clearance people were coming in just over an hour.

'I'll love you and leave you,' she announced, slipping her arms into her jacket. 'I'm moving house tomorrow morning, so I'm pretty busy.'

'Oh what a task,' said Molly. 'I do hope it goes well.'

'Yes, good luck,' added Leni. 'Very stressful business. Hope to see you soon.'

'You will,' said Carla. 'I'll be back for my elevenses on Brontë Tuesday.'

And so will I, thought Molly. Tuesdays were much improved, now that she had discovered this teashop and these nice people and Sherry was overseas in Greece.

Chapter 25

'You must be Shaun McCarthy. I'm Will Linton,' Will held out his hand as he introduced himself.

'Linton Roofing?' Shaun knew the name, vaguely recognised the man in front of him in the smart black trousers and expensive blue shirt, though he was sure he hadn't spoken to him before. Maybe it was the accent that brought him to mind. He knew Will Linton was from somewhere in the East End of London. He shook his hand.

'Yep,' said Will, nodding his head. 'That's me.'

'I'm so sorry about what happened to your business,' said Shaun.

'Ah, shit happens, mate,' said Will, lifting up his hands and his shoulders in a gesture of resignation. 'But now I need a job. Labouring, anything. I ain't proud.'

Shaun shook his head slowly. 'I'm so sorry, there's nothing. I've just taken a labourer on. I've got no jobs. Not at the moment, anyway. Have you tried up at Winterworld?'

'Yeah, they haven't got anything either.'

Shaun watched Will Linton's Adam's apple rise and drop as he swallowed. He had probably had to gulp a lot of pride down since his business failed.

'Look,' began Shaun. 'If you want to leave me your

number and if, by any chance, I need an extra pair of hands I'll ring you and give you the opportunity to say yes. It would be ground work though, not roofing.'

Perfect.

'Aw that'd be great,' said Will, reaching in his pocket for a business card. The home number on it had been scribbled out leaving only the mobile. Not much point in anyone ringing the house phone when it had been cut off.

'I'll get some new business cards eventually,' said Will, with a small self-conscious laugh. 'When I get a business. And a house. Thanks, mate. I really appreciate it.'

'It might only be a couple of days here and there,' Shaun called after him.

'I'll take it,' Will replied. 'I'll take anything.'

Will went back to his van and checked his phone and wished he hadn't. Nicole had texted to say she had filed for divorce and would he please send the signed papers back as soon as they arrived. He tried to form a polite reply but the words wouldn't come. After three deleted drafts he put his key in the ignition, turned it, then twisted it back to off again.

Will's throat was dry as sand. He could do with a drink. Teashops weren't really his style but something was pushing him to go in and have five minutes in a fresh space with a coffee to give himself a head-break from all that was going on. As he entered the Teashop on the Corner, a woman with long dark hair was coming out. Had good-looking ladies been on his radar, this one would have beeped a definite presence with her big brown Sophia Loren eyes. But women weren't on his mind, a coffee was.

Will Linton walked into the teashop and saw the card which had just been placed there for the vacant flat at Dundealin.

Chapter 26

The house clearance people had taken what they thought they could sell of Carla's furniture and given her ninety pounds for it. Watching them take it out – and it looked even shabbier in the daylight – Carla thought they'd been over generous. If she'd had any pride left, it would have taken yet another knock; but she didn't, and ninety pounds was ninety pounds. She would have to watch every penny, even if she was going to be sitting in a house which was totally bought and paid for. There would still be money for rates and water rates and utility bills to find, and there was a hell of a lot of work to do on Dundealin to transform it into her idea of a comfortable home. She knew she couldn't live with the mustard-coloured wallpaper in the kitchen very long without it making her go blind or insane.

Just before seven p.m. as Carla was raking through boxes trying to find her mobile phone, there was a timid knock on the back door. She opened it to find Mavis Marple there.

'I'm sorry to bother you, Carla ...'

'Come in, Mrs Marple,' invited Carla.

'I heard you were moving out tomorrow and I didn't want you to go without saying goodbye to you.'

'I was just about to put the kettle on,' lied Carla. 'Would you like a drink? I think I can lay my hands on a couple of cups.'

'That's very kind of you, dear, but I don't want to put you to any trouble.'

'It's no trouble. Sit yourself down,' said Carla, gesturing towards the shabby sofa which the house clearance man didn't want. She took a cup out of the box on the work surface and rinsed out the one she had been using. She had bought herself a new kettle: it was one of the fast-boiling types. Their old kettle had been so slow she could have grown her tea, picked it and dried it before it boiled.

'I was so sorry to hear about what had happened to you,' said Mrs Marple. 'It was a terrible thing. And for you not to be able to get any answers was a very cruel blow.'

The gossip machine had obviously been busy, thought Carla. Might you, could she blame it? Her story had more juice than a cartful of oranges.

'I'll get by. I'll have to,' shrugged Carla. 'Tea okay? Do you take sugar?'

'Tea would be lovely and no sugar thank you, with a little splash of milk. And make it very weak please. And half a cup will do me. I don't want to keep you.'

'I'm sorry I haven't got any biscuits to offer you.'

'I brought you some,' said Mavis Marple, pulling a box of Jaffa Cakes from her stiff aged handbag, along with a small crumpled paper bag which she set on the table.

'That's very kind of you,' smiled Carla as a lump leapt to her throat. Why a packet of biscuits should make her feel teary was anyone's guess. Mavis's ancient fingers worked to open them as Carla poured boiling water over the teabags in the cups.

'I hope you don't mind, but I brought you something,' Mavis said as Carla delivered a cup in front of her. She pushed the paper bag across the table. 'My father made it for me when he was in a prisoner of war camp. He brought it home and said it would always bring me luck, and it has. I've had a very long and happy life, so maybe it's time to pass it on to someone who needs it more than I do now.'

Intrigued, Carla carefully opened the packet to find a small cat with a long graceful neck whittled from black wood. It was beautiful, intricate and exquisitely detailed. Mavis's father must have had the eyes of a hawk to produce such fine work.

'Daddy made my mother a parrot. She was buried with it. She had a long and happy life too. He had a gift, I think.'

'Oh Mrs Marple, I couldn't take your daddy's pres—'

Carla's outstretched hand was pushed back. 'Yes you can. I want you to have it. I want you to have some of Lucky's luck. I always called him Lucky – not very original, I know, but it suited.'

Watch out for the lucky black cat. Carla shivered.

'Thank you.' Carla squeezed the old lady's hand. Her skin was tissue-paper thin and blotchy with brown spots.

'Thank you for always wheeling my bins in and out for me,' said Mrs Marple, 'You've been a lovely neighbour to have.'

'So have you, Mrs Marple. I was going to drop these off to you in the morning before I left.' Carla reached for a gift bag on the work surface. 'It's just a box of thank you chocolates. And a card.'

'Oh, how kind,' grinned Mrs Marple, who had a very sweet tooth. 'Well, I hope you are very happy in your new home, Carla. I suppose *she* will be moving in here?' She suffused the *she* with enough venom to bring down a rhino.

'I doubt it,' said Carla. 'I understand she has a big house of her own. She'll most likely sell this.'

'Wants a good lick of paint,' said Mrs Marple, sweeping

her eyes around the room. 'And some new windows. Your frames are rotten. I have to say, I never did think much to your hus ... to Martin. Shifty eyes.'

Carla tried to suppress a giggle. Bless Mavis Marple. She said it how it was.

'I wasn't entirely surprised to find out that he was doing the dirty on you.' Mrs Marple munched on her fourth Jaffa Cake. 'Although to be honest ...' She leant in closer as if she was afraid of being overheard. '... I thought who'd want him? He wasn't exactly Marlon Brando, was he? I always thought you were far too good for him.'

'Really?' Carla was surprised by that.

'Yes. You've got such a pretty face and were always so pleasant. He was ... sorry, I shouldn't speak ill of the dead but I'm going to, a miserable-looking bugger. But anyway, now you've got Daddy's black cat, so you have to look forward to good luck and not back at the bad.'

She took a mighty slurp of tea and made a delighted 'Ahhh' noise. 'So you didn't have a clue that he was married, then?' she said.

'No,' sighed Carla. 'Not a single tiny clue.'

'How very cruel. I was fortunate never to experience that from a man. My Albert was always such a gentleman.'

'You're lucky,' smiled Carla.

'And so will you be, now you have my black cat,' said Mrs Marple, resting her hand on top of Carla's and giving it a squeeze. 'Lucky will bring you a good man, I'm sure of it.'

'If you're ever passing, you call in and have a cup of tea with me. My new address is written on the card,' said Carla, unable to stop a tear escaping from the corner of her right eye, to be quickly followed by another.

'I will,' said Mrs Marple, rising to her feet. 'Now I'll let you get on. I've got Freda McClure coming around to watch a Rock Hudson with me in half an hour. Whatever the papers said, I never believed the rumours. He couldn't fake what he had with Doris Day.'

And with that Mrs Marple tottered off to go and get ready for *Pillow Talk*, leaving Carla alone with the remaining Jaffa Cakes and a lucky black cat.

Chapter 27

When the furniture van came the following day to take her stuff to the new house, Carla was amazed to see how few belongings she had. God knows what the delivery men must have thought at the embarrassingly small cargo. Carla thought she might feel a rush of emotion as she stepped out of the bungalow for the last time and put the key into the door, but there was nothing. Ten years of life with Martin ended with the turning of that key. She walked away from the locked bungalow without a single happy memory of being carried over its threshold as a bride, nor even a sad one of being sat curled up in a corner crying when she found out he was having a fling with the woman in the post office during the first year of their marriage. It was as if she had never lived a life with Martin.

She left the urn containing Martin's ashes on the fire-place. It seemed appropriate.

When Carla eventually found her mobile phone it was out of charge, so she didn't realise that two people had called expressing interest in renting the mini flat. Both men. When she had enough juice in her phone to ring her voice-mail to listen to the messages they had left, she found the first one sounded elderly and quite posh, whilst the second was a Londoner with a chirpy voice like Danny Dyer's. She preferred the first voice, which belonged to a Mr Rex Parkinson. She pictured him being very neat and quiet and respectful of property. She rang him back and they fixed up an appointment to view the flat on Friday. She wanted to allow herself enough time to move in and give the place a good clean. She had a good feeling about him but out of courtesy rang the second man, who happened to be Will Linton.

'I'm afraid I've already given first refusal to someone,' Carla told him.

Typical, thought Will. Missed the boat again by a breath; first with Shaun McCarthy, now with this lady.

'Aw, not to worry,' he replied. 'If he does refuse, could you ring me back?'

'Certainly,' said Carla. She stored his number in her phone just in case, but didn't think she would be using it.

Theresa had taken the day off teaching to help Carla move in. She was already at Dundealin when the delivery men arrived with Carla's meagre amount of move-in items.

'Jonty has made us a Greek salad for lunch,' said Theresa. 'I've put it in the fridge.'

Carla burst into tears.

'Oh now, stop being so soft and tell me which box the kettle is in,' said Theresa, slapping her friend on the shoulder. 'I'll make us a coffee.'

'Theresa, there's something I need to do first, if you don't mind,' said Carla, wiping her eyes. 'I want to hand the keys of the house over to Julie. Then my business with the Prides is totally finished.'

Theresa's hand stilled on the box she was opening, which had 'kettle' written on the side of it.

'Are you really not going to fight?' she sighed. 'I think you're mad.'

'I don't want any more than I've got here,' reiterated Carla. 'And guess what, I found some money hidden in Martin's pockets. Thousands.'

'Please don't tell me you're going to give her that as well,' Theresa jumped in.

'Am I heck. I might be mad but I'm not insane,' shrieked Carla. 'And I found a Cartier watch that he'd obviously bought for Julie's birthday. And no, I'm not giving it to her. I'm going to flog it to a jeweller.'

'Thank goodness for that,' Theresa breathed a sigh of relief.

'Really? You don't think it's stealing from her?'

Theresa stared hard at her friend.

'You are going to have to toughen up, Carla. Seriously.'

'She's lost him too. And she's pregnant. I don't want to stamp on her.'

'Go and hand the damned keys over then and have done with it,' said Theresa firmly.

'I've got some things arriving from Argos. A sofa and curtains and a dining table and other stuff.'

'Go. I'll sort it.'

'You're wonderful.'

Theresa, seeing water starting to gather in her friend's eyes again, flicked the cloth she had in her hand at Carla. 'I know. Now go.'

Chapter 28

She did a shop at the supermarket then once she was home, Molly spread the newspaper over the kitchen table. There was no good news it in at all. Some poor man had been slaughtered outside his front door and the drugged-up perpetrator had done it merely 'because he could'. A young child had been killed in a hit and run, a ninety-seven-year-old grandmother had been beaten up in her own home. It could be a terrible and cruel world, she thought, closing up the newspaper and reaching for her Midnight Moon romance novel instead.

She had only read two pages when there was a knock at the front door. As she walked down the hallway, Molly recognised the postman's orange coat through the frosted glass. He had a parcel for Bernard and asked if Molly would take it in for him. She signed for it and shut the door. But she couldn't settle back into her book. *What is wrong with me?* she thought. She was on edge for a reason she couldn't explain. She was about to put on the TV to watch her favourite antiques programme when there was a second knock on the door. She presumed it was the postman again. Molly was always taking in parcels for the neighbours who were out at work. When she couldn't see any flash of orange through the glass, she opened the door more cautiously and didn't slip off the chain.

A tall, slim elderly man with a thick steel-grey head of hair was standing on her doorstep wearing a suit that looked a good two sizes too big for him. He had piercing blue eyes that made her feel as light-headed as the first time he had used them to stare into hers. His smell wafted across to her, drifting up her nostrils, unclasping the lock in a part of a brain that said *do not open under any circumstances.* He was no longer the solid, strong-looking man with coal-black hair and Atlas-like shoulders she had last seen twenty-eight years ago, but she would have known him anywhere.

'Hello Molly,' said Harvey Hoyland. 'Can I come in?'

Chapter 29

Julie's address hadn't been hard to find. She was registered on the electoral roll as the single occupant of Pride Towers, Dinghill. The sat-nav led Carla out of Barnsley and onto the Wakefield Road, then right down the country lane to the tiny village of Dinghill, which was made up entirely of very grand houses. Brian Blessed announced vociferously that she had reached her destination as she turned in to a cul de sac of three prestigious new homes and parked outside the middle one, which bore the name of the house on the high brick wall.

Carla took a deep breath and exited the car. Pride Towers stood in a large ornate garden complete with working fountain, massive summer house and pond. Julie must have a gardener, thought Carla. Martin hated anything to do with greenery. He always left the mowing of their small lawn to her.

Carla's steps were nervous and unsure as they took her towards the gothic arch of a front door. She raised her hand to ring the doorbell and saw that it was shaking.

Julie answered the door almost immediately. She was dressed in a mauve velour lounge suit and fluffy slippers. Behind her in the vast hallway on the floor was a pram wrapped in plastic. It looked as if it had just been delivered. A pram for Martin's child – the baby Carla would never have with him.

'Oh, it's you,' she said.

'I've brought you the keys to the bungalow,' said Carla, her voice dry with emotion. 'And the ones for Martin's car. It's parked on our . . . his drive. The documents are in the bungalow on the work surface.'

'Oh,' said Julie. She seemed surprised. 'How quick.' Julie had obviously not expected her to roll over so obligingly. She held her hand out for the keys and Carla was about to give them to her when she realised they were both wearing wedding rings. Carla had been so used to hers, she wasn't aware of its presence any more.

'Just before I go,' said Carla, fingers closing around the keys again, hating herself for this momentary weakness, hating herself for what she was about to do. 'Did he . . . did Martin say that he was unhappy with me?'

Julie stared blankly at Carla.

'What do you want me to say to that?' she said eventually.

'The truth,' said Carla, annoyed at the desperation that had crept into her voice.

'He said he was bored,' said Julie with a tired huff. 'Bored rigid. He said that you were a nice person but he'd fallen out of love with you a long time ago.'

Tears began to roll down Carla's face.

'When was he going to tell me that he was leaving? Did he say?'

'The weekend he died. It crossed my mind he had told you already and you'd killed him when I didn't hear from him,' said Julie, staring hard at Carla. 'But you hadn't a clue, had you? No one could be that good an actress. It was my birthday on the Monday. He was going to leave you a note when he left for work that day to say that he wasn't coming back again and for you to contact his solicitor.'

'He wasn't even going to tell me to my face?' cried Carla.

'What would that have achieved except for a row?' Julie said with a humourless chuckle. 'There was no need for any more contact with you. He would have left you earlier, had your mother not gone and died.'

Carla gasped loudly, winded by the insensitivity of Julie's words. She made it sound as if it was a major inconvenience to her life that Carla's mother had passed away. Carla suddenly remembered that Martin had 'gone to work' the day after the funeral, telling her that he couldn't afford to take any more time off than was necessary as his job was on the line. A picture rose in her head of him arriving at Pride Towers bemoaning the fact that his plans had been delayed. How very selfish of Mrs Martelli to have had a stroke and died.

Without warning, a wave of anger whooshed through Carla blasting away any tears that were waiting in her eyes. To think that part of her had felt sorry for Julie. Now that part of her had been well and truly crushed underfoot by Julie's callousness.

'All yours,' said Carla, her top lip a rare narrow line of snarl. 'Martin's ashes are by the fireplace.' She dropped the keys into Julie's hand.

'Complete?'

'Pardon?'

'Are the ashes complete? Have you taken any out for yourself?'

Carla's eyebrows raised so high they were almost lost in her hairline. She fought the urge to say any more than, 'They are "complete", I can assure you.'

'Well, that's that then. We have nothing else to say to

each other do we?' And with that Julie's lips curved into a triumphant smirk just before she slammed the door in Carla's face. Their business was concluded. Their paths, they both hoped, had no reason ever to cross again.

Chapter 30

The teashop was empty, but it didn't matter because Leni was busy opening up boxes of newly arrived stock and marvelling at it. She never got tired of sourcing new things and taking delivery of them. Today's consignment included heart-shaped confetti which had been cut from sheets printed with the words 'Reader, I married him'. There were beautiful hard-backed notepads and journals and wrapping papers. There were compact brollies covered in umbrella-related book designs, cufflinks featuring tiny Ladybird book covers. And there were five heavily woven tapestry door curtains featuring shelves of books in their design which had arrived from Italy. She had been asked by an internet customer if she could find any and, though it had taken her almost a year, Leni had done it. She couldn't wait to advertise them.

She looked up as the doorbell sounded to see a slightly-built boy with untidy light brown hair, wearing a school uniform: a bottle-green blazer and black trousers. The blazer needed stitching at the shoulder and there was a button missing at the front.

'Good morning,' said Leni, smiling at him. 'Can I help you?'

'Got any Saturday jobs?' the boy replied, after a cough to clear his throat. 'And if you have, can I apply? Please.'

'Funny you should ask, I do have one and yes, you can,' said Leni.

'Oh, man, you've got a cat.' Leni watched as the boy bent down to stroke Mr Bingley's head.

'That's Mr Bingley.'

'Nice name. Suits him. Soft, inne?'

'Take a seat. I'll interview you now if you like.'

The boy pulled out a chair and sat down but he had to drag his eyes away from the contents of the cabinets. Leni could have sworn he said 'wow' under his breath. He rested his elbows on the table then immediately took them off again as if someone had snapped at him to do so.

'Let's begin with your name,' said Leni, lifting up a pad and pen from the counter. She had been about to put an advert in the *Chronicle* for a Saturday person, funnily enough, as the card on the noticeboard hadn't drawn any enquiries. The young man had perfect timing, it seemed.

'Ryan O'Gowan. And I'm fourteen. Just. Last month,' he said, pre-empting her next question.

'Where do you live?'

'Wombwell way. I got the bus straight up after school,' said Ryan.

'Have you had a Saturday job before?'

'No,' he replied. 'I did some errands for people on the estate to get some money for last Christmas but ...' his voice trailed off as if he had been about to go on and say something he shouldn't. 'Not a real job in a shop though.'

'Most of the help I need is for packing up things which people have ordered. I don't have that many customers in the teashop yet.'

'I don't mind what I do,' said Ryan.

'Where did you hear about this place then?'

'On the net,' said Ryan. 'I was looking up bookshops. This place came up, but it isn't a bookshop really, is it?'

Leni picked up on his disappointment.

'Ah, so you like books?'

'Yeah,' Ryan nodded. 'I read a lot.'

He didn't look like a reader, thought Leni. But she could have been wrong, of course.

'What's your favourite book?' she asked him.

'*Ninteen Eighty-Four*,' Ryan answered without even having to think about it. 'I thought it was brilliant. But I've read loads of books. All sorts. I'm going to be an English teacher one day.'

Leni nodded, not quite sure if she believed him, but she admired his plan to impress her, if that's what it was.

'So you'd prefer to work in a bookshop?'

'No, this place would be great,' Ryan said keenly, as if he were afraid that he had blotted his copybook. 'I'd love to work here.'

'The shop opens at nine,' she said. 'I'd need you till about five. I'll make sure you're well fed on your breaks and the wage is four pounds an hour.'

'Discount if I buy stuff?' Ryan added hopefully.

'We'll sort something out,' smiled Leni, coming out from behind the counter and presenting her hand. Ryan stood and wiped his hand down his trouser leg before shaking it.

'Do I start this weekend?'

Leni liked him on first impressions enough to give him the job.

'Yes please,' she said.

'Great,' he said. 'I'll be here on time.' He moved backwards towards the door, looking not at her but in the cabinets, at all the literary things she wouldn't have thought would be on a young lad's list of wants. He stopped at the postcards.

'Who are these all from?'

'My daughter. She's travelling around the world before she goes to university.'

He nodded as if the answer satisfied him.

'I'll see you Sat'day.'

'I look forward to it,' said Leni, resuming her unpacking duties.

Chapter 31

By the time Carla had got back to Dundealin, her furniture had arrived and Theresa was ripping plastic from the sofa.

'They've put the bed upstairs for you and set it up. I fluttered my eyelashes at them,' said Theresa, amazed at how composed and straight-backed Carla seemed. She hadn't expected her to return from Julie Pride's house looking like Boudicca. She scurried to put the kettle on. 'Oh and you've inherited a cat, did you know? I found the postman outside with a tin of pilchards. Apparently he's been feeding it every morning since the man who lived here "did a runner" was how he put it. Scraggy thin thing it is, but quite friendly. It was rubbing around my legs as I was standing on the doorstep.'

'The cat or the postman?' asked Carla.

'Silly,' chuckled Theresa. 'The postman is a bit of a chatterbox. He said he thought the guy who lived here might have done a runner with some diamonds. That's more detail than I got from Jonty. I shall have words with him when I get home.'

'Really?'

Mr Pink.

'So, how did it go?'

Carla sat down onto one of her four new cheap but cheerful dining chairs.

'Put it this way, I'm glad I kept the watch.'

'I would have slaughtered you if you'd given it to her,' said Theresa, taking the top off a new plastic bottle of milk. 'What was the house like?'

'Big and showy.'

'Surprise, surprise,' sniffed Theresa. 'You're very calm. Are you all right?'

'I think I'm on the mend,' replied Carla, with a cold snap in her voice.

'Oh my poor darling,' said Theresa with a heavy sigh. 'You've had a bloody awful year. Things are going to get much better for you now, though. I can feel it. They have to. I positively insist they do.'

'Oh, they will,' said Carla, with a confidence that put Theresa on edge. It wasn't natural that Carla had gone out of the door a sad and vulnerable woman and returned an iceberg. She was just about to ask, yet again, if her friend was okay when Carla offered up an explanation.

'Apparently Martin was going to leave me on the Monday after he died. His stress levels must have been up in the clouds, trying to appear normal.'

Good, thought Theresa, but she kept it to herself.

'He would have left me earlier had my mother not died.'

Carla's words hung in the air, a faint echo clinging to them. Theresa's eventual reply was almost breathless.

'She didn't actually say that, did she?'

'Oh yes.'

Theresa's mouth searched for the right words. 'Fucking bitch' fitted.

Carla held her hand up in protest. 'No, I'm glad she said it. Because any atom of sympathy I had for her has gone, along with any feelings I had for Martin.'

Theresa didn't quite believe the latter part, but nodded in support anyway. Anger was marvellous for masking heartbreak; and anger was so much easier to live with. Long may Carla be furious with the fat bastard.

'Good for you, darling. Neither of them deserves any of your headspace.'

Above the noise of the kettle and their conversation, Carla could hear a scratching sound at the kitchen door.

'What's that? Can you hear?' she asked Theresa who was spooning coffee into a cup.

'Cat?' asked Theresa.

'What cat?'

Theresa tutted. 'The cat that used to live here before Mr Costa del Sol abandoned it. The postman has been feeding it. I've just been telling you. Pay attention Mrs Pr . . . Miss Martelli.' Carla saw Theresa wince as her foot narrowly missed her mouth.

Theresa opened the door and in strolled a small black cat as if he owned the place. He walked over to the run of kitchen units by the side of the fridge and sat down. He was covered in raindrops and started to lick his paw and wipe them away.

'Cocky little sod,' said Carla.

'He's a cutie, isn't he?' said Theresa, who loved cats. She came over and gave him a stroke behind his ears. 'He doesn't look very old.'

'He doesn't look very healthy either,' said Carla. 'He's awfully thin. Have we got anything I can feed him? Do they eat bread?'

Theresa laughed. 'No. And I don't think they're partial to Greek salad either.'

'I think I've got some tuna in a tin somewhere,' said Carla, getting up from the table to look in one of the unopened boxes.

'I'll give him a saucer of milk,' said Theresa. 'I know you aren't supposed to, but I can't see one little dish doing him that much harm.'

Theresa folded some tin-foil into a dish shape and poured in some milk. The little cat started lapping it greedily as the women watched him. Then he climbed into an upturned empty cardboard box and settled down to sleep.

'Who the hell does he think he is?' said Carla, shaking her head.

Theresa hoped that Carla wouldn't turn the cat out. Both undernourished, both abandoned, both in need of a bit of human kindness. They were a perfect match for each other.

Chapter 32

It was a toss-up whether Molly was going to faint or go the whole hog and drop dead with shock. Every nerve in her body seemed to vibrate at the same time and her head felt as if a clutch of fireworks had gone off inside her skull.

This couldn't be happening, she thought. After all these years, Harvey Hoyland turning up on her doorstep? Twenty-eight years, to be exact. Bold as brass. And with a suitcase. How dare he? After all he had done to her. She was consumed by a swell of anger as pictorial bytes of their shared history fired like missiles through her brain. Harvey catching her before she fell on the patch of black ice and turning her heart up to five hundred degrees Celsius; Harvey telling her he was leaving her for another woman; Harvey sneaking off with her few precious pieces of jewellery, *her memories*; Harvey sending her that damned postcard from Blackpool that only said 'Wish you were here' on it.

Rage tore through Molly's veins obliterating every other emotion she was feeling.

'You have to be joking,' she said, and shut the door in his face.

'Wait, please,' he said, his words muffled through the glass panel, his image a thin, dark blur. 'Molly. I came to say I'm sorry.'

'Apology accepted,' said Molly. 'Now push off.'

'I'm dying, love.'

Though she wanted to ignore him and walk back to the TV, her feet wouldn't move. She slowly opened the door again, sliding off the chain. She knew he was lying. It wasn't exactly an original ploy. The newspapers and women's magazines were full of charlatans preying on the emotions of the trusting with tales of dying. She looked into his face and saw his sunken eyes and sallow skin and she knew that he wasn't well. He looked older than his seventy-two years. When she compared him with how fit and strong Bernard was, Harvey could have out-aged him by fifteen years.

'Thank you,' said Harvey, as the door fully opened and she stood there with her arms folded, looking as emotionally impenetrable as it was possible for Molly to appear. His hand came out to find the wall for support, but his legs gave way and he started to sink to the ground. Molly instinctively reached for him, looping his arm around her shoulder and then she was pulling him down the hallway and into her kitchen towards a chair. He felt like skin and bone; Molly could never have shifted him in his heyday – he'd been all rock muscle and solid. She left him on the chair whilst she went back to the front door to bring his battered suitcase inside, then she filled a glass with water.

'Here,' she said, putting it in front of him and then stepping backwards as if she expected him to leap up and attack her now that he had managed to gain entry.

Molly watched his hands extend out for the glass. They were old hands, thin and bony and shaking. She remembered how strong they once were. She remembered them threading in her hair as he pulled her mouth to his. She tried to cram those thoughts back into that *do not open* box in her head.

'Thank you,' he said again, taking a long sip before putting the glass back down. 'I'm sorry. I didn't mean for it to go quite like this.'

'What did you think would happen?' Molly snapped. 'You turn up here after twenty-eight years and expect what?'

'To say goodbye and sorry to you before I shuffle off this mortal coil,' said Harvey. 'I don't have a lot of time left. But I wanted ... *needed* ... to see you.'

'What's the matter with you?' said Molly brusquely. She was still reluctant to believe his story.

'Restrictive cardiomyopathy,' replied Harvey and reached into his pocket. When his hand came out, it was full of bottles of tablets. 'These are working less and less but I wasn't ready to let go until I'd made my peace with you.'

Molly swallowed hard. The evidence was stacking up but still she wasn't sure. She didn't *want* to believe him. Whatever she might think about him, she wouldn't have wished this on him. She picked up one of the bottles and read the label: *Lanoxin*. She recognised the name. A drug to help the heart beat stronger. His name was printed on the label.

'How long have you been unwell?' she asked.

'I've been on heart medication for a few years now, but my condition was managed. Then things started to get worse and I seemed to be more or less living at the hospital, getting poked and prodded at. I'd had enough of it. No more, I told myself.'

'Where were you staying?' *Are you still with her?* Molly wanted to ask, but couldn't quite bring herself to.

'I've lived all over,' said Harvey. 'London, Torquay, Spain, Germany, New York, even Shanghai for six months. I ended up in Portugal three years ago and settled there, sort of, but none of those places ever felt like home to me. They aren't though, are they? Thoughts turn to your roots when you're near the end.'

'Why the suitcase?' Molly bobbed her head towards it. 'Please don't tell me you're thinking of moving in with me.'

'No, no,' he replied quickly. 'I gave up my flat so I could move back and die in Barnsley. I've got a little bit of money. And this suitcase. That's all I amount to, but it's enough. I can't take it with me. I thought I'd go and stay in a room in the Vine or the Coach and Horses.'

'Both of those were knocked down an eternity ago,' sniffed Molly. She was swaying towards not believing him now. Was he really saying that he'd lived all over the world and wanted to die in Barnsley? She stiffened her back. Same old Harvey, despite the years and the tablets, thinking he can get anywhere on the strength of a few softly-spoken words and a plea to the heart.

'If you can tell me that you forgive me, Molly, I promise I will go and you'll never hear from me again.' He took another sip of water and for some reason his weakened state suddenly infuriated Molly.

'Just like that?' She gave a bitter laugh. 'All those years without a word and you expect me to say "absolutely, Harvey. Of course I'll forgive you. Off you go and pop your clogs in peace." Have you any idea how much you broke my heart, Harvey Hoyland? So much I never got over it and yet – yep – off you would trot to the bloody Pearly Gates with your conscience scrubbed cleaner than a whistle. Well no, I won't forgive you. No. I hope you rot in hell, Harvey Hoyland. You and *her*. I don't care.'

Harvey dropped his head as if it was weighted with shame.

'I'm sorry, I had no right,' he said and put his hand flat on the table and levered himself up. 'Molly, I shouldn't have come. I should have left you in peace. It appears I never learn.'

Then his legs gave way completely and he fell heavily to the floor, cracking his head on the table, and Molly knew that Harvey Hoyland wasn't joking when he said he was very, very ill. And that she'd been lying when she said that she didn't care.

Chapter 33

Theresa left the house at nine-thirty that evening. Between her and Carla every room in Dundealin was as spotless as a new pin; the furniture was in situ, the curtains were hung, her bed was made up, the carpets freshened up with Shake n' Vac and the ancient oven as clean as it ever could be. Jonty arrived after work and had great fun burning all the packaging in an old incinerator which he found in the garden. He was a typical bloke, happiest when employed in an occupation of controlled arson. The skinny black cat remained asleep in the cardboard box next to the radiator.

'What do I do with him?' asked Carla as she walked out with Theresa and Jonty to their car. The sky was growling and fat drops of rain were starting to fall from the doughy grey clouds.

'Are you going to throw him out on a night like this?' replied Theresa, raising her eyebrows. She knew there was more chance of Martin coming back from the dead.

'Well of course I wouldn't. Shall I put some newspaper down?'

'Good idea,' nodded Theresa. 'Give him another tin of tuna tonight and tomorrow go and get some flea drops just in case.'

'Yeurch. I'm not keeping him, Tez,' said Carla, holding up her hand in protest. The thought of fleas crawling in his fur made her shudder.

'I never said you had to,' said Theresa, all innocent blue eyes, although she knew that Carla had acquired a new pet.

Carla waved off her friends and then shut the door on the rainy night. The lounge of Dundealin didn't look that bad with the main ceiling light off and the low wattage wall lights on. There was still a lot to do, such as arrange for a telephone line and internet access; but at least the TV was working. She wished she had bought that Home Sweet Home picture from the teashop now. There was an alcove to the right of the fire which was ideal for it. She made up her mind to go and buy it in the next couple of days. It would be a marker of her new life; every time she looked at it she would be reminded that a line had been drawn under the old one and she was on the way up. She sat with a coffee, watching a programme about people who shared their homes with strange pets. There was a woman in America who had a tame lynx which sat on the sofa with her and a couple who slept with two pot-bellied pigs. The larger of the pigs reminded her slightly of Martin, she thought with a sudden snort of laughter. His belly was enormous and his nose was slightly flat at the end. And boy, could he snore.

Carla's thoughts started to stray towards Martin and she couldn't help but try and analyse what it was that she had actually loved so much about him. He was hardly Brad Pitt or Casanova. And she only saw him for two days out of every seven. Maybe her heart had kept being fond because of the absence? He used to be a fine, fit fellow with a cheery face. She'd fallen in love with his cheeky banter. Over the years she had watched his smile being whittled away by the long working hours and his waist grow thicker with all the pasties he ate on the road. She had started to feel sorry for him, pushed the boat out at weekends to give him some respite. She'd begged him to find another job but he never had. He said that it was better to stick with the devil he knew, and that he was putting his head down and getting on with it until pension time. Their relationship had been one-way traffic, she realised now, with hindsight. The changes in their marriage had crept up on her so slowly that she hadn't noticed them. Until it was too late.

Carla jumped as the black cat leapt up on her knee, turned a circle and plopped down on her lap. She was about to move him, then thought – why? He was soft and warm against her, purring softly; and it was a pleasant experience to be viewed as so comfortable. He was a sweet little thing and very friendly. In fact, when she thought about it, he'd given her more affection since he'd pushed his way into the house that morning than Martin had for weeks. When she thought some more, she realised that he hadn't shown her any real affection for a lot longer than that actually. He never gave her anything other than a perfunctory kiss on the cheek when he arrived home on a Friday night and left on the Monday morning. When they had sex, which had been infrequent, there was no cuddling afterwards or snogging during. He never brought her small gifts or flowers, and Carla loved flowers – and what's more he knew she did. She'd worked in a florist's for many happy years until the owner retired and closed up the shop. How had she missed the signs? They were screaming at her now. How could she have been truly happy with a man who gave her so little? She bet Julie Pride had wanted – and got – so much more.

A single fat salty drop landed on the cat's back but he didn't seem to notice. She sat and stroked him gently and sniffed back the remaining tears which were banked up in her eyes. She refused to waste any more on that man. But, my God, she really had been stupid.

Chapter 34

Molly had called an ambulance as soon as he collapsed and now Harvey was in Barnsley hospital. Molly had scooped up all the medicines from the table to take with her to show the doctors. Harvey wasn't lying to her, she found out after talking to them. He was a very poorly man.

She went in to say goodnight to him and found him asleep and covered in sticky tags and wires which were hooked up to various machines. He looked so old and thin lying there in hospital issue pyjamas. She would check in his suitcase when she got home and see if he had any of his own or if not she would nip into Marks and Spencer and buy him some. He wouldn't be the same size he used to be – she could still remember it. He'd had a seventeen-and-a-half-inch neck in those days, a fifty-one-inch chest. He wouldn't have now. He had been a big strapping fellow with an easy smile, George Clooney teeth and warm, sexy eyes the colour of a tropical ocean. She had fallen for him the moment her eyes rested on him. She had felt her heart react to the sight of him: it had stopped for a moment then gave a great big beat and she could have sworn she heard it whisper 'Good God.'

It wasn't all his fault, said a voice. *You should have told him. Maybe then . . .*

She shook her head, trying to rid it of that voice. She had never wanted to think that she might have had any hand in Harvey leaving her.

Returning home, she opened his suitcase and found, pressed between two jumpers, a photo – and it was of herself, her face tilted, her lips dark red and smiling, her skin like cream. She couldn't remember ever seeing that photo. *Did I ever look as lovely as that?* she wondered. She couldn't stop staring at it. She had always thought that she was punching well above her weight in landing a man as handsome as Harvey Hoyland, but she wasn't really. She shone from the inside when she was with him. He made her feel beautiful, gave her confidence; then had stripped her of it all when he left.

It wasn't all his fault.

She pulled out a pair of pyjamas which she found beneath the neat stacks of his shirts and trousers, all good quality but well worn; he had always been such a snappy dresser back in the day. His white shirts were like snow and ironed to perfection.

She lifted his pyjama top to her nose and inhaled. There lingered a faint familiar scent of him, his aftershave that transported her immediately to dancing with him, her body next to his. She had never been as happy ever as she was with him, or as unhappy as she'd been without him. And here he was again like a giant spoon, stirring all the settled waters inside her, disturbing the memory-filled sediment at the bottom until it swirled up and took over every thought she had. She didn't know what to do. She didn't know if she had any choice.

Chapter 35

Molly didn't sleep very well at all. She got up the next morning and tried to read the newspaper, but she couldn't concentrate. She rang the hospital and was told that Harvey was awake and was presently eating breakfast, no more detail than that. There were almost two hours until visiting time at the hospital and she was pacing about so anxiously it was a wonder there was still a pattern left on the carpet. She needed to get out of the house. She drove out to the little teashop with the gorgeous book gifts in the cabinets. She liked it there. And it would pass some time in the most pleasant way.

Leni greeted her warmly. 'How lovely to see you again. Please sit down and I'll be over to take your order in a moment.'

'Am I too early?' asked Molly, watching Leni switching on the huge coffee machine.

'Not at all,' smiled Leni. 'If the sign says open, everyone is welcome.'

*

Carla awoke with the annoying sensation that something was blocking her nose. She sat up bolt upright in bed after finding the black cat half-draped over her face. The damned thing had climbed upstairs and got into bed with her. The cheek.

She went downstairs to find a neat little poo on the newspaper she had left by the door. The cat trotted behind her and sat expectantly down by a cupboard in the kitchen.

'I haven't got any food for you,' Carla said to him but he didn't hear. He carried on sitting there, waiting and making her feel guilty enough to get dressed and grab her car keys.

Pets R Us seemed the best bet – a superstore with 'Everything for your pet friend'. Pest friend, more like. She had never gone shopping for a cat before. Which did they prefer – fish or chicken? Fine flakes? Bite and Chew or Lick and Chew, gravy or jelly? Whiskas or Felix – or would he want biscuits? She put a selection in her trolley and then walked on to the bowls. She didn't know whether to get a blue one or a pink one. Was the cat a boy or a girl? Would it give a stuff if it got the wrong colour? Still, she played safe and bought a yellow one, to go with her kitchen. Cat milk? They had special milk for cats? Should she get him a bed? Blimey – some of them were dearer than her own new double from Argos. And how big a litter tray did she need? And what sort of litter – clumping or non clumping? Pellets, anti-bacterial, grey, pink, organic? God – it was a minefield. And she supposed she'd better get one of those spatula scoop things as well. She collared one of the assistants to help her choose a flea treatment as they were stored in a glass cabinet. 'Don't forget the wormer,' the assistant advised. Carla's trolley contents cost nearly as much as her weekly shop at Morrison's.

She started to drive home, except that she was on automatic pilot and was almost outside Martin's house before she realised her mistake. She was just about to reverse, then decided to drive on, slowly, curious to see what the house looked like now that she was no longer living there. A scarlet Porsche was sitting in the drive. Julie's Porsche if the personalised number plate was anything to go by. A cocktail of emotions rose up and swirled inside her: a measure of hurt, a measure of betrayal, a measure of annoyance. Carla did a three-point turn and zoomed away from the estate before she felt any more of its poison. She decided to indulge in a spot of retail therapy for herself at the Teashop on the Corner and buy the Home Sweet Home sign.

*

Molly let the calm and warmth in the teashop pervade her bones. She felt every one of her sixty-eight years today, tired and stiff. She ordered a coffee and a toasted teacake. She wasn't really hungry but she hadn't eaten much yesterday at all. She was going to have to take some headache tablets in a moment and thought she shouldn't swallow them on an empty stomach.

She was in such a world of her own that she didn't even notice when Carla walked in, and so didn't acknowledge her when she bid her good morning. Only when Leni put the buttered teacake and the cup and saucer down in front of her did she come back into the room.

'I'm so sorry,' she called to Leni who had taken a step back to the counter. 'Thank you. Oh, good morning, Carla. I didn't see you come in.'

'You were lost in your thoughts there, Molly.' Carla smiled, but she didn't think Molly looked right at all.

Neither did Leni because in the next breath she said, 'I hope you don't mind me asking, Molly, but are you all right?'

'Yes, thank you.' Molly tried to smile bravely and failed. 'No, no I don't think I am.' She didn't mean to crumble in front of strangers but she couldn't stop herself. Margaret would have known what to do, but she wasn't here. And Molly needed to lean on something, someone, anyone. Her brain felt full of thoughts too big for her head to carry. She felt gentle fingers take hold of her hand and looked up to see that Leni was sitting opposite her, her lovely elfin face concerned and interested. Molly couldn't hold back.

'Years ago,' she began, 'I was married to a man I loved. But he left me. For someone else.' Molly bit her lip as she made the admission. 'It wasn't entirely his fault. I could have been . . . warmer. He was a man who needed . . .' She came back to the word again, for want of a better one: '. . . warmth. I never quite got over him, I think. And yesterday, he turned up on my doorstep with all his worldly goods in a suitcase and told me he had a heart condition that meant he didn't have long to live and he wanted me to forgive him. Then I told him to go away and he collapsed and he's in hospital. He's got nowhere to stay and . . .' She lifted her shoulders and gave a dry laugh. A tear rolled slowly down her cheek and landed on the teacake.

'Jesus Christ,' said Carla, from the next table.

'And you haven't a clue what to do?' suggested Leni.

Molly nodded eagerly. 'That's exactly it. I can't take him in to stay with me. It's impossible. I won't. Not after what he did. We divorced twenty-seven years ago. We have no ties to each other.'

Leni squeezed her hand softly. 'And yet you can't leave him to die alone?'

'He knew I wouldn't be able to,' snapped Molly, with a flare of anger. 'He's a crafty one, that Harvey Hoyland. A seducer.' She sniffed and raised her head up to tilt back the remaining tears that were trying to make an escape. 'I'm going to the hospital now. He's stabilised. I doubt they'll be letting him out today but they will eventually I presume,

and he'll need looking after; that's more than obvious.'
Molly growled. 'How dare he put me in this position? He's
a stranger to me now.' She looked from Leni to Carla, her
eyes pleading for direction. 'What should I do?'

Carla didn't think she would be the best person to ask.
She imagined Martin walking in through the door and
begging her for forgiveness. She wouldn't give him the
time of day. Or would she? Saying what she would do was
one thing, but when you were actually put in that position . . .

'Oh Molly, I honestly wouldn't know,' she gulped. Even
if she did, she would have been very reticent to say. It was a
hell of a responsibility to suggest that an old lady fling open
her doors to a dying ex-husband whom she hadn't seen for
over a quarter of a century.

'Could you turn your back on him?' asked Leni, gently.
She suspected that Molly's old love still had roots in her
heart.

Molly sighed. 'No. I don't think I would ever forgive
myself if I did.'

'Then you have your answer.'

Leni knew that life was so very precious. For Molly to
have a warning that her old lover's life was on the wane was,
in a strange way, a gift. Not everyone was granted the
chance to let go gently and have the time to say goodbye.

'I'm not sure that I'd forgive myself if I forgave him
either,' said Molly, her voice croaking with confusion then
she groaned. 'I'm lost.'

Carla opened her mouth to speak, then shut it again as
quickly. Maybe if she told Molly the truth about herself it
might give her some direction. But could she dare to shame
herself for a relative stranger? She glanced at Molly's worried
face and decided that she should.

'I'm not a divorcee,' Carla blurted out. 'I'm a widow. Sort

of. My husband died last month, and at his funeral I found out that I wasn't actually married to him after all because he never divorced his first wife and he was planning to leave me for her.' She realised that Leni and Molly were staring at her open-mouthed.

'My point being, Molly, that I wish I'd had the chance to let go of him myself. I'd have had to say goodbye one way or another, but being able to allow him to slip from my life rather than be wrenched from it . . . I'm not putting this very well . . . I could have coped with it all so much better.'

'Oh, you poor dear,' said Molly.

'I'm okay,' smiled Carla. 'I'm on the mend.'

Molly closed her eyes and nodded a slow agreement. 'I'll drive to the hospital then and take it from there,' she said.

'I hope it turns out to be the right thing for you,' said Carla.

'Well, time will tell, won't it?' said Molly. Where Harvey Hoyland was concerned, life was always more of a rollercoaster than a sedate boat ride. She had no reason to think that, despite their advanced ages, it would be any different now.

Chapter 36

Carla was surprisingly glad that she had told Molly and Leni about Martin. She didn't feel in the slightest judged by either of them, or stupid for having been duped by him. And if the telling of her story helped Molly, then at least some good would come out of the whole sorry mess.

The cat was waiting by the door for her when her car rolled into the drive of Dundealin. He was turning circles as she approached with her bags of cat shopping and the Home Sweet Home sign, his tail a shepherd's crook of welcome. She applied the flea lotion behind his neck whilst he was scoffing his chicken flakes. He didn't seem to mind.

Carla wondered if he was the lucky black cat which Pat Morrison had told her about. She'd consider herself very lucky if she didn't have flea bites after finding him in her face that morning.

*

Harvey was fully dressed and remonstrating with a nurse when Molly arrived in the ward.

'You really need to stay in bed, Mr Hoyland,' she was saying.

'I can assure you, dear lady, that I am leaving and yes, on my own bruised head be it. I most certainly am not dying in a hospital ward.' Then he saw Molly and he beamed. 'Molly, you're here. Please tell the Sister that you're taking me home.'

The nurse turned around and threw up her hands in a gesture of frustration.

'Just let me sign a consent form, or whatever they call them, and you can let me go,' said Harvey. 'I assume full responsibility for my own bodily and mental state.'

Molly knew that Harvey's worst nightmare was to die in hospital. They'd had the conversation many years ago when Harvey's mother died in the cardiac unit in Sheffield.

She sighed. 'Yes, I'm here to take him home.'

The Sister looked gobsmacked and who could blame her. Molly wondered what Margaret would have said if she were still a Matron and faced with this situation. Molly thought her answer would have depended on whether the person arguing with her was *alone*. She didn't think her sister would stand in the way of anyone determined to die his or her way, if they were at the very end with no hope of coming back from it.

'It's so wonderful to see you, darling Molly,' said Harvey bending over and resting his hands on his thighs when they reached the lift. 'They told me you'd rung this morning to see how I was. Are you taking me home? I always liked that house.'

'I'm taking you to *my* home. You know, you really aren't well enough to leave here . . .'

'Molly, trust me, I know I have a bit of life still left in me, but don't worry – I won't encroach on your time long term,' Harvey replied with a grin. 'Promise.'

Harvey was full of the joys of spring in the car. Molly wondered if they'd given him a blood transfusion. He had some colour in his gaunt cheeks and a sparkle in his eye.

'Beautiful house,' he said as Molly pulled into Willowfell's drive. 'It was like seeing an old friend when I turned up yesterday. We had some good times here, didn't we, Moll?'

'I'll put you in the spare room,' said Molly, not answering him as she switched off the car engine. 'The bed's made up, but it could do with an airing. You go and rest in the sitting room whilst I do it.'

'Thank you, I will,' said Harvey, getting out of the car.

Molly went upstairs and into the second bedroom, lifting and wafting the quilt to let some air reach the bottom sheet. She suddenly thought, *Harvey will die in this bed* and felt a chill whip down her spine. She tried to push the vision of him lying there out of her head by giving the quilt an extra-vigorous shake. It was a lovely room, east-facing, so Harvey would awaken to the sunshine squeezing through the pale green curtains.

He was asleep by the time she went back downstairs so she took up his suitcase and hung up his clothes and put his underwear in the drawers next to the bed. She left his other possessions in the case, which she put in the bottom of the wardrobe.

Harvey looked so peaceful in the chair, snoring softly, his thin fingers interlaced on his lap. Molly draped a throw gently over him then sat on the sofa and studied him. Even despite the weight loss and the ageing, she could see the younger Harvey Hoyland underneath all the changes. Oh, he was so handsome, so charming. The first time he had kissed her, she'd thought she was going to faint. After all that had happened to her, Molly had felt that she had found her prince. Prince Harvey. And when he put the engagement ring on her finger, she thought she would die with happiness. She wished she still had that ring with the oval sapphire and the tiny diamonds around it. But Harvey had stolen it from her, taken it to pawn or sell to clear his gambling debts, most likely. And it hadn't been alone in his cache.

The spell was broken. Awful thoughts started to bleed into Molly's mind. He had taken the locket Ma Brandywine had given her as an eighteenth birthday present too, as well as the rest of the contents of her jewellery box: precious gifts from Margaret and Bernard and pieces inherited from Ma Brandywine. And her wedding ring which she had ripped off as soon as she had found out he was being unfaithful. She had discovered them gone on the same day he had left. She had been so angry, so hurt.

What the hell was Margaret going to say when she returned from holiday and realised that her sister was giving free board and lodging to the man who had cheated her on so many fronts? She didn't dare think about it.

Chapter 37

By the end of that week Carla had internet access and a house phone connected. She then spent an hour on her laptop trying to find herself a job before Mr Rex Parkinson arrived to view the mini flat.

Despite the number of sites advertising positions, there weren't any vacancies for a trained florist. That was all Carla had ever done, give or take her first-ever job working in the office where she had met Theresa. Flowers were her great passion. She knew every name of every flower, which scents mixed, which made the perfect visual combination and for what occasion. Still, needs must. She would just have to get herself any job to earn some money until a florist position came available. But she wasn't qualified enough for any of the full-time positions and the part-time ones on offer were so lowly paid. Plus she'd lost her confidence. It had been years since the last time she'd had to apply for a job, and the thought of going out into the world and working for strangers filled her with dread. Rex Parkinson's arrival at her door at least had the effect of snapping her out of a cold sweat about rejoining the rat race.

He wasn't at all as she had imagined from his deep plummy voice. She had envisaged someone tall and stately with the air of an educated gentleman; but the man who arrived at her door was short and squat with a red rough face, scruffy jeans and a jumper that smelt fusty.

Nervous, she launched straight into her sales spiel after making perfunctory introductions.

'Well, this is the kitchen and dining area. We would both be using this.' She tried to imagine sharing her kitchen with Rex Parkinson and it didn't sit very comfortably with her. His eyes flitted around the room but he didn't say anything. He followed Carla upstairs and along the passageway to the mini flat.

'This area would be private to you.' She pushed open the door to the bedroom and Rex looked around, sniffing. 'Small, isn't it?' he said. Carla didn't think the room was small. There was plenty of room in it for a bed and furniture and it wasn't as if he had to use it as a lounge too. A point she made next.

'There's a separate sitting room downstairs, and a private area outside.'

Rex Parkinson walked down the staircase, missing the bottom step and almost falling.

'Dangerous, those spiral stairs,' he said. 'Not sure they're legal.'

Carla was sure that Jonty would have pointed it out if they weren't. She didn't comment, but went on to introduce Mr Parkinson to the room.

'And this is the lounge. There's a TV aerial socket in the corner.'

If Rex Parkinson was impressed, he certainly wasn't showing it. His eyes barely touched on the long French windows which allowed sunshine to flood the room.

'Bit expensive for what it is,' he said, stuffing his hands in his pockets and walking around. 'At least a hundred quid a month too expensive.'

Ah, so that's why he was being so negative, thought Carla. Well, she wasn't playing his game. The flat was fairly priced and she wasn't dropping it.

'Well that's the price it is,' said Carla, feeling slightly uncomfortable that this was heading down a bartering route. She was too soft and liable to give in to him, so warned herself that she couldn't afford to. Jonty had made her promise not to take any less otherwise it was barely worth renting it out.

'My offer is three hundred pounds a month,' said Rex Parkinson and thrust out his hand to shake on the deal. Carla noticed how bitten and grubby his fingernails were. Her own hand stayed at her side.

'I'm sorry, but no.'

Rex gave her a scornful laugh 'You won't get anyone to pay four hundred and twenty for this. Three hundred and I'll move in tonight.' He jerked his hand aggressively, demanding she seal the deal.

'I'm sorry but it's four hundr—' Carla began to repeat.

'Get that thing out of here!' Rex snapped, the hand that he'd held out to shake hers suddenly pointing instead. The black cat had followed Carla and appeared behind her on the spiral staircase. As if picking up what Carla was thinking, it hissed. 'I hate those things,' Rex Parkinson went on. 'They should all be bloody slaughtered.'

Carla grabbed her chance to free herself from this situation.

'Ah well, I think maybe this wouldn't be the house for you. I have six cats. And the rent is four hundred and twenty pounds. Never mind. I do hope you find something suitable.' Carla opened up the French window. 'I might as well let you out of this side entrance. So sorry it wasn't for you.'

She didn't give Rex Parkinson the chance to protest as she shuffled him out. She was very surprised at how forceful she could be when she tried. *Maybe if you had been a little bit more forceful in pushing for what you should have had in your marriage, you wouldn't be in this mess now,* said a nagging voice in her head.

She breathed a sigh of relief as she shut the gate behind the horrible, fusty man. She really didn't want to share facilities with him. She didn't want to share them with anyone, to be honest, but she had to. She picked up her phone to ring Will Linton, the reserve tenant with the *EastEnders* accent whose number she had thankfully saved.

Chapter 38

'I can come now and have a look, if that's okay with you,' Will said to Carla.

'That's fine,' came the reply. 'I'll see you very shortly.'

'Great. Thanks. Bye.' Will put down the phone and grinned. Well, that was a turn-up for the books. He had just had a call from Shaun McCarthy asking if he would come in and see him tomorrow as he might have some work, cash in hand of course. And no sooner had he ended the conversation than the woman had rung about the flat in Little Kipping. Dare he actually hope that his luck was about to change? He could have seriously done with a break. He had thought there was no way to go but up, until yesterday when he'd gone cap in hand to the rival roofing firm Scotterfield's. He had beaten Gerald Scotterfield to the Yorkshire Stone Homes contract. Gerald Scotterfield was now laughing up his sleeve and had been delighted to see him. For all the wrong reasons.

'How the mighty have fallen,' Scotterfield had grinned. He was ten years older than Will, but looked twenty thanks to a basic diet of beer, chips and cigarettes. Still, he thought he was cock of the walk for not making the same stupid mistakes that Will had. He'd ridden the housing slumps, come out laughing at the other end and so invested in all the trappings of wealth: flash cars, big house, Rolex watch. The only thing he didn't have was the glamorous trophy wife. He'd been with Kay since school and she was the homely, plump type, champing at the bit for grand-children.

'So you want a job here now, do you?'

'If you've got one,' said Will. Had he had any other options left whatsoever, he wouldn't have been here beg-ging this loathsome man. But he didn't.

'I don't know if we have, let me ask.' Scotterfield made a slow meal of taking out his phone and ringing his foreman, asking him to come to the scruffy prefab office. When he did so, Scotterfield introduced Will to him as the man who had won the Yorkshire Stone Homes contract and Will stood there whilst they flashed schoolboy secret chuckles at each other.

'We 'ent got no vacancies,' said the foreman. Scotterfield had known that already, thought Will then. He was just rubbing his face in the mud.

'Leave your number,' said Scotterfield. 'I'll ring you if something turns up.'

Will realised that Scotterfield would cut his own balls off with a rusty saw rather than offer him a job.

'Thanks for your time,' he said politely, trying not to let his humiliation show.

Scotterfield called to his back. 'Course, I'm not sure we'll have any work for a roofer that's scared of heights.' Will stopped in his tracks and didn't turn his head as he answered.

'I think you've got me mixed up with someone else, mate,' he said, hoping they wouldn't see his hand shaking as he pushed the door open. He could hear the laughter following him as he walked back to his van, as he was meant to. It had been a long time since Will Linton had last felt tears rise up inside him and he pressed them down with every bit of might he could muster. How the hell did Gerald Scotterfield know about his problem?

Will arrived at Dundealin within half an hour. What an odd-looking house, he thought. It wouldn't have got planning permission these days. It was so different to the other nearby houses and much further set back from the road. And it was totally private, enclosed by four walls that were higher than was allowed, he could see that at a glance. He pulled into the drive next to a red Mini.

Carla, who had seen him arrive, opened the door in greeting. The first impression she had of Will Linton in his crisp white shirt and clean jeans was a far more favourable one than she'd had of Rex Parkinson. He had a friendly smile, she thought. It lit up his face as he said hello and she moved aside to let him in.

Will thought he had seen the woman somewhere before. He recognised her eyes: large and dark and exotic. Like Sophia Loren's.

'I'm so glad you called,' said Will, walking into the kitchen and turning a full circle. 'My, this is a big bright room.'

'It's the kitchen,' said Carla, then laughed at herself. 'Obviously.'

'It's lovely. Nice big windows there. Lots of space.'

'Yes it's ... nice,' agreed Carla. Actually it was a very pleasant room, she thought. It was amazing how a good clean had transformed it. And the new mushroom-coloured curtains, cheap as chips as they were, looked fresh at the window. At least they drew the eye away from the mustardy yellow walls.

'You're not from round here then,' Carla asked, as she led him upstairs to the mini flat's bedroom.

'Naw, I'm a London boy,' said Will. 'Moved up north a few years ago to work, met my ex-missus in the area and so I stayed.' *That's the first time I've referred to her as my 'ex-missus'*, thought Will, marvelling that he could say 'ex-missus' without feeling any emotion at all. He felt as if his life had definitely moved on a step – and in the right direction.

'Oh, this would do a treat,' he said as Carla opened the door to the bedroom.

'There's a closet,' Carla pointed out. 'There's a rail in it for hanging things up.'

'Oh, that's smashing that,' said Will, sounding as if it really was. 'Plenty of room for what I need.'

'There's an en-suite. It's avocado, sorry about that.'

Will laughed. 'Don't see that colour much these days.'

'I wonder why.' Carla's laugh joined his and she thought that she liked the first impression of Will Linton. She could imagine sharing a kitchen with him, which was a positive sign.

'The lounge is downstairs, if you'd follow me,' said Carla, descending the staircase.

'How can anyone put such a lovely staircase in as this and not alter that bathroom,' chuckled Will, then corrected himself. 'Sorry, that was a bit rude of me.'

'It's fine,' said Carla. 'I've only just bought the place so I haven't had a chance to do anything to it. I totally agree with you.'

Will was even more enamoured with the lounge. 'Ah, this is the bees,' he judged it. 'Just the business. And a little bit of garden outside, I see.'

'Well, if you can call it that. But it's private. There's a gate but it's lockable.'

Will stood with his hands on his hips and imagined himself in this mini flat. He was surprised to find he could do it quite easily. Living in that huge multi-bedroomed house with no furniture was depressing the hell out of him. He could almost hear all the neighbours scoffing at him through the walls; he was no better than a squatter in their eyes. The sooner he handed the keys over to the bank, the better. His accountant had worked out that if they took everything he owned, he'd be financially clear of his obligations. At least he could keep the pound of flesh nearest his heart.

'The rent is four hundred and twenty, that's right isn't it?' said Will as they retraced their steps back to the kitchen.

'Yes that's right,' Carla answered, hoping this wasn't the start of more bartering. But it wasn't. Will reached in his pocket and pulled out his wallet.

'In advance I'm presuming? Do you want a bond or anything as well?' he asked. 'I haven't rented a house before. Don't know the score.'

'Erm, no,' said Carla. 'You ... you want the flat?'

'Do I?' he said, producing four hundred and twenty pounds. It was all he appeared to have in his wallet. 'It's exactly what I need. How soon can I move in?'

'Erm, soon as you like. I just need to get your signature on a couple of documents.'

'Tomorrow? Hello, what do we have here then?' He cut off attention to Carla to give it to the small black cat who was rubbing against his leg. He bent down and picked it up. 'Bit thin, ain't you?'

'I inherited him with the house,' Carla explained quickly, in case Will Linton thought she was an animal-starver. 'He'll be enormous in no time because he never stops eating. Well, I say *him*, it might be a *her*.'

Will lifted the cat up above his head. 'It is a him. Neutered tom. We always had cats when I was growing up.' He

Chapter 39

'Oh Mr McCarthy, Mr McCarthy,' Leni called, waving to him as she stood outside the teashop door. 'Can I borrow you for a moment please?'

Shaun downed tools and walked across to where she was standing, moving her arms around as if she were guiding a plane in. He wondered what she wanted, hoping it wouldn't take long. He wasn't in the best of moods. He was being messed around by someone who wanted the smallest shop unit one minute and then didn't the next. A woman had begged him to hurry on it only for her to start being difficult to pin down to sign for the lease. He'd even arranged to have the signage done for her as part of the deal. Then she had left him a voicemail saying that she didn't want it. Today she had sent him another telling him that she had made a mistake and would take it, if he dropped the rent. Shaun didn't reply. She could have it as soon as flowers grew in hell.

'Mr McCarthy. I have a problem with a door at home. It won't shut properly and when I tried to force it ... well, I made it worse. Would you be able to come and look at it? I'll pay cash.'

'Yeah, I suppose so,' replied Shaun.

'Oh fabulous, thank you, thank you,' Leni nodded with obvious delight. 'Whenever is best for you.'

'I can probably do it tonight. About six?' Then he could get it over and done with by seven.

'Perfect, if you don't mind working on a Friday night,' she replied cheerily. 'I wrote my address down in case you could,' and she handed over a square of paper with small neat writing on it. 'I'll have the kettle on ready. I might even throw in some cake.'

Shaun walked back to the other side of the square hoping it was a one-off quick job that wouldn't give him time for small talk or cake-eating. Not that he had anything to rush home for. A Friday night was just as lonely as any other for him.

Chapter 40

Spending the last night in the marital home Will had shared with Nicole was probably the easiest thing he had done in a long time. He was taken aback how many happy memories he had in this house when he sat on a kitchen stool and tried to count them, because there were hardly any. There were a few jolly dinner parties with people he had thought were genuine friends, who had dropped him like a hot brick when his business started to fold. There was lots of sex with Nicole in the bedroom, usually when she wanted something or had just got what she wanted: the sauna, the pool, the Hermès bag, jewellery. He couldn't even remember planning to ask her to marry him, she'd sort of inveigled a proposal out of him in Monte Carlo after he'd won thirty thousand Euros on the roulette wheel. In their euphoria she had suggested they were a lucky couple and should get married and he'd thought, why not? Nicole was pretty with long legs and he liked the way people looked at her and envied him for having her. So his winnings, and more, had been settled on a ring for her the following day in a Monaco jeweller's shop.

Sitting in the empty house, he'd had a lot of time to think and he didn't like what he'd discovered about the 'sorted' life he thought he'd had. Nicole had a great figure and looked good on his arm. But if he loved her so much, how come he didn't miss her now? They'd had luxurious holidays all over the world together, but they hadn't been companions, friends – not like his mum and dad had been. Nicole hadn't talked to him much about anything that didn't involve spending his money. They'd been two people braced together by marriage, but they were never a couple as he understood the word. They didn't laugh, play, talk. He didn't miss her friendship, because they hadn't been friends. He hadn't spilled out what happened to him at work when he got home because she was at a Zumba class or Pilates or having spray tans. They'd shared a house and his money and a lifestyle . . . but it wasn't a life. There had been no glue to hold them together apart from possessions, which made a very poor adhesive. He'd been an arrogant idiot really. No wonder he came so unstuck.

He didn't even think about Nicole any more, other than when a document arrived from the divorce solicitor for him to sign. She wanted a quickie so she could be immediately available for the next bloke with a Jaguar and a des res.

The total of Will's belongings fitted easily in his van. They consisted of a lot of designer suits, shirts, socks, shoes and underwear. His clothes were worth more than everything else he was taking. A few boxes of books, a laptop, toiletries, photos – not of Nicole, although she had kindly left a souvenir wedding photograph for him which he had filed in the bin. Family souvenirs, an inflatable mattress that would serve until he bought a new bed, a quilt and pillow, his one-of-everything from the kitchen, the TV and his armchair, a box full of other bits and pieces. That would do him for now.

God, he wished his family were here, standing behind him, looking into the van. He could imagine his dad raising

'She's on a cruise,' said Molly, not wanting to talk about Margaret now.

'I always liked her, though. And Bernard. Wonderful man. But I fear the feeling wasn't reciprocated. And I totally understand why.' He stared straight into Molly's dark blue eyes 'You were the only woman I ever loved,' he said.

He's just saying that because you're looking after him, said a voice inside Molly, pulling her back from the abyss her heart wanted to throw itself into again.

'Eat your soup,' she said.

'Aye-aye, cap'n,' he smiled.

Chapter 42

Shaun would have been lying to himself if he said that he wasn't intrigued to see where Leni lived, although he could have guessed it would be in the sort of cottage whose image would sit beautifully on a tin of chocolate biscuits. He wasn't far wrong, he was satisfied to discover. Thorn Cottage was situated on the outskirts of Maltstone. There were three houses on the row which once belonged to the workers on the nearby Clough Farm. Hers was on the far end, an old stone build, covered in honeysuckle with frilly curtains hanging at the windows.

'Hello, Mr McCarthy.' She was at the door before he had even braked. She must have been looking out for him. 'Tea or coffee?'

Oh, why not. He was gagging for a drink. 'Coffee please, if you don't mind. Black. One sugar.'

'It'll be with you in a flash,' she said. 'I'll just show you the job first. I know you're busy.'

He wiped his feet on the mat and walked into a pretty lounge. It couldn't have been more different to his own house, with all the plump soft furnishings and bright paintings of French café scenes. There was a dark brown rug in front of a blackleaded Yorkshire range, unlit for summer, but

Shaun reckoned it would kick out some grand heat in winter. Mr Bingley was asleep on the rug, his head on his paws, his tail curling around his huge body. It was a warm, cosy and inviting scene. Nothing less than he expected from Miss Green Gables.

He had read somewhere how to tell the difference between a female and a male snake: put them on a bed with a soft side and a hard side and the female would always slither to the warmer more comfortable part. A female snake would have loved it in Leni Merryman's house. Even a male snake might have changed his proclivities for this set-up.

Shaun was moved slightly to envy. He had lived in so many houses, never feeling like any one of them was a home. He bought shells of houses, tried to make them his own with alterations and redesigns and ended up selling them only to move on to another and start the process again. Every one felt cold and empty. There was something missing from all of them that he couldn't produce.

'Follow me, Mr McCarthy,' Leni said, crossing the room to a polished wooden staircase. 'It's up here.'

Photographs lined the walls in frames hung by pink and cream striped ribbons. Shaun realised at the top of the stairs that it was the same girl in various stages of growth: a baby in a white frilly dress, a giggling toddler sitting astride a rocking horse, a school photo where she was grinning, her front two teeth missing; a lanky teenager with long dark messy hair holding up a certificate in one hand and a pair of pink ballet shoes with the other; then astride a horse, taking a fence.

'It's this door,' said Leni. 'I've made a bit of a mess of it, I'm afraid.'

'Haven't you just,' Shaun affirmed, looking at the twisted hinge and wondering how she had managed to do that. He tried to close the door and found that it didn't fit in the frame. The wood had swollen and needed planing off in the middle, then the hinges needed totally replacing.

'I'll get your coffee,' she said, squeezing past him on the landing. There wasn't a lot of space; it was as compact as a doll's house. The door he was mending led to a room he presumed wasn't hers, because it had a single bed in it with a pink quilt and a furry pink throw draped over the top of it, and an obligatory teddy bear. There were shelves of books and a desk with a cream anglepoise lamp on it. It had to be her daughter's room, the one who sent her the post-cards. Anne, was it? Shaun thought Anne might just have outgrown this room. No wonder she was staying away at the other side of the world.

'Here you go, Mr McCarthy,' said Leni, returning with a drink, not surprisingly in a mug decorated with brightly coloured cupcakes. 'Is it a big job?'

'I'll have to do it over two nights,' he replied, more grumpily than he intended. 'I can't save the hinges. I'll take the door off tonight and then come back probably tomorrow.'

'Oh,' said Leni. 'I thought it might simply be a case of a replacement screw. There's no rush though.'

'Well, once I've started a job, I like to finish it,' said Shaun. 'Is this your daughter's room?'

'Yes, yes, that's her room. Those are her things, although she hasn't seen it yet, but I've decorated it the same as her old one. I only moved here a few months ago and she's been abroad. She's taking a gap year before she starts university. Or two. I sold my last house to fund the business. It was much bigger than this.'

Shaun took a mouthful of coffee. It was the freshly brewed stuff, he could tell.

'You must miss her,' he said.

Leni lifted her shoulders and then dropped them again. 'Well yes, but she's too busy having a whale of a time. No doubt after uni, she'll go and live somewhere exciting and lively. She won't want to come back here permanently after all the adventures she's had.'

Why decorate a room for her then if she's hardly likely to use it? he thought but didn't say.

'When you moved away from your home in Ireland you never went back to live there again, I presume?'

Shaun put his cup down and picked up his drill to take out the screws.

'Yeah. I moved away from exciting Ireland and came to exciting here,' he said. It sounded brutally sarcastic and he jumped in immediately to temper it. 'South Yorkshire always suited me fine. I came here for work, found plenty of it and stayed. I've been lucky.'

'How often do you go back?' asked Leni.

'I don't,' said Shaun, pressing on a screw until it twirled upwards out of its home. 'It wasn't exactly a scenic part of Ireland I came from. No rolling green hills or quaint villages.'

'What about family?'

'I have none,' said Shaun and took out another screw. Then another.

'Ah, that's sad,' said Leni, lifting the cup to her lips and picking up the tone in his voice that intimated no further questioning on the subject would be welcome. 'Would you like some cake, Mr McCarthy? I've got some milk chocolate or . . .'

'No thanks,' replied Shaun. 'I'm nearly done.'

'Shall I pay you now, or at the end?'

Shaun waved his hand. 'It'll do later, when I find out how much the hinges are.' He looked for somewhere to rest the door.

'Against there is fine,' Leni pointed. 'The only thing it will block is access to the airing cupboard.'

Leni went back downstairs soon to be followed by Shaun and his toolbox. Mr Bingley had moved onto the sofa and looked like a fat orange cushion. Shaun handed her the cup.

'Thanks for the coffee,' he said, noticing what a strange colour her eyes were – like mud with green flecks. Chocolate mint.

'A slice of cake for your supper,' said Leni, handing over a wedge wrapped in a cream serviette. 'An interim payment.'

He took it because it would have been rude not to, but he knew he wouldn't eat it.

'Thanks,' he said. 'I'll be around tomorrow at the same time.'

'It's Saturday night,' she said, 'I can wait. I wouldn't want to drag you out again at the weekend.'

'Doesn't matter to me,' said Shaun. 'My work-life doesn't have an off switch.'

Leni knew that feeling. Off switches were dangerous things. They gave you time to think.

'Well, if you're sure. Good night, Mr McCarthy.'

'Night.'

Shaun called in for fish and chips on the way home to his large, empty house. After supper he ate the cake and wished it had been a bigger slice.

Chapter 43

The next morning Shaun walked past Leni's empty shop, took a casual glance through the glass in the door and saw someone with his hand in the till who wasn't Leni. It was a boy, with light brown hair and a green T-shirt. And he'd seen that boy before. He couldn't remember where or when, but the fragment of memory didn't have a good vibe to it.

Shaun barged in through the door and marched so fast to the counter that Ryan, on his first morning at work, had no chance to react as his collar was grabbed and he felt himself being marched between the tables.

'I think you're in the wrong place, laddie. Come back here again and you'll find my boot right up your backside,' he growled.

'Let go of me, you knobhead,' said the kid, struggling now, but his skinny limbs were no match for the strength of Shaun.

'Mr McCarthy, what on earth do you think you're doing?' Leni's voice from behind his shoulder arrested his movement.

'This little swine had his hand in your till,' yelled Shaun, thinking that she didn't sound very grateful considering he'd probably saved her week's takings. About ten pounds in her case.

'He's my Saturday boy,' shrieked Leni.

'Yeah,' Ryan affirmed, swinging from side to side to break free of the hold on his collar.

'Saturday boy?'

'Yes, it's his first morning. Let him go, Mr McCarthy.' Leni slapped Shaun's hand and his fingers sprang open.

'Why the hell didn't he say?' snapped Shaun.

'Maybe he would have if you'd given him a chance.' She addressed Ryan. 'Are you all right?'

'Yeah,' he nodded. 'I'll carry on putting the change back in, shall I?' and he gave Shaun a pointed look of annoyance.

'Please,' said Leni, giving him a comforting rub on his arm as he walked past her. Then she turned to Shaun and for the first time, she wasn't smiling.

'I'm sorry,' he said, 'I thought . . .'

'It's fine,' said Leni. 'Crisis averted.'

'Where did you get him from?'

'He called in to see if I had a job.'

'Where does he live?'

'Why all the questions, Mr McCarthy?'

'I've seen him before and I can't place him.'

Leni sighed. 'He's from somewhere near Wombwell.'

'Bit vague.' Shaun called across to him. 'Where are you from?'

'Near Wombwell,' replied Ryan, not looking up.

'Whereabouts near Wombwell?' Shaun pressed. The boy was being deliberately unclear and there had to be a reason for that.

'Sort of just outside it.'

Shaun made an intelligent stab at a guess. 'You're from Ketherwood, aren't you?'

Ryan's head jerked up. 'No,' he said. But the upward inflection gave him away.

That's why I know his face, Shaun groaned inwardly.

'Tell me he's not one of the O'Gowan lot,' he said to Leni. 'I knew I'd seen him before. Although I bet I haven't. I've probably seen one of his brothers because they all look the f . . . same.'

Leni opened her mouth to answer, but Shaun didn't leave her space to.

'You wanna get rid of him now before you come in one morning and your stock is all gone.'

Then Ryan ran forwards, butted between Shaun and Leni and addressed them both, his head turning from one to the other.

'Yes, I am from Ketherwood. I knew if I said I was from there, you wouldn't give me a job. And yes I am one of the O'Gowan lot but I'm not like them. I won't end up in prison or selling drugs. I want to make something of me'sen. I've never been in trouble with the police, you can check.'

No one said anything and Ryan took it that his speech had fallen on stony ground.

'Aw, I'll get my coat,' and he turned away.

'You'll do no such thing,' said Leni. 'You'll carry on sorting out that change if you want a job.'

Ryan turned back to her and the corners of his lips lifted in gratitude, then he went over to the till.

'You're mad,' said Shaun, raking his large hand through his short greying hair.

'Sometimes you have to give people a chance. They don't always prove you wrong, Mr McCarthy. None of us is perfect.'

Shaun lifted his hands in surrender and his blue-green eyes flashed as big a warning to Leni as his next words did.

'Don't come running to me when it ends in tears. But if there is any damage or thefts on my land, I'll come straight here for him.'

And then he was gone, muttering the O'Gowan name under his breath.

Chapter 44

By eleven-thirty that morning, Harvey was stir crazy.

'Shall we go out into the sunshine? Have tea in a café somewhere?'

Molly huffed. 'You're supposed to be resting.'

'I have been resting and I can rest again when I pop off,' said Harvey, hoisting himself out of the chair. 'But I can't sit here and watch another *Columbo*.'

'There is a little teashop I sometimes go to,' said Molly. 'It doesn't have any outside seats yet but it's very nice.'

'Then lead the way,' said Harvey. 'I'll even pay.'

*

It was quite odd to have a man she didn't know at all moving into her house, Carla thought, but it would have felt a lot stranger had it been Rex Parkinson instead of Will Linton. The more she thought about Rex, the more she was glad he had been so stubborn on the rental price.

She had thought about asking Will if he wanted a hand moving in, then stopped herself because she knew she should keep her distance. But Carla, being Carla, found herself outside on the drive asking if he needed any help, and he gratefully accepted, as long as she left the heavy stuff to him, he said.

He didn't have a great many things to move in with. She wondered if, like her, he had walked out of his old life with only the bare essentials, ready to start afresh. She presumed from their conversation yesterday that he was newly separated or divorced. She noted that when he carried in the massive armchair, he managed it without any exertion. He might not have had bulging muscles in his arms, but he was obviously very strong.

'I need to get a bed and a sofa and things but I wanted to see where I ended up living and how much space I had first,' said Will, explaining why he had so little furniture. He looked embarrassed. Carla wanted to jump in and tell him that there was no need.

'Would you like me to make you a cup of tea or coffee?' she asked.

'Thanks, but I've got a kettle and I'll put it on here and get acclimatised to my new living quarters.'

'I'll leave you to it then,' she smiled. 'Oh, here are your keys. And your rent book. And your list of do's and don'ts.'

He looked slightly stunned.

'Joke,' she said, her turn to be embarrassed, admonishing herself for being too familiar. She was probably coming across as a total loon.

His face broke into a smile. 'Phew,' he said. 'I've stayed in enough boarding houses on jobs with those sorts of lists pinned to the back of the door to last me a lifetime.'

He was an attractive man, thought Carla. Crinkles around his eyes that aged him but in a good way. Cheerful grey eyes.

'Well . . . thanks,' said Will, taking the book and keys and thinking it was good to be in the presence of a female who smiled. He realised then that Nicole had never once made him a cup of tea or coffee in all the years they had been together.

*

Half an hour later Carla set off into town to buy a present for Theresa's birthday but the road into the centre was jammed with cars because there was a food fair on in the market. Carla took the first opportunity to double back up the road. Maybe she would find something in that lovely teashop on the corner.

She was thrilled to find Molly in there and not alone but with a gentleman, the one she had been talking about, who was ill, she presumed. He was very thin and had dark crescents under his eyes but he was working his way through an enormous piece of chocolate cake. Carla noticed that there was a young lad helping Leni today. He was walking very slowly towards Molly's table with two cups of coffee.

'Oh good morning, Carla,' said Molly. 'Harvey, I'd like you to meet a friend of mine. Harvey, this is Carla. For some strange reason we always seem to turn up here at roughly the same time.'

Harvey stood and extended his hand. 'Goodness and beauty gravitate towards themselves, I always think. Good morning, Carla,' he said. 'Charmed to meet you. Do join us. We're having coffee and cake.'

'Yes, and I'm not sure that triple chocolate gateau is on your diet sheet,' tutted Molly.

'Then I must have picked up the wrong one,' replied Harvey, casting a wink in Carla's direction.

Carla couldn't help smiling. How long did Molly say they'd been apart? And yet they looked like *a couple*. She wondered if people who saw her and Martin thought of them as a couple. Then again, who would have seen them?

She couldn't think of the last time they had been out together – for dinner, lunch or even for a coffee or a walk.

'And Carla, I'd like you to meet the newest addition to my staff,' said Leni. 'This is Ryan. He's our Saturday lad.'

'Nice to meet you, Ryan,' greeted Carla. Ryan nodded shyly by way of return, obviously not enjoying the attention.

The table next to Molly's had a half-eaten scone on it and a teapot.

'Mr Singh is in the loo,' said Molly. 'How strange we should all be here today.'

'He's in a very good mood,' smiled Leni. 'He's had a letter from his daughter.'

On cue, Mr Singh emerged from the toilet, jolly-faced as usual.

'My goodness,' he said on seeing Carla. 'We are meeting here yet again.'

'We've fallen into the same orbit around the teashop,' laughed Carla.

'Yes, well you can laugh, but I believe that happens,' said Mr Singh, retaking his seat. 'I have three times been on holiday to different places and met with people whom I knew. Quite extraordinary.'

'You look very happy today, Mr Singh,' said Carla, giving him the opportunity to show off his news.

'Ah well, I have a letter from my daughter.'

'How lovely,' said Carla, infected by his jollity. 'I didn't know anyone wrote letters any more.'

'She rings on the telephone,' he replied. 'But she knows her papa likes letters, so every month she writes to me too.' He sat down with a groan of contentment and took out an envelope from his pocket.

Molly watched Mr Singh holding up the letter, savouring the shape of it. She recognised that wonderful anticipation.

When they were courting, Harvey would send her notes in the post, even though he lived just a short bus ride away. He knew she read his letters over and over again. She wished now she had kept them, not been persuaded by Margaret to burn them in the garden in a bid to rid her heart of his spectre. It hadn't. It had only served to make her wish she hadn't destroyed them. All that remained was that postcard that said . . .

'Wish you were here, papa-ji' said Mr Singh, in complete synch to Molly's thoughts. 'She always writes that on the back. I wish she were here, but at the same time I want her to spread her wings and take flight in the world. Like your Anne. Doesn't it make you proud, Leni, that your daughter, like mine, is living, really living, life and seeing the world?'

'Oh my, yes, it does,' agreed Leni.

'Have you travelled much, Pavitar?' asked Molly.

'I always liked to travel very much with my wife,' replied Mr Singh. 'But not now. I don't want to travel alone.'

Molly drew from that that Mr Singh was a widower. She wondered if it was worse to be alone for so many years and be acclimatised to it, or suffer the shock of losing a partner late in life. She and Harvey had once made plans to travel all over the world when they could afford it, see the Northern Lights, drift on the canals of Venice, visit the Vatican, climb the Statue of Liberty, have champagne at the top of the Eiffel Tower. She had crossed a couple of these off her list, but it wasn't the same going with her sister and Bernard. Life with Harvey had been feast and famine – depending on whether his gambling paid off. It was mainly famine.

'What can I get you, Carla?' asked Leni.

'I'll just have a coffee, I think, but give me two minutes. I want to look for a present for a friend of mine first.'

Carla started at the nearest cabinet, next to the wall of

postcards pinned up in a higgledy-piggledy fashion to hide the missing top corners where the stamps once sat.

In the third cabinet, Carla spotted the ideal present for Theresa: A scarf woven with scenes from *Wuthering Heights*. Heathcliff's glowering face filled one end, the other – Catherine Earnshaw sporting some wild bed-hair. There was even some wrapping paper covered in small Top Withens buildings, the sky mean and moody behind it. Perfect. Theresa could take a little bit of Yorkshire with her when she went to New Zealand.

Carla carried on looking, though, fascinated by the things to buy. There were new things since the last time she had been: a set of china mugs featuring Dickens characters, coloured paperclips in the shape of Jane Austen's profile, a tiny bookshelf filled with all the books Agatha Christie had written in perfect miniature, a 'writers block' notepad that looked as if it had been made out of a chunk of wood, bracelet charms made from old typewriter keys. And – joy of joys – the most gorgeous journal in the world, replicating the cover of *Hard Times*, by Charles Dickens. It was exactly what she needed to record her plan of action to get her life back into some semblance of order.

'Found anything you like?' asked Molly. 'I could buy everything in this shop.'

'I'm going to have the *Hard Times* journal, the Top Withens roll of wrapping paper and the Heathcliff scarf, please.'

'Certainly,' smiled Leni. 'I'll get them ready for you whilst you're drinking your coffee.'

'Heathcliff. What a bastard he was.' Harvey's voice filled the teashop.

'For goodness sake, Harvey,' hissed Molly. 'Keep it down.'

'Well he was,' said Harvey, refusing to be hushed. 'I never understood why they always picked the good-looking actors to play him in films. He was an absolute psychopath. Quite the most unpleasant character I've ever read.'

'I totally agree,' said Mr Singh, excitedly accentuating his words with a waving finger. 'Laurence Olivier, Timothy Dalton, Ralph Fiennes – all very striking men.'

'And Cliff Richard. Don't forget Cliff Richard,' put in Leni.

'I think you mean let's forget Cliff Richard,' said Harvey.

'Cliff Richard? Surely not?' said Mr Singh, tilting his head in confusion. 'I can't remember that version.'

'It was a musical,' Harvey replied. 'Though with the best will in the world I can't imagine Cliff Richard hanging a dog.'

Molly shuddered. 'Did he hang a dog? I can't remember that part.'

'Cliff Richard didn't but Heathcliff did. What's-her-name's dog. The sister.' Harvey tapped the table in frustration at not being able to remember the character.

'Isabella.'

All eyes turned to Ryan.

'That's it, lad. That's the name,' said Harvey.

'You really do read then,' Leni smiled at him.

'I told you I did,' Ryan replied, shrugging his shoulders as he unwrapped a box of small metal lapel pins shaped like old typewriters and took them into the back room.

'But because he loves Cathy so passionately, we're supposed to wipe Heathcliff's slate clean,' said Harvey in a very mocking voice. 'Oh, you women do love a bad boy.'

Carla let loose a quiet dry laugh. She wasn't one of those women. She had recently realised how much of a bad boy she had been living with and it didn't make her excited in the least. She didn't want another bad boy. Nor did she want a good boy, because that good boy might really be a bad boy after all. She'd never trust another one of them again.

'I don't,' she said.

Milly Johnson

'Me neither,' agreed Molly and threw Harvey a disapproving look. 'Personally, I'd much rather have a Mr Rochester.'

'Shouldn't we be saving this conversation for Brontë Tuesday?' asked Carla.

'What's Brontë Tuesday?' asked Harvey.

'Every Tuesday there is a theme here,' replied Molly. 'It's Brontë Tuesday next week.'

'I can't wait until Tuesday,' replied Harvey putting his hands on his hips. 'I live in the here and now.'

'Me neither,' agreed Mr Singh, nodding his head heartily. 'Now, Mr Rochester didn't treat his wife very well, did he? He locked her up in an attic.'

'I have to defend him, I'm afraid,' Carla jumped in. 'He was seduced by two families into marrying Bertha Mason who kept it from him that she had hereditary madness. He could have put her in an asylum but he didn't. He kept her in the house and employed a carer. Admittedly she was a bit rubbish at keeping the door locked. Of course if you were to read Jean Rhys's *Wide Sargasso Sea*, you might feel more inclined to be on Bertha's side but . . .' Then she realised all eyes were on her and her mouth clamped shut. She wasn't used to being the centre of attention.

'Go on, dear,' urged Molly. 'I haven't read that book.'

'Well,' gulped Carla. 'Put it this way, if you like Rochester and want to keep liking him, don't read it. He comes across as a bit of a—' *Martin*. 'He doesn't come across well at all. In fact, he's a bit of a git. The sympathy is totally weighted towards her.'

'Then I definitely shan't read it,' said Molly. 'I like my Rochester gentlemanly and considerate. I would rather not see him any other way.'

Mr Singh laughed. 'Yes, I see I see. Maybe he isn't as bad as I remember.'

'And Rochester liked dogs,' put in Molly. 'He didn't hang them.'

'He was far from perfect though,' said Mr Singh. 'You have to give me that point.'

'Girls don't mind a little bit of imperfection,' called Leni over her shoulder as she walked into the back room for some fragile tape. 'Luckily.'

'A perfect man would be far too daunting,' added Molly, before she realised that Harvey was looking at her with barely concealed amusement.

'Flawed heroes are good. So long as they don't hang dogs,' chuckled Mr Singh.

'Well that's got my blood flowing, all this talk of Byronic heroes,' chuckled Harvey.

'We should make a move soon,' said Molly, who was aware that Harvey was getting far too animated, which couldn't be good for him. 'Could we have the bill please, Leni?'

'So it's Brontë Tuesday, is it? I hope we'll be here for that,' said Harvey, after swallowing the last piece of his chocolate cake. 'I could slag Heathcliff off all day every day. Bye Ryan. Don't let them work you too hard. Join a union and insist on plenty of tea-breaks.'

Ryan, putting some washed plates back on the shelf, grinned.

Molly hung behind for a second after Harvey had walked outside.

'Thank you for listening to me the other day,' she said to Leni and Carla. 'I think I did the right thing. I do apologise for his bad language. He was always so very . . .' *impassioned* '. . . loud.'

'He was enjoying himself and we were enjoying listening to him,' said Leni, waving away that apology. 'And what better place to have a literary argument than in here.'

'He seems a nice man,' said Carla, hoping he was, because she was the world's most rubbish judge of character. She'd thought Fred West looked like a jolly bloke when she'd first seen his face in the newspapers.

Molly caught Harvey up. He had started a new argument about Heathcliff and was chuntering away to himself about what might have happened in his missing years. Which seemed more than ironic to her.

Chapter 45

'Come and have your break,' said Leni, going into the back room where Ryan was pricing up items. 'You must be hungry. Cheese and ham toastie?'

'Yeah, great,' said Ryan, putting down the roll of stickers and following Leni into the by now empty tearoom.

'I thought you might. I've put one on for you.'

'Ta.'

'Tea, coffee, milk or orange juice?' Leni asked Ryan as she put the sandwich down in front of him.

'Er, orange please.'

By the time she had poured a glass out and taken it to him, the sandwich had disappeared.

'Goodness me,' laughed Leni. 'Were you hungry? Do you want another?'

There was a telling pause before he answered, 'No thanks.'

'I'll make you another,' smiled Leni. 'It's no trouble.'

She tried not to watch, but she couldn't help herself. He ate quickly, like an animal who was afraid that if he didn't get his food into him, it would be stolen away. She cut him an extra-large piece of chocolate cake. She figured he would enjoy that, seeing as he had been eyeing it up all morning. And she was right.

'Don't you have any breakfast before you come out?' she asked, pouring herself a cup of coffee.

'We don't do breakfast at ours,' Ryan said, through a mouthful of cake. 'I'm not that bothered.'

Oh, the arguments I used to have with Anne, Leni remembered. *Mum, I don't want any Ready Brek. I'm not hungry.*

Well you aren't going out of this house without a breakfast inside you, young lady.

I'll be sick if I eat it.

Compromise. Half a bowl.

I'll have a Weetabix then. How's that?

It'll do.

Ryan finished the cake and dabbed up all the crumbs with his finger.

'Thanks, that were lovely,' he said and stood to go back to work.

'Sit down and finish your drink,' Leni commanded. 'You've only had a ten-minute break.' He obeyed her. 'I'm sorry about what happened this morning. With the landlord, Mr McCarthy.'

'It's all right,' said Ryan with a resigned lift and drop of his shoulders. 'Everyone knows us. The O'Gowan name's always cropping up in the Chron.'

'Well, I hadn't heard of you,' smiled Leni softly.

'You must be the only one who hasn't. I can't really blame anyone for hearing the name O'Gowan from Ketherwood and thinking bad stuff. We've got a bit of a reputation.'

'I might need some help after work sometime if you're free and it doesn't interfere with any homework,' she said, moving on to another subject. She didn't want to embarrass him.

'Yeah, great,' Ryan replied.

'Saving up for anything?'

'A Kindle,' he beamed, without having to think about it. He drank the remainder of his orange juice and went straight into the back room and Leni thought she just might send him home with the rest of the chocolate cake.

Chapter 46

'Fancy meeting you here.' Will waved across to Carla as she was about to get into her car.

'Oh, what a surprise,' said Carla. 'You work here then?'

'Hoping to,' said Will. 'A few days' casual work carrying a hod.'

So he was a labourer, thought Carla. That accounted for the strength in lifting up that armchair. His arms were bare now and she could see his muscle definition. She hoped he hadn't spotted her looking at them.

'I've just been for a coffee,' said Carla, pointing back at the teashop on the corner. 'It's really lovely in there.'

'Yeah, I've been in before.'

Unable to think of anything witty or incisive to say, she settled on, 'Well, bye. See you later. Good luck with the job.'

'Cheers.'

Shaun was running late and was at the builder's merchants, one of the lads on site informed him. Will thought he might as well have a coffee in the teashop. He could just about afford one.

How the mighty had fallen.

Those words from Gerald Scotterfield had been playing over and over in his head like a stuck record since he had said them. They kept him awake for a good chunk of last night as he lay on the inflatable mattress with his new hollow-fibre quilt from Brenda's Bedding Shop covering him (obviously Nicole had taken the Hungarian goose down duvet). Even more cutting than the words themselves had been the derision in Scotterfield's piggy little eyes. He had enjoyed every minute of seeing Will brought low. Will decided in the middle of the sleepless night he could either let that vision crush him or use it to kick himself up the derrière. As he never wanted to see anyone looking at him in that way again, he chose the latter course of action.

He hadn't put any food in his cupboards yet. He'd go to the supermarket after meeting Shaun and stock up. Carla had left some shelves clear for him and said he was free to use the kettle and things like the washing-up liquid, sponges and tea-towels. Initial impressions told him that Carla would be a relaxed landlady and he hoped that her initial impressions were that he wouldn't abuse that. She was a nice woman, pretty, with a lovely smile, and he wondered what her story was. She must be as skint as he was, having to rent out half a house she had only just moved into.

He walked into the teashop and sat at a table.

'Afternoon,' said the cheery café-owner. 'Be with you in a minute.'

Will picked up the menu and spotted straightaway what he fancied. Two egg mayo sandwiches and a huge pot of tea. He relayed his choice to the young lad who appeared at his side within a few minutes, notepad and pencil poised. Then he looked around at all the lovely cabinets full of book-related things. Will hadn't read half as much as he used to in the past few years; he'd been too busy and too stressed out. He came from a family of serious readers. His mum loved her Midnight Moon romances and his dad couldn't get enough of his spy novels. His sister read Agatha Christie books over and over again and he enjoyed biographies and history. He'd always liked having books around; they were furniture to him, made a house a home. Nicole didn't read books, only fat glossy magazines full of models wearing designer clothing. Strangely enough, she had them all over the house, yet banned any books from the shelves, saying they looked untidy. Dear God, every day was bringing another reason why they had been a ridiculous match.

The egg mayo sandwiches came on hunks of soft granary bread with crunchy salt and pepper and were absolutely delicious. Will thought he could have sat all afternoon in the teashop, eating sandwiches and drinking tea. There was a lovely atmosphere in it: warm, inviting, calm. He wished he could bottle it and sprinkle it around his new flat so he would have a good night's sleep. He'd forgotten what one of those was. He got to his feet reluctantly to pay the bill after he spotted Shaun across the square.

'That was just what I needed,' he said, giving the young lad a two-pound coin extra, who held it in his hand as if he was scared it would blow up if he put it down.

'Your tip, you earned it,' said Leni. 'So you keep it.'

'Mint,' he said, delighted.

'New starter,' Leni explained with a grin. 'He's done brilliantly.'

'No cock-ups on my order, it was great,' said Will. 'Beautiful little place this. If the other shops he's building are as nice as this one, you should have a good footfall of customers coming your way, touch wood.'

'Thank you,' said Leni. 'I hope so. Feel free to call again and give me your custom.'

'I will,' he said and stuck his thumb up at the boy.

Will stopped to look in the cabinets as he walked out.

There was a notepad with the cover of *Five Little Pigs*. He had once snatched that book from his sister's hands and flicked to the back, teasing her that he was going to tell her who the murderer was. She had thrown her hairbrush at him and it had cut his eye open. He'd had to go to hospital, where he'd had two stitches, and his mother had made his sister go as well. Jackie had cried for the whole two hours that they had sat in Casualty and swore they'd never fight again, and they never had. God, he wished she were here fighting with him now, living her life, loving a man and children. Nicole had staved off some of his loneliness, being a point of reference in his life, a significant other to concentrate on and stuff up the gaping hole of sadness which the absence of his family had left him with. More and more he was thinking that was her main function for him, as his had been banker for her. He sniffed back the rising emotion inside him and crossed the square to talk to Shaun.

Chapter 47

'I must say I like your friends, Molly,' said Harvey, picking up the post from behind the door as they entered Willowfell. 'Wasn't Pavitar Singh a fascinating chap? I bet he was a doctor or a solicitor or something very highbrow in his heyday. Something about the way he carries himself.'

'Possibly,' said Molly, taking off her jacket and hanging it up on the hook behind the door. She had to confess that she was curious about Pavitar Singh too. He was always so beautifully dressed and was a very handsome man. She wouldn't have been surprised to discover he was an old Bollywood star.

'We must go back there again. I enjoyed it so much. All that book passion. My blood was flowing.'

'I noticed. Would you like a cup of tea?'

'I would indeed, please.'

Harvey followed Molly into the kitchen.

'And what a beautiful young lady Carmen was.'

'Carla.'

'Yes, sorry, Carla. Although Carmen suits her more, I think. Very Spanish looking.'

'Italian actually,' said Molly, pulling two cups out of the cupboard. 'Lovely girl. Such a sad story.'

She said it without thinking. Harvey picked up on it straightaway.

'Sad? In what way?'

'Oh, nothing,' said Molly, but Harvey wouldn't let it drop.

'I shall take anything you tell me to the grave,' he promised.

'I wish you'd stop saying things like that,' snapped Molly.

Harvey chuckled. 'Believe me, my dear, laughter sometimes really is the best medicine. Now tell me.'

Molly sighed, hoping she wasn't being disloyal to her new young friend by relaying her business.

'Carla found out that the man she was married to never divorced his first wife and was planning to go back to her. She discovered all this at his funeral last month. Isn't that awful?'

Harvey blew out two slow lungfuls of air and shook his head slowly from side to side.

'And you thought I was a cad,' he said.

'You are,' said Molly, putting a plate of assorted biscuits on the table.

Harvey reached immediately for a chocolate finger.

'That is sad. I hope she finds a nice young man soon to heal her heartbreak.'

He chomped on the biscuit for a moment then asked, 'Did you, Molly? Did you find someone after me?'

Molly put the teapot down on the table with an unintentional slam.

'No,' she said stiffly. *No one could ever make me feel like you did.*

'Not even a dinner date?'

'I had a meal with a local reverend one time,' admitted Molly. 'It wasn't a success.'

'I could see you as a vicar's wife.' Harvey winked at her. 'What went wrong?'

He wasn't you.

'He was ten years older than me physically and twenty mentally. We hadn't even got to dessert and he was planning the wedding.' Molly shuddered. Even now, fifteen years later, she could envisage that date in all its horrid clarity. The Reverend Clarence Cartwright had been persistent to the point of bullying in his efforts to fix up a second date with her. Once again she'd had to turn to Bernard Brandywine for help in getting him to stop pestering her. 'He was borderline stalking me.'

Harvey guffawed with laughter, slamming his hand down on the table.

'You're very giddy today,' noted Molly, trying to appear serious. Harvey's laugh was always so very infectious.

'I feel on top of the world for that debate in the teashop.'

Molly poured out the tea. 'It's a lovely little place. There are some quite delightful things in those cabinets.'

'I remember you always used to write letters on scented notepaper,' said Harvey.

'No one writes letters any more,' sighed Molly. 'It's all emails and texts. I do feel for the young ones, never knowing the thrill of waiting for a letter to arrive from a loved one.'

'I bet you'd buy all the contents of that shop if you could.'

'I would. Though I'd probably misplace them and they'd end up in an antiques shop in Holmfirth,' Molly said without thinking.

'What do you mean?'

'Oh, nothing,' replied Molly. 'My memory isn't what it used to be. I keep losing things.'

'Of value?' Harvey's eyebrows were raised.

What a strange question to ask, thought Molly. She gave him a small nod by way of an answer.

'Have you told Graham about me yet?' said Harvey then.

Molly wondered why he had leapt to the subject of her son from talk of the missing items. She hoped he wasn't insinuating anything by that. He didn't exactly have room to talk if he was.

'He's in Greece at the moment on holiday. He and his wife have a villa.'

Harvey was so surprised, the passage of the second chocolate finger to his mouth was temporarily interrupted. 'He has a wife?'

'Yes. Sherry. And they have a son at university.'

'Well, bugger me,' said Harvey, letting out a surprised whistle of breath. 'Is that them there?' He pointed to a photo on top of her display cabinet. It was a family portrait of the Beardsalls which Sherry had given her as a Mother's Day present a couple of years ago. He pulled himself out of the chair to take a closer look. 'Dear God, he hasn't aged well, has he? Is that shredded wheat on his head? Mind you, he'll be in his mid to late forties now, won't he?'

'If you aren't going to say anything nice . . .' Molly made a move to take it from him, but Harvey snatched his arm away.

'No, let me see. I promise, I'll play nice.' He studied the picture and Molly could almost hear the inner workings of his brain trying to form something positive to say. 'Well, there's a woman who likes her pies,' was what he came up with.

'She's been good for him,' said Molly, turning away before he saw the giggle escape. 'They're happy together.'

'And the young man. So like both his parents in looks. Poor sod.'

Molly took the photo from his hand and put it back in its place. 'That's enough,' she said.

'I'm sorry, Molly,' said Harvey. 'There was never any love lost between your son and me, but that was a long time ago. Does he look after you? That's the main thing.'

'Yes, yes, he's very good,' Molly lied. Well, he wasn't bad to her anyway. She would have liked to have seen more of him and less of Sherry. There was something about the woman she could never trust. She always felt as if Sherry had a hidden agenda every time their paths crossed.

'Well, that's all that matters,' Harvey said on a long drawn-out yawn.

'You've done too much. Finish that tea off and go and have a nap.'

'I will obey,' he said, lifting the cup to his lips. 'One more biscuit.'

Molly slapped his hand as it snaked towards the plate.

'No. I'm not going to be responsible for you going to an earlier grave than you should.'

'Molly, I do not want to extend my life by two hours by substituting the food I love for boiled cabbage. I shall die a bon viveur, as I have lived.'

Molly humphed and her arm shot out to lift the plate of biscuits out of his reach. Harvey gripped it en route and looked into her eyes.

'You, my dear Molly, have made my heart feel stronger today than it has done for a long time.'

Molly tried not to let the sadness show as he quietly finished his tea and then crossed the room and made a slow walk up the stairs to the bedroom with the pale green curtains.

Chapter 48

Shaun McCarthy arrived at Leni's house at six-thirty on the dot.

'Come in, come in,' she said in her usual bright and breezy way. 'I've just put the kettle on. Can I get you a coffee?'

'Please,' said Shaun. He walked into Leni's ridiculously cosy cottage to find that her portly ginger cat was sitting on the arm of the sofa and appeared to be watching Ant and Dec on the TV. His tail was tapping out a rhythm like a slow hand clap. Shaun didn't know if that was a good or bad sign. What he did know was that he would have killed to be as at peace as that cat, no worries in his brain, able to shut out the world and relax.

'Have you eaten? Would you like me to make you a sandwich, Mr McCarthy? Always plenty of food in my cupboards, as you would probably imagine.'

'No thanks,' replied Shaun, just as his stomach made a betraying grumble which could have been heard in Benidorm. He knew Leni must have heard it. Even the cat's eyes seem to widen in amusement.

'He looks happy,' Shaun nodded towards Mr Bingley.

'He's always happy,' said Leni. 'He's never been one for

doing much. I've had more animated cushions than him. My daughter chose him from an animal shelter when she was thirteen. It was love at first sight for both of them.'

That was enough cat and kid talk for Shaun. He gestured towards the staircase and Leni encouraged him to go up. This time the two other doors were ajar. Through one, he could see what must be her room: pale cream wallpaper, an ornate cream wardrobe and matching dressing table and a very bouncy-looking violet quilt on the bed. The curtains were lace, fancy – swooping swags and tails, very French-chateau inspired. Through the next door he could see a small bathroom, white suite, white tiles but with rolls of pastel towels on white shelves. Shaun's bathroom at home was white too, cold and clinical without a hint of cosiness about it. How had she managed to make a white bathroom so damned inviting?

He set to work straightaway. Leni brought him a coffee upstairs and a huge plate of biscuits which she put on the table just inside Anne's room, silently, without disturbing him.

Shaun tried not to be greedy even though he could have swept up all the biscuits and eaten the lot. He hadn't had time to stop for lunch today. He was behind schedule because one of his labourers had rung in sick – measles, of all things. Thank goodness Will Linton had been able to step in. He felt so sorry for the guy that he almost didn't ring, not wanting to humiliate a former company head by offering him such a menial position. But, as Will said, bills were bills and had to be paid. Shaun needed to get Spring Hill Square finished and start reaping in the rents before he commenced on another project. He always said that the development he was working on would be his last and it never was. Shaun McCarthy could no more have relaxed than he could have joined the Royal Ballet as their principal dancer.

Leni brought him up a second coffee after twenty minutes and a plate of freshly made sandwiches. 'Leave them if
you don't want them, I won't be offended, but your stomach sounded rather growly,' she said, her eyes twinkling with
mischief, and turned straight back downstairs.

Shaun didn't leave any. They hit the spot and stopped his
stomach yowling like a kicked wolf. He expected her to
make some comment when he took the empty plates and
cups down after he had finished the job, but she didn't.

'How much do I owe you?' she said, reaching for her
handbag.

'A tenner will be fine, for the hinges.' Anyone else and he
would have asked for more, but she'd made him all that
food. He had to charge her something though, in case she
saw a free job as a precedent. He didn't know her well
enough to judge if she was the 'take-the-advantage' type.
Taking the advantage reminded him of something he meant
to mention to her.

'It must be more . . .' she remonstrated.

'No it isn't, really. But will you take a piece of advice and
get rid of that Saturday boy? You don't know the O'Gowan
family like I do. The oldest brother is a headcase. He's
locked away for murder and you really don't want to know
the details. Another two brothers are in and out of prison
for drug-dealing and assault. There's a sister who had three
children by her eighteenth birthday, all taken into care. As
for his father . . .' Shaun shook his head. '. . . Bull O'Gowan:
not a nice man. You don't want to have anything to do with
him or anyone who has anything to do with him. That
would be my advice.'

'And what about Mrs O'Gowan?' Leni asked, without
reacting.

'Mrs O'Gowan left all her children for another man years
ago. Bull always has a woman hanging around him though,

but none of them seem to last very long. He likes them young. Eighteen and they're thrown out on the scrap heap for being too old and past it. Doesn't bode well for a stable upbringing, does it?'

'Well,' said Leni, sticking out her chin, 'that's even more reason for not letting young Ryan go. He said that he's different to his family.'

'He would, wouldn't he?' laughed Shaun. 'How can he be different when none of the others are? Too much bad blood. They're all con men, nutters and thieves.'

'Thank you, Mr McCarthy,' she said, with a tight smile that appeared anything but grateful. 'I do appreciate your concern, but I know what I'm doing.'

'You obviously don't,' said Shaun under his breath as she opened her purse.

Leni handed over a ten-pound note. Shaun could tell by the expression on her face that she'd heard him, but not listened. She'd learn. He'd done his duty and warned her, he could do no more. She'd realise he was right when the shit hit the fan. As it would. It always did with the O'Gowan family.

Chapter 49

'Found him,' yelled Harvey. 'He's a retired surgeon. I knew it.'

'Who on earth are you talking about?' Molly came out of the kitchen to shout up the stairs.

Harvey's head emerged from the study bedroom where he had been surfing the internet on Molly's computer.

'Pavitar Singh. I knew he must be either a doctor or a high court barrister or something. Very good reputation he had. There's loads about him on the net. His daughter's a surgeon too, in America. Beautiful girl.'

'What sort of surgeon was he?' called Molly.

'Transplants. Can you imagine the number of lives that man has saved? His wife was a general practitioner and his childhood sweetheart, apparently. She died ten years ago.'

'Does it tell you his inside leg measurement as well?' tutted Molly.

Harvey laughed. 'No privacy for the eminent. No wonder I'm not on the internet.'

Molly stayed silent. She knew he wasn't. She had looked his name up many times, dreading seeing it in an obituary, but there had been not a mention. She returned to the kitchen and was joined by Harvey a few moments later. He raised his nose, closed his eyes and sighed.

'You always did make the best Sunday dinners in the world.'

'You always were full of such flannel.' Molly opened the oven door and the steam rushed out at her. The goose fat was plenty hot enough for the Yorkshire pudding mix.

'Do you remember when we first got an oven with a glass door and I used to sit watching your puddings rise?' said Harvey, sitting down so he could do exactly the same as he did thirty years ago.

'Nope,' said Molly, though she could. He had been like a big kid, totally fascinated and shouting with glee at the puddings puffing out of the tins. He used to measure the tallest one and they'd try and beat the record. He could find fun anywhere. She hadn't laughed at anything for years after he left.

'Thank you, Molly,' he said to her back as she spooned the pudding mix into the tin recesses. She looked over her shoulder to see that there were tears in his eyes.

'Watch the puddings and stop getting maudlin,' she snapped, turning from him until her own tears had sunk back down.

Chapter 50

Carla rose early after having an awful dream about finding her bank account totally empty because Julie Pride had drawn it all out. She couldn't get back to sleep so she walked to the village papershop and bought a copy of the *Sunday World*. Will was drinking a coffee in the kitchen when she returned. He was dressed in work clothes.

'Morning,' he said with a wide grin.

'Morning,' Carla replied, thinking back to how Martin was at this time of day. He was totally incommunicative until his mood had been thawed out by a cup of strong sugary tea and two cigarettes. 'You're chirpy.'

'Don't like being idle. Feel much better when I'm working,' said Will.

'At Spring Hill?'

'Yep. The very place.'

'Did you sleep okay?' asked Carla, slotting some bread into the toaster.

'Like a tranquillised hippo. That inflatable mattress will be a hard act to follow.'

Carla smiled.

She didn't believe him wholly but he wasn't lying. For the first time in ages he had dropped off easily, slept soundly and dreamlessly and awoken to sunlight saturating curtains in a room that the bank couldn't take from him. He felt as if someone had loosened the noose around his neck by enough degrees to allow him to breathe again.

He downed the last of his coffee and put the cup in the dishwasher.

'Have a nice day,' he called.

'And you,' Carla replied.

She watched him bend to give Lucky a scratch on his head before leaving the house.

'Are you going to be lucky?' she asked the cat as he walked towards the cupboard where she kept his food and sat down expectantly.

Will didn't mind working on Sunday in the slightest. He'd take any day or even night to put some wages away so he could pay his rent and eat. He knew one of the other labourers, Duffo, working on site as Will had employed him a few times as well. He was a good worker, a cheerful man and a non-moaner. He didn't take any joy in finding his ex-boss working alongside him as a labourer. In fact he made a point of saying how sorry he was that Will's firm had folded and that he'd been grateful for the work he'd been given in the past. Will appreciated those few words of kindness more than he could say. He hadn't had many of them in the past months.

They worked well together and the day passed quickly and companionably. Will could feel his muscles responding to all the lifting and his mind clearing of some of his troubles. Plain hard physical graft was always good for making you think about the job in hand and nothing else.

'Do me a favour, Will,' Shaun asked him, just before the end of the working day. 'Give me your professional opinion and go check out the roof. Make sure those two sub-contractors did the job I told them to.'

Chapter 51

'That was a grand Sunday dinner we had today, Molly, love,' said Harvey, putting the newspaper down on his lap and letting his eyelids drop over his blue, blue eyes. 'Did I say?'

'About sixteen times.'

Molly was sitting on the sofa knitting.

'You should have let me wash up.'

'The dishwasher was quite capable, thank you.'

'I can tell you don't do them in the sink,' said Harvey. 'You always did have beautiful hands. You could have modelled with them.'

Molly gave a loud 'huh'. 'You always were a smooth talker, Harvey Hoyland.'

'It's true. Your hand always looked so delicate in mine.' He had stopped fighting keeping his eyes open now.

A ghost of a feeling flittered through Molly and made her shiver: Harvey's large warm fingers wrapped around her own.

'What did you do with it?' he asked drowsily.

'What did I do with what?'

'Your wedding band. And that pretty little engagement ring with the sapphire and the diamonds. Did you sell them? Or did you throw them away in a rage?'

Are you serious? Molly suddenly wanted to yell at him.
He knew very well what had happened to them. He had
left with them in his pocket. Then again, it was all a very
long time ago now. Maybe he'd forgotten that was his parting shot, his final kick whilst she was down, to take all the
jewellery which had meant so much to her.

'I can't remember,' Molly lied, sticking her needle aggressively into the back of a stitch.

'You always wanted an eternity ring. I never bought you
one.' He was almost asleep now. 'I was going to.'

'Yes, well there wasn't much point in buying me an eternity ring when we were only together four years.' *There were
a lot of things you were going to do. You were going to take me
travelling and see all the wonders of the world. You were going to
grow old with me.*

'I left mine with yours.'

'What?'

'I wasn't worthy to wear it so I left mine with yours . . .'

He was asleep. Molly carried on knitting as Harvey fell
into a solid slumber, snoring softly and contentedly. He'd
left what with hers? His wedding ring? Well, they both
knew that he hadn't, however much he might have tried to
rewrite history to make it more digestible. That's what men
like Harvey Hoyland do, Margaret would have said.

Chapter 52

Just before he went home, Will tried to climb the ladder again and once more he failed. It would be funny if it weren't so tragic. He contemplated going to the doctor's and rehearsing what he would say. He couldn't imagine fessing up to his phobia without envisaging the doctor collapsing into laughter. Will wasn't daft; he knew it was some form of anxiety and could be cured. But he wasn't one for sitting talking to counsellors and expounding his problems. He was a private person. His roofing mojo would come back eventually, but until then he'd have to stick to the ground.

Still, at least something in his life was going well. By Monday he was comfortably settled in his new living space. The day was particularly warm and the June sun was still pumping out its rays at seven o'clock. Will poured himself a beer and sat in his private square of garden with the unofficial salacious biography of a famous hell-raiser. It was amazing how enjoyable such a simple pleasure was. And if that wasn't enough, Carla asked if he'd like some stew because she had made far too much and he did – and it was delicious. He mopped up the gravy with some slices of white bread and felt as stuffed as a pig in the sunshine. It was the first day in months he'd totally and utterly relaxed.

Chapter 53

It was Brontë Tuesday at the Teashop on the Corner and Carla found herself driving to Spring Hill Square with a broad smile on her face. An old couple and a retired Sikh gentleman wouldn't have been on her traditional list of friends but there was something about the motley little group of people that gave her spirits a well-needed lift. She was delighted to find them already there, in time for their elevenses. Harvey was greedily tucking into a giant slice of Branwell carrot and orange cake.

This was Harvey's first outing for a couple of days. He had felt tired and weak since Sunday and hadn't resisted Molly's insistence that he rest. She was worried about him, he knew, but he had no intention of missing the best rejuvenating drug to date – good company.

'Ah Carla, just in time,' said Harvey. 'Pavitar has been talking rubbish about *Pride and Prejudice*.' He swivelled his head back to Pavitar. 'Darcy was an anti-hero in the first half of the book. Rude, condescending. Elizabeth was quite right to tell him to piss off.'

'Ooh, straight in at the deep end today,' Carla grinned at Leni. 'But I thought this was Brontë Tuesday.'

'It started off like that but it appears we have diversified into nice romantic heroes,' explained Leni. 'No Heathcliffs today. So far we've had a Gabriel Oak, a Mr Knightley, Jude the Obscure and Mr Bingley.'

As if he heard his name being mentioned, the feline Mr Bingley leapt up on the chair next to Carla and immediately assumed a sleepy curl position.

'I always found Jude the Obscure a bit wet,' said Carla.

'Wet as a fish's arse,' said Harvey, before he was elbowed sharply by Molly. 'What's your opinion of Darcy then?'

'Let the girl order before you start interrogating her,' snapped Molly.

'The specials are Branwell carrot or Wuthering milk chocolate cake,' said Leni. 'Ridiculous names, I know.'

'Can't believe you've called a cake after that waste of space Branwell,' snorted Harvey, then bit short what he was going to say about troublesome sons. It would have been too close to the bone for Molly.

'I'll go for the Wuthering and a latte please,' said Carla with a grin before turning back to Harvey. 'So far as Darcy goes, I'm totally with you. I suspect we are supposed to think he's boorish before Miss Austen makes us all eat our words. But he's very masculine. I think I could fancy him. She's so good on heroes. I don't like Thomas Hardy's men that much. I'll probably be damned for saying that I think Gabriel Oak is a bit wimpy too.'

'He needs a kick up his bottom,' said Mr Singh with a grin. 'Nice man but not much get up and go.'

'And don't get me started on Boldwood.' Harvey puffed out his cheeks. 'Totally deranged obsessive. Should have been in a mental home.'

'Calm down, Harvey,' said Molly crossly. 'He's a fictional character, not a neighbour you've having a dispute with about leylandii.'

'Thank God for that,' replied Harvey, nevertheless taking

Molly's advice and sitting back in his chair to rest his racing heart.

'What triggered the diversion from the Brontës then?' said Carla, giving Mr Bingley a scratch behind his ears.

'Leni has just received a consignment of next year's diaries featuring pictures of the most desirable heroes,' Molly explained. 'Now Maxim de Winter. I always found the thought of him very sexy.'

'He's not in the diaries, yet Heathcliff is. Darcy, obviously, takes centre stage,' Harvey said with a disgusted 'pfff'. 'Could we have another pot of tea please, Leni? I'm quite thirsty after all this discussion.'

'Certainly, Harvey,' said Leni, coming forward to take the empty teapot away.

'I haven't read *Jude the Obscure*,' said Mr Singh.

'Don't bother,' replied Harvey. 'It'll depress you. Unless you enjoy dysfunctional relationships, poverty, passive aggression and violence.'

'Maybe I will give it a miss,' said Mr Singh. 'I can see all that on *Jeremy Kyle*.'

'You watch *Jeremy Kyle*?' Carla was highly amused by that.

'I am hooked,' said Mr Singh. 'Especially the lie detector results.' He started to chuckle. '"Apart from the five people she knows about, have you slept with anyone else?"'

'How have we gone from a conversation about Jude the Obscure to Jeremy Kyle lie detectors?' Leni said with a broad smile, bringing a full, steaming teapot over to Molly and Harvey.

'My favourites are who has been doing the stealing from the family house.'

Carla thought Mr Singh might explode if he laughed any louder. Molly didn't say anything but imagined Harvey hooked up to a lie detector machine. The incriminating spikes would run off the paper.

Leni brought a wide wedge of cake and the latte to Carla.

'How is Anne?' asked Molly. 'Have you had any more postcards from her?'

'I had one at the weekend,' smiled Leni. 'She's fine. Enjoying the Greek sunshine.'

'Which university is she going to?' asked Carla. Oh, to be young again and at the threshold of life. She wished she were Anne.

'She has a place at Cambridge to read English,' Leni beamed.

There was a round of impressed 'wow's.

'Which college?' asked Molly.

'Robinson. It's the newest college, I think.'

'She'll be coming home soon then to start in September. Or do they start in October?' said Mr Singh.

'She's taking another year off. They encourage gap years there so it isn't a problem.' Leni wrung out a cloth and started wiping down the counter surface. 'She might never get the chance again to do all this travelling.'

'Yes, she must travel,' put in Harvey. 'I've been all over the world and never regretted it. Everyone would sell every- thing they have and get on a plane if they could see what I've seen.'

'She might meet a nice rich doctor in Australia and be swept off her feet,' smiled Carla. It happened to some people. Not everyone had crap love lives. Some women met decent men who didn't lie and were loved and respected.

'Life is there to be enjoyed, especially by the young,' said Mr Singh, taking a handkerchief out of his jacket in order to blow his nose on it. 'Before they begin to fear it and worry about it not always being there.'

'Anyway, seeing as it is Brontë Tuesday and we should respect that,' began Harvey, intent on steering the conversation around to where he thought it should be as he could sense a dip in the mood and wanted to zap it away. 'Charlotte, Emily and Anne – snog, marry or avoid?'

Chapter 54

By Thursday Will had been shopping and bought himself a proper double bed and a decent mattress, though it wasn't a flashy pocket-sprung top-of-the-range type like the one his marital bed had boasted. But, if anything, it was more comfortable. He always found the old one a bit firm. This cheap one would probably knacker up his back, but at least he was getting a good night's sleep, even if he couldn't shake off that recurrent dream about panicking at the top of ladders. And he joined a gym. He'd cancelled the platinum joint membership for the swanky Harrots gym near Penistone; Nicole's dad would have restarted her membership because she couldn't do without her spa treatments. But for Will, the This Is Sparta gym on a back street of Old Town was good enough. It had all the weights and machines he needed to batter his body and free up his head for a few hours a week. There was no fancy café with a super salad bar, no swimming pool, no vibrating plates, just a load of men in various stages of fitness and not a bottle of Evian spray to be seen anywhere.

He hadn't seen much of Carla the past few days. They both kept themselves to themselves, crossing paths occasionally in the kitchen. She was always pleasant, but he

thought that her eyes carried a lot of sadness in them, however much her lips might have smiled.

Carla was starting to panic about money. She might be on
the brink of owning the deeds to Dundealin, but there were
still water rates and council tax, electricity, gas, shopping
and car bills to pay. At the back of her *Hard Times* journal,
she had started a budget sheet with a column of outgoings
and incomings and decided that maybe joining a temp
agency might be a way forward, because what was stored in
the bank wouldn't go very far if all she had was Will's rent
coming in by way of revenue.

Carla headed off to Sheffield on Thursday morning. She
drove her car down to the station, parked up then caught
the train into the city centre and walked up to The Moor
where 'Workpeople' was situated. The office was very
impressive with its almost totally glass front. Her appointment was at eleven-thirty and she was exactly on time.

She didn't have to wait long before she was escorted to a
desk by a woman whose name badge read 'Faye' who then
typed her details into a computer. Faye, bless her – thought
Carla – tried not to look discouraging about there being
hardly any job opportunities for a thirty-four-year-old
woman whose only real skill was in making bouquets and
wreaths.

'No positions available working with flowers at the
moment,' Faye sighed, scrolling through information on the
monitor. 'I've got some data entry work at the West
Yorkshire Bank. Five days in Wakefield starting Monday.
Lollipop lady. Volunteer at Helping Hands charity shop,
obviously that's unpaid. Erm ... Vera's Sandwich café in
Brightside need a part-time worker: ten-thirty to two p.m.
five days a week. Office cleaner, four hours per week.'

'I'll take the data entry,' said Carla. She knew she would

be bored out of her skull, but at least it would get her back onto the job market and earning a wage.

'Okay, I'll ring them,' grinned Faye, happy to have helped someone out. She obviously enjoyed her job, thought Carla, who knew how good it was to have a job you liked. And how grim it was to have a job you hated.

She caught the train home, avoiding the shops as she knew she'd find loads of things she wanted because she had no money to spend on them. Sod's law.

Chapter 55

Molly, usually a light sleeper, was amazed to find that when she woke on Saturday morning there was a note from Harvey on the kitchen table informing her that he had gone into town and wouldn't be long. *What on earth did he have to go into town for?* she thought. Then a bite of panic stung her heart. He hadn't left, had he?

She hurried upstairs and into his room, flinging open the wardrobe doors, expecting to see empty coat hangers swinging, but his things were still there. Her whole body seemed to sigh with relief.

Molly went into her bedroom to look through the window to see if, by chance, she could spot him walking down – or up – the road but she couldn't. She wondered how long he had been gone and if he was all right. She had a sudden vision of him collapsed in the market and a circle of strangers crowded around him. Maybe she should go and try and find him, she decided, but then again he didn't have a key to get in if he returned home before she did. She would just have to wait.

It was when she passed her dressing table that she noticed the lid wasn't square on her jewellery box. She lifted it up to find that three of her rings were missing.

*

Ryan arrived half an hour early. He was wearing a red polo shirt that had been ripped on the side seam and badly repaired with orange cotton. Leni suspected it might be his own handiwork.

'Morning, early bird,' she greeted him. 'Would you like some crumpets before you start?'

'Please,' he said and ate three. From the blissed-out look on his face, Leni wondered if he'd ever had real butter before in his life. Some of it had dribbled and made dark circles on his shirt.

'Your mum isn't going to be very pleased at those,' Leni pointed out, before she remembered what Shaun had told her about his mother being absent.

'I do me own washing,' he replied.

A sad ache passed like a cold cloud across Leni's heart. Poor lad, she thought. She wondered what home life was like for Ryan. Who cooked his meals, who changed his bedding, who kissed him goodnight?

Her thoughts were interrupted as the large figure of Shaun McCarthy entered the shop, his expression full of suspicion.

'Morning,' he said, looking from Leni to Ryan and Leni knew that he was checking to see that all was okay, but she managed to answer his greeting politely enough.

'I came to see if there was any chance of ordering some breakfast. The site office toaster has decided to die.'

'Yes, of course,' said Leni. 'How many slices would you like?'

'Er . . . sixteen please.'

'Yep, no problem. I'll get my assistant onto it. He'll bring it out to you. Four slices at a time.' And she smiled as if making the point that her assistant was going to offer a totally reliable service, despite him being a notorious O'Gowan.

Ryan was wary of Shaun, that was obvious, and Shaun was quite happy that he was wary of him. It might keep him from trying any underhand tricks, knowing that someone was onto him.

Shaun watched the lad walking back to the teashop after delivering the last four slices of toast. He didn't have a cocky swagger like his father and his eldest brother Fin, who had been in Broadmoor, the last that Shaun had heard. Bull O'Gowan bragged about it, which proved to Shaun that as far as headcases went, he wasn't far behind his son. He'd also been reliably informed that Leslie O'Gowan, the second oldest brother, was out of prison. Not for long, Shaun thought, as Ryan went back into the teashop on the corner. No, it was impossible for the skinny lad with the thin arms and the grease-stained top to be anything other than dysfunctional with his family history and background. Nature and nurture had both failed him.

Didn't anyone give you a chance when nature and nurture both failed you? whispered a quiet voice inside him.

Shaun picked up his trowel. Voices like that he could do without. He didn't want to remember so he made it a point never to look back, he only ever kept his eyes, and his thoughts, forward.

Chapter 56

Molly couldn't work out if she was more cross than disappointed, more hurt than angry. She knew those rings had been in her jewellery box and there was no reason why they would be anywhere else but there. Harvey must have taken them, there was no other explanation. That's why he was so damned secretive in going into town by himself. She hoped he'd exerted himself and was taken to hospital where she would go and visit him and find those rings in his pocket and ... what then? Would she turn him out of her house? Shout at him as he lay on a hospital bed that she never wanted to see him again – however ill he might be? Damn him. Damn Harvey Hoyland. She felt hot tears of frustration spring to her eyes and she defied them to make a showing.

She hated him for stamping all over her heart again. Leopards didn't change their spots, hadn't she learned that by now? Even after all these years, Harvey Hoyland's spots were so familiar, she could have drawn a portrait of them all in her sleep.

She heard a car pull up outside, hurried to the front window and saw Harvey getting out of a taxi. A cold feeling of dread gripped her and threw her whole body into a state of panic. She didn't know what she was going to say to him when she saw his lying face. She was equally, if not more, furious with herself for being taken in by him. Again.

Molly, calm down, she urged herself, breathing as slowly and deeply as she could before she hyperventilated. Outwardly, when she checked in the mirror, she looked composed, even if inside her heart was tearing around like a bucking bronco.

Harvey was breathing heavily when he walked in. Whatever he had done had fully exhausted him.

'Where have you been?' she asked, struggling to keep the annoyance out of her voice.

'Town,' he replied. 'I fancied a bet.'

Oh, well that explains it. She wondered which pawn shop her rings would be in by now.

'I won,' he grinned. 'A hundred and fifty pounds. And I only had a fiver each way on it. I saw the name and I couldn't resist.'

'What was the horse called?'

'Troubles of the Heart. Now I really do need to go to the toilet, Molly, if you'll let me pass please. I'll answer all your questions and no doubt get the sharp end of your tongue when I come back downstairs.'

His tread was slow and laboured on the stairs. Molly paced up and down waiting for him to return. She knew she would have to say something to him about her jewellery. He seemed to take an age to come back down again. He walked into the lounge, bold as brass, with a relieved smile on his face.

'Oh my, that's better. Now what were you saying?'

'I was asking you where you had been.' Molly's impatience was seeping out through the cracks in her composure. Better that than tears of disappointment. 'And you were telling me that you'd been to a betting shop.'

'Yep. That's about it.'

'Was betting on a horse worth getting up at the crack of dawn for in your state of health?'

'Well, the betting shop didn't open until eleven, so I wandered around the shops for a while. Barnsley town centre has changed in the past few years, hasn't it? My goodness.'

'Why get up so early if the betting shop didn't open until eleven?' Did he think she was an idiot?

'I couldn't sleep so I thought I'd go out and catch the bus into town. I hardly thought it appropriate that I woke you early and asked you to drive me to a betting shop, knowing how much you always disapproved of my habit of gambling,' said Harvey, going into the kitchen to put on the kettle. 'Tea?'

He was infuriatingly chipper. Well Molly decided that she was going to bring him down a peg or two. Ill or not ill, he couldn't go around stealing from her when he was a guest in her house.

Without answering him she marched upstairs into her bedroom and grabbed her jewellery box. Once downstairs, she slammed it on the kitchen table making the cups and saucers he had just put out give a short shocked dance.

'I had six rings in this box,' she began with a very tight expression. 'Do you want to guess how many I have now?'

Harvey's eyebrows dipped in confusion. 'Erm . . . six?'

'Let's count them, shall we?' Molly opened it and took out a ring. 'One . . .'

She found another. 'Two . . .' and moved her necklace out of the way to retrieve the third with the opal. 'Three.' Strangely that opal ring was one of the missing ones she hadn't been able to find. She gulped. There were three more rings in the box. A cold wash of shame drenched her.

'And three plus three makes six?' said Harvey. 'Is this some sort of dementia test to make sure my heart hasn't affected my brain?'

Molly was only glad she hadn't come out and made a point-blank accusation. He must have realised where this conversation was going. Worry nudged the embarrassment away. She had been sure there were only three rings in there, just as she was sure that Royal Doulton figure was on a shelf and her pen and compact were in her handbag. She'd had another 'episode', it seemed, and now was the time to go and see a doctor and have a test done for Alzheimer's.

'You've got too much on your mind,' said Harvey, pulling out the chair for her. 'Sit down and stop nattering. I merely fancied a little outing by myself and some thinking space. Now, have we got any chocolate biscuits left?'

That was it, said Molly, sinking onto the seat. She had too much on her mind, that was all. But she was so sure there had only been three rings. So sure.

Chapter 57

'Shaun, Shaun!'

Shaun's attention was diverted from choosing between the mixer tap he was holding in his hand and another. He looked up the aisle and saw her, waving, making an awkward bouncy run towards him and then he felt her arms around his neck and her lips press deep into his cheek.

'Well, how are you?' She held him at arm's length and beamed at him. Rosie, his ex-wife.

'I'm fine,' he said. 'I see you are pretty fine too.'

Rosie patted her solidly rotund stomach. 'Two months to go. A girl.'

'Well, that's good,' said Shaun, wondering how he could be struggling for something to say to a woman he had been married to for two years.

Apart from the change in her usually trim figure, Rosie looked exactly the same: swinging blonde ponytail, big blue eyes, and a trademark perma-smile. Pretty, bubbly, warmth oozing out of her. Once upon a time he thought that's what he wanted, thought she would be good for him.

'So what are you doing in Plumber's World?' It seemed an obvious question.

'I'm here with the builder to choose a bath for our en-suite,' she replied, still smiling, eyes sparkling as they took him in. She rubbed his arm. 'Oh it is good to see you. You look great. Is a lady putting that twinkle in your eye?'

She was fishing, thought Shaun. There was no twinkle in his eye, they both knew it.

'No,' he said. He noticed she was wearing a wedding band. He was glad she had found someone to love her and give her a child. He knew he had broken her heart and from the way she was looking at him, he also knew she would let him break it all over again. She had told him over and over that she would never love anyone as much as she loved him – he was her soul-mate, her everything.

'Well, you look happy anyway, Shaun. Plenty of work?'

'Too much.'

'That's good, that's really good. Especially in this climate. How many builders can say that?'

Her hand had slipped to his wrist and her fingers were circling it, not quite daring to hold his hand. He knew she was waiting for something – any sign of affection that implied they still had some connection. She had adored him to the point of obsession and he guessed that he still lingered in her heart. But he couldn't give her anything back. She was a stranger to him now. Really she always was.

'Well, I better get on and leave you to picking out your bath,' he said, pulling his hand away to scratch at an imaginary itch on his head. A sigh of disappointment snagged on her smile that he didn't want to chat any more, that she might as well have been stood behind a firewall. She reached up and kissed his cheek again, forcing him close. Her perfume was the same, heavy and spicy and cloying.

'Goodbye, Rosie. Good luck with the baby.'

'I hope you find someone, Shaun. Someone you can love.'

He saw tears blooming in her eyes as he walked away and

he hated himself for being so cold. But there was no chance to ever be warm with Rosie – there was only frost or stifling heat.

He had met her in a pub in town. One of Shaun's workers had been getting married and he had agreed to join them for a drink. The plan was that he would show his face, drink a pint with the groom and then go home. Then he met Rosie.

She said she had fallen in love with him at first sight, spotting him across a crowded room. She spoke in lots of clichés. She latched on to him as he was ordering a round, batted her eyelashes at him and persistently talked to him as he waited to be served until he had given her some attention.

She looked good. She was all blonde hair, big blue eyes and pouty pink mouth and was wearing a dress that made the best of her slim figure. The only other person who had ever shown Shaun any real kindness was also called Rose; it seemed like an omen. Shaun had had relationships before, all short-lasting, all usually ended in a flurry of frustrated accusations about his inability to commit and his emotional detachment. Ironically all he wanted to do was settle down and have a home; yet as soon as he was in a relationship, he found himself looking for an out.

He thought that maybe it was time to try harder, give it his best shot – and who better than with a pretty, kind, warm woman who idolised him. Rosie put him on a pedestal and he forced himself to open up to her, told her about his loveless upbringing, how every time he began to settle in a foster home he was taken from it and placed somewhere else, eventually ending up in a home for boys which was little better than a holding pen. Opening up to Rosie had been the beginning of the end.

Rosie embarked on a quest to fix him, heal him, change

him. He felt smothered by her constant attempts at therapy. If he never saw another fecking candle scented with de-stressing oil in his lifetime it would be too soon. Books lined the shelves: *Letting People In. Men Who Cannot Love. The Injured Inner Child.* He became her life project. Even when he told her that enough was enough, she went underground: her attempts became less obvious but she didn't stop.

He *did* want to love her, she was the perfect wife, but he couldn't. Then he discovered that she had stopped taking the pill and he panicked. A child would be good for them, she said. It would help him focus outwards instead of inwards. He started to wake up feeling as if someone were pressing a pillow over his face. She was giving, giving, giving, but why did it feel as if she were taking, taking, taking from him, leeching from his history, making him her project, her life's work? He didn't want a child. He couldn't stay with Rosie, not even for the sake of a child: she was suffocating him with her giant caring heart. What if he couldn't love the child when it arrived? What if something happened to Rosie and him and the child ended up in foster care and the whole cycle happened again? He knew he had to get out soon. He stopped sleeping with Rosie; she got more frustrated and hurt because of his emotional with-drawal. He didn't want to smash her heart by breaking up and tried to do it by degrees, but he was killing her with his coldness as much as she was stifling him with sunshine. They split up.

Seeing her again brought it all back, those horrible fears that she might get pregnant deliberately. She had no inter-ests outside him, nothing to talk about but therapies and theories – she was even planning to conceive a child as a form of treatment. He often dreamt that his child had been born and was unhappy, suffering and would grow up unable to love, to connect. Just like its father.

He paid for the tap and walked out of the shop. There was a pink Volkswagen Beetle painted with yellow roses in the car park with plastic eyelashes on the headlights. He knew that it must be Rosie's car.

He got in his van and took a deep breath before starting the engine. He was damaged beyond repair, he knew that. He would have been better off staying with his *durty whore* of a mother, not being fed, not being washed, not being looked after properly, for then at least he would have had connections with people, a sense of home and a heart that worked. Shaun McCarthy was adrift with no anchor. It was more of a curse than a life.

Chapter 58

After the first hour in her new temping job, Carla was bored rigid. On the second day she wanted to grab her handbag, walk out and find refuge in Leni's teashop, with the others. What theme had Leni decided for today? she wondered. Would today be Tolstoy Tuesday? Or maybe a tribute to D. H. Lawrence? But instead Carla sighed, treated herself to a compensatory coffee from the machine and carried on pumping numbers into her PC. After five days she was ready to hang herself from the fluorescent light on the ceiling. She found herself making tally cards of how many quarter hours were left until home-time. When the clock nudged its big hand on five o'clock on the last day, Carla didn't wait another second to down tools. She made as dignified an exit as she could, even though she wanted to turn the sort of cartwheels that would have had Olga Korbut ringing her for tips. Never had she felt a Friday feeling like it.

There was a little corner shop on the way to the train station. She called in, picked up a bottle of over-priced red wine and contemplated buying herself a bunch of flowers. But the offerings were pathetically skinny – they couldn't have cheered anyone up.

Carla missed floristry so much. She had loved her last job

working in Marlene's Bloomers where Marlene Watson, the owner, was quite happy sitting in the back room smoking her fags and reading *Hello* and *OK!* for the last few years of her working life. She left the running of the shop totally down to Carla, knowing that her business was in safe hands. Even though she was quite shy by nature, Carla was perfectly capable of dealing with customers in the shop. She loved delivering the buttonholes and bouquets to excited soon-to-be newly-weds, some young and some not so young. She was brilliant at putting together a quick bouquet for someone who wanted to buy an impulse present. She loved the smells and colours and shapes of the flowers, the packed velvet heads of roses, the phallic anthuriums, the pungent stargazer lilies with their oriental perfume, the jaunty birds of paradise, the giant-headed sunflowers. There wasn't a flower that Carla couldn't recognise or wasn't able to put together with others for best effect.

Despite her misgivings, she bought one of the scraggy flower sprays. She'd make it her mission tonight to fashion something presentable out of them.

The train was cancelled and when it eventually arrived it was full to the brim with commuters so Carla not only had to stand, but she had to endure being crushed against the bulk of a large man who kept coughing on her without covering up his mouth. The train dumped her at Barnsley station at quarter to seven and she was drenched by the time she reached the car, thanks to a flash summer storm of heavyweight proportions.

The lights were on in Dundealin when she pulled up in the drive. For a few moments she sat in the car with the wipers on and marvelled at it. The odd-looking house had become a cosy haven that she couldn't wait to get in to. She switched off the engine and dashed to the front door, getting even wetter than before.

Will was in the kitchen snapping the ring-pull off a can of coke.

'Bloody hell, is it raining?' he laughed, watching her drip all over the floor.

'It's terrible,' said Carla. 'It was at full pelt when I crossed from the train station to the car park and I thought that was as bad as it could get, but apparently not.' She eased off her coat to find the rain had soaked through her blouse. She made a quick check that she wasn't treating Will to a Miss Wet T-shirt private show before hanging it up, but it was mainly her sleeves that were soggy. She should change, but first she pulled the wine out of the carrier bag and Will instinctively reached behind him to get her a glass out of the cupboard.

'You look as if you need a big one.' Then he added, 'glass of wine, that is.'

'I need a massive one. Wine, that is,' smiled Carla, screwing off the top and pouring out the liquid. 'Would you . . . ?'

'Nah thanks. Just opened this. I think your flowers might be a bit water-drunk.'

The bunch looked even more sorry now it had been saturated.

Carla tipped her head back and took a long, long sip of wine. It was a little on the cool side, but it was dark and fruity and still hit the spot. She felt it spread around her system and up to her brain where it zapped away all images of numbers out of her head.

'What do you do for a living, Carla?' asked Will. He had been curious and now was an ideal time to ask.

'Well,' began Carla after another glug, 'I'm doing some temping at the moment. Office stuff. I've spent five days in a bank inputting data.' She shuddered. 'By trade I'm a florist though.'

'Didn't put *them* together did you?' Will winked as he pointed towards the apology for a bouquet.

'I did not,' said Carla with mock fierceness. Will chuckled. He could see Carla quite easily as a florist; he couldn't picture her in a bank, sitting in front of a computer though. 'How come you're not a florist any more then?'

Carla took out a towel from the drawer and used it to wipe her hair and dab at her face. She hadn't checked but she bet her mascara had run and she was standing there talking to her lodger with a face like Pierrot.

'The lady I worked for retired. And there don't seem to be any vacancies in that line of work so I've had to diversify.'

'Ah, that's a real shame. Did you work for her a long time?'

'Fifteen years.'

'You must know your stuff.' He looked impressed.

'I do,' said Carla proudly.

'You should set up on your own. Be a shame to waste all that experience.'

Carla gave a hoot of laughter. 'Me? With my own shop? I wouldn't know how to start.'

'I'd like to say that working for yourself is the best job in the world, but I'm not sure I'm that qualified any longer.' Will gave a little laugh of his own.

'You've worked for yourself then?' asked Carla, not getting his joke.

'Most of my adult life. Built up my business then lost the lot by putting all my eggs in one basket. Lost the house, lost the fancy car, lost the wife. Now I have nothing left to lose except my honour. Even lost my ability to climb a ladder.'

Carla's eyes widened. 'What?'

'I've become scared of heights.' There, he had admitted it to someone else besides Nicole. He surprised himself with the ease with which he confessed it. It didn't feel half as embarrassing saying it to Carla as it had to his wife.

'God, that's awful,' said Carla. 'I'm presuming it's a symptom of anxiety. If so, it's probably a temporary thing. Sortable, if that's a word.'

'You think?' He remembered Nicole's reaction, which had been very different. She had ridiculed him. *You're losing money hand over fist and now you've lost your nerve. What's next? Because let's face it, you haven't that much left to lose have you? You're a fucking joke, Will Linton.*

'Are you going to see a doctor about it?' asked Carla. Nicole hadn't suggested that, obvious as it might have been. She had flounced off and refused to talk about it, and he had been embarrassed enough to not bring it up again either.

'I thought it might go away by itself, but it hasn't. I keep testing myself to see if my mojo has come back. Even went into B&Q the other day and started climbing their ladders. God knows what the security guards watching the CCTV must have thought.'

Carla put her hand over her mouth to still the laughter.

'I'm sorry,' she said. 'I wasn't laughing at you, just the way you're saying it.'

Will grinned too. 'Couldn't make it up, could you? Ain't life a bag of laughs sometimes.'

'You're telling me,' said Carla. 'I'm the widow of a man I was never married to.'

'Eh?'

No one could have been more amazed than Carla to find herself launching into the tale of Martin and the funeral and Julie Pride so easily, to reassure her lodger that it wasn't only for him that things were screwed up. There was a certain comfort to be had in knowing that even on life's scrapheap, there was good company to be found.

*

She's working late again, thought Shaun. He could see her through the teashop window, wrapping a parcel. He considered that she might be looking out of the window and thinking that he was working late and wondered if she was working late for the same reason he was: that he didn't want to go home because there was nothing there for him.

Home for Shaun was a large, heavily gabled house at the end of a lane between Higher Hoppleton and Maltstone. Gothic in appearance, it had been empty for years, run down, neglected, forgotten; a project only for the insane to take on, which was where he came in. It was yet another house he wanted to put roots down into, another house big enough for a family – for some reason he always picked family-sized houses. Shaun McCarthy was a master builder, there was nothing in the building trade that he couldn't lend his hand to. He could put a roof on, dig out a cellar, rebuild walls, construct staircases ... but he couldn't make a house into a home. Fallstones was a perfect mix of the old classic and new practical. He had stripped it of everything but the original features worth saving and, where needed, had matched in cornices and ceiling roses and made them look as if they had been there since day one. Architecturally it was stunning, but it still felt cold, cavernous, empty inside. There was no feeling that Fallstones had ever been lived in, even though local reputation was that it was haunted by an old lady who had died there over a hundred years ago. The atmosphere in every room was that of the Dead Sea, as if nothing could live in it. Not even spectres.

Shaun McCarthy was an expert at taking the run down, the unwanted, the forgotten and crafting it into something fresh, beautiful, wanted. He could do it easily with buildings, but not with his own life.

*

Carla had just got to the part of the story about taking the keys to Julie Pride when her hand flew to her mouth to stem the words rushing out.

'I am so sorry,' she said, realising how long she had been talking for. 'I don't know why I'm boring you with all this.'

'I'm not bored at all,' said Will, getting up and bringing a wine glass to the table. 'Go on then, I will have one with you.'

'Help yourself,' Carla invited.

'Thanks.' Will tipped the bottle into his glass after he had filled up Carla's. 'You know, I'm strangely comforted by the fact that there are other people at a stage in their lives when they should be sorted but find they have to start all over again. There must be a lot of us about.' He looked straight into her eyes and she saw how grey and warm his were. Nice eyes, kind eyes.

'True,' said Carla, feeling a blush creep over her cheeks. Will Linton was too easy to chat to. She couldn't imagine sitting in her kitchen talking to Rex Parkinson like this.

'Like I said, you ain't boring me,' he repeated, sensing she hadn't believed him when he said it the first time. 'If anything, I'm fascinated. It's like the plot of a film. You should write it all down and make a book out of it.'

'Not me,' laughed Carla. 'I love reading them, but I've never been interested in writing. And if I read this one, I'd abandon it for being too far-fetched.'

'Listen,' coughed Will. 'I was going to treat myself to fish and chips tonight. How about I get two lots and you can tell me the rest of the story?'

'Oh,' said Carla, about to say that she was all right thanks, but somehow the words metamorphosed in her throat. 'That sounds nice. Although that's really all I have to tell.'

'Well, you can eat instead of talking, then. Or you can make something up,' he smiled. He has a nice smile, thought Carla. White, even teeth, full bottom lip. The word *sexy* slipped into her head but she batted it away. She didn't want to go down that route, thinking about this man that she hadn't known two minutes having a sexy smile.

'I'll get me coat,' said Will. 'My treat.'

'Well, I'll butter some bread in that case.' Carla jumped up. 'And put the kettle on. You have to have tea, bread and butter with fish and chips. And lots of salt and vinegar.'

It's Nicole's birthday today, thought Will, as he took his waxed coat down from the peg and noticed the date on the calendar next to it. Last year he was on a sunny beach in Bali with her, this year he was having fish and chips with his landlady. His money troubles had been just starting to become uncontrollable. His head had been full of worry as he stared out across the blue sea and wished he hadn't blown so much cash on the holiday. Nicole was oblivious to everything but the sun and the opulence. The only night he'd slept properly was the night he got blasted on two of the bottles of ridiculously expensive champagne that Nicole had ordered, and even then he woke up worrying how much his hangover had cost.

And yet he was sleeping like a log in Dundealin in his new cheap bed. There was still a lot of paperwork to sort out from the loss of his business and the sale of all his assets but now he could see the distant glow of a lighthouse, guiding him to security.

Despite the rain, despite the lack of champagne, despite the absence of his trophy spendthrift wife, at the moment Will Linton really didn't feel that a fish and chip supper with a pretty, kind lady such as Carla was a comedown from his past life. His comforts were small, but by God they felt good.

Chapter 59

The next morning Carla was aware that she was walking around Little Kipping Stores with a big fat smile on her face, a lovely residue from the evening she had spent in Dundealin with Will, a bottle of wine, a pot of tea and two lots of fish and chips. Talking with him and eating together in the convivial kitchen as outside, the rain had lashed at the window, had lifted her spirits unbelievably. They'd talked some more about Martin and Nicole and they'd laughed. Carla would never have thought she could find any humour in her situation, but Will Linton had located it like a heat-seeking missile. Will's take on Mavis Marple, the vicar with the Louis Spence voice and two rival wives both brandishing red roses had her belly-laughing. Then he started taking a comedic view of his own story – telling her everything from walking in to find his house stripped of its contents, including the box of Christmas baubles, to storming over to greedy Nicole's parents' house and being chased up the staircase by her blubbery dad. It had been the sort of evening both of them needed. She had gone to bed delighted that Will Linton was her lodger.

As Carla turned into the bread aisle, she saw a familiar figure studying loaves.

'Fancy meeting you here,' said Carla, deliberately nudging her trolley gently into Molly's.

'Oh, hello dear,' said Molly. 'Where were you on Tuesday? We did miss you. Harvey and Pavitar got far too animated discussing *Howard's End*.' Carla burst out laughing which in turn made Molly chuckle. 'If you know what I mean,' Molly added. 'It's Bram Stoker day next Tuesday. You will be coming, I hope?'

'I shall,' replied Carla adamantly. 'Alas I had some temporary work last week. In a bank.'

'Sounds fun,' said Molly, flatly, whilst raising her eyebrows.

'Oh, it was fabulous,' nodded Carla in mock agreement. 'Harvey okay?'

'He seems very well, touch wood, thank you. Though I'm not quite sure if these literary discussions are good for him. He isn't a great lover of E. M. Forster, though it appears Pavitar is, very much so. We could have done with a referee at one point.'

'I'm sure they're very good for him,' smiled Carla.

'Maybe in moderation, but Pavitar was as defensive over the writer's plot devices as Harvey was scathing. It wasn't pretty.' She shook her head and sighed.

'They didn't really fall out, did they?'

'Oh no, Carla. Normal service was resumed as soon as the cake was served up. The moment of truce was a welcome one on that day.'

Carla shrugged. 'I'm so sorry I missed it, though I don't think I would have been able to contribute much. I've only ever seen *A Room with a View* on the TV and I could have taken it or left it, to be honest.'

'Like me then, on the fence on this one,' smiled Molly.

She looks lovely today, thought Carla. Molly was wearing

a pale blue dress with a green cardigan resting on her shoulders. Her eyes were dark blue and shining.

'Harvey is watching a cricket match. I have absolutely no interest in the game,' said Molly, waving the sport away with her long elegant hand. 'I thought I'd use the time to stock up on a few things, not that we need anything really except a loaf of bread.'

'I just nipped out for some cat food and milk,' said Carla. 'Shall we go for a coffee at the Teashop on the Corner? Do you have time?'

'Oh I'd like that very much,' replied Molly with delight. 'I'll pay for these and meet you up there.'

Leni and Ryan were restocking the cabinets when Carla walked in.

'Oh good morning,' beamed Leni. 'You were much missed last week. I nearly had to phone the army.'

'I've just met Molly in the supermarket and she was telling me,' laughed Carla. 'She'll be here in a moment. We thought we'd have a coffee together.'

'Lovely to see you. You weren't ill, were you?'

Bless, thought Carla. It was nice to have people concerned about her.

'No, I was doing some temp work. Data entry.'

Leni pulled a face. Even Ryan pulled a face.

'Yep, it was that good,' nodded Carla. 'Don't let me stop you, I'll wait for Molly,' she added, seeing Leni about to rise from her knees.

'We've just had some beautiful poetry-themed things delivered,' said Leni, resuming her kneeling place. 'Cufflinks, wallets, ties, notebooks, address books, desk calendars. I've been thinking how very handsome Lord Byron was. Ryan, would you be a love and fetch me the Stanley knife from the back room please?'

'Bit of a bugg ... bad boy with the ladies,' replied Carla, correcting herself mid-sentence. She waited for Ryan to be out of earshot then said quietly, 'Still, I would, wouldn't you?'

Leni chuckled. 'He was rather gorgeous, if his portraits do him justice.'

'Prefer Keats' stuff,' said Ryan, coming back holding the knife.

'Oh, do you now?' Leni winked at Carla. 'And which is your favourite of the Keats poems?'

'"The Pot of Basil",' replied Ryan without having to think. 'There's some dodgy lines in it but it stuck in my mind.'

Then Molly walked in and brought a blast of warm sun-shiney air in with her.

'Hello Molly,' greeted Leni, now standing up. 'Ryan's just been telling us that his favourite poem by Keats is "The Pot of Basil". Have you heard of it?'

'It's the one where the woman plants her dead lover's head in a pot and grows herbs in it,' Ryan grinned.

'Ugh,' said Molly and Carla together.

'Of all the lovely poems that Keats wrote and you pick that one out, Ryan,' tutted Molly. She saw Ryan stifling a giggle as she picked up the menu and fanned herself with it.

'My, it's warm outside,' Molly said. 'That storm last night has really cleared the air.'

'I'd like a pot of vanilla tea, please,' asked Carla. 'I think that will be more refreshing than coffee today. Nothing to eat for me. I had fish and chips last night and I think I'm still digesting them.'

'I haven't had fish and chips for ages,' said Molly, drawing in a whistle. 'Make that pot for two. Sounds lovely.'

As Leni poured hot water over the vanilla tea-leaves she noticed Shaun through the window. He was wearing khaki combat trousers that showed off strong calves and a white short-sleeved T-shirt that stretched over his muscular frame. Leni dragged her eyes back to the task in hand. She found herself secretly looking at Shaun McCarthy too much these days.

'Why don't you take a break, Ryan? Grab yourself a piece of cake and there's some cans of pop in the back fridge,' she said.

'Can I go and sit on the grass outside?' he asked.

'Of course you can.'

'So Ryan, when do you break up for the summer holidays?' asked Molly as he lifted the dome up over a very tall chocolate cake and began to cut himself a slice.

'End of July,' he said.

'Are you going on holiday?' asked Carla.

He looked at them both as if they were mad. 'No. We don't go on holiday.'

Carla and Molly and Leni exchanged glances of silent sympathy. Every one of them could have hugged the boy.

'Well, you can always make up for that,' said Molly with a rush of positivity. 'I didn't really go anywhere until I was in my twenties. I was over forty when I went on a plane for the first time.'

'I'd like to travel,' said Ryan, going into the back for a drink. 'I will, one day.'

'Good for you,' said Leni, bringing a tea tray over to her customers.

Carla poured. Leni had given them an accompanying plate of tiny cherry shortbread biscuits. Life felt good today. It was as if some of the outdoor sunshine had found its way inside her. Ryan took his cake and can and went to sit on the grass square outside the shop.

'What a lovely boy,' said Molly, her eyes following his slight frame. There was something about the lad that made the tears well up in her eyes. She thought of what Harvey had told her about his early loveless life with not a lot of food on the table.

'He is,' Leni agreed.

Molly wiped her eyes on a serviette, apologising to the others as she did so.

'Don't you worry,' said Carla, reaching over to give her arm a comforting rub. She suspected – rightly – that Molly was ready for crumbling under the pressure of trying to be brave.

'Oh, I feel silly,' said Molly, sniffing back tears that refused to stop. 'I don't know what's the matter with me.'

'Is it Harvey?' asked Leni. 'Is that what's upsetting you, Molly?'

Molly dropped her head and nodded.

'Oh, you poor love.' Leni handed her a fresh serviette.

'He's fine, the picture of health,' half-laughed Molly then. 'He gets a little tired now and then but he seems far more robust than the rules say he should be. It's me who's losing sleep.'

'What exactly is wrong with him?' Carla asked softly.

'It's a heart condition,' replied Molly. 'Nothing can be done except to keep up with the medication. I feel as if I'm living with a time bomb. He's accepted what's going to happen, I can't.'

Molly wiped furiously at her eyes. They were starting to become sore. She was angry for disgracing herself in public like this.

'Trying to keep a stiff upper lip constantly must be very difficult,' said Leni, taking a seat next to Molly.

'It is,' Molly agreed. She didn't add that she thought she was losing it and that she'd been on the brink of accusing Harvey of stealing her jewellery when he hadn't. At least he hadn't *this* time. And from what he said recently, he didn't believe he had stolen from her before either. That had confused her. She didn't know if he was wily or going funny in the head as well.

Carla nudged the cup of tea closer to Molly's hand. 'Have a drink,' she urged, then immediately felt annoyed with herself. As if a slurp of tea would make this situation any better. And she thought she had problems not being able to get a job. But Molly lifted the cup to her lips anyway.

'That's lovely,' she said.

'How British of us,' smiled Leni softly. 'Cup of tea cures all.'

Molly let loose an unexpected burst of laughter. 'How kind you both are,' she said. 'Thank you.'

'Anytime you want to escape and have some space, you come here,' said Leni.

'Look, here's my mobile number,' said Carla, scribbling onto a serviette. 'You call me if you want a natter. And don't think twice about it.'

Ryan came back in and Molly turned her head away so that the boy couldn't witness that she had been crying.

'That was quick,' said Leni.

'It's too hot,' he said. 'I like it better inside.'

'You could do with some sun on that pale skin,' Carla teased him. *And some meat on your bones*, she added mentally.

'I suit being this colour,' he grinned. 'My dad's girlfriend is orange. Except for her hands that are whiter than me.'

Carla let loose a hoot of laughter and Molly's and Leni's joined it. It was a moment of jollity that was well needed and they all blessed young Ryan for giving it to them.

Chapter 60

Leni was pinning up another postcard when Molly and Harvey walked into the teashop.

'Oh please let me see,' said Harvey. 'Where is she now?'

'Don't be so nosey, Harvey Hoyland,' Molly admonished him.

Leni handed over the postcard. She had cut the stamp out of the corner as usual.

Dear Mum, and Mr Bingley,
Greetings from Crete. Glorious sunshine
yet again. People wonderful, doing lots of
swimming in the sea. Loads to do. Wish you
were here with me.
Lots of love, Anne. XX

'Ah, Crete. What a lovely island. Not my favourite but close to the top.'

'That reminds me,' said Molly, opening her handbag. 'I've got a bag of stamps for you to add to your collection for the blind dogs. Only ordinary first and second class, I'm afraid. No foreign ones.'

'Blind dogs?' Harvey laughed until he set himself off coughing.

'Oh, you know what I mean.' Molly sighed as she thought about Anne's postcard. 'How lovely to be young with all your life in front of you. I planned to do so much with mine. Funny how it works out in the end.'

Mr Singh was already in situ and pouring a cup of tea. 'At last, my literary friends are here for Bram Stoker Tuesday.'

'Don't you go working yourself up,' Molly gave Harvey a quiet warning as he sat down. 'I don't think Bram Stoker would appreciate your death on his conscience.'

'Oh sit down, woman,' twinkled Harvey. 'I feel as if my heart could go on forever when I'm battling with Pavitar.'

Mr Bingley was asleep on the next chair and Molly gave him a stroke. He woke up momentarily, though not enough to open his eyes. He raised his head lazily and then replaced it on his paws.

'The specials today are Vampire red velvet cake and Whitby white chocolate and raspberry pie,' Leni announced.

'I'll have them both,' chuckled Harvey, casting his arm in a large flamboyant arc.

'You will not,' said Molly.

'Not good for the body but very good for the soul,' said Mr Singh, lifting up a spoonful of the white chocolate pie to his lips.

'I'm past caring about that,' replied Harvey, banging his chest wall. 'Restrictive cardiomyopathy. With complications. Doctors can do bugger all which gives me more or less carte blanche to do what I like.'

'Really?' said Pavitar Singh, putting down his spoon. 'Are you taking your medication regularly?'

'I am,' Harvey said firmly. 'I am not, however, going for check-ups just to be prodded and poked. I hate hospitals. I hate waiting around in hospitals watching thin, poorly people in cheap dressing gowns. I hate drips, medicines, those bleepy machines, the food. I never realised that anyone could make such a cock-up of marrowfat peas but they seem to manage it in hospital.'

'Then perhaps we should not argue so forcibly,' said Pavitar Singh.

'Oh yes we should,' replied Harvey, wagging his finger. 'You won't use the poorly card against me. I thought better of you than that, Pavitar.'

'As you wish. Prepare for war then, friend.'

Mr Singh lifted up his cup and toasted Harvey's prolonged good health. Harvey was grateful that he hadn't taken the opportunity to lecture him. Pavitar Singh was already high up in his estimations, but he went a little further for not pulling out the doctor advantage and using it.

Leni had just served Harvey and Molly with tea and cake when Carla walked in.

'Oh Carla, turn back and go out,' Molly waved at her. 'It's about to kick off in here this morning.'

Carla smiled and wasn't deterred.

'Good morning,' said Mr Singh and Harvey together.

'Morning. And what trouble are you two causing today?'

'Well, it's Bram Stoker day, although I think our conversation could extend to other books about the supernatural,' said Harvey, pulling down on his jacket lapels as if he were a professor about to deliver a lecture.

'Like what?' asked Carla, taking a seat next to Mr Bingley.

'Cathy's haunting of Heathcliff,' Harvey replied.

'And Jane Eyre, hearing Rochester calling out her name three times when she is on the brink of saying that she will marry Mr St John Rivers,' added Mr Singh.

'Frankenstein,' Carla clicked her fingers with enlightenment.

'Marley's ghost,' suggested Molly.

'Coffee?' Leni mouthed at her.

'Yes please and a slice of . . . is that red velvet cake?'

'It's vampire cake,' winked Leni.

'Of course it is. I'll have that please.'

'I do like a bit of the supernatural in my books,' admitted Pavitar. 'I am quite fascinated by psychic phenomena.'

'Molly's twin sister is a psychic,' said Harvey without thinking, much to Molly's obvious horror. He immediately covered his mouth with his hand. 'Sorry, I forgot it was a secret.'

But it was too late. All eyes were eagerly fixed on Molly to explain.

'Big mouth,' grumbled Molly.

'Molly, I am so sorry,' said Harvey, but his apology was making everyone extra keen to discover to what he had been referring.

'She isn't a vampire, is she?' asked Pavitar with a twinkle in his large brown eyes.

'Well, Molly?' said Carla. 'You can't leave us in suspense like this.'

'Oh, it's nothing,' said Molly, wafting her hand as if she was wasting everyone's time by trying to explain. 'She just . . . sees things.'

'Dead people,' put in Harvey, much to Molly's added annoyance.

'Dead people?' echoed Mr Singh, wiping cake crumbs from his beard.

'Oh fiddle . . .' Molly puffed out her cheeks. Harvey really had put her in an intolerable situation.

'This stays in this room and goes no further.' Molly waited for everyone to nod in agreement before she started.

'When my sister started nursing in her teens, she used to see people sitting at the sides of patients in their beds at all times of day and night and, though she presumed they were visitors at first, she couldn't help feeling there was something different about them,' she began to explain under duress. 'They brought a prickle of electricity into the air,' she said. It didn't take her long to realise that she was the only person who saw them. When she reported them to the sister for being present after visiting hours, the sister thought she'd gone loopy because she couldn't see what Margaret saw, so Margaret learned to keep her mouth shut and hoped whatever was causing these visions would go away. All the patients the *visitors* stayed with died very soon afterwards. The only possible conclusion was that they were people who had already passed, who had been close to the patients and had come to take them on – to the next place. Margaret never mentioned it to anyone outside the family. She is a private and down-to-earth woman and it upset her for many years, until she learned to live with it. There, now you know.'

'Wow,' said Carla. 'What a gift.'

'It was a long time before she recognised that it *was* a gift. She could give the patients with the visitors at their side the sort of end-of-life care they needed and a little bit more of her time. It was hard for her to see medical staff battling to keep them alive when she knew it was useless and yet her nursing background compelled her to try also. There was never an instance where a patient with one of those visitors didn't die. You can't beat death.'

'Nope,' said Harvey. 'But you can give him a good run for his money.' And he lifted the last piece of his cake to his mouth.

'But, please will you forget what I've just told you all?' asked Molly. 'I would feel very disloyal if she ever found out I'd told anyone.'

'It's forgotten, Molly,' said Carla, wondering if someone had been hanging around the garage on the day that Martin had his heart attack, and who would be most likely to come for him. His mother, she supposed. Horrible, great nasty lump of a woman. Maybe, when she came down to the garage, she tripped and sat on him and that's why he went so fast. A giggle bubbled up in her throat and she coughed it down. What the hell was the matter with her?

Molly felt Harvey's large warm hand fall over her own.

'I'm sorry,' he whispered. 'It was out before I could stop it.'

'Oh, I don't suppose it matters,' sighed Molly, turning to Mr Singh. 'Maybe you knew my sister, Mr Singh. Margaret Brandywine. She was a matron before she retired. At the Northern General Hospital in Sheffield.'

Mr Singh raised his eyebrows. 'Yes, I did know her. Very efficient nurse.'

'Of course Margaret is much larger,' put in Harvey. 'More your Peggy Mount type of figure to Molly's Pat Coombs.'

'No one knows who they are, you old fool,' said Molly.

'Oh, I do,' called Leni.

'Me too,' added Carla. 'I remember watching an old film with my nan and it had Peggy Mount in it. All about ladies who cleaned and started dealing in stocks. Lovely story. I can't remember the name of it.'

'*Ladies who Do*,' Mr Singh chirped.

'Dear God, you have an amazing memory, Pavitar,' said Harvey, giving him a round of applause.

'Well, we've gone from vampires to Peggy Mount today,' smiled Leni. 'That's quite an achievement.'

'I think I'd rather come across a vampire than Peggy Mount,' said Harvey. 'And Peggy Mount rather than Margaret Brandywine.'

'Wonderful nurse,' mused Mr Singh. 'I would never have known she had seen such visions.'

'Surely you don't believe she did, Pavitar, being a man of science?' asked Harvey.

'Maybe once upon a time,' said Mr Singh. 'But now . . . I want to believe.' He hoped when his time came that his beloved Nanak would be sitting beside him, waiting for him to join her. Margaret Brandywine's story had given him hope that she would be.

*

Will saw Carla's Mini edge out of the car park and instinctively lifted his hand to wave, but he was too far away to be seen. He enjoyed her company so much. He thought he had been through a lot, but she had lost far more than he had. At least he had some closure. He could wave goodbye to everything he had and walk forwards with all ends tied, but her brain must be full of questions, teeming like impatient eels. That was some mental torture to find her life torn to bits behind her back. At least his had been shredded in front of his face.

He was painting the walls of the smallest unit in the square – a relaxing job, easy on the brain. He was savouring the headrest: no scrabbling together of figures for bankers, juggling accounts to make sure his workers were paid, lobbying debtors for payment. There was none of that as his brush glided up and down the wall as he clocked up another hour's pay.

He had replayed his fish and chip evening with Carla a few times now. He didn't think he would ever find any humour in his situation, but telling his story to Carla he'd had an actual stitch in his side from laughing at Barnaby Whitlaw's aubergine face as he'd stood in Nicole's bedroom doorway trying to play the hard man. And Penelope telling him to shoo. And he had to admit that his chest had puffed up a little when he'd told Carla what he had said to Nicole to make her give him his family's jewellery back, and Carla had made the comment: 'Bloody good for you.'

He knew he could be loud sometimes and hoped he hadn't overstepped the mark laughing at Carla's narrative of the events of her husband's funeral. Maybe in the cold light of day, she would regret telling him. He hoped not. That laugh they had shared had done his spirit wonders.

Shaun wasn't smiling today, though. Someone had been to view this unit with the prospect of renting it and rejected it for being too small. That was the fourth or fifth knock-back he'd had on this space.

Will carried on painting until the sun dropped low into the sky, mellowing into a large orange blur, the colour of a marigold. It was the sight of it that planted the seed of the idea into his head.

Chapter 61

Molly pushed the front door open and retrieved all the post jammed behind it: junk mail mostly, she was sick of it. A bank statement and a postcard with various scenes of Dubrovnik on the front of it.

Dear Molly. What a wonderful time we have had. We really did wish you were here and you will be because we will have to bring you next time. Remember, we will be home on the 7th, about 3 p.m. We have both missed you, darling. Love Margaret and Bernard XXX

The seventh – twelve days away. What was Margaret going to say when she saw who was sharing her house? And why.

Molly reminded herself that she was sixty-eight years old and not sixteen. Margaret had always looked after her though, taken the lead, made sure she was all right. But she wasn't a bully. Margaret only ever had her best interests at heart and she was compassionate and kind. *Except where Harvey Hoyland is concerned*, a snipey voice in her head whispered.

And what would Sherry and Graham say? Graham had never liked Harvey. He had been a boy of fourteen when Molly met Harvey. Secretly, and very unfairly, she had hoped that his hostility to her new husband was rooted in jealousy that Molly was sharing her love with someone else, which must mean he wanted it for himself. But, deep down, she knew that was a hope too far. Graham didn't like Harvey because Harvey wouldn't let him get away with cheeking his mother, emotionally blackmailing money out of her and disrespecting her. Graham repaid Harvey's defence of his mother by flushing his treasured goldfish down the toilet. He denied it, but the fish didn't sink and its poor pitiful dead body floated in the pan as indisputable evidence.

Molly thought back to that horrible day the month before Graham's eighteenth birthday when Harvey had found the fish in the toilet pan. She had never seen Harvey's temper unleashed before then. She'd had to hold him back from doing God knows what to her son. His eyes were mad white balls of fury, leaking tears at the corner as he screamed at Graham. *Get out of this house before I do the same to you, you evil little bastard.* Graham had smirked and walked slowly out as if daring Harvey to come at him. Graham was six foot two and wide as a door then; Harvey was an inch smaller and more than twice his age, but if he had got to him, he would have torn Graham to pieces. But Graham was smug in the knowledge that his mother would never let that happen.

That was the last time her son and Harvey had seen each other. Three weeks later Harvey was gone, and Joyce Ogley the barmaid from the White Lion had taken off with him. Graham paid her a visit that day and, though she knew he couldn't be anything other than glad that Harvey had left, he hadn't lectured her, but instead he had put arms around his mother and comforted her until she cried herself to sleep. It was when she awoke that she discovered that Harvey had stolen from her as well. Graham had seemed genuinely disgusted that Harvey could have walked out with her jewellery – presents from the Brandywines, her sister, the wedding ring that she had taken from her finger. He knew what those things meant to her. It was the only time Molly could remember her son giving her any unsolicited affection.

She watched Harvey walk across to the armchair he had claimed as his own. His back was stooped today, she noted, as if his spine had curved by degrees during the night. He flopped down and closed his eyes as he rested his head against the chair back.

She'd expected him to go for everything he could get out of her in the divorce. A man who could steal from his wife would do that. He could have forced her to sell Willowfell and claimed half of it, but he hadn't asked for a penny via his solicitor. That had always surprised her.

'Who do you reckon will be sitting here releasing prickles of electricity into the air when it's my turn to go?' he asked Molly.

'Don't talk like that,' snapped Molly.

'The devil himself, I think,' smiled Harvey, not moving his head nor opening his eyes.

'Yes, well, you're probably right. Can I get you a tea?'

'I'm not a bad man, Molly. Just a weak one.'

'Are you telling me that you want a weak tea or are you saying you're a weak man?'

'I'm a weak man who likes strong tea,' said Harvey, drowsiness creeping into his tone. 'I never loved Joyce, you know. I only wanted . . .'

'I'll put the kettle on,' said Molly, taking a stride towards the kitchen before he said any more.

'Molly, don't.' Harvey's eyes sprang open and he sat forwards, wincing as he did so as if in some pain. 'I want to say this and make sure you hear it. And believe it. You were the only woman I ever loved. I know you didn't love me the same, but I hoped you would learn to. If I could have had any wish granted, it would have been that you loved me as I loved you.'

His voice was soft and heartbreakingly tender and landed with laser precision in the middle of Molly's heart.

'I did love you,' she replied softly, blinking madly to stop the tears coming. 'Don't ever think I didn't love you. You broke my heart when you left. It was still breaking when you arrived back at my door.'

Harvey shifted forwards. 'What was it then, Molly? Why wouldn't you let me hold you? Why were you so warm out of bed and so cold in it? I wanted to touch you. I wanted us to have a real marriage. You wouldn't talk to me.'

You wouldn't talk to him. For the whole of your marriage you rejected him, Molly Jones. He was starving for your love. He went with Joyce to make you sit up and notice, you always knew that, Molly, didn't you? Molly didn't like the voice that she had stuffed down hard inside her finding its way out. She had loved Harvey Hoyland with her whole being and that, ironically, was why she couldn't talk to him.

'There's more to marriage than sex,' she snapped defensively.

'I know,' he nodded slowly. 'Anyway, you don't have to worry that I'm here for any belated conjugal rights. I can barely raise a smile on the tablets I'm taking, never mind raise the *Titanic*.' He looked at her tenderly with eyes that once made Paul Newman's look dull. 'I just wanted you to know that there was no one to compare with you, Molly. You were – *are* – the sweetest, kindest, loveliest girl a man could ever meet and I wish we could have made it work. If

THE TEASHOP ON THE CORNER 273

I had my time to live over, I'd have stayed with you, sex or no sex.'

Molly took a breath. 'I'll put the kettle on, although you'll be asleep by the time it's boiled, I shouldn't wonder.'

She saw his head give a slow nod of disappointment. She still wouldn't talk to him, she knew that's what he was thinking. Time was running out. Molly stood by the slow-boiling kettle and knew she shouldn't leave it like this.

Chapter 62

Theresa called in to Dundealin after giving her last lesson, curious to see what it looked like now that Carla had had a little time to settle into it.

'My, my, my – I can't believe how different it looks.' Theresa turned a full circle in the lounge and beamed proudly. There were pictures hanging on the walls now, stylish black and white prints of Parisian scenes, and a cosy red rug in front of the sofa.

'Cat Rescue charity shop purchases, except for that Home Sweet Home sign,' said Carla. 'It's amazing what bargains you can find when you're being frugal. When I can afford it, I'm going to get a decorator in to paint every wall in the house white. It'll look so much nicer then.' Maybe she should ask Will, she suddenly thought. He could do with the money as much as she could do with the emulsion.

'No luck with a job yet, darling?' Theresa gave her a sympathetic rub on the shoulder.

'Well, I'll do what I have to until something permanent comes along. Data entry, cleaning, whatever. I'll take what I can. Hopefully a good job will come up soon. Someone must want an assistant florist.'

'Of course they will, very soon, I can feel it in my waters.

I think you're doing marvellously,' said Theresa, walking towards the kitchen. 'The house feels cosy, and you say that your lodger is okay?'

'He's very nice,' smiled Carla. 'I'm comfortable with him around.'

'What's his history, then? Why is he renting the flat?' Theresa pulled out one of the dining chairs and sat down on it.

'He used to be a roofer but his business folded. Wife walked out on him when he lost his money.'

'Money. The root of all sodding evil,' huffed Theresa. 'I would like to bet you a pound to a penny – if you'll excuse the pun – that Martin wouldn't have hung around that woman if they hadn't won the bloody lottery.'

'We'll never know,' sighed Carla.

'Quite honestly, I don't know what she saw in him. He was a gloomy tosser. And he'd let himself go. At least when you first got together he was quite a smart fellow, even if he wasn't exactly David Beckham.'

Carla snorted with laughter.

'You can be so evil.'

'I'm cross for you,' said Theresa, nudging a stray red curl back from her face. 'It was cruel what he did. And how *she* knowingly put up with him spending the weekend with another woman ... well I simply can't work it out.'

'She told me, she enjoyed the break from all the sex,' said Carla, filling the kettle up with water.

'Wha-at?' Theresa burst into laughter. 'I thought you said—'

'I did. We hardly ever.'

'Well, lucky you, that's all I can say. Who'd want that big sweaty hippo grinding on top of you?'

Carla could barely fit the kettle back on the charge-point for laughing.

'When he grew that beard he must have thought he was Russell Brand.'

'Stop it, Theresa, I'm getting a stitch.' Carla was now bent double.

Theresa looked over at her friend crying with laughter and smiled. At least it was tears of mirth for a change. She hadn't deserved what she had gone through. She so wished Carla would reconsider coming to New Zealand with them. With any luck she'd meet a fit, tanned Kiwi who would fall in love with her sweet nature and her sultry smoky voice and live happily ever after, just like she and Jonty.

'Anyway, tell me more about this Will.'

'There's nothing to tell,' replied Carla, wiping her eyes on a square of kitchen roll. She didn't want to wax lyrical about how well they got on because Theresa would start making 'ooh' noises and reading things in their 'relationship' that weren't there. 'Lucky likes him.'

'Lucky by name and Lucky by nature,' chuckled Theresa, glancing over at the cat asleep in a bed that hooked over the kitchen radiator. He had one of his front legs extended straight in front of him, Superman-style. He was well and truly at home again in Dundealin. Probably more than he ever had been before.

'The offer still stands. If you want to come with us to New Zealand and start again over there . . .'

'Oh Tez. That's your dream, not mine.'

'And what is your dream, Carla?'

'I don't know. I lost any dreams I had along the way somehow. I'd just been plodding on, taking each day as it comes, thinking the earth underneath my feet was solid, like an idiot.' Carla puffed out her cheeks and let out some sad air.

'I worry about you,' said Theresa.

'Don't,' replied Carla, taking two cups from the draining board. 'I'm fine.'

'Have you any money left?'

'Yes, though not enough to do what I want to do with the house. Besides, I'm bored being at home. I like to work, I want to work.'

They both heard the front door open. Theresa's eyes opened wide and she whispered, 'Is that your lodger?' She was dying to see what he was like.

Much to Theresa's delight the door into the kitchen started to open. Then an arm extended through it holding a chocolate Swiss roll in a box.

Theresa and Carla both looked at each other, wanting to giggle. Will, having no response to his action, pushed the door open slowly, saw that Carla had a highly amused friend sitting at the table and he swallowed hard with embarrassment.

'Sorry, I thought you were by yourself, Carla.' He coughed.

'No,' twinkled Carla. 'This is my friend Theresa.'

'Delighted to meet you, Will.' Theresa stood and extended her hand. Had her pupils grown any bigger, they would have enveloped the room in a black hole.

'I ... erm ... thought you might like this,' he said, holding up the Swiss roll. 'I wanted to ask you something. I thought we'd have a coffee and ... It'll wait.' He handed over the box and then scratched his head in a gesture of embarrassment. 'I'll go out to the gym now. Nice to meet you,' said Will with a bashful wave in Theresa's direction. 'See you later, Carla.' And with that he closed the door.

Theresa waited until she heard Will's feet on the stairs before opening her mouth.

'Ooooh,' she trilled. 'He *is* nice. Chirpy cockney type. Perfect balance of gentleman and bit of rough. You never said he was a tall lean man machine.'

Just what Carla didn't want to happen.

'And fresh out of a marriage and, like me, not looking for any sort of romance whatsoever,' she admonished the giddy Theresa.

'Still . . .'

'Still nothing, you. Behave.'

'He brought you a Swiss roll and wants to talk to you.' Theresa nodded towards the said dessert which made Carla hoot.

'It's hardly an engagement ring.' Though she did wonder what he wanted to ask her that prompted him to buy a cake to discuss it over.

Later, when he was back from the gym. Will popped his head around the kitchen door where Carla was putting a load of washing in. 'Has your friend gone?'

'Oh yes, ages ago.'

'Can you talk?'

'Yes, I can,' replied Carla with amused curiosity. 'Coffee?'

'Please.'

Carla spooned some granules into two cups. She was all coffee-ed out actually, but she didn't have to drink it. She could simply sit with it whilst Will said what he had to say, which apparently warranted a Swiss roll accompaniment.

The awful thought skipped across her brain that maybe the cake was a softener, and he was going to ask to be released from his rental agreement.

Will was very heavy-handed when cutting the slices of Swiss roll. Carla had to ask him to cut hers in half. Then they sat down at the table and Carla braced herself for what Will had to say.

'Okay,' he began, clapping his hands, as if he were about

to sell her something. Which in a way, he was. 'There I was painting a wall and I had an idea.'

'Which was?' prompted Carla. Was he going to ask if he could emulsion his flat?

'I'll start from the beginning,' said Will, chomping into his huge slice of cake. 'Imagine the scene: this woman definitely one hundred per cent wants to rent a unit from Shaun. No question of backing off, wants to move in asap, begs him to get it ready, so he rearranges his schedule to finish it off so she can have it and he can get his rent. He even makes her a bleedin' sign for the front. Only she backs out at the last minute. And he's fuming.'

'I'm not surprised,' said Carla.

'This unit is really small. He's going to have real problems renting it out. Architect cock-up apparently. Still, it's got a front room, a back room, a loo and a sink. And a nice big front window. Someone else comes to look at it, rejects it for being too small. And someone else after that.'

'Ok-ay.' Carla nodded slowly, not sure where this was going.

'Long story short – it'd make a great shop for a florist.' Will sat back and folded his arms, letting that sink in. 'What do you think, then?'

Carla's brain took a few seconds to work out what he meant. 'For me, you mean?'

'That's what crossed my mind.'

'I couldn't . . . I couldn't rent it.'

'Why not?'

'Because . . . because I . . . I work for other people. I'm not the sort of person who has her own shop.' She laughed. She couldn't help herself. What a ludicrous idea. Her – Carla Martelli – owning a shop.

'I thought you managed a business for years.'

'I did but ... I had a boss ...'

'Who sat on her bum and did nothing, you told me.' Will interrupted her.

'Well, yeah but ... I just couldn't do it.'

Couldn't you? A strange whispery voice sounded in her ear. *No, I couldn't,* she answered back. She might have known everything there was to know about flowers, pre-pared display pieces that won awards which Marlene Watson claimed as her own. She might have run Marlene's Bloomers single-handedly whilst her boss sat in the back room watching every soap from Australia, Britain and America on the colour portable with her packet of fags for company. She might have gone to the markets at five a.m. to pick the flowers, estimating how many they'd need, and getting it almost right every time. But to run her *own* shop? That was just mad. Anyway, even if she thought she might be able to, and she wouldn't think that, she didn't have the money. Well, she did, but she couldn't gamble spending the savings that she needed to cushion her until she had a job. She was supposed to be working to earn money not invest-ing in a business and spending it.

'I think that Shaun would give you a month's free rent,' added Will, as if reading her mind. 'To have the unit occu-pied makes the other unfinished units more attractive. You can always ask and he can only say no.'

Once again Carla's mouth opened to say that she couldn't really. But no sound came out.

'Just go and have a look and see what you think,' said Will. 'It may not seem like it now, but I've always had a great instinct for a business opportunity. I did ask him, on your behalf, and he said that you can go and have a look tomorrow.'

Absolutely not. That was a ridiculous idea. Carla wasn't the sort of person who was in charge.

'Thanks but no thanks, Will. It's not me, running my own business.'

'Well it was just an idea,' said Will, not forcing the issue. After all, he didn't know Carla well enough to try to convince her otherwise.

Chapter 63

Ryan had a school bag with him when he turned up for work on the Saturday morning and a serious look on his face.

'Mrs Merryman,' he started, 'is there any chance I could do my homework on the computer in your back room in my breaks?' he asked.

'Yes of course you can,' she said, thinking that was an odd request. Why couldn't he do it at home?

'My laptop broke,' he said, as if he had just heard her ask aloud. 'I'd put most of it on my memory stick but I need to finish it off.'

'Ah, I see. Well, you stay after work if you like, to finish it. You can print it out as well, I won't charge you for the ink.' She winked at him.

'Ta.'

He wasn't quite himself today, she thought. There was a frown on his brow as he went into the back room to dump his bag and Leni noticed how much of his socks were showing below his trousers, though they were hanging off his waist. He had a dirty mark on his face as well, which she hoped he would see in the mirror in the back room and save her from having to point it out.

was deeper than a wardrobe leading to Narnia. Another night the back room was a huge garden full of freshly blooming flowers and she had woken with a feeling of true euphoria, which faded as soon as she realised she was jobless. Her mobile rang and she didn't recognise the number, so she let voicemail pick it up in case it was Will reminding her that he had made her an appointment with Shaun. When she replayed the message she found it was from Workpeople, asking her if she would be available for a few more days of data entry starting Monday.

Carla fed the cat who was fussing around her as if he had been ignored for days, then she sat with a coffee that she had no intention of drinking whilst weighing up her options. The thought of going back to the bank made her heart feel as heavy as a concrete brick. She wanted to work with flowers again so much. Was running her own florist shop that distant a dream? Damn Will Linton, she thought as she threw her purse and a notepad into her handbag.

She drove up to Spring Hill extra carefully because her whole body felt shaky. She arrived at the square just before ten-thirty so she called in to see Leni at the Teashop on the Corner. Leni was taking an order from an elderly couple, so Carla peeked in the cabinets. There were some paperclips in the shape of the Brontë sisters' profiles now, joining those of Jane Austen. Not that any of them particularly looked like whom they were supposed to, but they were a lovely novelty and the tin they came in was very covetable. There were some earrings in the shape of small inkpens, a table runner with the quote 'If music be the food of love, play on' embroidered on it and the most adorable purse resembling an airmail letter, complete with stitched address on the front. This shop was dangerous to a bank balance, thought Carla, tearing herself away and to the table. She ordered a small coffee but nothing to eat. She felt sick with nerves.

As she waited for her drink to arrive she stared through the window at the small shop unit nearby and imagined it being hers. She envisaged pulling up in a van and offloading all the flowers she had picked at the wholesalers that morning. She saw herself answering the phone: *Hello, Carla's Flowers. No . . . that wasn't right. Martelli Flowers? Hello, Black Cat Flowers. Nope. Hello . . .*

'Hello?' Leni's voice broke into her reverie. 'Earth calling Carla.'

'Sorry, Leni. Thank you.' She wondered if she should tell Leni about the shop unit and get her opinion on it. After all, she was a woman who worked for herself.

She opened her mouth, but shut it again fast. What if Leni laughed in her face at the idea of her opening up a business in the same square? Then again, Leni seemed too nice to do that, even if she did think Carla was daft to even think it.

'I'm here to view that unit over there,' Carla blurted out with a sudden burst of bravery.

Leni didn't laugh with derision at all. 'Which one? The little one? Oh, how exciting for you. What sort of shop would it be?'

'Yes, the little one. I'm thinking about starting a florists. I've worked in floristry for fifteen years, although I've never had my own shop.'

'Then it's about time you did,' smiled Leni. 'If you don't know what you are doing after fifteen years, then there's something wrong.'

'Do you think I could?' asked Carla, which was a ridiculous question, she told herself as soon as the words had left her mouth. How would Leni know the answer to that? 'Sorry, that was a daft thing to say.'

'I think you need a slice of my coffee and rum cake this morning. It's filled with confidence-giving drugs.'

'It's true – I have no confidence,' confessed Carla. 'I came from a very traditional family, where the men were the bread-winners and the women were destined for domestic duties.'

'Don't tell me,' Leni held her hand up to stop Carla saying any more. 'Then you met a man for whom that set-up was ideal. And any secret ambitions you might have had got buried under your obligations.'

'Am I that obvious?'

'You're not the first and you won't be the last.'

'You sound as if you're talking from experience,' Carla said, taking a long sip of coffee.

'I eventually realised that there had been enough people in my life trying to hold me back without myself being one of them.'

'You're divorced, I take it?' Carla smiled.

'Oh yes.' Leni looked happy about it too. 'I work best under my own steam.'

'I don't know if I'm able.'

'There's only one way to go when you hit rock bottom,' said Leni, making the point of looking through the window across at the shop. 'And that's upwards.'

'Should I go for it?'

But even if Leni didn't know the answer, she was no less than encouraging. 'Sometimes you have to take a leap of faith, Carla. You know your craft; Mr McCarthy doesn't charge stupid rents. It all boils down to whether you can afford to buy the stock, and can you drum up enough busi-ness to sell it.'

'I think I can,' said Carla.

'You know you can,' Leni corrected her.

'Yes, I know I can,' Carla said, feeling a swirl of excite-ment inside her. She had to go up and forwards. The road backwards led to data entry jobs in banks, and the likelihood of having to sell Dundealin and rent somewhere and say goodbye to Will. *Blimey.* She hadn't realised until then how awful that would be. She wasn't sure she was comfortable having him so embedded in her plans for a happy life.

'Do you mind if I ask – have you had your own business for a long time, Leni?'

'I don't mind at all,' she replied. 'I was the manager of a bookshop for many years. The owners installed a café in it and it was terrible. I thought I could do better, but doing it is very far away from planning it. It wasn't a well-paid job and I was divorced and my ex-husband didn't pay any maintenance so, to find some extra cash, I started, in my spare time, importing novelty stationery to sell on the internet. Annie was only young then but she used to help me pack it up and just to amuse ourselves really, we'd plan having a shop where everything for sale was book-related and in the middle would be a small teashop with lovely cakes and proper sandwiches.

'Then I began to find that I was earning more money and getting far more satisfaction out of doing my part-time job at home than I was in my full-time job during the day. So I decided to hand in my notice and go for it. I'll be honest,' she laughed, 'it took me a while to build up to take the leap. I was terrified that all my orders would dry up and I'd have to sell my house and that Annie and I would end up out on the street. But, I was determined to make it work. I wanted to make sure that Annie didn't have to take out any student loan when she went off to university. But, with her gone ... travelling, I found I was quite lonely. Then I saw this place advertised. It was too far away from where I lived in North Yorkshire, so I sold up, moved here and took out the lease and I opened up the little teashop that Annie and I had planned.'

Carla's anxiety levels were spiking. What was she even doing here? Leni was competent and brave, Carla was a total wet lettuce.

Through the window, Carla saw a man approach the small shop unit and stand there, taking a look at his watch. He was early but it had to be Shaun McCarthy. She took out her purse.

'This one's on me,' said Leni, pushing the five-pound note away. 'Good luck.'

'Thank you, Leni. Bless you.'

Carla walked out of the shop and across the square with legs shakier than those of a new-born giraffe.

Chapter 66

Molly drove to Spring Hill. It was the only place she could think of to go. She needed to be somewhere that felt as comforting as an old cardigan because she was chilled to the bone as she slipped the car into gear and set off. She walked in to the Teashop on the Corner, her body scrunched up as if she were in pain, and she was.

Leni glanced up and smiled. She held on to that smile even though the usually cheerful Molly looked pale and shivery.

'Everything all right?' asked Leni, adding tentatively, 'Harvey not with you?'

'No. Not this morning,' said Molly with an over-casual tinkly laugh. 'I fancied some time to myself. Morning Ryan. And how are you today? Busy?'

'I'm all right, ta,' he called, going into the back room with a pair of scissors he had just collected.

'He's parcel-wrapping today,' explained Leni. 'Now, what can I get for you?'

'A nice pot of tea, nothing to eat, thank you.'

Leni prepared a tray. She arranged some freshly made shortbreads on a plate as well. Glancing over at Molly, she knew that all was not well. Molly had something on her mind, the weight of it was almost visible on her shoulders, pushing them down.

'There you go,' said Leni.

'Thank you, dear.' Oh how Molly wished Margaret were here to talk to. Then again, maybe not. She could hardly expect Margaret to give her an unbiased view. And Molly was more than partly to blame for that.

'Leni,' Molly's fingers curled around Leni's as she put down the plate of biscuits. 'Thank you.'

'Thank you for what, Molly?' Molly obviously was thanking her for more than the tea.

'Thank you for setting up this wonderful little teashop. It's one of my favourite places to be.'

'That's a lovely thing to say,' beamed Leni. She could see that Molly was close to tears. 'Shall I get a cup of tea and join you? I could do with a break. We've had a bit of a rush on this morning for once.'

'Yes please.' It had been a long time since Molly had been in more need of some warm and gentle female company.

Chapter 67

Shaun McCarthy held his hand out.

'Miss Martelli?'

'Yes, that's me,' she said with a nervous chirp.

'Come on inside, why don't you?'

He had a lovely lilting soft accent, thought Carla, like Liam Neeson. Although she preferred Will's voice, which was quite gritty and deep and always seemed to have a laugh hiding in it ready to spring out.

Carla walked into the shop unit. An architect's cock-up, Will had said. Dundealin was an architect's cock-up as well. Was it a sign? Or was she merely a magnet for architects' cock-ups? It was small, a quarter of the size of Marlene's Bloomers. The front part of the unit was big enough for the purpose of a florist. The back part was larger than she expected, with a sink at one side of the back door and a loo at the other. Yes, this would do very well indeed for a florist shop. *Her own florist shop.* A swell of giddiness rose up in her. She beat down all the doubts that threatened to spoil her vision of her own business with an inner war-cry of *Yes I can do this. Yes I can make this work.*

'I had got it ready for a woman who wanted to open it as a cupcake shop. Then she realised that there was a teashop in the same square and changed her mind. I had checked with Ms Merryman first to make sure there was no conflict of interests and there wasn't but . . .' He huffed with annoyance. 'So, there you have the story on that one. I can let you have it for a good price, I'm not greedy. I just want to get the units filled.' Then he told her what he expected for the rent and it was less than she had imagined.

Yes, yes yes. She wanted to bite his hand off, but she supposed she should act against nature and play it slightly cool. She forced a sigh out of her lungs and formed her features into a contemplative arrangement.

'Hmm,' she said, crossing her arms. 'The unit is a little smaller than I imagined.'

Shaun blew the air out of his cheeks. If he heard that line one more time, he would scream.

'Six weeks rent free, no bond,' he offered.

'Done.' Carla couldn't hold back any longer. She was so rubbish at bartering.

'You worked me a bit there, didn't you?' Shaun's blue-green eyes were narrowed, but there was a twinkle playing in them.

'Hard-headed businesswomen do that,' smiled Carla as a thousand champagne bottles popped their corks inside her.

'I don't suppose you want any signage?' Shaun asked, picking up a long wooden plinth and turning it over to reveal what the cupcake shop should have been.

Carla stared open-mouthed at the words FRENCH FANCY. If that wasn't an omen, what was?

Chapter 68

Leni poured herself a cup and checked to make sure that Ryan was doing all right in the back room. He was fine but still quiet, as if he had things on his mind. She could feel the tension in the air.

Leni took her tea over to the table to find Molly dabbing at her eyes with a linen handkerchief. She was laughing with nervous embarrassment and apologising.

'Molly, what's wrong, my love?' Leni's gently concerned voice was like a key to the door that held back a mother-lode of the older woman's hidden feelings. The years hadn't hushed or weakened them. They wouldn't be held back any more.

'I'm so sorry. Here I am again, making a fool of myself,' Molly tried to smile away her emotion. 'I don't know, I haven't cried for years and suddenly I can't seem to stop.'

Then Carla burst into the shop brimming with news about what she had just agreed with Shaun. When she saw that Molly was upset her euphoria was pushed right down.

'Hello, Carla dear,' said Molly, her lovely dark blue eyes swimming with tears.

'Molly. What's wrong?' She looked to Leni for guidance. 'It's not Harvey, is it?'

'Molly, you're among friends,' said Leni, taking one of Molly's hands and placing it between both of hers. It felt tiny and chilled and full of delicate bones. 'Why don't you start with why you're here today? What you needed to get away from.'

Molly nodded slowly.

*

Harvey slid his finger into the flap of the first envelope and ripped it along the edge. It contained one sheet of lined white paper. The letters were wild loops of anger, written quickly and from a crushed heart.

> Harvey Hoyland,
> I didn't think it was possible to hate someone so much, but I do. You have killed me by leaving me to run off with a woman I know you will despise within weeks. What you have done has hurt me as much as you intended it to, so well done. 'Once a thief, always a thief,' was what Margaret warned me before I married you and she was right. I hate you, I hate you, I hate you for what you have taken from me and I hope you both rot in hell.
> Molly Jones.
> Please note that I will never use the name Mrs Hoyland again.

The ink had bloomed in places and he knew that tears had been falling from her eyes when she wrote this. He could see the small scratches where her pen had ground letters into the paper, he could feel the pain in every character formed. He had hated her too when he left. Hated her for driving him to the warm waiting arms of another woman when it was only Molly that he wanted.

Chapter 69

'I've given Harvey some letters to read that I wrote after he'd left me. And I'm frightened. So very frightened.'

'What are you frightened of?' asked Carla, gently.

'That I'll disgust him. That he'll realise I'm not the woman he thought I was.' Molly could not wipe her tears away fast enough. 'There's so much I should have told him. I locked it away and it festered and damaged everything. It damaged my whole life. *He* damaged my whole life.'

*

Harvey opened the second letter.

Oh my darling, I miss you so much. The pain is ripping me apart. If I could see inside myself, I know there would be a hole in my heart that will never mend. I cannot sleep, I cannot eat. My mind torments me with visions of what you are doing now with her. I see you laughing, I see myself pushed to the back of your brain, out of sight, out of mind. I have forgotten how to smile.

I jump out of my skin when anyone comes to the door but it is never you. Or when the phone rings, or when the postman stops at my door. I want to see you so much but I would die if I saw you with her. I know I would not survive the sight.

He shook his head. Guilt filled him that he had hurt her so much. He didn't even think she cared that he had gone. He had imagined her in Margaret's house, the both of them huffing: 'Good riddance to bad rubbish.' He had no doubt that Margaret had warned her about him: an ex-jailbird wasn't going to be good enough for her sister, even though he had been toeing the straight and narrow path since being released ten years before he had ever met her. Molly Jones was a lady and she deserved more than he could ever have given her. God hadn't bestowed upon him a brain like Bernard Brandywine that brought in a salary huge enough to build Molly the house *he* should have provided her with. But he could give her all the love she would ever need. If only she had taken it from him.

He opened another letter.

A postcard arrived from you last week. All you had written were the words 'wish you were here.' Did you know what it would do to me to hear from you? Did you not realise I would rip myself apart looking for a hidden message? Why are you writing to me when you are with another woman? Are you really missing me? I cannot tell you what it did to me to receive it. I had begun to accept that it was the end and you tore me apart all

*over again with those four words. It was
cruel to give me hope. I felt drunk on it
when I heard from you, filled with light
which slowly faded over the next days
when nothing followed. You plunged me into
a sickening darkness worse than you did
when you first left. I would kill you if I saw
you again.*

He remembered writing that postcard on the morning he
walked out on Joyce. He had been on the way to the bus
station and the jolly postcard with the little boy riding the
donkey on it had caught his eye. Molly didn't love him
enough to forgive him. It wasn't fair of him to ever compromise her dignity to ask her to.

Wish you were here summed it up perfectly. He wished
with all his heart that she were. But as soon as it left his hand
at the post box, he knew he shouldn't have sent it, because
she would be confused by it. He learned from that that he
was a selfish bastard, self-serving, scarily impulsive. If that
didn't tell him she deserved better, nothing would. He
folded up the letter and picked up the next.

*

'My sister has the nicest husband you could possibly wish
for,' smiled Molly through her tears. 'Bernard has been a
knight in shining armour to me as well as her. He built me
a house in their grounds to live in after my first marriage
broke down. He gave me the deeds, it's all mine, my security. He met Margaret at a dance when we were sixteen and
he was nineteen. I think we both fell in love with him on
the spot, but it was Margaret who caught his eye. She was
always much more sure of herself than I was, feistier, fun. I

was quiet and skinny and always in the shadows. I couldn't have him, so I looked for someone like him and I thought I found him in Edwin. He was tall and broad and dark-haired and came from a rich family, like Bernard did.' Molly quickly held her hands up in protest. 'Don't get me wrong, it wasn't his money that attracted me, it was his refined manner, his confidence. Just like Bernard. He swept me off my feet. Things moved too fast. I was very innocent. I didn't know if what I was feeling was right or wrong. I supposed it was love.'

*

I didn't tell you the whole truth about so many things and I wish I had because I know it would have made a difference. I once said to you in an argument that you were just like Edwin, can you remember? You weren't. You were nothing like him. I never told you what he was really like. I thought you would think I was a stupid girl for the mistakes I made. And you were so worldly. I wanted you to think I was wiser than I was too. I am now, but it's too late.

*

'I didn't know anything about men, courting, relationships,' said Molly. 'Margaret was so happy, so content and I wanted to be like her. On our third date, I let Edwin . . .' She didn't say the words, but she didn't need to, the others understood. 'I wanted him to. I wanted to feel normal. But I didn't. He was clumsy, rough. I thought the problem was me. I fell pregnant straightaway and there was no question in his mind that we shouldn't be married. I thought I'd grow to love him, that everything would be all right, that I'd grow to enjoy . . . *it*.'

'Oh Molly.' Leni reached into her pocket for a tissue as Molly's hankie was saturated.

'I know, I'm a stupid woman. I never spoke about it. Not even to Margaret. Whatever happened in our marriage was supposed to stay in our marriage and Edwin was . . . was not a man you disobeyed. Plus I had little Graham to think about. I had to make my marriage work. I didn't want him to grow up with a broken family. But Edwin was so brutal.'

'You must have been in hell.' Leni's lovely face was so full of genuine concern that Molly could hardly bear to look at her.

'How can you not think that I am the most ridiculous woman in the world for staying with him?' she asked.

'Because sometimes our perspective gets lost without us realising it,' replied Leni. 'Time and distance help us find it again.'

*

I don't think my son ever loved me. Even as a baby he wouldn't take comfort from me. He wouldn't breast-feed, he wouldn't settle in my arms. It was as if he didn't recognise me as his mother and mistook his grandmother Thelma for her. I don't know if he picked up on my being a constant nervous wreck but he resisted my attempts to cuddle him whereas he would hold out his arms to his grandmother.

Edwin was frustrated with me. I screamed out one night for help and Thelma rushed into the bedroom only to tell me that I would wake the baby. I didn't see how distorted my life had become until many years later. It was as if they were a sealed family unit, Thelma, her son and grandson and I was an unwanted outsider. It broke my heart that my child wasn't bonding with me.

Everyone thought I was so lucky having a husband who didn't want me to go out to work. I expect they imagined me being a lady of leisure. I didn't set foot outside the house for a month once. It would have been more but Bernard and Margaret forced their way into the house, worried about me. I laughed off their concern, but they weren't fooled.

The things Edwin called me were worse than what he did to me physically. One particular horrible night I knew I had to get out. Edwin was asleep and the baby was in the cot in his grandmother's room. I wish now I had grabbed him and raced out, but I was terrified Thelma would wake up and shout for Edwin. I have always felt shame that I left my son, even though I knew he was idolised and secure and I intended to fight for him when I was safe. I was his mother but I left him.

*

'But you couldn't do anything else. You would have done it, if you could have,' said Leni.

'I have told myself that so many times over the years and I've never believed it once,' replied Molly. 'I should have unlocked the door, opened it ready and grabbed my baby. I wish I could tell you how many times I've replayed that scene with a different ending.' She coughed and Leni rushed to get her a glass of water.

'I ran to Bernard and Margaret. I said I'd left Edwin but I never told them the whole story why, although I supposed they guessed most of it. I was so conditioned into not saying anything. You see it on the news, don't you? These poor girls who have the chance to escape a kidnapper and they don't because they're brainwashed into a perverse sense of loyalty.'

'And your baby?' asked Carla gently.

'Not even Bernard could get him back for me. Edwin was very well connected, shall we say. His father had been a mill-owner, a very powerful man, and a mason. Edwin threatened to have me sectioned. He knew I wasn't in any fit state to pass any psychological testing. Plus he had his loyal mother to back up any story he made up. The court agreed that my son should be brought up by his grand-mother and his father and that I should have supervised visitation rights. My boy was as good as lost to me. It was a constant battle to have Edwin hand him over when he should. He hoped I would give our son up totally and get out of their lives, but I clung on. And I could never tell my son that the father he worshipped was a brute, not that he would have believed me anyway. Edwin loved his son, indulged him, would have died for him, would have killed for him. Instead, I have to live with my son thinking that I was a weak woman who ran away and left him and lost him as a just consequence.'

'I think you're being very hard on yourself,' said Leni. 'I'm sure as he grew up, your son realised all was not as cut and dried as his father had presented it.'

'Edwin died when our son was twenty. Thelma survived him by three years, becoming more poisonous with every day. Only once did my son ever put his arms around me and that was on the day when Harvey left me. I saw a precious glimpse into a world that day where my son truly loved and cared for me. I treasure that day because I never saw it again. You're so lucky, Leni, having a daughter who loves you and misses you.'

'I'll get some more tissues for you,' said Leni, standing quickly before Molly saw her eyes mist over.

Chapter 70

When I met you, I thought all my Christmases had landed at once. You were everything Edwin wasn't: funny, caring, gentle. I wish I hadn't told Margaret about you once being in prison. I only wanted to impress her with how much of a strong character you were, coming from a rough background and yet having the ability to change. Of course, it made her wary that I was getting myself into another mess. She thought you'd lead me into bad ways. Bernard was very fond of you from the off. In his profession he had seen many people change paths, for the better and the worse.

I was so happy with you. I tried to make you happy too, but I couldn't. Oh my love, I wish you were here with me now. I want you to understand that it wasn't you to blame, it was me. I made you leave, my darling. It was all my fault.

Harvey pinched the tears out of the inner corners of his eyes. So much pain and regret suffused Molly's words. He should have known that there was something that ran deep inside her that changed her as soon as he crossed a barrier. She would let him cuddle her and kiss her, but he felt her resistance in his arms when his tongue traced her lip or his hands began to stroke her. When he tried to love her like a husband, she stiffened like a corpse. He felt as if he were violating his own wife. His own sweet Molly so gentle and smiling and affectionate out of bed, so icy within it. Then the frost began to follow Molly from their bedroom. She grew as cold during the day as she was in the night. He began to understand. She hadn't told him how much of a pig Edwin Beardsall was. She must have been frightened that all men were the same if her only experience of sleeping with someone was that. She must have believed that all men had two sides, a seducing angel and a brutal devil and she was bracing herself against his dark side manifesting itself. He should have guessed there was something wrong. He should have made her talk to him. They could have gone to a doctor. If he'd known she loved him but couldn't show him, he would have waited.

He opened another letter which dropped from his hands as his eyes cleared the first sentence.

My pen is trembling in my hand as I write this, my love.

He picked it up and as he scanned the body of the letter he closed his eyes against her words.

'Oh no, Molly. My poor love.'

Chapter 71

'However much I loved Harvey, and I did and I still do, I couldn't bear him to touch me . . . like that.'

'It's to be understood, dear Molly,' sighed Leni. 'You went through so much in your first marriage. It was bound to scar you.' Her hand was gripping Molly's as much as Molly's was holding on to hers.

Molly gave a single cough of humourless laughter. Then she dropped her head and her shoulders shook with tears.

'I'm so frightened, Leni. I'm scared stiff of facing that I've wasted so many years. I buried something away that refused to die, that has shifted and turned in its grave instead and laughs at my idiotic attempts to ignore it and forget it. Today Harvey will know and he will understand so many things and have some peace in his heart for himself, but he will also hate me. I let everyone think the end of my marriage was completely down to him. It was wrong of me. I have never forgiven myself for it. He couldn't possibly have healed me. I was damaged beyond repair.'

'No one is, Molly,' said Carla.

'I was,' came the weary reply.

'You can have help. Even after all this time, you know.

There are people specially trained in helping victims of domestic abuse.'

Molly shook her head slowly. 'I'm afraid by the time I met Edwin, the damage was already done.'

*

Oh my darling, Harvey.
    This is the last letter I shall write to you and the hardest. I am glad you will never read it because it will change the way you think about me forever. I love you so much and I always will but I cannot show it. When a root is spoiled, the flower cannot grow straight. I hope you can forgive me for not telling you. All you wanted was my love and I had it in abundance for you and yet there will always be an impenetrable fence between us.

Harvey's hands were shaking as he held the letter. *Not that, not that, not that.*

*

'I was always a daddy's girl,' smiled Molly. 'Margaret was a total tomboy, but I liked to sit with Father watching him. He made models of planes. He was very good at it.

'I was about twelve when it started,' said Molly, looking Leni, then Carla, straight in the eyes. 'Mother was out shopping and Margaret was playing on her bike in the park. Daddy and I were alone in the house. He was disgusted with himself, I know. But it didn't stop him doing it again.'

'No,' said Carla. 'Oh Molly, no.'

Molly's hand was squeezing Leni's hard as if she was afraid she would fall if she let go.

'All the clichés followed: that I was his special girl. That we must not ever say anything to Mummy because she wouldn't understand and would be very angry with me. And if I ever told anyone else I would be sent away to a home for naughty girls and would never see Margaret again.'

Her eyes were dry now, hard and dark like stones.

'It was as if there were two people inhabiting his body: my daddy who was smiley and funny and the man who ... did ... those dirty things. Just after my fourteenth birthday I saw him staring at Margaret in the way he stared at me when ... when he wanted ... I panicked and I ran to my mother for help. I was so scared for my sister that I told her what Daddy did to me and she slapped me and screamed at me that I was evil and if I ever said anything like that again they would put me in a children's home. I had no doubt from the look on her face that she would, because she was angry, just as Daddy said she would be. And I couldn't risk Margaret being left alone with Daddy.'

Molly hadn't smoked for forty years but she wished she could have a cigarette now and feel the smoke hit the back of her throat, absorb the nicotine hit.

'And so our lives continued. He left Margaret alone because he had me. I was a much safer bet to be yielding than my wilder, confident sister. Whilst I was compliant, Margaret was safe and she and I were in no danger of being parted. That is what he made me believe. And then when we were sixteen we sneaked out to a dance and Margaret met Bernard Brandywine, dragged along there by his friends. Oh, he was such a looker. Tall and broad, with thick black hair, and he treated her like a princess. Daddy, of course, was furious when he found out that a man was "sniffing around his daughter". He barred her from seeing him, but Margaret being Margaret used to climb out of the window and run off to meet Bernard.

'Then one day Daddy caught her and he beat her – and me for trying to stop him. When Bernard hadn't seen Margaret for a few days, he and his father and mother came around to the house to make sure she was all right. They felt something was very wrong and forced their way in; Bernard and his mother came up the stairs and as soon as they saw the state we were in they helped us pack a suitcase each. Mr Brandywine was having a huge altercation in the front room with my parents whilst we gathered together as much of our stuff as we could. My parents stood back as we walked out with the Brandywines and I'll never forget the look on my mother's face: pure hatred. Those wonderful people took us into their beautiful home and the rest, as they say, is history. I loved them so much. Margaret and I started our lives again.'

Leni wiped her wet cheek with the back of her hand. 'And what of your parents?'

'There were no police involved. I think the Brandywines thought that going to court would be too much for us. They wanted us to forget and hoped their love would undo all the damage, although they never knew the full extent of how much damage there had been. Only Margaret and Bernard knew what happened to me. I told them when we were safe with the Brandywines and Daddy would never be able to hurt Margaret or send me away from her.

'We didn't speak to our parents again. Occasionally we saw them walking through town, but they never acknowledged us. They sold the house when Margaret and I were in our twenties and they moved away. I don't know if they're still alive or not. Margaret says that she never thinks of them, but I do. Part of me wants to go back to those days when I was watching Daddy put together those model planes and hope that things progressed along a different path. I loved him so much.'

Carla didn't know what to say but wished she could give Molly some comfort. She felt numbed by what she had just heard. Her own father was strict and old-fashioned but loving as a father should be. She had never had cause to be afraid of him and couldn't imagine what growing up would have been like if she had.

Molly checked the delicate gold watch on her wrist. 'I expect Harvey will have read all the letters by now. He will know everything, the whole sordid lot.'

'And he will still love you, Molly,' said Leni insistently.

Molly reached behind for her jacket over the back of the chair.

'We shall soon see, won't we?'

*

Harvey couldn't have guessed why Molly was so disgusted by sex, but now he knew and he folded up the last letter, replaced it back in the envelope, tied it in the ribbon with the others and then he had sobbed into his large hands. His poor darling girl had gone through all that and he'd never known. He wasn't a violent man, but if Molly's parents had been in front of him now he thought he could have killed both of them.

He sat in the sunshine and skipped back through his memories of Molly as a beautiful woman of thirty-six, who blushed when he talked to her and how good she felt in his arms. He had honoured her and not taken her to bed until their wedding night, and there he had tasted the first sour notes of their relationship.

He looked up to see that same beautiful woman standing

in front of him now, her hair silver where it had once been golden, her shoulders slightly stooped, but she made his heart thud as much now as she had back then. He pulled himself out of the chair and walked towards her, his arms out. Molly moved into them, Harvey pushed her head into his shoulder and they stood there, silently, together, with no words spoken for there was no need of them.

Chapter 72

'I hope she'll be okay,' said Carla, looking at the clock on the teashop wall. She reckoned that Molly should be home by now.

'I hope so too,' replied Leni. 'Who would have guessed that she was carrying all that around with her?'

'And I thought I had skeletons in my closet,' sighed Carla, drinking the last of her coffee. 'Martin's shenanigans are nothing compared to what we've just heard. Really puts things into perspective, doesn't it?'

She caught sight of Will through the window holding a broom. He'd had his share of skeletons too. Even young Ryan must have had a few, coming from the infamous O'Gowan clan. Maybe not everyone did though. Leni, for instance – she was far too smiley to have bones hiding in her closet.

'How did you get on with the shop?' asked Leni, remembering why Carla was there in Spring Square.

'I'm going to take it,' replied Carla, feeling slightly guilty about having good news to celebrate after all she had heard from Molly.

'That's great news,' smiled Leni. 'You'll be my new neighbour.'

'I'll like that,' Carla returned and meant it. 'Now, if you'll excuse me. I need to go home and plan.'

When she left Leni's teashop she went over to find Will and tell him the good news. He had been delighted for her and said that he would make her a counter. Then she had rung Theresa, who had whooped down the phone and then told her off for holding back for so long before taking the plunge.

Now Carla was sitting in her lounge with the *Hard Times* journal she had bought from the Teashop on the Corner, half resting it on Lucky's back, who was taking up prime position on her lap. On the left-hand page she had a list of all the essential equipment she would need to set up: flowers, display vases, ribbons, wrap, raffia, gift cards, country baskets etcetera. Oh, and a phone line. She could use an ordinary cash box – there was no point in splashing out on a fancy till – but she would definitely require a credit card machine. She needed to replenish her florist's toolbox which was essential for last-minute repairs, alterations and additions especially on bridal flowers, and she had plenty of books which would be handy for would-be customers to refer to and get an idea of style.

On the right-hand side she had a list of ideas on how to drum up some business. She still had the orders book she had taken as a souvenir from Marlene's shop after she'd retrieved it from a pile of paperwork to be burnt. So many of her old clients had told her to contact them when she started to trade again, promising that their custom would follow her.

Jonty and Theresa would help get her name out there, she knew. She would set up a site on the internet; maybe the *Barnsley Chronicle* would run a feature on her in exchange for a bouquet. She could forget the incompetent *Daily Trumpet* who would no doubt get all the details wrong. And what could she call the business?

A nasty voice hit her from left field. *Who do you think you are kidding?* And she thought it sounded like Martin. She had once thought about setting up a part-time bouquet delivery service from home and those were the very words he had said to her: Who do you think you are kidding? Then he told her not to be so silly and go make his tea.

Carla felt a spike of anger as she recalled how stupid he had made her feel. Maybe if she had ignored him, she would be running a chain of florist shops now.

Who do you think you are kidding? That voice again.

'You aren't here any more, Martin,' said Carla to the air. 'And I am going to do it. So there.' She felt marvellous just for daring to say it and punched the air in triumph. Life was for the living and she *was* living and Martin wasn't. So stuff him.

Chapter 73

'You sure?'

'Very.'

'Here goes then.' Harvey cast the bundle of letters into the lit garden incinerator. The edges began to brown and smoke and curl and they watched mesmerised as all Molly's words of pain and confession were devoured hungrily by the orange dancing blades of fire.

It was a warm, balmy night but Harvey noticed that Molly was shivering. He took a step closer to her and put his arm around her shoulder.

'It was the right thing to do,' he said.

'I know,' she replied.

'You aren't going to live in the past any more, are you?' He gave her a gentle squeeze. 'It can't hurt you now, Molly. You must never look back again.'

'I won't.' His arm felt good around her shoulder. She let herself be pressed closer to him.

'I'm so glad I came back,' said Harvey. 'I wouldn't have laid quiet in my grave if I hadn't said goodbye to you. I would have done a Catherine Earnshaw and knocked at your window.'

'I've got triple-glazing. I wouldn't have heard you,' sniffed Molly.

Harvey threw back his head and laughed. Then he kissed Molly tenderly on her hair.

'Let's go in and cover ourselves with blankets and fall asleep in front of a film like the couple of old farts we are.'

Molly nodded. That sounded good. She cast a last look into the incinerator as they passed it. The letters were totally gone, save for a few smoking black flakes in the bottom.

Chapter 74

Carla was in the kitchen when Will landed home. Hearing him enter she turned around and grinned.

'I was just about to open a bottle of celebratory fizz if you'd like a glass. Not champagne, it's Prosecco, which I actually prefer. And to be honest, I can't tell the difference.'

He smiled.

'I'd love a glass.'

That sadness in her eyes was gone today, thank goodness, and there was a shine to her that he hadn't seen before, as if a light had been turned on inside her and illuminated all her features.

Lucky jumped on his knee as soon as he sat at the dining table. Carla took the bottle out of the fridge and unfastened the gold wrapper at the top of it, twisted off the wire and then grimaced as she tried to twist the cork out. Two minutes later she was still twisting.

'Give it 'ere,' Will beckoned. 'I hope you're better with bouquets than you are with bottles.'

'I couldn't be any worse,' said Carla, wincing as the cork popped.

She took the bottle from Will as Lucky was too comfortable on his knee to be moved. She slowly poured two
glasses and he lifted his and chinked it against hers.

'Here's to . . . what's your shop called, then?'

'I don't know yet,' replied Carla, after taking a mouthful
of fizz. 'I haven't got a name.'

'When are you moving in?'

'Soon as possible. I'm going to be very busy buying
equipment and ringing up my old clients. And designing
some business cards. It's going to be mad next week.'

Will chuckled. It was good to see her smiling. She looked
like a different person to the one who had shown him
around the flat at their first meeting. He searched his brain
for a suitable word to describe her and found it: *glossy*. She
was shiny and glossy today.

'I think this merits a Chinese,' he said, on the spur of the
moment. 'Can I treat you? Some of your good luck may
rub off on me if I do.'

'Lucky.' Carla raised her finger. 'That's it. The Lucky
Flower Company. That's what I'll call it.'

The black cat on Will's knee didn't acknowledge his
future fame. He had everything he needed in life and it
didn't include flowers.

Chapter 75

Molly awoke on the Sunday with a happy heart and to slices of sunshine pushing through the curtains where they didn't quite meet. Harvey was already up and was sitting in the garden with a pot of tea and some toast.

'Ah, good morning, Molly,' he greeted her with a beaming smile. 'Isn't it glorious?'

'Beautiful,' said Molly, lifting her face to the sun.

Just as Harvey was about to tip the teapot over the second cup he stopped. 'Let's go to the seaside,' he said. 'We can be there before lunchtime.'

'Don't be ridic—' Molly started to answer, then cut off the protestation. Why not? *Life is for the living.* She clapped her hands together. 'All right. We'll go to the seaside.'

'We'll have fish and chips on the prom.' Harvey grinned. 'I might even buy you a cornet.'

'I'll get my handbag,' said Molly, a thrill of excitement tripping down her spine. She hadn't been this impulsive in over twenty years.

She had felt as light as a feather since returning home from Leni's teashop yesterday. Harvey had been waiting for her with his arms open and she moved into them and let him hold her.

'I love you, Molly Jones,' he had said to her later, when they were sitting on the sofa together. 'I will always love you and nothing in your past will ever alter that.'

'If only I'd—'

He shushed her. 'If only you had done this, if only I had done that . . . but we didn't. And we can't go back. But we have a little forward time, so let's enjoy it.' And they had sat watching a Burt Lancaster film together on the sofa, holding hands like teenagers, both feeling safe and content.

Chapter 76

Shaun was looking through his accounts in the pre-fab building which served as the temporary office for the site. Working at the weekend was the norm for him, he couldn't remember the last time he had spent a Sunday at home, lazing, reading the newspapers, doing what other people did. There were few rest days for Shaun McCarthy.

The king was in his counting house, counting out his money. Shaun was happier in the company of work. It gave him a thrill to see a healthy set of figures on his balance sheets, knowing that he could finance the next project. Every pound he earned was a cock-a-snook in the face of the priests and teachers who told him that he would never amount to anything. That he was 'illegitimate scum who came from scum and would beget scum'.

He heard a knock on the door. A quiet, hope-I'm-not-disturbing-you knock.

'Hello,' he called. He suspected it was Leni Merryman. No one else was around on the site today but him and her although he didn't have a clue what she might want.

The door opened slowly and in she walked, carrying a plate covered with foil.

'Hello Mr McCarthy,' she said, smiling brightly. 'I hope

you don't mind me dropping in like this, but I'm shutting up shop early today and I thought you might like these. Chicken and ham pastries. And a slice of ginger and lemon cake.'

'I thought you usually took your cast-offs to the homeless,' Shaun replied, immediately annoyed with himself for sounding scathing and ungrateful. He had meant it as a joke, but it hadn't come out that way.

'I've only got those couple of pastries to give away today,' she replied, still cheery, as if she hadn't noticed. 'You can throw them away if you don't eat them.'

'No, no, that's very kind of you.' He stood to take them from her but she came forward and saved him the trouble.

'They're fresh,' she said. 'I baked the pastries this morning and the cake yesterday but I had a nice little run of customers this morning. Cyclists – all hungry from their ride.'

Shaun found himself trying to hide a wry smile. Had this been any other woman on the planet, he would have thought she was flirting. He wasn't an idiot where women were concerned, he knew their subtle manoeuvres to winkle their way into a man's heart: the soft encouraging sounds they made when they were rapt in every word a man said, the small seductive kindnesses they offered up. He didn't consider himself handsome but his strong features sat well with each other and women seemed to like the rough cut of him: his tall strong physique, his firm jaw, his nose broken in a fight years ago, his piercing blue-green eyes. He looked like a man who wasn't afraid of trouble, because he wasn't. For some the draw was his Liam Neeson soft burring accent; or his aloofness, because human nature demanded that what people couldn't have, they found intriguing. For others, the attraction was his money and that type he could sense a mile off. It amused him that he – Irish bog scum, as he'd been so often called in the past – would ever have made enough money to interest a woman.

He noticed that when his eyes locked with hers, her head turned, she blinked, her gaze skittered away. Had he got it wrong? Was she flirting after all? Wasn't that a sign?

For a second he entertained the theory that she might be double-bluffing and appearing as uninterested to spark his attention, but no – this was Leni Merryman they were talking about, and he felt no manipulations were afoot. The woman had spare pastries and cake and she had brought them over to him as an act of consideration. It was as simple as that. She was as transparent as the window behind her.

She pressed the heel of her hand against her temple and he suspected she might be going home early because she had a headache.

'Overdone it today?' he asked.

'Bit of a migraine stirring,' she replied. 'I'll be okay after a lie down in a dark, quiet room.'

'I get those too,' he said. They sprang on him whenever he slowed down and gave his body time to rebel. So he didn't slow down.

'Well, goodnight. Or rather good afternoon, Mr McCarthy,' said Leni.

She looks tired, thought Shaun. That smile on her lips looked more difficult to sustain today.

'Thank you,' he replied.

'Pleasure.'

He watched her walk back to the teashop on the corner, her step less springy than usual and he wondered what else she had in her life but work and her cat. Then again, he didn't even have the cat.

Chapter 77

They ate fish and chips sitting on a bench on the prom, watching children playing in the sand and riding donkeys. Why did fish and chips always taste so much better outside in the paper, covered in far too much salt and vinegar?

'I haven't had these for . . . well, I can't remember when,' said Molly, licking her fingers.

'You haven't lived.'

'No, I haven't really, have I?' replied Molly, sadness tingeing her words.

'Time to start then, lass.' Harvey nudged her. 'Make a list: Paris, Rome and Venice and all the other places we planned to go to.'

Molly laughed. 'Yes, let's go to them all.'

'No, you go without me,' said Harvey, staring straight ahead to the horizon. 'Promise me you'll see all those places when I'm gone.'

'I will not,' huffed Molly. 'Wandering around by myself like a lost old woman. What do you take me for?'

'I'll be with you,' said Harvey, scrunching up his fish and chip wrapper and putting it into the bin at his side. 'I'll send those white feathers down from the sky to prove that I'm watching you. Go on a cruise. Fly to New York. Do it for me. We can compare notes in the afterlife.'

Molly tried to hold on to her composure, but he was making it hard.

Harvey stood up, seeing the slight tremble claiming her bottom lip. He held out his hand for her to take.

'Excuse the vinegary fingers.'

Molly closed her equally vinegary fingers around his.

'We never let each other go, really, did we?' said Harvey.

'No,' smiled Molly.

'Do you think it's because deep down we knew that we'd get our second chance?'

'Maybe,' said Molly, standing. Is that what this was? Their chance to get it right this time?

'Come on. I want to feel the sand between my toes and then the sea washing it away,' said Harvey, pulling her towards the stone steps that led down to the beach.

'I suppose you want to ride a donkey as well.'

'I never did get to ride a donkey,' Harvey replied. 'I never had a holiday when I was a kid.'

Poor Harvey, thought Molly. He hadn't been given a lot of love in his life and yet he'd been full of it himself. Too much of it, greedy for it, drinking affection up wherever he found it like a dry dog supped water.

She helped him take off his shoes and socks and kicked off her sandals and together they walked along the silky golden sand towards the gentle rush of the waves and stood there letting the sun warm their bones.

'Why did you send me a postcard of a boy on a donkey? Was there a reason? I always thought there must be one, though I never worked out what it was.'

Harvey didn't move his eyes away from the horizon.

'The one thing I always wanted to do when I was a lad was to ride on a donkey, but I never did. I always envied kids at school who said they'd been to the seaside and ridden one along the beach. I never even saw a real donkey until I was a strapping eighteen-year-old, far too big to fit on one of their backs.'

His voice was weighted with such sadness that Molly closed the gap between them and slipped her arm into his. He turned towards her and looked into her still lovely dark-blue eyes.

'I think that over the years a donkey ride became a symbol of yearning for what I would never have. I'd never be little enough to ride on a donkey just as I would never have been able to return to you.'

Behind them, the gentle tinkling of the donkeys with their bells became louder, and when they drew level Molly waved at the donkey man.

'But you did return to me,' said Molly, an idea in her head. 'Wait there.' She walked over at speed to the donkey man.

Harvey watched her explaining something to him and then they both waved over. He padded towards them, eyebrows dipped in question.

'Get on,' said Molly.

'Don't be daft. I'd flatten the poor thing.'

'Your feet might trail on the floor, mate, but you must be only six stone piss-wet through,' said the donkey man. 'You should see some of the sizes of the kids these days. Right fat-arses. Thank God these are beasts of burden.'

'Poor donkeys.' Molly stroked the nearest donkey's ear.

'They're like oxen,' said the donkey man. 'They don't mind. I know what weight would be too much and you aren't it. Come on, I'll help you.'

He lifted Harvey onto a donkey who had the name 'Neddy' painted onto his bridle and put the reins in his hand.

'Now you, missus.'

'Oh I didn't mean me . . .'

'Oh come on, Molly,' urged Harvey with a chuckle. 'We can pretend we're in the Grand National. Put the shoes down on the sand and mount your steed.'

'Oh . . .' Molly gave a resigned smile and let the donkey man help her onto 'Bobby'. And then the donkey man led them down the beach laughing like loons, not caring who was watching them or what they were saying. Life was here and now and it was good.

After their donkey ride, they sat on a deckchair with an ice-cream, listening to the sound of the sea and the seagulls and horses trotting down the prom, pulling their tourist carriages. Then they went into the amusement arcade and fed lots of two-pence pieces into the coin cascade machines. Harvey couldn't get rid of his: he kept winning, so Molly helped him spend them. The machine churned out a load of tickets which could be redeemed against prizes. About three million of them were needed for a pen. Harvey gave them to a delighted small boy already clutching handfuls of them, then he put a pound in a creepy-looking fortune-telling machine and a card plopped out of the bottom.

'Apparently I'm going to have a long and happy life,' he read. 'Lying bugger. At least about the long. He got the happy bit right though.' He mused to himself. 'It's certainly been an eventful one. Too much booze, too much gambling, too many women, a lot of beautiful sights and one true love, but at least it's been a life. And this is the happiest I've been in a long time. With you.'

Molly took his hand. 'I haven't been this happy in a long time either, Harvey. I'm so glad you came home to me.'

'Talking of which, let's go home, shall we? I've had enough today.'

'Yes, we've done a lot.' She pulled him out of the arcade and they walked hand in hand in the cooling sunshine towards the car park. Harvey stopped suddenly and turned around for a last look at the town with its gaudy colours, the chime of the donkey bells on the beach, the arcade machine tunes, the bangs and whirrs and scents of fried onion and doughnuts. Another wonderful memory notched up. One of his best.

'Grand,' he said. 'Just grand.'

Chapter 78

Ryan arrived at the teashop on the corner at four o'clock after school on Wednesday. He looked extra pale, Leni thought, and so thin. His green blazer must have been a hand-me-down because it was so obviously the wrong size. He was almost lost in it.

'Hiya,' he greeted. 'That bloke's got a problem with me, hasn't he?' He thumbed behind his shoulder across the square and when Leni peeped out of the window, she saw Shaun standing there.

'Oh, ignore him,' she said.

'I'm not like the rest of them, you know,' said Ryan, taking off his blazer. His shirt had a black line of pen down the sleeve. He caught Leni staring at it.

'It's Sharpie. I can't get it off,' he said. 'My other shirt's the same.'

'It's impossible,' agreed Leni. 'Would you like something to eat before you start?'

'Can I?'

'Of course you can. Toasties?'

'Yes please.'

'Go and put your stuff in the back room. I want you to

open those boxes in there by my desk. They should be bookends. You can wait until after you've eaten though.'

'Might as well get started.'

Shaun McCarthy entered just as Leni closed the lid on the grill.

'Hello there,' she grinned at him. 'Are you here for shopping, sandwiches or spying?'

He narrowed his eyes at her.

'Some thanks for making sure you're all right,' he mumbled.

'I'm perfectly fine, Mr McCarthy.'

'Was that the O'Gowan boy I saw coming in here?'

'It was.'

'That's okay then. Just checking.'

'Are you going to check on everyone who comes in?' Leni was still hanging on to her smile. He felt a prickle of annoyance that he amused her so much.

'Yes, I think I might.'

It was as big a mystery to him as it was to her why he should bother. She wasn't his responsibility – God forbid. If she wanted to get herself mugged by the most notorious family in the area, why should he really care?

'Would you like a coffee, Mr McCarthy, whilst you're on surveillance duties?'

'You're very kind, but I'll pass.' He gave her a smile of his own. The one he saved for the VAT man.

Leni noticed how straight and white his teeth were. They would suit a proper smile. She wondered when he had last thrown his head back and laughed.

Ryan emerged from the back room holding a wooden bookend. He stopped in his tracks when he saw Shaun McCarthy.

'It's okay, Ryan,' said Leni. 'Mr McCarthy didn't realise it was you coming into the teashop. He thought it was a hoodlum out to murder me.' She dropped a sly wink for Ryan's eyes only.

'Well, I'll get back across the way then,' said Shaun. 'Oh, you're going to be joined by a florist on the square. Thought I ought to let you know.'

Leni grinned. 'I had heard and I'm really glad. For you too, Mr McCarthy. One less shop to find a tenant for.'

'Two, actually,' replied Shaun. 'Your next-door neighbour is going to be an antiques emporium.' The man had signed on the dotted line that afternoon. It had been a good day for Shaun McCarthy. Somewhere in a parallel universe, another Shaun McCarthy would be buying a bottle of champagne and taking it home to crack open with a good woman and celebrate.

'Wonderful,' said Leni. 'I love antiques.'

The grill pinged, indicating that Ryan's toasties were ready. Shaun McCarthy left her to it, pondering if there was anything in Leni Merryman's life that wasn't either 'wonderful' or 'lovely'.

Chapter 79

Harvey was still talking about their visit to the seaside three days later. He chattered like an over-excited child. Molly thought they must have started putting E-numbers in fish and chips these days.

'That is the best day out I can ever remember,' he said, sitting on the garden chair, tilting his head to the warm light of the afternoon.

Molly watched him replaying the events of Sunday in his head and smiling. He had caught the sun on his face and it had chased away that awful pallor.

'There's a new restaurant open in Maltstone. Italian. Shall we go and test it out?' he suggested.

'I was going to cook some chicken.'

'Oh, chicken, schmicken. Who wants to cook on a glorious sunny night like this? Let's push the boat out.'

'Oh all right,' said Molly, thinking that sounded a good plan. She was enjoying her days with Harvey more than she could say. Yesterday they had been to the Teashop on the Corner and talked for a full hour about Daphne du Maurier books with Mr Singh. Dear Carla wasn't there because she was running around getting things for her florist shop, which everyone agreed must have been so exciting for her.

Then they had come home, drawn the curtains, turned the front room into a cinema and watched the old black-and-white version of *Rebecca* with Laurence Olivier and Joan Fontaine. Mrs Danvers gave Molly the heebie-jeebies as much as she always had. Today they had been for a stroll in Higher Hoppleton Park and had taken a bag of cake crumbs to feed the ducks and geese, then called in at the antiques shop in the village and poked around for treasures. She tried not to think of all the other wonderful days out with Harvey she could have had, if things had been different.

'It's called Piccola Venezia. Shame it's not the real Venice.'

'Beggars can't be choosers.'

'One day it will be the real thing for you. Don't forget to look around for those white feathers. Or an Embassy Tip packet. I always smoked those. I could blow an empty box your way, that ought to convince you that I'm around.'

'You're a fool, Harvey Hoyland.' Molly shook her head in exasperation and stood. 'I'll go and freshen up if we're going out.'

'I'll wait here for you.'

He watched her walk into the house. She still looked the same from the back as she had done thirty-two years ago, reed-thin and straight-backed. A pain stabbed him in the side and he leant over to ease it. His repeat prescription would be due soon. He knew it wasn't worth picking up more tablets.

Chapter 80

'Okay, matey, that'll do I reckon. Your two hours are up,' said Leni, going to the till and pulling out Ryan's wage.

'I've got another quarter of an hour,' said Ryan, looking at the clock on the wall. 'I spent the first fifteen minutes here eating.'

'You must be the most conscientious worker I've ever known.' Leni knew he was over-compensating for his family's reputation. She held up the money. 'Do you want me to put this in the safe for you? I haven't forgotten about the extra fiver by the way.'

'Please,' said Ryan, picking up the scissors and putting them neatly in the drawer. He always cleared up after himself.

'I'll run you home.'

'No, it's all right. I'll get the bus.'

Leni glanced at the clock and made a calculation. 'The next bus won't be here for another half-hour. I insist. The least I can do is make sure you get home safely. I don't want your moth . . . family being cross with me.'

Ryan mumbled something under his breath which Leni didn't quite catch but she could guess at the essence of it.

'Come on. I'm going to lock up myself and have an

early-ish night. Here.' She handed over a small brown paper bag. 'There's a slice of carrot cake in there for your supper.'

'Aw, cheers, Mrs Merryman, thank you.'

'You can call me Leni, you know. I'm not your teacher.'

'Okay.'

Leni set the burglar alarm and locked up. She waved an instinctive cheery good night to Mr McCarthy, who was carrying a bag of cement across the square. She tried to ignore how much it hurt her to think that she rubbed him up the wrong way. She usually kept her distance from anyone that might affect her, but she had failed at the teashop. Based on their shared love of books, friendships with Molly, Harvey, dear Mr Singh, lovely Carla and Ryan had crept up on her when she wasn't looking, uniting them all with gentle unthreatening bonds. It was different in the case of Shaun McCarthy though. The sight of him made her insides tingle as if her nerves had been ruffled by a soft, warm wind. She didn't want them to. She didn't want to be drawn towards him. She didn't want her eyes to drift over to the window in the hope of seeing him across the square.

She knew he was an unhappy man, she could feel it coming off him in waves when she was near him. It was almost a forcefield warning people to stay away. But Shaun McCarthy would never need worry on her account. Her heart was on a chain and the door would only open so far.

Leni felt Shaun's eyes on her as she slipped into the driver's seat of her car. He thought her a silly chirpy woman, she knew, and it wounded her that he did so.

Ryan climbed into the car with his school bag, which badly needed replacing. One of the seams was torn and held together tenuously in the middle with a safety pin.

'Any homework to do?' asked Leni, making conversation as they headed through town.

'Done it,' replied Ryan. 'I do most of it in my breaks at school. I can use the computers.'

'Very wise,' said Leni. 'Then it's all out of the way and you have plenty of free time in the evenings. What do you like to do?'

'Watch TV, read,' said Ryan. 'I stay in my bedroom mostly.'

'No friends to go and see?'

'My best mate lives at the other side of Darton. I've been there a couple of times but his mum is a bit posh. Don't think she's that keen on me.'

Judging you on your clothes no doubt, thought Leni with an inner pang. Ryan was such a good kid, she knew. Polite, studious, decent, but people who knew the name O'Gowan would have difficulty seeing past that.

'It's next right,' said Ryan as they passed the Ketherwood Fried Chicken shop. Five youths were hanging around outside drinking from cans, rubbish pooled at their feet. One of them was holding a lead attached to a sturdy Staffordshire Bull Terrier with a spiked collar.

'Honest, you can leave me here, it's not far to walk.'

'I'll drop you at the door,' Leni said adamantly, turning right where instructed.

'I can . . .' Then Ryan sighed. 'Okay. Right again at the offy.'

Leni knew he was ashamed about where he lived. The Ketherwood estate was grim. A lot of the houses were boarded up and most of the ones that weren't looked uncared for, with grubby net curtains hanging at windows, cracked panes of glass in doors and squares of garden devoid of grass and full of detritus.

'It's this one,' said Ryan, pointing to a semi-detached with a battered black Ford Fiesta with one red door parked outside it. It appeared that the wooden front door had been kicked in at some point as it had been patched with a bolted-on metal panel.

'Thanks, Mrs Merryman,' said Ryan, jumping out of the car then turning back to say, 'Don't hang about here.'

Leni watched him open up the door with a key, caught a glimpse of grimy walls and broken skirting board before he shut the door again. She could have cried.

Chapter 81

Molly and Harvey dined on an Italian feast fit for Garibaldi himself in the beautiful high-ceilinged conservatory part of the restaurant. A male opera singer with backing tapes provided musical entertainment. Occasionally he came forward to hand the mike to a diner but the offer to join in was always laughingly declined. Until he approached Harvey.

Diners temporarily downed their cutlery to listen to the deep powerful voice, in word perfect Italian, coming from the thin elderly man. Molly had forgotten what a beautiful voice he had and marvelled that in his state of health he could hold the melody with such precision. It was as if the sound came from a part within him that was untouched by illness; *his soul*.

'Time to Say Goodbye'. Of all the songs to sing. Why did it have to be that one, she thought. A song about a lover dreaming of the places he wants to travel to with his love, from whom he is separated by death. So he takes her with him in his heart, knowing that one day they will be reunited in the afterlife and then they will sail on ships together. Molly swallowed hard on the ball of emotion which threatened to choke her as his pure and remarkable voice filled the room, and she knew she would remember the sound forever.

The diners gave Harvey a standing ovation, the opera singer hugged him, even the owner came out from the back to shake his hand. The room was brimming with conviviality and joyous surprise. The owner gave Harvey and Molly a free dessert each and two coffees. Molly thought she could have stayed in that restaurant forever, but when she looked across at Harvey she saw that his eyes were getting tired.

When they left the restaurant, the sun was fast darkening to a ripe orange and sinking into the horizon, as if the moon was shooing it away from his territory.

'I don't want to go to bed yet,' said Harvey when they reached Willowfell.

'How about a brandy in the garden?'

'That sounds perfect.'

Molly had two huge balloon glasses which had never been used and still sat in their presentation box. Tonight might be the night to finally christen them. By the time she had got them out and poured the brandy, Harvey was asleep on the swinging chair.

She shook his arm gently and received no response. Nor did she the second time. She panicked and grabbed at him with both arms and he snorted whilst his eyes sprang open.

Molly pressed her hand on her heart. All this would kill her before it killed him.

'I was having a lovely dream,' said Harvey, stretching out his long wiry arms. 'I'd been for an Italian meal with my ex-wife.'

'I had the same dream,' said Molly. 'He scared her half to death and then they had brandies on the garden terrace.'

'I hadn't quite got to that bit,' said Harvey. 'Did I tell you that I once had a coffee with Placido Domingo on a train to Madrid? He signed a serviette for me. I have it in my suitcase. There's a zip compartment. Placido is in there with some other souvenirs from my travels.'

He had done so many things in his life and Molly knew she wouldn't have time to hear the half of them.

They sat in quiet contentment enjoying the warm hit of the brandy under a high bright moon until after midnight.

'That was what I call a perfect evening,' said Harvey, pulling himself to his feet with a yawn and holding out his hand to help up Molly.

'It was,' nodded Molly. 'It was.'

The answering machine was flashing when they walked into the house.

You have one new message, said the plummy-voiced announcer when Molly pressed the button.

'Helloooo, Mother,' came a woman's squeak. 'Just to tell you that we're coming back on Friday night. We've had such a terrific time. I'll call up to see you on Saturday morning. Bye-ee.'

Sherry. She and Graham would be home in two days.

Molly decided she might need to take a nightcap up to bed with her.

Chapter 82

Once again Carla was up early, too excited to sleep. She fed Lucky and let him out, then let him back in because he started scratching at the door as soon as she shut it. He wasn't a very outdoorsy cat. He seemed to prefer life inside.

Over the past days, she had designed some online business cards. They weren't very expensive and that would probably be reflected in the quality, but they'd certainly do to begin with. She had rung her old contact Sheila at Forrester's Floral Supplies in Sheffield, had a catch-up chat and then she ordered a starter pack of vases, ribbons, wrap, baskets and various Oasis shapes. She was back on familiar territory and it felt good. She even managed to negotiate a discount and got some further money knocked off for collection of goods. The delivery prices were ridiculous and Carla was determined to see profits coming in as soon as possible, which wouldn't happen if she threw money away. She had also ordered a card payment machine and this morning she was going to work through her address book and let old customers know that next week she would be trading live as The Lucky Flower Company.

Each day was a mad whirl of organisation and she loved every second of it.

Chapter 83

From the moment she awoke on Saturday morning, Molly was like a cat on hot bricks.

'I wish you'd relax,' said Harvey, watching her stride across to the front window and nudge her nets out of the way for the hundredth time. 'Why are you so jumpy about your daughter-in-law coming?'

'Because she'll go home and tell Graham that you're here and he'll come over and . . .' She didn't know what would happen after that. All Molly knew was that there would be trouble.

'I'll hide when she arrives,' said Harvey, calmly. 'I'll go into the study bedroom and read the newspaper. I promise I'll sit quietly in the corner on the rocking chair.'

'Would you mind?' asked Molly, feeling her shoulders untense slightly at the thought of buying herself some extra time. 'She only usually stays half an hour. And don't rock. It makes the floorboards creak.'

'Of course I won't mind and I promise to stay still,' chuckled Harvey. 'Although I would have liked to have seen the legend in the flesh. Dressed flesh, obviously.' And he shuddered.

'The sooner she comes the sooner she'll go ... oh she's here. Quick, Harvey.'

Harvey toddled up the stairs as speedily as he could. 'I'll be as quiet as a little mouse,' he called over his shoulder. 'Enjoy.'

'Enjoy, ha!' Molly batted the word back at him with a small explosive sound. She didn't enjoy Sherry's company at all. She was constantly on edge waiting for Sherry to get around to saying what she had really come for. She was starting to suspect that despite the villa in Greece, despite the his and hers BMWs, despite the double-fronted house in a posh part of Bretton, Graham's financial situation wasn't as healthy as it was cracked up to be. That would explain all the 'this house is too big for you, Mother' casual statements with barbs attached and all the comments along the lines of 'what a lovely retirement home Autumn Grange is'. Then again, he inherited a fortune from his father and grand-mother. He couldn't have lost it all, could he?

Sherry came waddling up the path in a skirt that was far too short for her. At least her varicose veins were less noticeable now her legs were tanned.

She rang the bell and walked straight in as usual. 'Hello, Molly,' she called and leant towards her mother-in-law to kiss the air near her cheek. Her ghastly perfume enveloped Molly like a cloud of mustard gas.

'You look well,' Molly forced herself to say. 'Your hair's gone lighter in the sun.'

'Oh we've had a fabulous time. Gram and Archie send their love. They say they'll see you soon. I've brought us an éclair each. Let's go and have a cup of tea and a catch-up. You can tell me everything that's been happening to you whilst we were away.'

'Oh there's nothing to tell, really,' shrugged Molly, fol-lowing the enormous-bottomed Sherry into the kitchen.

She had put on even more weight on holiday. Her hips stuck out like two donkey panniers.

The chair groaned as if in pain when Sherry sat down at the table and took the éclairs out of the bag, licking the chocolate from her fingers whilst Molly boiled the kettle.

'I think we're going to sell Dream Hall and move somewhere smaller,' said Sherry. She said it casually, but Molly knew there must be more to the story. The large house with the gaudy frontage was their main status symbol. They wouldn't have let it go lightly, whatever Sherry was trying to tell her.

Dream Hall. What a ridiculous name for a ridiculous building. Sherry had had the front façade painted with a pink bottom half and a yellow top half. It sat in their garden like a giant trifle.

'Oh?' Molly poured the hot water into a warmed teapot.

'Yes, it's too big for just Gram and me. We're rattling around in it now that Archie's at university and unlikely to want to live with us any more.' Sherry took a mirror out of her bag and started pincering at a rough hair on the edge of her lip with her French-polished nails. 'And much as I've enjoyed my holiday, I said to Gram I said, "I'm getting a bit bored with Greece. Maybe we should sell this as well and have holidays in other places".'

So they *were* having financial problems. She waited for more.

'I'm looking forward to a smaller house. Less to clean and why waste all that money heating rooms you don't use? We don't need a games room any more. No one has played snooker for years.'

'I totally agree,' said Molly as a spark of mischief ignited within her. She was feeling the influence of Harvey Hoyland far too much. She dropped a nugget of bait into the conversation to see if Sherry would bite. 'I feel that I need a smaller place too.'

She saw Sherry jerk forward in her chair, her interest sparked.

'Do you? Is that how you feel?'

'Yes, I'm rather lonely. I wouldn't mind the company of other people my age.'

Molly, you naughty woman, she giggled inwardly to herself.

Sherry bit hard down on her éclair. The cream squished out of the sides as if the cake had grown wings. Sherry extended her tongue and licked down two lengths. She could catch flies with that tongue, Molly imagined Harvey saying.

'I would love a house this size,' Sherry said, through a mouthful of choux pastry. 'We should live here and you should move into Autumn Grange.' She let loose a tinkly laugh as if she had made a joke, but Molly knew that Sherry's head was already knitting plans together.

'Oh yes, Autumn Grange. I remember you telling me about that place.' She nodded in contemplation and smiled as she did so.

'They have social clubs up at Autumn Grange. Do you remember me telling you? For non-residents as well. You should go up there and make some friends.'

'Yes I think I might,' replied Molly, although she had no intention of doing so. She didn't want the éclair either. She cut the end piece off and ate it out of politeness.

Sherry had finished hers and was eyeing up Molly's.

'Don't you want that?' she asked.

'I did have rather a large breakfast.'

'Waste not, want not.' Sherry lunged for the bun. She seemed incredibly jolly – as if she'd just had some great news. 'They're from our local patisserie. I hope we don't move too far away. I don't think I could survive without my weekly fix. Then again, you've got a lovely bakery around the corner, haven't you? In fact I think it's even better than ours.' She devoured the second éclair in two bites, with the ease of an anaconda swallowing a ferret.

'Have you had some good weather over here? You look very mocha.'

'Do I?' replied Molly.

'Yes, you do. Very well, in fact.'

Molly heard a small creak upstairs. Harvey had rocked on the chair, she could tell.

'I think I'll have another cup of tea, please. I'm a bit dry after those éclairs. Would you put the kettle on again, Mother? I think I'd like a fresh brew if you don't mind.' Sherry rocked to her feet. 'I'll just pay a little visit. How can you be thirsty and want the toilet at the same time? Seems mad, doesn't it?' Again that frothy laugh. She was a very happy bunny.

And with that she waddled up the stairs, leaving Molly to make a fresh pot of tea. It appeared that Sherry Beardsall was going to be there for another twenty minutes at least.

Upstairs Harvey tried not to rock in the chair. He broke off attention to his newspaper on hearing footsteps on the stairs and remained as still as he could, his ear trained to pick up every sound. He heard the bathroom door open and then, a second later, he saw the door to the room he was sitting in creep open and an enormous fleshy woman with a mop of white blonde hair tiptoed incongruously into the room. She didn't see him because he was half-obscured by a wardrobe door and had a tartan cover pulled up to his nose. But he needn't have worried because she didn't even glance at his side of the room; her attention was firmly fixed on the large desk.

As Harvey watched, she pulled something out of her skirt

pocket and started poking it into the lock of the desk drawer. He wondered if she had tried to open it before, failed and come back with a more specialised tool to trigger the lock. As she bent over to see if there was something blocking the hole, Harvey was presented with a sight that he never wanted to see again. A woman with an arse like two giant uncooked dumplings should never wear a G string, he decided.

'Fuck,' the woman whispered under her breath. 'Fuck fuck fuck.'

Harvey really tried to keep his mouth closed, but the brake badly needed attention.

'You won't find any pies in there, my dear. Only a last will and testament and the house deeds. Or maybe that's what you are looking for?'

Sherry spun around, saw the man in the chair, threw whatever she had in her hand up in the air and screamed as if he were a poltergeist.

Seconds later the house shuddered as Sherry thundered down the stairs and crashed into Molly who was on her way to see what the commotion was all about, though she could make an intelligent guess.

'Ring the police. You've got a burglar upstairs.'

Oh, Harvey.

Then Harvey appeared in the doorway and Sherry screamed again. 'There he is.'

'He's not a burglar, he's a guest,' explained Molly, casting an evil eye at Harvey.

'A guest?' exclaimed Sherry, her face screwed up with revulsion. 'What do you mean *a guest*?'

'Delighted to meet you. Name's Harvey Hoyland.' Impishly, Harvey extended his hand which Sherry viewed with disgust.

'Harvey Hoyland? *The* Harvey Hoyland? The Harvey Hoyland you were married to, Molly?'

I'm going to kill you, Harvey Hoyland, when Sherry has gone.

'Yes,' Molly was forced to say.

Harvey, realising that Sherry wasn't going to shake his hand, dropped it back by his side.

'Sherry was looking for pies in your desk, Molly,' he twinkled.

'We're not having this,' growled Sherry, grabbing her handbag from the table. She was bright crimson in the face and the whites of her eyeballs contrasted madly with it. 'I'll see what my Gram has to say about this.'

'Do give him my best,' said Harvey called after her, with the smoothness of Cary Grant. 'Tell him he still owes me a goldfish.'

Sherry teetered out of the house, rattling her car keys, and stomped down the path towards her car.

'That was a very telling conversation you had with her, my love,' said Harvey, watching Sherry through the window squeezing her bulk into the driver's seat. He hoped the car had reinforced suspension. 'Heard every word through the floor. Voice like a bloody foghorn, but thank goodness for that. Selling up their assets, eh? And trying to bung you in an old people's home. What does that tell you, I wonder?'

'Oh Harvey, what have you done?' said Molly, slumping onto a chair and burying her head in her hands.

'I'm lancing a boil,' said Harvey. 'I don't want to leave you at the mercy of those two. So I'm bringing it on, as the youth of today say.'

Chapter 84

'Will, it's bad news, I'm afraid,' said Shaun, not comfortable at having to deliver it. 'My labourer is coming back full-time tomorrow.'

Will nodded his understanding.

'Look, Shaun, I'm really grateful for the work you've given me already.'

'If I need you again, I'll give you a ring,' said Shaun. 'I was talking to John Silkstone, who's a building contractor in Oxworth. He mentioned he might have something suitable soon.'

'Well, I appreciate that,' Will smiled. 'And if I stop passing out when I get above the twelfth rung, I'll get in touch with him.'

'You ought to see a doctor about that,' said Shaun. 'I'm sure it's fixable.'

'I shall,' said Will. He'd have to. Or he'd starve.

Back to the drawing board after today then, he thought. Who would have reckoned he'd ever be worried about keeping a roof over his head in his profession?

*

'My dear Molly, please don't panic.'

But Harvey might as well have told the tide to stay back. Molly was mentally following Sherry on her way to Dream Hall. She would burst in and tell him all about finding Harvey in the bedroom and Molly could envisage Graham going the same shade of beetroot purple that his father had when he was enraged. Graham would pick up his jacket and follow Sherry out to her car to 'sort this out immediately'. By her calculations, they would be here in ten minutes maximum.

She turned from the window back to Harvey, his mood annoyingly buoyant as he sat in the armchair conducting an imaginary orchestra with his foot.

'Are you sure that's what you saw? Tell me again.'

Harvey dropped a loud sigh. 'Yes I'm very sure. Sherry tiptoed in, as far as a woman of that size can tiptoe anywhere, and she made straight for your desk and started poking around in the lock with this.' He held up the tool which he had retrieved from the floor after Sherry had dropped it. It was like a Swiss army knife, except all the arms looked suspiciously like various kinds of lock-pickers.

'What was she doing in that bedroom in the first place?' Molly muttered to herself. So she'd been right to suspect that Sherry might be snooping around upstairs when she had heard all those tell-tale creaks before.

'I'm no Brain of Britain, my love, but I wouldn't be surprised if she'd had a few cracks at opening that desk already and returned with some specialised equipment this time. Do you keep anything important in it?'

'Yes, all my bank books, premium bonds, some cash for emergencies, passport, house deeds, will.'

'Yes, I suspected as much. You remember when you told me that things of value were going missing ...'

But the conversation was cut short as the squeal of a car tyre dragged Molly's attention back to the window.

'I knew it, they're here. They must have flown.'

'Good, you'll get some answers sooner rather than later then, won't you?' said Harvey, rising to his feet. He wouldn't have admitted this to Molly but he was very curious to see what the years had done to Graham. He couldn't imagine that they'd ironed him out into a decent man who really did care for his mother. Well, his death might be imminent, but he could pay Molly back in some way for her kindness. He could give her some temporary protection until her sister and Bernard came home at least.

Harvey took a deep breath and prepared to meet with his ex-stepson. He was strangely excited. His illness had made him warrior-fearless. There was only one enemy he intended to fall prey to – the last one. He heard Sherry twittering shrilly like a budgie on speed and saw Graham's giant bulk pass the window and the room darkened as if there had been a solar eclipse.

The colour had drained from Molly's face. She felt shaky and panicky. Graham had a loud and scary shouting voice and a clever way of running rings around her verbally. Molly caught a glimpse of his face through the window and he looked furious – and extra-purple. Graham charged into the room, his jacket, bought at a time when he could close it in the middle, was now open and framing his swollen gut like a pair of pin-stripe curtains. He halted and Sherry, unable to stop her momentum at such short notice, barged into his back, which inflamed him even more.

'Well, well, well,' he said. 'If it isn't you, Ronald bloody Biggs.'

'Graham,' coughed Harvey, straightening his back. 'You haven't changed a bit. Alas.'

Graham's head swivelled around to Molly. 'Mother, what

do you think you are doing having *him* in your house? Have you completely lost your mind? Can't you remember what happened last time you had anything to do with him? You nearly had a nervous breakdown. I had to pick up the pieces.'

A picture flashed through Molly's mind of Graham's arms around her, his voice soft in her ear: *Don't worry, Mother. I'll look after you* and she was momentarily weakened by it.

'That was a long time ago, Graham,' said Harvey. 'Things have changed.'

'You haven't changed,' screamed Graham. 'Look at him, Mother. I bet he hasn't got a penny to his name and he's wormed his way back into your house. Why do you think that is, Mother? Hmm? Hmm?'

'He's after your money, Molly dear,' said Sherry, her voice a soft, reasonable antidote to her husband's fury. Good cop, bad cop.

'I most certainly am not. Absolutely no use for it at all,' replied Harvey.

'You don't fool us,' Sherry hissed. 'Once a liar, always a liar. Once a thief, always a thief.'

Harvey let loose a trill of laughter. 'I went to prison once and that was ten years before I even met Molly and I never went back. Now if we are talking about thieves, I suggest we discuss why you, dear lady, were picking at your mother-in-law's desk lock.'

Sherry's voice rose in volume. 'Oh, don't you divert attention away from yourself. You're the only thief in this room and you know it.'

'What were you doing in my bedroom, Sherry?' Molly heard her own voice and couldn't believe she had been brave enough to speak out.

'I . . . I noticed you didn't have a key. I was going to have one made for you. As a surprise,' Sherry said confidently, as if it was a pre-rehearsed answer.

Molly's counter-parry was delivered in a calm, confident voice totally at odds with the tremors claiming her whole body. 'How do you know I didn't have a key? You must have been in that room before to notice there wasn't one in the lock.'

'Of course I went into the room before. I do check around to make sure everything is okay, you know. *I* wouldn't run off with your jewellery.' She purposefully narrowed her eyes at Harvey.

'I do have a key. I keep it safe out of the way of intruders.' Molly's voice was packed with unsaid accusation.

'Don't you dare imply that my wife has anything but your best interest at heart,' said Graham, advancing with his finger extended.

Harvey pushed Molly behind him to a position of safety.

'How's business, Graham? Doing well, are you?'

Graham froze and his eyes widened to their maximum. 'And what's that supposed to mean?'

'Selling up a lot of assets, I hear. This house would be worth a pretty penny to you. What's the plan? To shove your mother in an old people's home and bleed her bank account dry?'

Graham had grown so purple now that his head looked in danger of exploding like a giant grape. 'How ... how bloody dare you suggest that ... that ...'

He was rattled. Harvey had hit the nail on the head. He could read Graham like an open large-print book. But then, he always could.

'Oh, don't tell me that you're terrified your mother might be manipulated into leaving me everything she has, instead of you?' Harvey opened his arms as if he meant to put them around all that Molly owned. 'That's the real reason you're so furious, isn't it? You're not defending your mother, you're safeguarding your inheritance. Well please don't worry, dear boy. I'm dying, as it happens. And I can't take Molly's money with me, even if she stuffed my shroud full of it.'

Sherry was silent for a moment, then she nodded slowly as if she had worked out what Harvey was up to.

'Yes, of course you are. So that's how you managed to get around Mother. The old sympathy card. Very clever.'

Graham was so angry he couldn't talk. Instead, he let loose a series of half words, gasps, and unintelligible sounds.

Harvey turned to Molly. Something was buzzing around his head and wouldn't stop. 'What did she mean just then by: "*I* wouldn't run off with your jewellery"? and then making the point of looking at me?'

'You know bloody well what I meant, you thieving scumbag,' snarled Sherry.

'It doesn't matter,' said Molly. 'It was a long time ago. I've forgotten it.'

Harvey's interest spiked. Sherry's words had obviously been more loaded than he initially thought.

'Molly, what did she mean?'

Sherry opened her mouth and Harvey raised his finger to her. 'You be quiet. I want to hear from Molly.'

'It doesn't matter, Harvey. I think I understand.'

He wanted to hurt her by taking her jewellery, punish her for rejecting him. It was never his prime concern to gamble it away, she knew now. He wouldn't have crushed her like that. That's why he tried to make himself believe he hadn't done it.

Harvey's brow pleated with puzzlement. 'Molly, I have absolutely no idea what you are talking about.'

Sherry started to applaud his confusion. 'Oh don't tell me you're going to blame an early stage of dementia for forgetting.'

'Leave it, Sherry,' snapped Graham. 'We'll see what

Auntie Margaret has to say about all this.' He took hold of his wife's sleeve and attempted to tug her out.

'Whoa. You'll wait there until I get my answer,' said Harvey. 'Molly?'

'Oh, for Christ's sake,' Sherry gave a dry snicker. 'We know all about it. Not only did you walk out on this poor woman but you took all her most precious possessions with you as well.'

Graham pulled harder at Sherry's arm, but her feet appeared glued to the floor.

Hearing it said aloud, especially from the sneering mouth of Sherry, Molly winced.

'What jewellery?' Harvey looked genuinely mystified. 'Molly? What jewellery?'

Molly couldn't look at him. She didn't want to witness Graham and Sherry's enjoyment at his shame.

'Her wedding ring, her engagement ring, presents from the Brandywines ...' Sherry's mouth formed into a triumphant crescent: she was relishing this.

'What?' It was Harvey's turn to be on the back foot. 'You think I would steal from Molly?'

'Ha.' Sherry laughed. 'Once thieving scum, always thieving scum.'

Harvey's hands came out to either side of Molly's face and he forced her to look into his eyes. 'Molly, I swear that when I left, I put my wedding ring in the box with yours. I wasn't worthy to own it. I never took a penny from you.' He laughed soundlessly. 'Please tell me that you haven't believed all these years that I would or could do that to you?'

Molly could barely see him through the mist of tears. She didn't know what to believe. But what was true was that Harvey had walked out of her life without laying claim to anything he had a legal right to, something that had always puzzled her. But if he didn't take the jewellery, who did?

No one had been in the house but Margaret and Bernard and she trusted them with her life.

No, no. It couldn't be. Surely, no.

She remembered Graham's visit the day Harvey had left and the concern her son had shown.

She recalled Graham directing her attention to the empty jewellery box and insisting that there was only one conclusion to be drawn.

'No, no, not that,' Molly cried out. Hurt and disappointment and guilt rose like a huge wave inside her, engulfing her stomach, making her nauseous.

'What is it, my love?' asked Harvey tenderly as Molly's features went through a metamorphosis in front of him. The water in her eyes cleared, her lips narrowed, her jaw hardened. Molly's head swivelled on a smooth slow arc to her son and she said, 'It was you, wasn't it, Graham? You took my jewellery that day.'

'You're deranged, Mother. Get a grip.' He couldn't meet his mother's eyes. 'Come on Sherry, we're going. She won't listen to us.'

'My own son,' Molly could see it in his twitching features, guilt flicking at his eyelids, making them blink madly. He always did that as a little boy when he lied.

The hurt inside her flipped to a raging torrent of anger. She picked up the nearest thing to hand – a cushion from the sofa – and launched it at her son where it hit him squarely in his face. He tottered backwards, and Sherry reached for his arm to steady him.

'Get out! Get out of my house,' Molly yelled with a ferocity in her voice than no one in that room had heard from her before.

'You attacked your own son,' Sherry growled. 'If that isn't an indication that you need some help then I don't know what is.'

'Oh yes, I am mad, very mad indeed,' screamed Molly, picking up another cushion and taking a step towards Sherry with it. 'I'm so mad I could be murderous.'

Graham towed Sherry quickly down the hallway and out of the door. Molly strode behind them, roaring at them.

'How could you, Graham? You let me think that Harvey took it, but *you* did. You stole it from me and let me believe ... all those years ... my own boy!'

Graham threw open the car door and swung his great mass inside. Molly rammed on the glass with her fist, not caring that it hurt, wishing she had the strength to break it and reach in and force him to look at her and tell her it wasn't true.

'How could you? How could you?'

The car started to reverse at a wild speed down the drive and out onto the road. Graham was driving before he had even fastened his safety belt on, he was so eager to escape. Molly stared after the car and she felt something in her die, choked by betrayal. She felt Harvey's arm around her and she turned to him and sobbed on his shoulder.

'Come on, love. I'm so sorry. I'd have let you think it was me to spare you this upset if I'd known.'

'No, no. I'm glad I finally realised what happened.'

But Molly didn't know if what she said was true. Her heart was breaking. For so long she had thought the thief was Harvey and she had learned to live with it. It was as if she had just found her treasures gone all over again.

She thought of the Royal Doulton statue. She knew what had happened now without a shadow of a doubt. Sherry had taken it, and her pen and the silver compact too and God knows what else had gone missing. In the midst of her anger, Molly felt a warm gentle rush of relief. She hadn't been going daft after all. No doubt the Beardsalls would have let her think she'd been going doolally too. All the easier to shoe-horn her into Autumn Grange.

'Let's go and get a coffee at the Teashop on the Corner,' she said. 'I need to get out of the house.'

'Sounds good to me,' said Harvey, lifting up her dear hand and kissing it.

Chapter 85

When Mr Singh came into the teashop he was carrying a bag which looked very much as if it contained a book.

'Good morning, Leni, where is young Ryan?' he asked.

'Stuffing his face in the back,' replied Leni and called him. Ryan emerged with a worried expression on his face as if he had been summoned to account for some misdemeanour.

'Don't look so worried,' laughed Mr Singh. 'Ryan, I have brought you a present.' And he held out the bag. 'Go on, take it.'

'What is it?' asked Ryan.

'If you open it, you'll find out.'

Ryan stepped forward and took it. He opened it carefully and pulled out the book inside.

'It's my favourite novel of all time – *Nineteen Eighty-Four*,' grinned Ryan.

'Not only that, but a first edition, first impression, dated 1949.'

'Mr Singh,' gasped Leni. 'That's worth a lot of money.'

'Alas, not as much as if it had been signed by Mr Orwell, who was sadly hospitalised with tuberculosis just after the book was published and never came home again. But, I suggest that you keep it safely and sell it when you need some funds for university.'

Ryan was stunned into a temporary silence.

'I won't sell it,' he said eventually, holding it like the precious thing it was.

'You have my permission to do so, though,' replied the old surgeon.

'Thanks loads,' said Ryan, almost breathless with joy. 'It's fabulous. Can I keep it here, Leni?'

'My safe is going to be full of your stuff,' Leni winked at him. 'Course you can.'

Ryan almost skipped into the back room.

'That was a kind gesture, Mr Singh,' said Leni. 'Whatever you want today is on the house.'

Mr Singh pulled out his favourite chair. 'You will never make any money, Leni, giving your cakes away.'

'I'm sure that letting you have a slice of cake and a pot of tea today won't bankrupt me,' she smiled at him. 'Now, what's it to be? St Clements or clotted cream mousse pie?'

He was tucking into the pie when Harvey and Molly arrived.

'So lovely to see you,' he greeted them. 'You look well, Harvey.'

'I haven't felt this good in years,' replied Harvey, looking over to check that Molly was all right. She had been quiet in the car, still shell-shocked, he imagined. He wondered when the next instalment of trouble would be. He had no doubt that Graham and Sherry would be out mixing things up with Margaret as soon as she returned. He had that hurdle to cross yet.

He had just ordered two toasted teacakes when Carla bounced in with a broad beaming smile.

'Someone's happy today,' greeted Molly.

'I've been over to the shop to start moving things in,' said

Carla, the smile so big now, her lips could barely contain it. 'I'm opening Wednesday.'

Mr Singh and Harvey applauded. 'That's wonderful,' Mr Singh praised her.

'I know,' Carla clapped her hands together with glee.

'I intend to be your first customer,' said Harvey, behind his hand so Molly couldn't hear.

'You'd be very welcome,' said Carla. She was hungry this morning. All the excitement had given her a proper healthy appetite that she hadn't had in a long time. She ordered a huge piece of the chocolate pie. Today was not a day for dieting.

Through the window Leni could see a van with the name *Northern Deliveries* sign-written on it on the other side of the square.

'Oh, that's for me,' she said. 'Excuse me.' When she went outside to wave over the driver, Mr Singh suddenly leapt up out of his seat and shouted for Ryan.

'Quick everyone, look, whilst Leni is busy,' he said, pulling a folded page from a newspaper from his pocket and handing it over to Harvey. 'Not a word to her. I have recommended the Teashop on the Corner for this.'

Ryan peered over Harvey's shoulder to see that it was a page from the *Daily Trumpet*, featuring a competition to find the most welcoming café in South Yorkshire. The prize was five hundred pounds and a full page of advertising in their new Thursday magazine supplement.

Molly nodded with approval. 'Oh, wouldn't it be lovely if Leni won. She deserves some extra business.'

Carla nodded in agreement. Leni was a darling. She wasn't sure she would have had the guts to take the lease for the shop had Leni not tipped her over the edge towards the decision.

Mr Singh lifted a finger to his lips. 'Not a word,' he

warned Ryan. 'I want to see the surprise on her face when she wins.'

Ryan grinned. He was in a happy mood. After today's wages, he would only be ten pounds short for his Kindle. And as luck would have it, Leni had given him a voucher cut from yesterday's paper. With it he could get ten pounds off a Kindle if he bought it at Tesco. He was going to catch the bus straight from work and buy it.

'She's coming back,' warned Carla, and they all assumed their former positions just as Leni walked in with a handful of small packages.

Harvey noticed that Molly hadn't eaten much of her tea-cake.

'I don't want you to be upset, my love,' he said.

'All these years I thought you—'

Harvey shushed her. 'I acted like a scoundrel and it was an easy conclusion to draw. And you were manipulated by Graham when you were vulnerable. I'm only glad that I didn't die before you realised the truth. I remember how much you treasured those few pieces.'

He wondered who was wearing that beautiful engagement ring now with the diamonds and the oval sapphire which he had chosen for her because it was the same colour as her eyes.

'To think that my own son . . . I always hoped he had some love, some respect for me . . . but I've been fooling myself on that score too. I don't want to leave him anything in my will. I feel like selling up and blowing the lot of my money on something frivolous.'

'You should,' said Harvey. 'Go travelling. See the world.'

'It's too late in life,' replied Molly. 'I'm too old now.'

'Too old? Don't be daft, woman. There are some things it is never too late for: holidays, good friends, happy endings.'

He turned to Mr Singh. 'Pavitar. Please tell Molly that she isn't too old to buy herself a round the world ticket.'

'Not at all,' said Mr Singh with a deep merry chuckle. 'I would be happy to come with you and carry your bags.'

'There you go, I've even found you a chaperone,' laughed Harvey. Then, he suddenly folded over, pressing his chest.

'Harvey,' Molly cried.

'It's all right,' Harvey said, straightening up and letting slip a white lie with his next breath. 'Only a smack of heartburn. Nothing to worry about.'

'You should be resting,' said Pavitar, his serious professional head on. 'It's easy to think you are more well than you are and overdo things.'

'I've never felt better,' Harvey insisted, his eyes bright and twinkling and fixed on Molly. His lovely Molly. Oh, how he adored her. He hoped he would last until Margaret came back home. He wouldn't rest in his grave knowing those fat greedy vultures Graham and Sherry were circling.

Ryan had rushed over with a glass of water.

'Bless you, lad,' said Harvey. 'You're a good boy. I should like to be in one of your classes when you're older. I think you'd make an excellent English teacher. One of those superb pedagogues you remember for all the right reasons.'

'I had an English teacher like that,' put in Molly. 'Oh, she was wonderful. Miss Cole. She was a terrifying woman with a very hairy upper lip but she brought every book we read alive. Oh, I remember reading *Great Expectations* and thinking what a fascinating creature Miss Havisham was.'

'Do you know that book, Ryan?' asked Mr Singh.

'Yep,' said Ryan. 'Pip's sister was awful. She's like my brother Leslie. Right bully.'

'Yes, Ryan, she was. I always did want to kick Joe up the bottom and tell him to stop being so henpecked,' Molly smiled.

'Can I get you anything, Harvey?' asked Leni, her face full of concern.

'I have all I need,' said Harvey. He would miss this little world of warmth and camaraderie. He wondered if God would allow him to visit occasionally on a Tuesday, to sit invisibly in a chair and drift past the cabinets full of literary gifts and listen to the banter about Marley's ghost, that bastard Heathcliff and old cobwebby brides. Harvey Hoyland thought he could handle death quite easily if he could do that.

Chapter 86

Leni called a cheery Sunday 'Good morning' to Shaun as she walked across the square from her car to her teashop. He waved back with some reluctance, as if his politeness had won over his will. She wondered if there had ever been a Mrs McCarthy and if she had broken his heart and that was why he pulled away from the world.

She put the cat basket down and opened the door for Mr Bingley. As usual, he took his time about leaving the warm blanket inside. And when he did, he walked straight across to his regular bed in the corner.

Leni attached a new postcard to Anne's wall.

Hope all is well at home. Sunshiney and
lovely here, mummy. Give Mr Bingley a
big kiss from me.
Wish you were here.
Loads of love
Anne X

Leni stood back to look at all the postcards. Her vision instantly blurred with tears.

'Oh Annie, I miss you so much,' said Leni, her hand

coming out, touching the latest of the postcards. She thought of her daughter, slim and tall like her ex-husband, but with her colouring; dark hair, eyes a combination of green and muddy brown. She turned quickly away and towards the day's work. She had a lot of photographs to take of the new stock for the internet site. There was no point being maudlin, wishing her daughter was here with her.

*

Margaret and Bernard had barely got through the door at three-thirty p.m. when the phone started ringing.

'Oh for goodness sake, let the answerphone pick it up,' said Bernard. 'It can't be anything important.'

'There are nine messages saved,' said Margaret, crossing over to it and seeing the number flash. She pressed the play button.

'Auntie Margaret. If you are there, can you please pick up,' came a horribly familiar voice through the machine speaker. 'It's about Mother. It's urgent, I must speak to you.'

'God, it's Graham,' said Margaret. He never rang so it must be serious. She didn't even realise he had her number.

The second message was also from Graham. 'Hello, hello. Are you there, Auntie Margaret? Uncle Bernard?' Then followed a mumbled impatient aside about old people not having mobile phones before the receiver was put down.

'Are all of them from him?' asked Bernard, more concerned now.

'Can you please ring me, Auntie Margaret? It's about Mother. I have to talk to you. She's gone mad.'

Margaret and Bernard looked at each other.

Without hearing more messages, Margaret lifted the receiver and dialled the repeated number listed on the incoming call register. She pressed the speakerphone button so Bernard could hear too. It was answered almost immediately.

'Graham, Graham, it's Margaret. We've just this minute got in from holiday. What is it? What's wrong?'

'Mother has gone barmy,' screeched Graham. 'I don't think it's unreasonable to have her mentally assessed. I'll be over in ten minutes. Don't go over to her house until you've seen me.'

'Graham ...' But he had gone.

Margaret put down the phone. Bernard was looking at her expectantly.

'I didn't catch the last part of what he said. He was half-hysterical. He's coming over straightaway, and then what? We better go over to Molly's and see what's wrong.'

'He said not to and to wait for him.' Margaret was worried. What on earth could warrant Graham being so concerned over his mother? It didn't bode well at all.

Chapter 87

Leni was in the back room pricing up some notepads when she heard the shop door crash open and slam shut again. She got up from the table and walked into the teashop and there she found Ryan sitting at a table, his head down on his arms, his shoulders shaking with sobs.

She rushed over and pulled up a chair at the side of him.

'Ryan, whatever is the matter? Are you all right, love?'

'No, I'm not,' said Ryan, lifting his head. His face was red and tear-stained as if he had been crying for a long time. 'He's taken my Kindle and flogged it.'

'Who has?'

'Our Leslie. Me brother. He took it out of my room when I was asleep. The box is missing as well. He's flogged it. And he's going to kill me because I've thrown his wraps down the bog. I'm dead.'

Ryan's head dropped down again and he howled.

'Oh love,' Leni said, and put her hand on his shoulder. And Ryan sobbed harder, then suddenly turned to her and threw his arms around her and cried into her neck. And Leni held him tightly and thought how slight he was for a boy of fourteen.

As if suddenly embarrassed by his weakness, Ryan pulled

abruptly away and wiped his nose on the back of his hand.

'Sorry,' he said. 'I'm just so bloody angry. I hadn't even had a chance to download a book.'

Leni handed him over a serviette. 'Let me get you a drink of orange juice. You wipe your eyes and sit there for a minute.'

'Will you lock the door?' asked Ryan, his voice hiccupping with sobs.

'Yes, of course I will,' replied Leni, crossing to the door to drop the latch. Shaun's warning about the O'Gowans flared in her brain and she felt a heavy knot of panic form in her stomach. Especially as, framed in the pane of door glass, she saw a black Fiesta with one red door screech into the grassy middle of the square and then someone got out and started striding purposefully towards the shop.

Chapter 88

Margaret hadn't seen Graham for a few years now, but he hadn't changed, apart from having added a couple more stones of lard to his gut. And his hair had thinned and remarkably got less grey and more yellow-blond. She found herself instinctively curling back her lip and tried, for the sake of politeness, not to. Had she been a cat, the hairs on her back would be standing up and her tail fuzzed to five times its normal size.

Nevertheless she and Bernard listened as objectively as possible to Graham and Sherry's shared account of the nightmare which occurred in Willowfell the previous day.

'She attacked Gram,' Sherry reported, palm flat on her enormous chest as if attempting to still a racing heartbeat. 'His own mother. Physically attacked him.'

'More than that, Sherry. She actually issued a death threat.'

'That doesn't sound like Molly.' Bernard's eyebrows were dipped in concern.

'It didn't look like her either. She was possessed. Possessed by that . . . that man. She was accusing Gram of all sorts. Screaming at him.' Sherry's hand flew up to her forehead. 'It gave Gram a migraine last night. He was nearly sick on the sheepskin rug.'

Margaret was having a real problem fathoming all this out. She was pre-disposed not to believe anything Graham said, but then he could hardly lie about having seen Harvey Hoyland in the house. And he certainly must have been extremely concerned to search out his aunt for help. *Harvey Hoyland.* How had he managed to inveigle his way back into her sister's life? And why – at this time of their lives?

'What was she accusing you of, Graham?' asked Bernard, his calm, calculating barrister's head on.

'Theft. Can you believe?' Sherry answered for him. 'She actually accused Gram of all the things she knows *that man* did. I tell you, we were that far off ringing up to have her sectioned,' and she pincered her thumb and finger, leaving the minutest gap between them.

'She went for me,' said Graham. 'I felt frightened of my own mother.'

'And she was about to go for me too,' added Sherry. 'She had this wild look in her eyes. It was as if she'd suddenly been turned into Russell Crowe.'

Bernard looked at the twenty-eight-stone, six-foot-two man and his rotund five-foot-ten wife and tried to imagine them in a physical confrontation with five-foot-five, seven-stone Molly. She couldn't have done them much damage even if she'd gone at them full pelt.

'It's all that Harvey Hoyland's fault,' put in Graham. 'It has to be.'

'Oh and you haven't heard the best of it,' said Sherry, her chin wobbling like a turkey's wattle. 'He says he's dying. He's actually had the nerve to use that line and the sill ... Molly believes it. He's totally brainwashed her.'

'I think it's best we all go across to Molly's house,' Bernard said calmly, needing to see this phenomenon of a rabid gladiatorial Molly for himself. He didn't wholly trust

Graham's account, but he was concerned about Harvey being back in Willowfell.

Margaret was silent with a steely expression on her face. Bernard recognised that look as one to beware of. The Terminator wouldn't have had a chance against his wife in full matron mode.

'Let's go then, shall we? Now,' she said. No one dared to disobey.

Chapter 89

Leni didn't have time to drop the latch before she was thrown backwards with the force of the door opening and Leslie O'Gowan exploded into the teashop.

'You fucking little bastard!' Leslie launched himself at Ryan who moved like a whip out of the passage of his brother's closed fist. Mr Bingley jumped down off the chair next to Ryan and in an effort to get out of the way, wrong-footed the elder O'Gowan, who banged his knee hard on a table leg. Now Leslie's fury was diverted to the cat. Swearing, he pulled back his foot to kick it but just before it made contact, Ryan barrelled into his brother's side, pinning his arms by clinging on to him with all his might, giving the cat the opportunity to speed off into the back room.

'Get off you little twat,' Leslie screamed, shaking off his brother until Ryan landed on the floor. Again Leslie aimed a kick, which was thwarted this time by Leni, who smashed him on the arm with the cake stand she had just picked up from the counter, complete with half a chocolate pie.

'Fucking 'ell,' winced Leslie, grabbing his arm in pain, then looking down in horror feeling his fingers squish into a mass of mousse adhering to his sleeve – a three-hundred-pound Stone Island sleeve at that – which ratcheted his anger up several notches. He shoved Leni and she crashed hard into the wall, then as he turned round, his younger brother rammed into his stomach sending him flying backwards. Leslie tried to right himself from falling but his foot slid forwards on a patch of cake until he was virtually doing the splits. Then Leslie felt himself hauled upwards to his feet and slammed against the wall and a man with scary blue-green eyes was gripping his shirt at both sides of his neck.

'Get fucking off or I'll kill ya,' spat Leslie, lips peeled back from his cheesy teeth.

'Oh you will, will you? Well, I'll tell you what I think shall I? I think you better leave,' said Shaun with arctic menacing calm. 'And I also think you better not come back here ever again.'

'Do you know who I fucking am?' Leslie sniffled, the intimidation effect totally cancelled out by the sight of pastry and mousse smashed flat on his head.

'Oh yeah,' Shaun laughed, very unpleasantly. 'I know exactly who you are, Leslie O'Gowan. And you want to ask your daddy who you've just threatened. Then stand well back whilst he shits himself.'

Leslie lifted his head, locking eyes with the man who was holding him as firmly as chain. He didn't recognise him, but there was something about him that told him he would be wise to take a step down from his high horse. That accent was chilling, the expression on his face was even more so.

'Now, I won't see you or that skip of a car anywhere near here again, do you hear me, Leslie O'Gowan?' It wasn't a request from Shaun. It was a very definite order. 'Do you?' he asked again, shaking him.

'All right. Let go.'

Shaun took a step backwards to let Leslie move. He strode off, head down, still full of swagger. Then at the door, he turned, made brave by distance from the Irishman, and lifted his finger to Ryan.

'Don't you fucking come home.'

Shaun stepped forward, Leslie threw open the door and walked out at speed. Seconds later, they heard the blowy exhaust as the Fiesta raced off.

Shaun turned back towards Leni and Ryan.

'Are you all right?' he addressed them both.

'I think so,' said Leni. 'Thank you.'

'It's fine. You don't grow up like I did without learning how to fight. What the hell was all that about?'

'He nicked my Kindle,' said Ryan, 'so I threw his wraps down the toilet.'

'I presume we aren't talking cheese and tomato wraps?' said Shaun, bringing a breath of light relief to the heavy atmosphere. He was shaking his head at Leni and she knew he was going to say that he told her so. The O'Gowan family were trouble and it was only a matter of time before she realised it too.

God she was so frustrating, thought Shaun. He'd told her what was sure to happen and it had. It was lucky he was still on site. What if he had been a normal man and not heard O'Gowan's car pull up because he was at home where he should be on a late Sunday afternoon? What sort of five-foot wee idiot tries to step in the fighting line of a twenty-year-old O'Gowan nutter? Especially to stop him hitting someone she barely knows?

'Not so sniffy about me being on surveillance duties now, are you?' he levelled at Leni.

'No,' she replied. He saw that she was shaking and his hand almost came out to her arm. Almost.

'Now what?' Shaun said.

'Ryan, is there anyone I can ring to come and fetch you?' asked Leni gently.

Ryan shook his head from side to side. 'Nobody.'

'Just great,' said Shaun, lifting his arms and dropping them.

'Then he'll come home with me,' said Leni. 'There's no way he's going back to that man.'

'Are you mad?' That was taking do-gooding to an insane degree, thought Shaun. How could she take in a virtual stranger from *that* family? Was she asking to get murdered in her bed? He turned to Ryan. 'Where's your father?'

'He's living with Orange Shannon.'

'I'm presuming that's his girlfriend. You'll have to go to him then.'

'No chance,' said Ryan. 'I don't even know where they're staying.'

'Jeez,' Shaun shook his head with impatience. 'Where's your sister?'

'Dunno. Haven't heard from her since last year.'

'What about aunties and uncles?'

'Dun't have any.'

'It is not possible with a family your size that there is no one to look after you,' said Shaun, almost laughing with disbelief. Then something rapped on the inside of his brain as if to remind him of his own circumstances. *Hello Shaun McCarthy – are you in there? Shaun McCarthy who couldn't remember how many brothers and sisters he had. Or what happened to his mother. Whose birth certificate says that his father is unknown.* Chances were, being poor Irish Catholics, that he had aunties and uncles aplenty, although not one of them had stepped in to look after him.

He had never had the slightest inclination to try to find his family. They were linked by blood only. And in these days of promiscuity and careless contraception, so were half the population probably. He could never understand why, on those TV programmes, people reconciled with a relative they'd never seen, acted as if they were suddenly fused into one being of shared history and experience. How could they? Blood wasn't thicker than water. It was merely a different colour.

'There's only our Leslie.' Ryan's head dipped and Shaun saw a tear-splash land on his trousers. 'Fin's in prison and our Josh is on remand.'

'What a surprise,' said Shaun.

Unbidden he heard the echo of a soft female voice in his head: *Treat a person as if they were what they should be and they will become that person.* Sister Rose-Maria. That old nun with the wrinkled face and thin lips and the kindest eyes he had ever seen in his life. *Shaun McCarthy, don't let your past experiences harm your future. You can't escape what has happened, but you can learn from it.* She looked at him with her wolf-grey eyes not only as if she could see right into his soul with them, but as if she liked what she saw there. *You've got a good heart, Shaun. Don't be like the others who think their past is all the excuse they need to waste their future. Look forward, not backwards.*

She was as wise as an owl and smelt of clean soap, which was as sweet to him as any perfume when he was a boy. He wished he could have told her how much her compassion had meant to him and that it set him on the right path. Sister Rose-Maria gave him the first seeds of his self-worth and over the years they had taken root in his soul.

'Ryan. You'll come home with me tonight. All right?' said Leni. 'We'll work out the rest later, but I think for now that might be the best move.'

Ryan nodded and tried to wipe his eyes without anyone seeing him.

Shaun watched Leni search in her bag for her car keys. Her hands were trembling.

'You can't drive home in that state,' he said. 'I'll take you.

If you give me the keys, I'll get one of the lads to help me get your car to you later.'

'Thank you, but I'll be fine,' Leni smiled and promptly dropped the ring of keys on the floor.

'You want to risk crashing with a wee boy in the car?'

Leni, bending to pick up the keys, momentarily froze as if his words had immobilised her. When she was fully straightened she lifted her eyes to his and said, 'Yes, you're right. We will be happy to accept a lift. Thank you.'

Shaun held out his hand for the key, which Leni separated from the keyring before giving it to him.

'Come on then. Lock up. I think you can safely call it a day.'

Leni touched Ryan gently on the arm. 'Are you okay coming home with me?'

'If you are,' said Ryan.

'Come on then,' said Shaun. 'I'll take you both home.'

Chapter 90

Margaret marched straight into her sister's house to find Molly alone in the kitchen washing up. She looked like the same old Molly, from the back at least, and not a woman frothing at the mouth who had grown horns on her forehead and had been overtaken by a demonic force.

Molly turned around and any joy she might have felt at seeing her sister and Bernard was dampened by the sight of Graham and Sherry behind them.

'Molly,' said Margaret, not approaching her sister for what would have been a natural hug of greeting. 'How are you?'

'I'm fine, Margaret,' replied Molly suspiciously, her eyes flicking across the crowd now in her kitchen. 'Did you have a good holiday?'

'Oh please dispense with the small talk,' said Graham with a spray of saliva. 'I've told Auntie Margaret all about it, Mother.'

Molly folded her arms and she leant back against the sink. 'Oh you have, have you, Graham? Told your Aunt Margaret how you let an innocent man take the blame for stealing from me, when all the time it was you? Did you tell her that bit?'

'See?' Graham threw up his hands and swivelled his head from his aunt to his uncle.

'Oh and, Sherry, I worked out that you stole my Royal Doulton figurine. I found it in an antiques shop in Holmfirth. How many other things have you taken from the house that you thought I wouldn't notice?'

'Pardon?' Sherry's cheeks were suffusing with colour.

'Molly dear, what's been happening whilst we were away?' said Bernard. 'Are you all right?'

'I'll tell you what's been happening, shall I?' Molly's eyes narrowed to dark slits as they locked on to her son and his enormous blubbery wife. 'Harvey came to see me because he's dying of a heart condition. I took him in. He caught my wonderful, concerned blancmange of a daughter-in-law over there trying to break into the desk where all my private documents are kept. I'm presuming it isn't the first time she's been snooping around upstairs because I've heard her walking about in there before, and things have been going missing from the house. So off she goes scurrying to Moby Dick there and both of them are thrown into total panic because suddenly their inheritance doesn't look one hundred per cent safe any more. God forbid I might spend some. That's what's happened. No doubt they've come to you with some cock and bull story about me going bananas? Are they attempting to get you on side to have me sectioned, Bernard, so they can apply for power of attorney and shove me into Autumn Grange to rot in a corner?'

'You aren't well, Mother. You physically attacked me,' yelped Graham.

'Oh for goodness sake, I threw a cushion at you, you big wet lettuce,' Molly tutted, shaking her head at the absurdity of it. 'I tell you what, that's nothing compared with what I'd like to do to the pair of you after finding out that you've both stolen from this house. Did you know that he'd done that to me, Sherry? And you, *Gram,* were you aware that your wife was pilfering? I always wondered what force had drawn you two together and now I think I can guess. You're both a pair of blooming crooks.'

Margaret turned to face her nephew. 'Is this true, Graham?'

'Don't be ridiculous. My mother seems to have lost the ability to determine lies from truth. Harvey Hoyland is no more dying than I am. He's still as big a charlatan as he ever was and she needs protecting from him. Be honest, have you ever seen her like this?' He appealed to his aunt and looked as if he were about to cry. 'Throw him out, Auntie Margaret. It's your house after all.'

'It's your mother's house and always was,' said Bernard firmly.

'I've had enough of this,' snapped Margaret. 'Where is he – the man at the centre of it all? In here, presumably?' She strode off in the direction of the lounge, Sherry and Graham trotting behind.

Harvey had his hands in his lap, his head on his chest as he dozed.

'Oh yes there he is, sitting in the armchair, sleeping like an innocent baby,' sniffed Sherry.

Harvey's eyes flittered awake but before he could lift his head and say a word, Margaret spun on her heel and addressed Graham and Sherry.

'You two – out. This is your mother's business, not mine and certainly not yours. Leave.' She flapped her hand at them.

'You are joking,' humphed Sherry. 'After everything we've just told you?'

Margaret's expression told Sherry that she most definitely was not joking.

Sherry gave an incredulous laugh. 'This is ridic—'

'I said OUT.'

Margaret's voice was enough to make the Beardsalls scuttle towards the door.

'You haven't heard the last of this,' spluttered Graham as a parting shot.

'Oh, I think we have,' said Margaret. 'Bernard, make sure they've left.'

'Hello Margaret,' said Harvey, his eyes now fully focused on proceedings. 'You haven't changed.' But he said this with a fond smile.

'As for you,' Margaret turned to Harvey, 'you need to rest. Molly, if those two come anywhere near you, you ring Bernard and me straightaway.' And her arms came around her sister and she squeezed her tightly. 'I've had the most wonderful holiday but I've missed you, darling,' she said tenderly.

Chapter 91

'Where are we going?' asked Leni, as Shaun turned right when he should have turned left on Higher Hoppleton Lane.

'I've left my drill. I'm calling home to get a spare. You need a bolt on your door.' He'd noticed on his last visit that she didn't have one. He thought she might benefit from some extra security, especially now.

'Did you see our Leslie slip in the chocolate cake, Mr McCarthy?' came Ryan's giggle-filled voice from the back. 'He must have split his nuts.'

'Ryan.' Leni's voice was disapproving.

'Cat all right?' said Shaun, trying not to let the smile show on his face.

Ryan was poking his finger through Mr Bingley's carry case. 'He's purring. Leslie missed him. I'd have killed him if he had hurt him.'

'Thank you for this, Mr McCarthy,' said Leni again. 'It's much appreciated.'

Shaun made a grunting noise as if embarrassed by her gratitude. He drove on in silence until he swung into a twisting private road and braked outside his gothic-style house.

'This where you live? Wow,' said Ryan, seemingly very

impressed. 'Any chance I could go to your toilet, Mr McCarthy, please?'

'Erm, yeah, of course. Come in.' Then, without thinking, he extended the invite to Leni. 'Come in yourself, and wait if you like,' he said, then wished he hadn't. He was only going to be a couple of minutes – he didn't have to say that.

Leni got out of the car and followed Shaun and Ryan down the path to the front door.

'It's like the house in *Psycho*,' said Ryan, his head at a severe angle as he looked up at the high roof.

'Thanks very much,' said Shaun, not attempting to hide his indignation.

'In a good way though,' added Ryan, hopping from foot to foot now.

Shaun pushed the door open to let Ryan in first. 'Straight forward through the kitchen and it's the end door you need.' Ryan sped off. Shaun stood aside to let Leni in. 'Take a seat, I'll not be a moment.'

'Thank you,' she said. There was none of the usual strength in her voice, he noted. She was as meek as her cat. He saw her sit down tentatively at the large kitchen table and wondered if she was in pain. She'd possibly hurt her back when Leslie O'Gowan threw her against the wall; not that he could ask to inspect any injury. A sudden vision of him seated where she was, Leni standing between his legs lifting her blouse to allow him to search for damage rose unbidden in his head. He thought her skin would be pale and soft and fragranced.

Shaun strode off fast as much to escape the image as to be quick and get his drill, which, as luck would have it, wasn't where he thought it was. Then he remembered that he'd left it in the garage.

As Leni waited in the kitchen she looked around admiringly

at the size of the room and the design. She guessed Shaun McCarthy had made the units himself. They were rustic oak, designed to look as if they'd been there for many years. It was a kitchen she suspected he didn't use that much because of how pristine it was. She wondered if he had refurbished the house for himself or with a view to selling on. It was certainly a big chunk of building for a single man. The kitchen was perfect and she imagined the rest of the house would be finished off to the same standard, but it was lacking something – little touches that turned a house into a home, that softened and comforted: flowers in a pot in the windowsill, a cushion on a seat that indicated it might be a reading chair, pictures, well-used recipe books on a shelf.

Ryan appeared in the kitchen doorway, puffing out his cheeks with relief.

'I feel better now,' he said.

'Good,' said Leni with a gentle smile.

Shaun appeared. 'Got it,' he said.

'You have a lovely house, Mr McCarthy,' said Leni.

'It's all right,' said Shaun, following her to the door, catching the light honeyed perfume that trailed behind her.

*

Bernard and Molly were in the kitchen making chips and fried eggs, lots of bread and butter and a big pot of tea. Harvey had waited until they were both out of earshot before he asked the question.

'So, Margaret, who did you see waiting for me?'

'What do you mean?' Margaret replied with gruff indignation.

'Someone is here, aren't they? To take me across the river Styx.' His blue eyes fixed on hers and his eyebrows raised to their limit.

'Don't be daft. I haven't seen anything like that for years.'

'It would be a comfort to know,' Harvey said. 'Unless it's an old bloke with a handlebar moustache and a walking stick. That would be Uncle Selwyn. Vile old bugger.'

'There's no one but us in this room,' said Margaret, her back as stiff as her voice. 'Now, was that true about you not taking our Molly's jewellery when you left?'

'On my life,' said Harvey, 'which doesn't sound like much of a guarantee at the moment, but no. I wouldn't have done that. I knew those pieces in her jewellery box meant the world to her. I even took off my wedding ring and left it with hers in the box before I went. I thought she could at least sell it.'

'We always thought it was strange that you didn't try and get money out of her when you divorced. We presumed you'd taken the jewellery to hurt her because you knew it meant so much to her. Or to sell to pay off your gambling debts,' she added the last phrase with a sniff.

'No, never.' Harvey shook his head slowly from side to side. 'I went to prison once for theft and I came out a changed man. Thieves are the scum of the earth. People and their things are often very entwined, I've learned. When you take someone's possessions, you can rip their heart out as well. That's why I've always travelled light. My treasures are all in here. Memories,' and he tapped the side of his head.

Harvey's eyes locked on to Margaret's and he saw in them that she believed him. A slow smile spread across his lips and he said, 'Thank you.'

She knew what he meant by that.

'There are things I wish I'd said to you, Harvey,' she blurted, her voice shaking with rare tearfulness. 'About Molly. I've never forgiven myself . . .'

'She told me,' smiled Harvey. 'She told me it all.'

'But too late.' Margaret wiped the single tear that was racing down her cheek.

Harvey raised his shoulders and dropped them with a sigh. 'I'm glad I got to know eventually, in the end. It gave me answers to all the questions I'd been pondering about for years. We will part as friends. I hope you and I will too.'

The conversation ended as Bernard came into the room with a tray full of bread and butter, chips and egg.

'I'm ready for this after all that rich food we've had,' he laughed. 'What a feast.'

And Molly and Margaret, Bernard and Harvey broke bread together for the first time in twenty-eight years. And the last.

Chapter 92

If Ryan's eyes grew to saucers when he saw Shaun's house, they were positively dinner plates when he walked into Leni's cottage.

'This is bloody lovely,' he said.

'Oi you, no swearing,' Shaun admonished.

'Sorry,' Ryan made an embarrassed grimace at Leni.

'Ah, don't you worry,' smiled Leni. 'Would you let Mr Bingley out of his carrier please, Ryan? Sit down and put on the TV if you like.'

Ryan took off his shoes and placed them neatly by the door, then he unhooked the catch on the cat carrier. Mr Bingley made a lazy exit and plonked down on the mat in front of the black iron range. Ryan picked up the remote and clicked on the TV.

'He's at home too quick,' said Shaun, unfastening his toolbox and taking out a bolt.

'I'd rather he were like that than scared to move,' said Leni. 'Can I get you a drink? Coffee? Tea? Hot chocolate?'

Shaun asked for a hot chocolate. The cottage was a hot chocolate sort of place, he thought. Leni made three hot chocolates, presuming that Ryan wouldn't say no. She brought them out with a plate of soft-baked cookies which she set on a small table at the side of the sofa. Shaun didn't take a sip until he had fitted a bolt to both the top and bottom of the front door, though it didn't take him long. The chocolate was thick and creamy and for a moment Shaun wished he could take a seat at the side of Ryan on that big cushioned sofa. Sister Rose-Maria had once brought him a cup of hot chocolate when he was ill with mumps. She had a Crunchie hidden in her pocket for him too. Chocolate wasn't allowed in the dormitories usually. It was the first time he had ever had a hot chocolate and it was even nicer than he thought it would taste.

'That'll help get you on your feet,' said Sister Rose-Maria. 'I put an extra spoonful of chocolate in and the bar is a wee present from me for doing so well in maths. I hear you got top marks in the class.'

I did it for you, he was desperate to say to her. *I wanted to show you that I could do it*. But all he really said was 'Thanks, Sister.' And she had chuckled and fixed him with her bright, bright cheerful eyes and somehow he thought she knew what words were inside him reserved for her, even though they wouldn't come out.

'I'm proud of you, Shaun McCarthy. Now eat that chocolate quickly before anyone sees and we both get into trouble,' she had said and ruffled his hair before levering herself to her old feet. And he thought his heart would burst like a balloon inside him with pride. A little went a long way with a starving child.

Shaun checked the front windows. They had locks on them. How could anyone have those and yet a door that a five-year-old could have broken into with a hairgrip?

'You need that door lock changing as well. I'll come and do it soon for you.' He sipped his chocolate and the warmth spread all the way inside him, right down to his toes. 'I'm presuming the back door is the same as this one.'

Leni gave him a puzzled look. 'I don't really know about locks.'

'Okay to go through?' Shaun closed his toolbox, picked it up and gestured to the kitchen.

'Yes of course.'

Her kitchen would have fitted six times into his own at least but it would have given it a lesson in how to be welcoming. Bright yellow checked curtains hung at the windows and a jar of freesias sat in the middle of the small kitchen table, diffusing their sweet heady scent. There was an orange teapot on the table, painted to make it look as if it were a sleeping ginger cat. The door was obscured by a thick brocade curtain woven into a pattern of books on shelves. Leni pulled it to one side.

'Can I make you a sandwich or something?' she asked, as Shaun bent once again to his toolbox.

'I'm fine,' he replied. 'I'll get something at home.'

'That's a lovely kitchen you have to cook in,' Leni remarked.

'I don't cook that much,' said Shaun, plugging in his drill.

'It's a big old house, too. I wish mine were that size.'

'No you don't,' Shaun said, seeing Leni wince and fold over slightly. 'I rattle around in it. Did O'Gowan hurt you?'

'I'm sure it's only a bruise,' she replied. 'If you'll excuse me, I'll just bob in and see if Ryan is okay.'

He watched her as she smoothed her hand over Ryan's hair, enquiring if he was all right. The boy had landed right on his feet here. He wouldn't want to go back to the family home in Ketherwood with its stench of cannabis and grime. And who could blame him? What would *he* have felt like if any of his foster homes had had a house as comforting as this and a woman to greet him with a smile? He didn't know how any of those had ever passed muster to take on children. One house had been so cold he had to sleep in his plimsolls as well as his socks and there was never any water warm enough to take a proper bath in. He imagined Ryan would have a soak later in water hot enough to steam the whole house up, scented with half a bottle of bubble bath that smelt like ice-cream.

'Okay, I'm done,' said Shaun. 'I'll come up with your car later. I'll put the keys through your letter-box so as not to disturb you.'

Leni made a sudden move towards Shaun and he took an instinctive step backwards. 'I was just taking that ball from your coat,' Leni explained. Shaun looked at his sleeve to see a furry ping-pong attached to it.

'It's Mr Bingley's sticky toy,' said Leni.

'Oh.' Shaun pulled it off and handed it to her. He had embarrassed her, moving away from her so quickly as if she revolted him. If only she knew that he wanted her to lean towards him. He wished he could have sunk his nose into her chocolate brown hair and breathed her in. God he was fucked up. He needed to get out of here.

'What do I owe . . .'

Shaun held his hand up. 'It's fine. If you have any funny business with his family, don't hesitate to ring the police. They aren't reasonable. You can't talk to them so don't even try.'

'I promise,' said Leni. 'Thank you.'

Shaun reached for his toolbox. Ryan was now sitting with Mr Bingley on his knee, eating biscuits. If only Shaun had had a temporary mother in his childhood like Leni. Maybe then he wouldn't have grown up into an ice-man, he thought to himself as he walked out of the warm cottage and into the cool July night.

*

He returned an hour later with Leni's car and a couple of black bin bags. It appeared that Leslie O'Gowan had dumped everything his younger brother owned on the teashop doorstep. Shaun gathered up the clothes, school uniform, the socks with worn soles and holes, the tatty trainers, the books, the school bag, a water bottle which looked as if it had been stamped on, some ripped up papers and certificates. He knocked on the door and handed them over without accepting the offer to come in. He thought that he might have been tempted not to leave again if he stepped forward into the warmth and light of Leni Merryman's space.

Chapter 93

'Come and talk to me for a moment,' said Harvey, seeing Molly pass the doorway as she crossed from the bathroom to her bedroom. 'Wasn't that lovely today, having a meal with Bernard and Margaret?'

Molly walked into the room in her pink fluffy dressing gown and matching slippers. Her long snowy hair was loose and lay on her shoulders.

'You look like a young girl,' he grinned, patting the bed cover.

Molly sat down at his side. Harvey took up her hand.

'You are the most perfect woman I ever met. You have a heart as big as a planet.'

'Stop it,' said Molly, giving him a good-humoured slap with the hand he wasn't holding.

'You were quite formidable today too. You could have given Muhammad Ali in his heyday a run for his money.'

Molly grinned. 'Do you know, I think I could have.'

'Did you really love me, Molly?'

She gazed deep into his intense blue eyes and saw again the fit, strapping man she had fallen head over heels with at first sight.

'More than you ever knew,' she replied with a soft smile. 'More than I ever knew.'

'I want you to pack as much life into your years as you can, Molly. You've got a lot of catching up to do.' His fingers smoothed over her hand. He used to love holding it whilst they were walking down the street. He was so proud that someone like him could have landed such a prize as lovely Molly Jones.

'I feel as if we've packed years into this past month,' said Molly, savouring the sensation of his large warm fingers around her own. She used to love holding his hand whenever they walked anywhere. She felt as if she truly belonged to him then, in the nicest possible way. 'And I've loved every second of it.'

'I love you,' Harvey said. Then his face contorted with terrible pain and Molly screamed in fright.

*

Leni felt a flash of panic as she opened up the door to Anne's room. It was *Anne's room*, but she had to put Ryan in here. She hadn't thought forward when she had suggested he sleep here. It was wrong. This was Anne's room, full of her things.

'This your daughter's room?' asked Ryan.

'Yes,' said Leni, her voice constricted with sudden alarm. 'You okay?'

A quiet voice inside Leni told her to get a grip. 'Yes, I'm fine,' she said. 'I'm sorry about all the frills and the pink.'

'I won't touch any of her stuff, you know,' said Ryan, as if he was afraid she might be silently warning him.

'I'd appreciate that,' said Leni. 'But I'll clear out a drawer and some space for you to use. You settle in and I'll get you a towel and a toothbrush.'

'Am I going to school tomorrow?'

'I think I could see to it that you had tomorrow off,' replied Leni wondering what she was going to say to the school to make that possible. Should she ring up and pretend to be his sister? She didn't want to alert any authorities that might swoop in and take the boy away to strange foster parents. For now he would be safe with her and Mr Bingley. In Anne's room.

Chapter 94

Margaret and Bernard came straight over as soon as Molly telephoned them.

'Have you rung for an ambulance?' Margaret asked as soon as she saw Harvey's face. He seemed to have aged twenty years in the hours since she had seen him last.

'No. No ambulances,' cried Harvey. 'I won't go to hospital. I'm staying here.'

Molly's eyes were imploring her sister to make him see reason, but instead Margaret turned to Harvey whilst she rolled up her sleeves.

'Then you've got me as a nurse,' she said. 'Don't say I didn't warn you.'

Harvey's face broke into a smile. 'Molly, can I have some water please?'

'Yes, of course.'

As soon as she had left the room, Harvey held out his hand towards Margaret. She took hold of it and sat down on the bed.

'Margaret. We both know there's no use in ringing for an ambulance because someone is here for me, aren't they? I need to know. Who is it?'

Margaret looked at Bernard who was standing in the doorway.

'Please, Margaret. It would be such a comfort.' Harvey's hand squeezed hers.

'It's a woman,' blurted Margaret, nodding towards the chair in the corner. 'She's sitting very straight. She's elderly, white hair in a tight bun. She's got a grey cat on her knee.'

Serenity spread across Harvey's features. 'How many legs has the cat got?'

'Four,' replied Margaret.

'How many ears?'

'Two.'

'How many eyes?'

'Two. But there's something wrong with the left one. It looks disfigured.'

'You passed the trick questions,' Harvey said with a tired chuckle. 'It's my Nana and Mouser, although I don't think he ever caught a mouse in his life, too bloody spoilt. Nana died when I was five, but I have always remembered her. I was the apple of her eye. It will be so good to see her again.'

Margaret tried to stay strong but tears were sliding down her face. God, she hated having this ability. Now more than she ever did.

'Molly, hurry up, my love,' she called out to her sister.

'I'm here, I'm here.' Molly appeared in the doorway with a tumbler full of water.

'He's fading, Molly,' said Bernard.

Margaret moved away so that Molly could sit at Harvey's side and took the tumbler of water from her. She knew Harvey hadn't wanted it.

Molly took both of his hands in hers.

'Don't leave me,' she sobbed.

'Ah my beautiful girl,' said Harvey. 'You have to promise me that you'll have adventures.'

'I will,' she said, tears pouring down her face. 'I promise.'

'Time to say goodbye, my lovely.' His voice had dropped to a sound barely more audible than a breath, the smile on his lips was closing down before her eyes. She felt his fingers tighten around hers, then they relaxed. Molly held them against her lips kissing them madly, trying to imbue them with life; but Margaret could no longer see the old lady and the grey cat with the funny-shaped eye. That meant Harvey had gone too. He had whispered away from them to another adventure.

Chapter 95

Leni ironed the last of Ryan's shirts. She couldn't get them white, even on a boil wash. She stitched missing buttons on his trousers and his blazer but he needed a totally new uniform. Thank goodness it was almost the end of the summer term. She wondered if he would be with her when the new school year started in September or if his family would claim him back after calming down.

She knew she would be in real trouble with the school if they found out she had lied when she'd rung that morning and said that she was Ryan's brother's girlfriend and that their telephone number had changed. The woman on the end of the phone hadn't seemed to suspect anything though and merely thanked her for letting them know. Leni knew she hadn't really thought this thing through, but what else could she do?

Ryan must have got up to go to the toilet during the night and left his door ajar because Mr Bingley had sneaked in and was asleep on his bed, curled up behind Ryan's legs. The boy was dead to the world. Mr Bingley used to curl up behind Anne's legs just the same. Leni quietly opened the wardrobe and hung the ironed clothes inside, then turned to look a second time at the sleeping shape beneath the quilt and tried to imagine it was Anne, home with her again. Leni closed the door gently and went back downstairs.

Chapter 96

Carla was a mess of excitement and nerves as she loaded up her car on Monday morning. Will came into the kitchen as she was lifting the last box that would fit in her boot.

'Oh God, I didn't wake you, did I?' she said, horrified, because she knew he wasn't working today.

'What? This is a lie-in for me,' he replied. 'I'm used to early mornings. Here, let me,' and he insisted she hand over the box. Martin wouldn't have done that. He wasn't what she would have called 'a gentleman'. She was beginning to wonder what Julie Pride had seen in him when they'd met up again. Maybe if he hadn't won the lottery the relationship really would have fizzled out after the initial flare up of old passions after all.

'I could come and help you, if you like,' said Will as he shut the boot. 'I haven't got anything else to do today.'

'Oh don't be silly,' smiled Carla. 'Not that I don't appreciate the offer.'

'Well that's settled then,' said Will. 'I'll follow you up in the van and bring the rest of the boxes.'

'You don't take no for an answer very well, do you?' she grinned.

He didn't say anything, just winked at her and Carla hurried into her car before he saw her blush.

When she got to Spring Hill, she intended to get a couple of toasties and some coffee from the Teashop on the Corner, but was surprised to see that it wasn't open, which was odd. She hoped everything was all right with Leni.

Carla unpacked the box with the new kettle, the coffee and the cups in it first and was about to pour out when Will arrived with the last two boxes and the sweeping brush.

'It's taking shape isn't it?' said Will, looking at the vases ready waiting for the flowers.

'Yep,' grinned Carla. 'I'm getting my phone line put in this morning and the credit card machine installed this afternoon.'

'You just tell me what sort of counter you need and I'll make it,' said Will, taking a retractable tape measure out of his jacket pocket. 'Won't take me that long. It'll be a bit more professional looking than this table.' Carla had bought a cheap table to set her on for the time being. It would do the job but the thought of a proper purpose-built counter was making her quite giddy.

'I've got some dimensions together.' Carla reached for her notepad. 'Do you need money for materials up front?'

'Naw, it's okay,' said Will with a slow grin. 'I know where you live.'

'Thank you,' said Carla, almost breathless with excitement. 'I can't believe after all these years I am actually going to have my own shop.'

'What about the sign over the door?'

'That's coming first thing Wednesday morning, apparently,' replied Carla. 'And I've decided to have a uniform. Black dress and a white apron. Sort of French-maidy.'

Will puffed out his cheeks. 'That sounds great.'

'Oh God.' Carla was thrown into panic by his reaction. 'I

didn't mean in a pervy way. It's classy. It's got a black cat on the bib thing.'

Will let loose a booming laugh and Carla's joined it.

He didn't admit to Carla that the idea of her in a French Maid outfit was the reason why he suddenly had to go out to his van and take a few moments.

'Everything is happening so fast,' she said when he came back in.

'Yep, and there was you trying to convince us all that you wouldn't be able to run your own place.'

Will seemed to be as thrilled for her as she was, thought Carla, looking at his cheery face.

'Will you be able to manage it all by yourself?' he asked her.

'I might need a part-time assistant. I'll see how it goes,' said Carla. 'If I need help that means I've got good business coming in and can afford it.'

A bucket of self-doubt splashed in her face. *Oh God, I hope I'm doing the right thing*, she thought to herself. Where would she go and what would she do if it all died a death overnight?

It won't, said another voice. A stronger voice. *You're going to be just fine.*

*

Ryan eventually woke at eleven a.m. He might have slept longer had Mr Bingley not decided to snuggle up to his face and his whiskers tickled him awake. He came downstairs yawning, with mussed-up hair and pyjamas that had seen much better days and walked into a kitchen that was rich with the scent of cakes baking.

'That was a mint sleep,' he announced to Leni, who was washing up her giant mixing bowl.

'Glad to hear it. Now, would you like some breakfast?' she asked. 'Or are you going to skip straight to lunch?' She made a pointed look at the clock.

'Breakfast would be nice, thank you,' grinned Ryan.

'Bacon, eggs, sausage? Beans on toast? Omelette? Cereal?'

Ryan's eyes rounded. 'A bacon sarnie?' he half-asked, unsure that Leni wasn't joking.

'Crispy or not crispy? Teacake, toast or bread?'

'Er . . . crispy, and . . . teacake, please.'

'Coming up. Help yourself to orange juice in there.'

Ryan walked tentatively over to the fridge which Leni had just pointed to.

'Go on, there's nothing in there to bite you. Glasses in the cupboard to the right,' she called.

He poured himself a full half-pint of orange juice. 'I like this stuff with bits in. Tastes more real,' he said, lifting the glass to his lips and sipping. From the look on his face, he could have been drinking Cristal champagne.

He wolfed down the bacon sarnie as if he hadn't eaten for a fortnight, then dabbed at the crumbs on his plate with a dampened finger.

'I've washed your clothes and put them in the wardrobe,' Leni said, taking the plate from him and dropping it in the sink.

'God, it's like a hotel,' said Ryan. 'A nice posh one. Can I go and watch some telly please?'

'You go and fill your boots,' said Leni. 'School tomorrow, though.'

But not even the 's' word could dampen Ryan's spirits. He and Mr Bingley watched TV whilst Leni worked on her laptop until it was time for tea. He couldn't remember having a day when he'd been as warm and fed and content as this ever.

Chapter 97

By four o'clock Carla had a working phone line and a credit card machine installed. She had experienced so many tremors of excitement that her bones had almost forgotten how to stop shaking. She wondered if Harvey would honour his promise to be her first customer after all. She allowed herself a moment's reverie where she was taking his credit card and he was typing in his pin number so that he could purchase a huge bouquet for Molly. It was all too weird.

Two months ago she had been Mrs Carla Pride – or so she thought – wife of a not too successful salesman with an okay-ish life, although now she realised that she had settled for much less than she should have. She had been content with the crumbs of affection that her 'over-worked' spouse sprinkled from his table, but she had loved him and supported him hoping that the powers that be at work would eventually recognise his devotion to the company and give him the big fat pay rise he deserved.

Now she was two stone lighter, outright owner of a strange little house that once belonged to a diamond smuggler, standing in her own florist shop and landlady to possibly the nicest man on earth.

Her thoughts drifted to Will, presently away buying materials to make a counter for her. They followed him quite a lot if she dared to admit it to herself. He was a true prize as a tenant: he was considerately quiet when he had to leave early in the mornings, paid his rent on time and even wiped down work surfaces after he had used them – Martin would never have stooped so low. Will Linton wouldn't be single for long. Some very attractive woman would spot him and fall for him and soon he would be asking Carla if he could be released from his rental agreement and he would leave her at the mercy of having to find another tenant. Oh, she hoped that wouldn't be too soon. The thought of not seeing his cheery, cheeky face in the kitchen, hearing him sing in the bath, or chatting to him as the kettle boiled was too sad to think about – especially as she was so happy at the moment.

The idea of him leaving Dundealin made Carla realise she had become far too fond of Will Linton, far too quickly.

Chapter 98

Just after tea, Leni and Ryan both felt a stab of cold fear shoot through them on hearing the sharp knock at the door, although a second later they heard a strong Irish voice say, 'It's me, Shaun.'

Leni jumped up to unbolt the door.

'I came to see that everything was all right with you,' he said as Leni moved aside to let him in.

'Yes, yes, fine and dandy,' replied Leni. 'Come in.'

'Have you got that injury looked at?'

'No,' Leni shook her head, dismissing it. 'It's okay. Really, just a bruise on my back. Can I get you a coffee?'

He wanted to say no, that he'd popped by because he happened to be in the area and it seemed natural to check. He didn't want to get involved. Even though he wasn't in the area and had made a special trip over.

'A wee one would be good, thank you.'

'Ryan?'

'I'm all right, ta. Hello Mr Mac.'

'Hello,' Shaun half-grunted in reply.

'It was strange not seeing the teashop open today,' said Shaun, following Leni into the kitchen.

'I should have put a notice in the window,' mused Leni. 'I hope I didn't miss much custom.'

'The lady at the flower shop called over, I saw. Didn't see anyone else.'

'Ah she must be so excited. Two days to opening.' Leni spooned some coffee into two cups. Shaun's had Mr Rochester's face on it, Leni's had a quotation from *Persuasion: But if Anne will stay, no one so proper, so capable as Anne.*

That summed Leni Merryman up perfectly, thought Shaun. Capable. Her boat coursed confidently through life with its sails slicing through the wind with no account of waiting storms. That's why she had useless locks on her door and was stealing a boy from the roughest family in South Yorkshire. She made King Midas look like Mr Bean.

'Have you thought any more on what you are going to do about the boy?' asked Shaun quietly as he reached behind him and nudged the door between the kitchen and lounge shut.

'The way I see it, Mr McCarthy, I can't *do* anything other than what I am doing.'

'I get the feeling you haven't really considered what you're dealing with,' said Shaun, a sharp impatient note in his voice.

'You think I should drop him back off at a home where he obviously wasn't cared for?' Leni's large mud-coloured eyes rounded at him.

'Do you think his family aren't going to want him back when they find out any child benefits stop coming to them?' Shaun tried not to raise his voice, but it was getting increasingly difficult with Mrs Idealistic here. 'They might not care about the boy, but they'll give a damn about the money they get for him.'

'They can keep drawing their money. I don't want it.'

'Did he go to school today?' Shaun asked, but he knew the answer already. Leni had stayed at home with him, it was clear, and that's why she hadn't opened up the teashop.

'I kept him off. Yesterday was traumatic for him. He'll be going tomorrow as normal.'

'Normal?' Shaun dropped a dry laugh. There was nothing normal about this set-up. 'I bet you didn't ring the school and explain the truth of it. You'll have pretended to be his step-mother or his sister, no doubt.'

She didn't respond, which gave him all the answer he needed.

'Oh, Leni, you'll be wrapping yourself up in a web of lies and it'll do you no good at all. The authorities will have to know what's going on. His doctor, his school need to know a change of address. And when they do, the benefits people will be down on the O'Gowans like hawks wanting their money back. And they'll come looking for you. Because that's what they're like. Nothing is their fault, so you'll be to blame.'

Shaun raked his hand over his cropped peppered hair. Her ship was going to get a cannonball in its side before long. She was too intent on being a do-gooder to see it coming and it would sink her. He didn't want that to happen to her.

Leni put the coffee down in front of Shaun none too gently. It splashed up over the top and landed on the table. She noticed he had called her Leni for the first time and the word coming from his mouth had a strange effect on her.

'I'm taking it one day at a time,' she replied, her voice tight. 'All I know is that what I'm doing feels right. At least right for Ryan. If I turn him in to the care authorities, the chances are he'll be whisked away to strangers. I can fight my own battles, he can't. I can keep him for a couple of weeks without informing anyone, I checked on the internet. We will see what happens after that.'

She hasn't a clue what she's getting into, thought Shaun. He had warned her about employing an O'Gowan and she hadn't listened then and she had no intention of listening now. Maybe if he had left her to get her face smashed in it would have made her realise that the world wasn't made up of cakes and nice china cups and arty-farty stationery. She needed a reality check. He didn't know why he was even bothering to have this conversation, really. It was none of his business. She was nothing to him. But he still didn't want her to get hurt – physically or otherwise.

The coffee was milky and he was able to drink it straight down without it burning his throat. He set his empty mug on the table.

'Thanks for the drink. I'll be away.'

'Thank you,' said Leni, calmly now, the tightness gone from her voice. 'I mean it. You've been very kind.'

Shaun shrugged away the compliment. Leni led the way to the front door. Ryan was playing Candy Crush on an iPad. He waved at Shaun and smiled. Shaun saw in the boy's eyes that he'd been given semi-hero status. An O'Gowan looking up to someone who wasn't another O'Gowan – that was a first. Then he remembered how the string of a boy had tackled his brother to protect the cat and Leni. That wasn't typical O'Gowan behaviour. Then he recalled how Leni had thrown herself at O'Gowan to protect the boy. As a proper mother would do.

As Shaun opened his car door he looked back at the cottage and saw Ryan and Leni framed in the window. He hoped the authorities didn't find out about him. It was better that he stayed in a warm, kind house than experience anything like what he'd had to put up with. He humphed to himself. *Care.* Whoever came up with that word to describe the system he'd been through should have been strung up.

Chapter 99

Molly felt more lost and lonely than she ever had in her whole life. Even with her beloved sister and brother-in-law glued to her side, she didn't know what to do with herself. The house felt empty without Harvey's laugh, his presence, the scent of his aftershave in the air. Molly had sunk her nose into his jacket and inhaled hoping to feel him near again, just for a second, but instead she had felt his loss even more.

Dear Bernard had insisted on dealing with the coroner's office and the funeral director and Molly knew that Harvey could be in no safer hands.

'Darling, is there anything I can do for you?' asked Margaret. 'Do you want me to ring Graham?'

Molly answered by way of a mirthless peal of laughter. 'No. Definitely not.'

She had no doubt that she would hear from her son again though. She expected him to try and prove she was insane and unable to handle her finances. Well, he could shove his power of attorney plans up his giant jacksey. Molly would be ready for him if he tried that one. She had reserves of long-saved fury to vent and a clarity of thought now that she didn't have in her younger days.

Her life had been tossed up in the air these past four weeks and nothing would ever be the same. For so many years her life had felt as if it were running on the wrong rails, a gauge that she had tried to fit to, but never had. Now she knew why; Harvey's return had shifted her life back onto the proper track. He had gone but their brief time together had left her with a precious legacy. She felt she no longer had to try to love a son who would have seen her shoved in an old people's home as soon as he had papers signed to say she was doolally. She had learned that Harvey had loved her and never stopped loving her and would have still loved her had he known what had happened to her in childhood. She thought by telling him that she would feel grimier than ever, but he had made her feel clean, as if all the dirt of the past had been scrubbed from her.

'Margaret, dear, would you take me to the teashop on Spring Hill tomorrow. I'd like to let the people there know about Harvey. They were his friends,' said Molly.

*

Will had worked hours into the night to make a counter for the shop to Carla's specifications. He had cleared a space in the shed and used it as a workshop. She was absolutely delighted with it when he drove up to Spring Hill the next morning and unloaded it out of the van. He found himself comparing her giddy delight with Nicole's reactions whenever he'd given her anything. She had received her presents – and there were a lot of them – with the merest modicum of thanks, as if they were the expected norm. The name Tiffany on a box wouldn't even prod one heartbeat out of sync. And here was a woman leaping about like a Bichon Frisé on amphetamine because he'd knocked together a few pieces of wood so she could put her

Chapter 100

After getting Ryan safely off to school with half a pigsworth of bacon buttie inside him, Leni drove over to Spring Hill, unlocked the shop and walked into her lovely welcoming little world. The only traces that remained of that unpleasant business with Leslie O'Gowan were a few lumps of chocolate pie and cream on the floor and wall that were quickly wiped up with a cloth and the mop. Miraculously she found the glass cake stand still intact and laughed to herself.

She loved the Teashop on the Corner so much. Anne would be so proud of her. She wished she would walk through the door, all sunshine-skinned and smiling. Leni imagined her staring into the cabinets and exclaiming in that full-of-joy voice that she *must* have that handbag, *oh my God, Mum, I've changed my mind. I have to have that Kindle cover instead. Quick get the key, Mum, before I burst with the anticipation.*

Annie always loved opening the boxes of delivered stock at home, seeing the goods. They were both book and stationery mad and every delivery was like a mini Christmas for them.

You need a shop, Mum. You'll be lonely when I'm at uni. It had been Anne's idea.

And now Leni had that shop. And her daughter had never seen it.

Today, she had decided, would be Thomas Hardy Tuesday. Casterbridge custard cake and Obscure coffee and walnut gateau were on offer.

Mr Singh was already there when Will and Carla came over. He was inspecting the cabinets, searching for things to buy that he didn't need but merely wanted to own.

'Come in, come in, how lovely to see you,' he greeted Carla, as if he had suddenly acquired ownership of the teashop. Behind the counter, Leni winked at the couple.

'Carla, look at this, isn't it beautiful?' said Mr Singh, pulling her gently by the sleeve towards the cabinet. He pointed to a wooden writing slope. 'It has secret compartments. It is an exact copy of the one used by Thomas Hardy and today there is ten per cent off. I think I might have to buy it. What do you think?'

'What would you use it for?' asked Will, appraising the workmanship. It was a damned good copy of Victorian woodworking.

'I don't know,' said Mr Singh with a gurgle of a laugh. 'You buy stationery and then work it out later.'

'Exactly,' called Leni. 'There is a lot of coveting going on in the stationery world.'

'Mad,' said Will, shaking his head but smiling.

'You must buy it, of course, Mr Singh. Oh by the way this is Will, my . . .' Carla began to introduce the man at her side and then verbally froze. *Friend* sounded a little presumptuous. *Lodger* sounded slightly condescending. She plumped for 'master counter-maker. I now have a proper reception desk.'

Mr Singh seized Will's hand in a strong man-shake. 'Delighted to meet you,' he said.

'You're in a very good mood today, Mr Singh,' said Leni.

'I am going to be a granddad,' he beamed. 'My little Siana is pregnant. I am going to be *Babba Singh*. Doesn't it sound wonderful?'

'Oh Mr Singh, what fabulous news,' said Leni, clapping her hands together. 'I think that is cause for a celebration. Tea and cakes are on the house for you all.'

'No, no,' protested Mr Singh.

'Oh I insist,' said Leni.

'You are going to be bankrupt soon, I think,' said Mr Singh with a sigh.

'Not whilst you're buying all my stationery,' laughed Leni.

'I wish Molly and Harvey were here,' said Mr Singh. 'I would like to share my news with them also.'

*

Margaret unclipped her seat belt and was about to get out of the car when Molly's hand on her arm stopped her.

'Margaret. When you first walked into the lounge on Sunday with Graham and Sherry, when Harvey was sleeping, was there anyone with him? Is that why you sent Graham and Sherry packing?'

Margaret opened her mouth to protest but she couldn't. She had remembered what Harvey had said about wanting to know because it would be a comfort to him. She couldn't deny her sister the same.

'You saw someone, didn't you?' pressed Molly.

'Yes,' Margaret sighed. 'I saw an old lady. His grandmother, apparently. She died when he was five, Harvey said.'

'A grandmother? I didn't even know he'd met any of them,' said Molly.

'He said that she was a loving, kind woman.'

'I didn't think anyone was kind to him in his family,'

huffed Molly. 'I know he didn't have a lot of love.' Tears spilled over her eyelids.

'Well, his grandmother obviously loved him. She was the one who came for him,' said Margaret. It hurt her to see her sister so sad. She'd been upset too many times in her life.

'Was he happy when you told him?' asked Molly.

'Yes darling. He was.'

'I'm glad,' nodded Molly and her face broke out into a smile. 'Doesn't it give you hope that there's a place to move on to from here? I'll see him again, won't I?'

'I believe so,' said Margaret, reaching for Molly's hand, 'unless I've been imagining these people all my life. Now come on and let's see your friends.'

Margaret linked Molly's arm as they walked across the square to the Teashop on the Corner. Molly pushed open the door and saw Mr Singh standing with raised arms obviously waxing lyrically and passionately about something.

Mr Singh and Margaret recognised each other immediately.

'Matron!' He bounced over and seized her hand to shake it vigorously. 'How lovely to see you again after so many years.'

'Mr Singh,' smiled Margaret, real pleasure in her voice.

'I don't believe it,' Mr Singh beamed at Molly. 'I just wished you were here and here you are. Where is he? Where is Harvey?'

Carla noted that the woman with Molly, although stouter, was very like her. This must be Margaret, the sister Molly protected as a child, the woman who protected Molly as an adult. Harvey wasn't with them. She knew straightaway what must have happened.

'He's gone, Pavitar,' said Molly.

'Oh no. No no no,' said Pavitar Singh, the smile seized and thrown from his lips. 'Dear Molly.' He strode forwards and put his arms around her. Molly felt his tears on her cheek.

All the joy at hearing Pavitar's news gave way to a heavy cloud of real sadness engulfing them. Leni looked felled. *Life is a bastard sometimes*, Carla thought. Harvey and Molly had found each other after all those years and barely had the chance to enjoy it. She thought that if she happened to meet Life in the street, she just might have given it a hard kick in the balls.

'Carla, dear, would you do the flowers for Harvey's funeral? It's on Friday. I know he would have liked that.'

Carla's mind flashed back to the smart elderly man telling her that he would be her first customer. She nodded and said as she wiped at her tears, 'It would be an honour.'

Chapter 101

After work that night, Shaun drove past Leni's house to make sure that all looked peaceful and there weren't any signs of O'Gowans. In a way he wished there were. The boy was one of theirs and they should be turning up at Leni's cottage and demanding he go back with them. What sort of family let one of their own go so easily? That familiar picture of his mother crying, collapsed on the floor being held back from attacking the people who were taking away her children flitted across his mind. He had always wondered why he had never seen her again. Did she fight to see him? In his imagination she had. No woman who was in such distress would have given up easily, he reasoned. He had convinced himself that she had been thwarted at every turn by the authorities and then died of a broken heart. He hadn't ever wanted to find out the truth was any different to that.

There was no sign of disturbances at Thorn Cottage. Through the large picture window he could see Ryan sitting on the sofa and Leni delivering a tray to his lap. The lad had landed on his feet all right there.

He slipped the car into first gear and released the hand brake. What was it about the woman that was getting under his skin so much? He found he was thinking about her far more than he wanted to. Even his house wasn't the same since she had walked into it, as if she had left a residue of light and warmth behind when she left. He opened the door to his kitchen half expecting to see her still sitting at the table, waiting for him. He didn't want to admit to himself that she had shaken up something within him, changed him. He didn't need a relationship, especially with someone so bloody perfect for whom a glass wasn't only half-full, it was brimming with hundreds and thousands and exploding confetti. He was a mess emotionally and no one would raise him to their level, he could only drag them down. He would snuff out her light and her smile if he got too close. It had happened before and it would only happen again. It was better that he fought against the bewitching attraction she held for him.

Chapter 102

By five o'clock on Wednesday morning, Carla was in the market choosing flowers and she was in seventh heaven. She was not alone; Will had taken her in his van as she could really stock up with the extra space the back of his vehicle afforded her. She would need to trade in her car for a more practical work vehicle as soon as possible. A picture of a white van with 'The Lucky Flower Company' lettered on the side, and the image of a black cat, petals around his head, loomed up in her mind and she felt a delicious thrill tremble through her. It didn't feel real – she, Carla Martelli, with her own florist business.

Harvey's funeral was going to be held on Friday and she needed to buy lots of white roses and scented lilies tomorrow, so she would check out what was on offer today. She wanted them to be as fresh and sprightly as possible. She intended to do him proud. His floral tributes would be perfect – it was the least she could do for Molly.

Will was fascinated. 'How do you know what to buy?' he asked, looking around at the early morning trading.

'You get a feel for it after a few years,' answered Carla. 'Obviously you have orders to fulfil and then you need to make sure that you have plenty, and a variety, of flowers to make emergency bouquets if anyone calls in on spec.'

She was delighted to find that her gut instinct was still working and telling her to make sure she bought her ger-beras from Daffo-Jill. Hers always seemed to last a couple of days more than those obtained from anywhere else.

'Lovely to see you again,' called a few of the stall-holders. Daffo-Jill gave her a big hug and took some business cards from her. Carla felt snugly back in her old comfortable niche.

'Bloody 'ell. How many sorts of red roses are there?' Will asked, seeing a stall that had lots of different varieties.

'Ooh, quite a few,' said Carla, pointing to a couple of boxes. 'Those are very popular and are called "Passion" and these gorgeous full-headed velvet ones are "Grand Prix". They're my favourites. Beautiful scent.'

Will recalled walking into his old house on Valentine's Day with three dozen red roses for Nicole. She had raised an obligatory smile and said *thank you* and given him a peck on the cheek, and hours later they'd still been wrapped up in their cellophane because she hadn't transferred them to a vase. She had just had her nails done, was her excuse. The cleaner had done it for her the following day.

At the same time Carla was thinking that Martin had never bought her a single flower in all the time they'd been together. She wondered if he had ever bought Julie any. She would never know. She really ought to stop torturing her-self with questions that would never be answered. Martin was almost totally out of her head. Time would remove the remaining stubborn vestiges.

'Thanks for this, Will,' said Carla as they carried boxes out to his vehicle. 'I need to get a van.'

'Happy to help until you do,' replied Will. And he was, too. Carla was so grateful, and so careful to ensure that he knew she was grateful, and she was eager to do him a good turn as payback. He wouldn't have thought it presumptuous to say that they were friends.

'I'll make it up to you. Not quite sure how,' smiled Carla. 'Want a bouquet?'

Will laughed. 'Bouquet of bacon and eggs would be good.'

'I can do that,' beamed Carla. 'There's a café down the road called The Greasy Spoon but it's really nice and does a top breakfast.'

'That's the sort of payment I like,' grinned Will, closing the back door on the van. He had no job, no money, no home of his own and just the prospect of a paid breakfast to look forward to; but somehow he felt bloody marvellous.

Chapter 103

What an enigma Shaun McCarthy was, thought Leni, watching him across the square through the window. Why did she feel that she annoyed him so much? And why, if she did annoy him so much, was he looking out for her? She was sure she had spotted his car on the road where she lived the previous night. Was he checking that she was okay? It wasn't normal behaviour. But then, who really was she to know what the norm was?

Leni had made a cake for Carla which she intended to take over later. She had decorated it with many coloured sugar-paste flowers and iced the words 'Welcome to Spring Hill Square' on it. The four sides of the cake were studded with tiny edible black cats. She put the cake tin on the counter and made herself a strong coffee. She hadn't slept particularly well, worrying about visits from the O'Gowan brothers; but she put on her best perky face to get Ryan off to school with four Weetabix and a croissant inside him. That boy could eat for England. She decided that she would close the shop for an hour that afternoon and go to Penistone Mill and buy some blue bedding for him. She had given him a key so he could get into the cottage after school. She could imagine what Shaun McCarthy would say about that. He would expect her home to be overrun with drug dealers and emptied out within the day.

Shaun was shouting up at a man on a ladder who was doing something on the roof. She studied him. He wasn't magazine-cover perfect: his nose had a bump in it as if he'd been in one too many fights and his face was always cast in a glower, but he was handsome in a strange way, if not a traditional one. He was powerfully built with eyes that were as bright and piercing as lasers and she knew that under that hard shell of an exterior was a caring soul, she could testify to that. Then again, he acted towards her as if she were a female version of ringworm. She couldn't work him out. He turned quickly to the shop as if sensing she was staring at him and Leni threw herself backwards so she wouldn't be seen. She didn't want him to even suspect that he was on her mind. Whatever ripples of warmth the sight of him might bring to the insides of her, her heart was unavailable. There was no point in even pretending otherwise.

*

By nine-thirty a.m., Carla already had two orders for bouquets to be picked up at lunchtime: a florist in Maltstone had let the very annoyed customer down and he wouldn't allow them to make it up to him, choosing to shift his business instead. The advert she had taken out in the *Barnsley Chronicle* had paid for itself already.

'You go and do your flower thing in the back, I'll man the phones,' commanded Will, seeing that Carla was on the verge of getting into a flap. Plus the sight of her in that black dress and white apron was doing things to him that it shouldn't. It wasn't that it was low-cut or short, quite the opposite, but it did show off Carla's Italian curves to their very best. She managed to look classy and sexy and sweet all at the same time. 'Go on,' he urged when she didn't move.

Carla opened her mouth to protest, heard a voice inside her brain say, *don't you dare turn him down you silly cow,* and shut it again. If this first day was anything to go by, Carla decided that she might need an assistant sooner rather than later.

She listened to Will take a call and smiled to herself. His chirpy cockney accent certainly helped amplify his charm.

'What do you mean your old man doesn't buy you flowers? You should treat yourself to a bouquet as well, love. Every woman deserves flowers . . . Course I buy my missus some blooms. Way to a gel's heart, you can keep your chocolates. Nothing more romantic than a nice big bunch.'

He put down the phone after closing the sale. 'Ker-ching,' he called to Carla. She laughed.

'You're enjoying yourself, aren't you?'

'I most certainly am,' said Will. 'Flirting for a living. I was born to it. Oh, here we go again.' The phone was ringing. 'The Lucky Flower Company, how can I help you?'

Carla twisted some yellow ribbon around the first complete bouquet as she listened to Will's half of the conversation. It was better than a radio play.

'Well, that's very kind of you to give us a go. My missus has been in the flower game since she was a kid . . . best in the business she is . . .'

Missus?

'Totally agree wiv ya, love . . . Funny you should say that, we've just had some business from a firm who were let down . . . not good, not good . . . Well that is great to hear that we can expect more business from you if we make your mum happy and we will . . . Yep . . . got that . . . she's seventy on Friday . . . she must have had you in her fifties then from the sound of your voice . . .'

Carla raised her eyes skyward. What cheese. But the customer was obviously loving it.

'Two hundred quidsworth? That is one serious bouquet ... Are we looking at any particular colours ... ? A mix ... nice traditional arrangement or something a bit avant garde ... ? Traditional – as I thought ... Oh, I think we can throw the delivery in for nothing ... Yep, let me get my pen and take down a few details ... Mrs Ellen Jacobs, Chloe House ... as in the perfume? Love that ... Maltstone ... It's off the main Maltstone Road to the left of the White Rose Corner Shop, private drive ... we'll find it, don't you worry, my darling ... Certainly, Visa is fine ... if you'd give me the long number on the front first.'

A two hundred pound bouquet? Carla gulped in a good way. She went out front when Will came off the phone.

'Who was the customer? Elton John?'

Will read from his notepad. 'No, a Mrs Julie Pride.' He looked up to see Carla had turned into a frozen open-mouthed statue. 'Carla? You all right, love?'

Carla was in total shock.

'*Carla?*' Will prompted.

Carla took a deep steadying breath. 'You've only gone and sold a bouquet to Martin's wife,' she said in mock-cockney.

'Jesus. Want me to ring her back and say you can't do it?'

Carla's lips spread into a slow smile. She clamped her hand over her mouth to stop the giggle jetting out of it.

'You are joking. I'm quite content to take her money. And her future money. Did I hear you say something about more orders if she's happy?' She didn't wait for Will to answer. 'Oh she'll be happy all right. I'll give her mother the best bouquet she's *ever* seen.' Carla laughed. 'Dear God, you couldn't make this up.'

'I expect you'd like me to deliver it though,' said Will. 'I think the future orders might dry up before they start if she suspects she's buying flowers from you.'

'Would you?' asked Carla. Without thinking she put her arms around Will's neck and kissed his cheek. 'What would I do without you?'

It all happened so fast that neither of them, when dissecting it later, could remember who made the next move but suddenly their lips were touching, pressing together, Will's hands were around Carla's back, pulling her closer, then just as abruptly they sprang apart.

'I'm so sorry,' said Will.

'So am I,' said Carla, feeling a blush overtake her whole head, neck and then her shoulders. 'Forget it.'

'Heat of the moment,' said Will, embarrassed that Carla seemed so eager to erase that moment.

'Absolutely,' replied Carla, wanting the floor to rise up and drag her down. Will was obviously totally horrified about what had just happened.

Then a knock on the door rescued them. It was Theresa with a bottle of champagne.

Chapter 104

Bull O'Gowan was easy enough to find. He might have moved house but he still used the same watering holes in Ketherwood where he enjoyed being a big fish in a small pond. Shaun tried the Duke of Wellington first, a dive of the lowest order, but he wasn't in there. He had more success with his second port of call: the Fighting Cock. Bull O'Gowan was sitting at a table with a skinny, over-tanned girl in a very short skirt. If the empties on the table were anything to go by, Bull was on his fourth pint.

Shaun was aware of eyes on the back of his neck as he strode over to Bull, a nickname that O'Gowan enjoyed because of the wild, unpredictable nature of such a huge beast. O'Gowan's natural build was a long streak of piss like the rest of his family, but he'd gathered bulk over the years first through muscle-building, then through bad diet. Really he was more hyena than Bull: a sly, vicious, scavenger.

'I want a word,' Shaun said, a statement, not a request. Bull's head slowly lifted to see who had the audacity to address him so and when he saw that it was Shaun McCarthy, the expletive that he'd been about to spit out stayed put behind his lip.

'Fuck off,' he said to the gum-chewing, tangerine-skinned

girl at his side. Although she looked older, Shaun guessed she was only about seventeen. Bull liked them young and pliant. She tutted in displeasure but obediently moved to the bar. Uninvited, Shaun sat, occupying the chair she had just vacated.

'It's about your boy, Ryan,' Shaun began, not waiting for Bull to get the first word in.

'What's he fucking done?' Bull said, twisting in his chair to fully face Shaun, puffing out his chest so anyone watching them – and they would be – would see that he wasn't threatened by the Irishman. Bull and Shaun had crossed paths just once, years ago, and Bull hadn't come off well at all. The truth was that Shaun was one of the few men that Bull was wary of. Shaun might not have been as wide or as tall as O'Gowan, but he had cement running through his core. And word was that he knew some nasty bastards in Ireland. Bull didn't want to cross him again, but neither did he want anyone to know that.

'He hasn't done anything,' said Shaun. 'Your Leslie has thrown him out on the street. A friend of mine has been putting him up.'

'Leslie's a nutter,' said Bull. 'The lad will be better off away from him.'

Shaun couldn't keep the anger rising in his voice. 'That it, is it? That all you've got to say about it?'

Bull threw up his hands in exasperation. 'What do you want me to fucking do about it? I don't live in the house any more.'

'I don't want you to do anything about it,' said Shaun, his voice now calm but brimming with menace.

'Then why are we having this conversation?' Bull took a slow controlled sip of his pint.

'The lad has been taken in by the woman he works for on Saturdays. She's very fond of him.'

'Money. I get it,' Bull half-laughed, half-grunted. 'She can fuck off.'

'She doesn't want your money.'

Bull's bloated features scrunched up with confusion. 'Then what?'

'She doesn't want trouble from your family.'

Bull lifted his glass again. 'Why would she have any trouble?' and he drained his pint, his great Adam's apple rising and falling like a fairground test-your-strength machine marker.

'Family ties? Loyalty?' Shaun spat at him, frustrated by the huge man's dimness.

Bull let loose a loud, unpleasant bark of laughter. 'Family ties to who? I'm not his fucking father. Have you see him? His head's always stuck in fucking books. Does that sound like an O'Gowan to you?'

Shaun stopped himself from laughing in the big man's face. How could he be that oblivious to the family resemblance? Strip back the years and build-up of blubber and there was no mistaking that Ryan was Bull's son. All the O'Gowan boys had Bull's cat-shaped eyes, high cheekbones and wide mouth, although his were now buried under fat. Shaun might have wanted to hammer that fact into Bull, but that wouldn't help Ryan's case.

Bull gave a long beery burp then stretched to the side and shouted to his girlfriend. 'Shan, get me another in.'

Shaun stood up. There was nothing much else to say here.

'So you have no problem with her making a formal arrangement to look after the boy?'

'Not a paedo is she?' Bull's smirk died on his lips as soon as he registered the flash in Shaun's eyes. 'No,' he said. 'I ain't got a fucking problem.'

'Good,' said Shaun. 'I wouldn't want her to have any

trouble. None at all. She's a very good friend of mine.' The inference was clear: mess with her and you messed with Shaun. 'I'll hold you directly responsible if any one of you lot even look at her in a bad way.'

Bull's girlfriend brought the pint to his table. Bull picked it up and delivered the edge of the glass to his mouth in a smooth arc but Shaun could see the slight tremor in his hand. And Bull knew that he could see it.

'Enjoy your drink,' said Shaun, turning. He had to get out of the place before he exploded. There was a wild, angry place inside him primed to rage. How could anyone give up their child so easily? He half wanted Bull to stand up, tower over him, scream at him, *who the fucking hell do you think you are trying to take my lad off me?* He would have walked away, made Leni realise that family – however dysfunctional it might be – was family and the boy belonged with his own. He might even have respected Bull for seeing him off. But he'd been little better than Pontius Pilate washing his hands of his boy, his own son. Shaun didn't want to believe what he had just witnessed. Because it was all too easy to apply to himself.

Chapter 105

That impulsive kiss they shared for seconds had a ridiculously long-reaching effect. Will and Carla were politeness itself to each other afterwards, but the dynamic had altered between them. There was an awkwardness that hung in the air like a stench.

When they got home, Will went off to the gym and Carla didn't see him for the rest of the evening. And he didn't travel into work with her the next day but said he would meet her there mid-morning. Carla wished she could have rewound time to the moment before she hugged him. Her head was all mixed up now and she felt that a cloud of sadness had appeared above her. On the drive from the flower market, she decided to act as normally as possible, as if nothing untoward had happened. She tried to smile rather than grin when she saw Will walking across the square to the shop at ten.

The second day of trading at The Lucky Flower Company started off slowly, throwing Carla into a worried panic, but then someone called in for an on-spec bouquet just before lunchtime which Carla put together whilst the lady waited. There was a spray on order to be delivered at one so Carla went into the back room to make it up. Will had just put the phone down from a man requesting an anniversary bouquet for the following week when the door-bell tinkled and an unwelcome sight appeared in the shop doorway.

'Well, well, well, I did hear rumours but I wouldn't have believed it had I not seen it for myself. Mr Linton Roofing – a chuffing florist.'

Gerald Scotterfield's sneering face was grinning so hard that his lips were nearly splitting. With him was one of his side-kicks, who laughed at everything he said but alone wouldn't have dared even make eye contact with Will; a wimpy little pilot fish clinging to a shark's back.

Will's brain was telling the rest of his body to keep calm and ride it out.

'I'm helping a friend,' he said as casually as he could. 'What's wrong with that?'

'How's the ladder-climbing? Get dizzy reaching up to them top shelves, do you?' Behind Gerald pilot-fish man in his donkey jacket tittered into his hand.

In the back, Carla stopped what she was doing and lis-tened, not knowing whether to venture out into the front or not. She decided to stay where she was for now.

'Yep. It's a condition called *vertigopia majora*. Comes from years of overworking,' said Will, quite impressed with him-self for making that up on the spot. 'You're pretty safe from getting it, Gerald.'

'Ooooh,' mocked Gerald. 'If you look out of the window, you just might see my new Lotus. Why work hard when you can get others to do the work and you cream off.'

'How the hell can you fit your fat arse in a Lotus?' chuckled Will. 'That why you brought the shoe-horn with you?' Will pointed to the skinny man whose grin instantly faded.

'Anyway, enough of the small talk,' said Gerald, switching

subjects. 'I'm here to give you some business. Thought you might like to send a bouquet to my new bird. Nice big one, full of red roses. Hundred quidsworth.'

'Quite happy to take your order, mate,' said Will, picking up a receipt pad and pen. He didn't like the way that pilot fish had started to smirk again. He should have seen the next part coming really.

Gerald began to slowly dictate the details. 'It's to a Miss Nicole Whitlaw, The Views, Hare Avenue. You know, the road behind the park.'

Time seemed to stand still for a long moment. In his mind's eye, Will saw his hand drop the pen and pad, felt his body leap like a cougar over the reception desk, his arm extend and his fist crash into Gerald's spotty, pudgy face. But in real time, Will felt no more than a single heavy thud of heartbeat as his body instinctively reacted to the mention of Nicole's name. But that was all his senses were going to afford her, and he was as astounded by that as Gerald was.

Will slowly raised his head and said in a voice as straight as a spirit level on the flat, 'You sure you only want to spend a hundred quid? I used to get her hundred and fifty quid bouquets.'

'Make it hundred and sixty then. I can afford it,' Gerald batted back, and for his benefit, Will raised a couple of perfectly impressed eyebrows.

Pilot fish watched quietly as Gerald peeled off eight twenty-pound notes from a big wad retrieved from his pocket. 'I'll have a receipt,' he said.

'I've made it out for a corporate expense, so you can claim it back on your tax,' smiled Will, handing over a written slip of paper.

Gerald snatched it out of his hand and turned to the door. 'Don't you be putting any fucking worms in it or anything,' he called over his shoulder.

'I won't even grace that with a reply,' said Will. 'My missus prides herself a bit more than that.'

Gerald's hand stilled on the door and he swivelled slowly around and a smile crept over his thick wet lips.

'Missus? Not my ex is it? That would be too ironic.'

'Naw. But then again sloppy seconds have never been my thing, Gerald.'

Touché, thought Carla in the back and clenched her fist in supportive victory.

That wiped the smugness right off Gerald's face. But Will didn't feel entirely happy to have won the point.

'Enjoy working with your pansies,' Gerald spat.

'You too.' Will made a point at nodding towards the pilot fish. 'Onwards and upwards, Gerald.' Will forced out his cheeriest and smuggest grin.

Gerald's eyes swept from wall to wall. 'You call this fucking upwards?'

'You have no idea, mate,' nodded Will.

When Carla heard the door close on the customers, she crept cautiously into the front.

'I wasn't eavesdropping, but I did hear most of that. Are you all right, Will?'

'Least I know where Scotterfield heard about my fear of heights from. My dutiful ex-wife. It was bugging me.'

He looks sad, thought Carla. Then again, who could blame him?

'That must have been difficult to hear: that he was buying flowers for her. You could have told him to stuff the order. I would have totally understood.'

'Naw,' Will held up his hand in protest. 'Bothers me less than you think. I'm angry at myself for saying the sloppy seconds line. Kay Scotterfield is a decent person, she doesn't deserve me talking about her with that sort of disrespect. She'll be absolutely gutted that he's left her.'

'He doesn't sound a very nice man,' said Carla. She'd taken a peep through the keyhole to see what Gerald looked like too and the face fitted the voice. He had wet-looking fish lips and a combover that made him look ten years older than he was. She wouldn't have matched him with the glamorous Nicole, whose picture she had found on the internet after taking a sly peek.

'He ain't,' said Will. 'But he has everything Nicole most values in a man: lots of money, lots of people working for him, big house, posh car; and he won't believe his luck that he's landed her so he'll be chucking presents at her left, right and centre. He'll think he's got a proper trophy.' He laughed. God he'd been such a fool and it was so obvious now. Seven years ago, he'd been Scotterfield, unable to believe his luck that a woman of Nicole's calibre couldn't leave him alone. He'd been sucked into her circle of people trying to outdo each other, to be the wealthiest, have the biggest house and the most luxurious holidays. He'd taken his eye off the ball, over-gambling his luck to be 'king of the set', and why? He didn't even like them – they weren't his sort of people. He'd lost sleep, lost weight, lost everything – for an illusion of happiness.

'You want them delivered?' asked Will, pointing to the bouquet which Carla was holding. 'I'll do it for you. Could do with the fresh air.'

'Erm, great,' said Carla. 'I'll get you the address.'

He might have said he was okay, but Carla thought he looked anything but. She fought her natural urge to give him a comforting squeeze. The last one had ruined everything.

Chapter 106

Shaun saw Leni leaving Carla's flower shop and called to her.

'I wanted a quick word,' he said. 'About the O'Gowan boy.'

He saw her stiffen.

'Oh yes,' she said, tightness in her voice.

'I bumped into his father,' said Shaun. He supposed a tweak of the facts would do no harm. 'We had a wee chat. You won't be getting any trouble from his family.'

'Oh thank you,' she said, and he knew that he'd shocked her. Maybe she had been expecting another lecture from him. 'That was very kind of you.'

'Obviously in the short term that takes the pressure off, but maybe you ought to formalise things if you are serious about fostering him.'

'Yes, yes,' she replied, her brow furrowed. He'd assumed she would huff and tell him to mind his own business.

'I'd think carefully about it, of course.' He saw that defensive look spark up in her eyes again and held up his hands in a gesture of peace. 'Look, if these social workers think that you're acting not in the boy's best interests, they could take him away and you might never see him again.'

The angry look waned. 'I know,' she said with a long drawn-out sigh. 'How can they let him go so easily, Mr McCarthy? He's a good boy. A fine boy.'

'One that you haven't known two minutes,' said Shaun, trying to sound sensible rather than biased. 'I don't want to . . .' *see you get hurt* '. . . see this get any worse for anyone.'

He was trying to not sound as protective as he felt. He didn't need to be. Ms Merryman could look after herself, he had no doubt. Besides which, he didn't want to worry about her. She was nothing to him but a tenant. He needed to keep reminding himself of that until it stuck in his thick skull.

'I appreciate your concern,' said Leni. 'I believe in him.' She broke the subject off and changed to another. 'I've just come from the florist shop. It's lovely in there. Have you seen what Carla's done to it?'

'I'm not concerned,' said Shaun sharply. 'As long as everyone pays their rent to me, they can decorate their units in unicorns and fairies for all I care.' And with that he strode away, fighting off the ever-thickening strands of involvement that were binding him to Leni Merryman.

*

After delivering the bouquet to a woman whose pupils dilated more at the handsome delivery man than at the birthday flowers, Will drove to B&Q and made his way over to the familiar ladder section. There were no staff around and even if there were, the way he felt at the moment, he would have been brazen enough to set a ladder up and do what he was about to do in front of them.

He couldn't remember ever before being so self-searching as he had been since yesterday, when he and Carla had kissed in her shop. It had knocked him to the core to discover how much the simple touching of their lips had affected him. It hadn't so much mixed him up as straightened him out.

He'd been sleeping, eating and smiling again since he moved into Dundealin and he'd credited the peace in his soul to dropping all the stresses of his debts. But he'd only been partly right, because he realised when he kissed Carla what a huge contribution she had made to the spring in his step. Her kindness, her gentleness, her friendliness, her humour, her acceptance of him, a skint roofer with a fear of heights, had been a massive reason why his spirit felt as light as a helium-filled balloon. Helping her kit out the shop, sharing fish and chips with her, enjoying her presence in the house were all simple pleasures that made him feel like a man again. She was a bloody gorgeous girl and he had been acting like a tongue-tied teenager in her presence since they'd kissed. He'd never once felt like that with Nicole – they'd gone from nought to sixty on the first date.

Will lifted up the ladder and rested it against the wall and began to climb it. And he kept on climbing it until one of the sales staff saw him above the display shelves and ran over before he fell off and health and safety came down on them like a ton of bricks.

Chapter 107

Carla lifted the bottle of champagne which Theresa and Jonty had brought her yesterday out of the fridge. She hadn't wanted to drink it by herself on the opening day, but tonight, she thought she just might pop out the cork and sink the whole lot, even though she knew it would make her blasted and very probably sick.

Will had left the shop at four saying that he was going to the gym and she didn't expect to see him again that evening. Plus he had helped her in the shop for a couple of days, and she hoped that he didn't presume she'd want the favour to carry on indefinitely and so was trying to subtly extricate himself. She hadn't tried to second-guess his feelings before the kiss: why had things changed so much now?

She was untwisting the wire at the head of the bottle when she heard the outside door open and close again. She thought he would go straight to his flat, but he came into the kitchen instead, carrying his gym bag over his shoulder.

'You're cracking it open, then?' he said, flicking a finger towards the bottle.

'Erm, yes. Would you like a glass?'

She asked but she knew he would refuse. He would have something more important to do.

'Yeah, why not. I'll get the glasses out.'

Oh, that was a shocker. So was the fact that he set three on the table.

'I thought I'd get an extra one, for the guest,' he said.

'The guest?' Carla was confused.

'The massive great fat elephant in the room. It's going to crush my bleedin' lungs if someone don't get rid of it.'

Carla felt her heart jump as if it were a horse just clearing Bechers Brook.

'Carla,' Will sat down at the table. 'Yesterday when ... we ...'

'Oh don't worry,' Carla waved her hands over-dramatically. 'Totally understand. You don't need to explain. It was a funny day, Julie ordering flowers, emotions running high ...'

'Carla, shut up a minute.'

Carla's jaw snapped shut.

'I didn't expect it.'

'I didn't either but ...'

He reached out and put his finger across her lips. 'Shush. Let me speak. Please.'

She nodded and he removed his hand. 'Carla. You're so ... so ... bloody wonderful,' he said and saw her big brown eyes widen at his words. 'I've been thinking how happy I am. I thought it was just the fact that I've got rid of all the crap that was weighing me down – the bills, the business, the worry – but that isn't all of it. Being around you makes me happy. I even climbed a bloody ladder today. Right to the top. The bloke in B&Q nearly had a fit.'

Carla blurted out a laugh. It was a lovely sound, he thought. She even laughed nice.

'Look.' Will raked his hand through his fair wavy hair, a nervous gesture. 'I'm not on the rebound, but I'm still married. Legally. Even if my wife is knocking off my arch enemy. Not that I give a flying toss about that because Nicole don't even cross my mind. My head just wants to think about you.'

He heard Carla give a little gasp and he was encouraged by it. That and the fact that she wasn't screaming and running away from him.

'I'll be up and on my feet again soon, I know I will. I'm not the type to stay down for long; but I have to say now, poor as I am, that I am the most content I've ever been. I don't have anything to offer you, Carla, but I ... I want to take you out to dinner. Won't be the Ivy. And I want to kiss you again. And I think, if you want that, it might be nice to take things slow. Like learning to climb a ladder again.'

'A rung at a time?' said Carla, her voice a rush of joy-laden breath.

'Exactly,' said Will with a sparkling lop-sided grin. 'One lovely sure-step of a rung at a time.'

Chapter 108

Mr Singh was waiting outside the church when the flower-filled hearse arrived. He was wearing a beautifully cut black suit and a black turban. He looked even smarter than usual, which was quite an achievement because he was always immaculately dressed.

Molly managed a sad smile by way of greeting. 'I'm so glad you could come, Pavitar,' she said as he bent to her and put a soft kiss on her cheek, then offered his arm to her without saying a word. He was too upset to speak.

'One of Molly and Harvey's friends from that little teashop,' Margaret explained to Bernard. 'Used to be a surgeon. Marvellous doctor.' She turned her head to look at the flowers in the hearse. They were absolutely beautiful. 'The lass has done a good job, hasn't she?'

'Yes, she has,' said Bernard. He too was choked up. It was all so sad. He wished Molly and Harvey had had more time together. He felt that it was too little compensation that they parted loving each other again.

Carla had left the shop in Will's hands. He had insisted she go to the funeral. Leni had also shut up shop and was there looking odd in black, as everyone was so used to seeing her in bright colours. She looked tiny in her smart coat, a black flower pinned behind her ear.

Mavis Marple had turned up too. She was a professional funeral-attender, after all. She enjoyed the hymns and the occasional drama, and, if she was lucky, the buffet afterwards. She spotted Carla and rushed over, her arms open ready to hug the younger woman.

'How lovely to see you,' she bubbled. 'Your old house has been sold. Very nice couple moved in. He used to be high up in Yorkshire Water but he's deaf now. She's from Thailand. Between you and me I think he bought her. But they seem happy enough. She's called Nom, he's called Norm. Bet that causes a few mix-ups. They've got one of those new cross-breed dogs – a Rotthuahua I think she said. Very funny-looking thing.'

'Have they?' replied Carla, politely, though she had no wish to know anything about the bungalow, in fact, it was as if she had never lived there. More and more her old life with Martin was feeling like a dream because she was no longer the same woman who was married to a man who gave her so little. She was moving on at a rate of knots. She didn't care what Martin and Julie had had or done together, she was just glad she had found a new life whilst she was still young enough to enjoy it. She felt as if she had been let out of a dark box and was now getting fully accustomed to the light.

'Whose funeral is it then? Do you know?' Mavis whispered at her usual thousand decibels.

'It's a very dear old gentleman called Harvey Hoyland,' replied Carla.

'Name doesn't ring a bell,' sniffed Mavis. 'Are they having a buffet after, do you know?'

'A small private one at his brother-in-law's house.'

Mavis huffed whilst giving an Elvis sneer. She wouldn't be able to go to that one then. She hadn't had any breakfast either so she could have a good feast. That was a disappointment.

They all filed into the lovely old Maltstone church. Unlike the last funeral Carla had attended, there were no dramatic scenes to spoil the dignity of the occasion.

Harvey had left a letter outlining his desired funeral plans, which were very short and simple. He had chosen his favourite hymn and requested a cremation rather than a burial.

The letter was in the same pocket in the suitcase as an envelope containing his will and the serviette signed by Placido Domingo. There were also photographs of him at Base Camp Everest, posing with Judi Dench, Sean Connery, Sir Ranulph Fiennes and, as identified by a stunned Bernard, the Sultan of Brunei.

After hearing the story of the impromptu opera, Margaret suggested they play the song, 'Time to Say Goodbye', but Molly refused. She didn't want to think of Harvey's funeral when she heard that song; the memories she would recall were of the night in the restaurant, the diners applauding, his voice and presence filling the room. The song was beribboned in happy full-of-life memories in her head, not sad ones.

So the small select congregation sang 'To Be a Pilgrim', and Bernard read a poem by Henry Scott-Holland which he had heard once at another funeral and thought the words would be a perfect fit for Harvey – and Molly.

Death is nothing at all
I have only slipped away into the next room
I am I and you are you
Whatever we were to each other
That we are still
Call me by my own familiar name

Speak to me in the easy way you always used
Put no difference into your tone
Wear no forced air of solemnity or sorrow
Laugh as we always laughed
At the little jokes we always enjoyed together
Play, smile, think of me, pray for me
Let my name be ever the household word that it always was
Let it be spoken without effort
Without the ghost of a shadow in it
Life means all that it ever was
There is absolute unbroken continuity
What is death but a negligible accident?
Why should I be out of mind
Because I am out of sight?
I am waiting for you for an interval
Somewhere very near
Just around the corner
All is well.
Nothing is past; nothing is lost
One brief moment and all will be as it was before
How we shall laugh at the trouble of parting when we meet
    again!

Pavitar held Molly's hand which felt as tiny and chilled as a new-born bird in his large, solid one. Margaret held her other and Molly felt the warmth from them both coursing through her like electricity and was strengthened by it. She was surrounded by such dear people – her family and her new friends who were already more important to her than her own son.

The vicar was a young man who delivered a wonderful speech made up from information he had gathered from Molly and the Brandywines. He began by saying that Harvey Hoyland was like Austin Powers – an international man of mystery. No one would know the full story of his life now, but it was obviously a grand one. Harvey Hoyland was a man who loved adventures. He was flawed, impulsive, bohemian but he had a good and loving heart. And he died peacefully in the place where he was loved and accepted and cared for.

After the cremation service, Pavitar, Carla and Leni went on to the Brandywine house and they all raised a glass to Harvey's memory.

'Thank you for coming,' Molly said to them all. 'We haven't known each other all that long, but I feel that you were true friends to Harvey and myself. You helped make the time we had together very special.'

She had cried and cried over the past days, but at the funeral she hadn't at all. She would miss him but he had changed her and for the better. She intended to fulfil her promise to him and travel. She wanted to see the sights which he had and she knew she would sense him at her shoulder when she did so.

When everyone had gone, Margaret insisted that Molly should not be alone.

'Go and pack a few things and come back over here.'

'Would you like me to come with you, dear?' asked Bernard.

'No, I can manage,' said Molly, not even wishing to put up any resistance to Margaret's offer. She had always felt safe and secure in the old Brandywine house. It would be the perfect place to recharge her batteries.

The answering machine on her phone was flashing when she walked into Willowfell. When she pressed the button, a female voice started talking.

Hello, this is a message for Mr Harvey Hoyland. I wonder if you could give Sylvia a ring please on Barnsley 534878.

Molly was in no mood to return the call or even to

muster up enough curiosity to wonder what that was about, at least not today. She replayed the message and wrote down the number on a notepad though. Then she went upstairs to change out of the black dress and pack a bag.

She pushed open the door to Harvey's old room. His cologne was on the dressing table. It wasn't an expensive one, but it suited him: it smelt of forests and open air to match the ridiculously free spirit he was. Molly screwed the top off and inhaled and imagined Harvey tipping it into his hands to slap onto his cheeks before they went out to the Teashop on the Corner. He had always been shaved and clean and as smart as his old suits and shirts would allow him to be. She pulled out one of his drawers which was full of socks, all paired into balls. He had few belongings, a couple of ten-pound notes in his wallet only. He had turned up at her door with that battered suitcase and not much else to his name. At least he hadn't had a poor man's funeral. Carla's flowers had been stunning and Bernard had made sure everything had been arranged perfectly. She thought Harvey would have approved.

His will stated very simply that everything he owned he left to Molly. She knew it wouldn't have been very much at all. Stored with that envelope and the one containing his succinct funeral plans, she had found a third in his case, addressed to *My Molly*.

She hadn't felt strong enough to open it before. Now she did. She slit the seal and pulled out the folded paper inside written in his strong slanting hand.

My Lovely Molly
 It is my turn to write a letter to you. If you are reading this, then I am gone and our outings to that wonderful Teashop on the Corner are at an end for me. But they must not be for you. I want you to start by

taking my ashes to Venice – there, that is a command. You cannot go to such a beautiful city alone so you have my blessings to take Pavitar with you. What a wonderful man. I should be happy if you were to become good friends or more. I want you to love and be loved, Molly. I want you to make up for lost time.

Be warned, my love, you will not enjoy this paragraph.

Twenty-five years ago, I recklessly put all the money I had in my wallet at the time on a seven-horse accumulator. Yes, I can imagine what you are thinking now, and how much your head is shaking, but I was an addict for the adrenaline rush. And my – what an afternoon it was, the reckless exploit of a lifetime. It was as if every horse was enchanted and flew across the finish line. I won a lot, and I do mean a lot, of money. And I used it to travel around the world and back again. It was all bloody marvellous. But never perfect, because you weren't there with me and I always missed you.

I hoped that one day I might have the courage to come back to you and take you to the other side of the world but my cowardly hand had to be forced by my condition. I regret that so much.

Molly, my dear, there is a lot of money still left and it is all bequeathed to you, as you will see in my will. On the reverse of this letter are my bank details. Use the money to travel. And start by taking me with you to Venice so that I can lie in the waters there. I think I should enjoy bobbing around with the gondolas.

Live for us both, my darling. I wish I were with you, but know that my heart will stay with you always. Thank you for making my last days so perfectly precious.

All my love – eternally.

Harvey xxx

Molly's legs gave way and she sank onto the bed that Margaret had stripped. Tears dropped onto the letter, then stopped as quickly as they had started.

Yes, I will live for us both, she heard her own voice, strong and loud, inside her say. Her head started buzzing with plans. She would tie up her money and make sure that her niece Melinda inherited the house. Graham and Sherry wouldn't be getting a penny when she shuffled off this mortal coil. She wouldn't wait for Margaret and Bernard to take her on a cruise, she would book one herself. And yes, she would start by going to Venice. She heard Harvey's words whisper to her: *That's my girl.*

Chapter 109

Leni walked into Anne's room with an armful of blue sheets and a blue quilt cover. The material was a print of old boys' adventure books.

She put them down on the chair and started to strip the pink covers off the bed but found she couldn't do it. This was Anne's room. It was here waiting for her to return. There would be no place for her to sleep if this became Ryan's room. And it would start becoming that if she took off the pink covers and put blue ones on.

She looked around at his few possessions, sharing space with Anne's knick-knacks. There was a letter on the desk bearing the school insignia on the right hand side. She picked it up and read it.

Dear Ryan

We are happy to announce that you have been chosen to receive the year literary prize as recommended by your English teacher Mr Birtwistle. This is a tremendous achievement, especially as this is the third year in succession for which you have won it. There will be a prize-giving ceremony on Monday 15th July at 11am if you would like to invite your parents.

Well done, Ryan. Your head of year Mr Threlfall and myself
are delighted for you.
    A Brookland
Principal

Monday. Ryan hadn't said a word to her. But then again,
why should he? She wasn't his parent. She doubted anyone
had ever been to school to witness him receiving a prize.
Maybe he just didn't expect anyone to support him. It
crossed her mind that he had deliberately left it there for her
to see, but she didn't think Ryan had it in him to be that
artful.

She was getting too involved with the boy, she knew. She
couldn't let him replace Anne.

She took a deep breath, whipped off the pink sheets and
put on the blue as quickly as possible. Her eyes rained tears
as she did so.

Chapter 110

Molly stayed with her sister and Bernard until she felt strong enough to return to her house on Monday. They reluctantly let her go.

Molly pushed open the door to Willowfell expecting to feel Harvey's presence lingering there, but she didn't. It was as if he had never been there. He had moved on, taking every trace of him away, as he had done twenty-eight years ago. But this time she didn't feel sad and weakened but strong and empowered. She had things to look forward to. *Live was for the living*, he had told her and she was going to make damned sure she lived it to the full over the next years.

The answering machine was flashing that a message had been recorded. Molly pressed the button to retrieve it and primed herself to hear Sherry's whine, but she was wrong.

Hello, this is Sylvia again with a message for Mr Harvey Hoyland. Could you please give me a ring on Barnsley 543878.

Molly remembered that the woman had rung before. She picked up the phone and dialled. A cheery young female voice answered.

'Good morning, Waterhouse and White. Can I help you?'

'Erm, yes, could I please speak to Sylvia.'

'Yep. I'll just get her for you.'

Waterhouse and White? Were they solicitors? The name rang a faint bell but Molly couldn't think where she had heard it before.

'Sylvia speaking.' It was the woman who had left the messages.

'Hello,' began Molly. 'I wonder if you can help me. You've left a couple of messages for Mr Harvey Hoyland at this number asking him to return your call.'

'Ye-es.' Sylvia's voice acquired an immediate tone of caution.

'I'm afraid he passed away,' said Molly.

'Oh dear, I am sorry,' said Sylvia. Concern now ruling her tone. 'Am I speaking to Molly?'

Molly's forehead puckered in confusion. 'Yes. Yes, you are.'

'Would you be able to come to the shop?' said Sylvia. 'You'll need to bring a form of ID with you but I have something for you. I'll explain when you arrive.'

Sylvia was there to meet Molly when she arrived at Waterhouse and White, which was a jewellers tucked away on a back street off Old Sheffield Road. It was a shop that belonged to another era: very old-fashioned, with a pawn division around the back. Tens of clocks hung on the walls, tick-tocking the time.

Sylvia shook her hand and smiled sympathetically. 'Would you come through to my office,' she requested, lifting up a wooden leaf attached to the counter so that Molly could follow her into a small back room furnished with an old desk, a chair at either side of it.

Sylvia closed the door to afford them some privacy.

'I'm very intrigued by all this,' said Molly.

'I'm so sorry for your loss,' said Sylvia. 'I wish we could

have got this to him sooner. But, these things do take time. Hopefully we've done him proud. Would you mind if I saw some identification? Protocol, I'm afraid.'

Molly took out her passport, two utility bills and her driving licence but Sylvia was satisfied enough with the first form of ID. As Molly was putting everything back in her handbag, Sylvia reached down and unlocked a drawer at the side of her. She took out a package and out of this, she brought a small dark blue oval box and set it on the table in front of Molly.

'Mr Hoyland was most specific about the design. He said it was "in keeping".'

Molly reached over and lifted the velvet box. She opened it to reveal an eternity ring set with oval sapphires and diamonds. It would have matched her beautiful engagement ring, had her son not stolen it.

Her hand flew up to her mouth and she hiccupped a sob.

'It's . . .' she couldn't find the word as she lifted it out. It fitted her ring finger exactly.

'He brought some rings in with him to check the size,' said Sylvia. 'I'm so glad it fits. It's the nicest eternity ring I think I've seen. So exquisitely simple. He was so excited about giving it to you.'

'Thank you,' said Molly, hardly able to raise any volume in her voice.

'He was quite a man, arranging that in secret for you, wasn't he? Such a romantic thing to do for someone you love,' said Sylvia, handing Molly a box of tissues.

'He was one of a kind,' replied Molly with a tearful smile. 'Just like this ring.'

Chapter 111

'And the Literacy prize goes to a young man who is a star in the making. Ryan O'Gowan has secured this award for the third year running. Ryan, come up and receive your prize.'

Ryan stood up to applause from his peers, teachers and other parents at the back of the school hall, hearing one set of hands clapping more loudly than the rest of the others put together.

'Well done, Ryan.'

He recognised the voice above the noise, ringing out like a bell. He looked to the side and he saw her in the crowd, her big smile, her proud eyes, her bright red coat and his heart leapt so high that it threatened to jump out of his mouth. He visibly started to glow, with gratitude, with love as he accepted his prize from the Principal, shaking both his hand and that of his Head of Year, then stood between them whilst they posed for a photograph for the school halls of fame. He waved to Leni, his eyes shining. He didn't think he had ever felt happier. This was a *mint* day – which would be made better only by the fact that there was a brand new Kindle wrapped up in blue paper on his bed awaiting his return.

Chapter 112

Molly was sitting in the garden imagining Harvey going into Waterhouse and White with a design for the ring that he might never see her wearing. She was studying the bright diamonds and the dark blue sapphires, moving her hand this way and that so the sunlight twinkled and bounced off them, when she heard the squeak of the back gate opening. She looked up to see Pavitar Singh.

'I am not disturbing you, am I?' he asked with caution. 'I knocked at the front door but heard no answer.'

'Dear Pavitar, come over and sit down,' said Molly. 'How lovely to see you. Can I get you something to drink?'

'No, I don't want anything,' said Pavitar, bending over Molly and kissing her cheek. 'I came to see how you were.'

'I'm very well,' smiled Molly, patting the space at her side on the swinging bench. 'Enjoying this beautiful summer day.'

It had been a week since the funeral. Pavitar hadn't expected to see her at the tearoom, but he was concerned, all the same.

'I was just thinking that I should go out and visit my friends again,' said Molly.

'We have missed you,' said Pavitar.

'It's funny, but I've been smiling more than I've been grieving this past week. I've even been looking at holiday brochures. I promised to take Harvey to Venice.'

'I am going to the United States to see my daughter and my new grandchild when he or she arrives,' said Pavitar.

'That's wonderful,' said Molly.

'I thought I would stay for some time then fly to Canada and cruise to Alaska.'

Molly's jaw dropped open. 'My, what a trip that would be.'

'Well, you are very welcome to come with me,' laughed Pavitar. 'A more charming travelling companion I cannot think of.'

Molly's laugh chimed along with his.

'I'll go and pack my bag right now.'

Pavitar stopped laughing. 'Really, Molly. Why don't you come with me?'

Molly stopped laughing too. 'Seriously?'

Pavitar threw his arms up. 'Why not? My family would make you most welcome.'

Molly raised her eyebrows and let loose a giggle.

'Why not indeed,' she grinned. She clapped her hands down on her legs. 'Yes. I will.'

'Oh my goodness,' chuckled Pavitar. 'I only came to bring you some news and now I am going to Alaska with you.'

'Oh. What news is that?' asked Molly.

Pavitar took a letter out of his pocket. 'This arrived on Tuesday. I'm so excited about it. Look.'

Molly read:

Dear Pavitar

Thank you for recommending The Tearoom in the Corner for the *Daily Trumpet* Award for Most Welcoming Café in South Yorkshire award. You may wish to attend the venue on

Tuesday 23 July at eleven a.m., as it has been chosen as the winner and we would like to interview you on site and take photographs. We would ask that you keep this information to yourselves so we can employ the element of surprise to the café owner who I understand is Miss Lorraine Merryman.
Best Wishes
Jeremy Spector
Editor

'Oh that's lovely, Pavitar,' she said. 'Give or take the errors. Such a good bit of news after all that has happened.'

'Don't worry. I rang and put them right on all the mistakes.' He lifted Molly's hand into his own. 'You look as if you have lost some weight, dear Molly.'

'I probably have lost a bit,' she sighed. 'But I shall have an enormous slice of cake tomorrow morning at the teashop. I promise. And I shall be all right, yes. I'm going to make sure I have a lot of things to look forward to. Now, have a cup of tea with me, Pavitar. I've missed our chats. Are you reading any good books at the moment?'

And Molly and Pavitar sat in the sunshine, drinking tea and talking. As good friends do.

Chapter 113

Whilst making cakes, the night before Virginia Woolf Tuesday, Leni bobbed her head out of the kitchen to check on Ryan. He was lying on his stomach on the sofa, reading his new Kindle, Mr Bingley a huge contented ginger cushion on his back. The sight of him brought a flurry of tears to Leni's eyes. How much longer would she be allowed to keep him? She really did need to alert the authorities, she knew. She had avoided Shaun for over a week now, knowing that he was bound to ask what was happening.

It would be the end of the summer term on Friday. She couldn't expect Ryan to go to the teashop with her every day for six weeks, but she couldn't leave him alone in the house whilst she worked. Maybe she should go part-time in the summer, or set someone on to help? It was all getting horribly complicated. And there was Anne to think about too. She didn't want Anne slipping into the background. Anne was her daughter, her priority.

Ryan's certificate of achievement was framed and hanging on the lounge wall. Leslie O'Gowan had torn up the certificates from the other years and they were past salvaging, so Leni had made a plaque to stick on the bottom reading 'Three Years Running'.

Shaun's warning that she would be heading for a heap of trouble if she didn't do this the right and proper way was ringing louder in her head with every day that passed. She made the decision that tomorrow she would ring the authorities and hope and pray that they'd do the right thing for Ryan and find him a good home. He shouldn't be with her, really. She didn't want him caught up in the big swirling dark mess that was her life.

Chapter 114

On the big day, Pavitar picked up Molly at ten o'clock and they called in at The Lucky Flower Company to tell Carla and Will what was going to be happening at eleven. Will immediately went over to inform Shaun. The advertising would be good for the whole of Spring Hill Square. Shaun had news of his own – he'd just had a call from the local housing developer John Silkstone asking about sub-contracting some roofing work. Shaun said he was too busy, but he knew a man who might want the job. Will thought he might buy his landlady's lucky black cat a large slice of salmon for his tea tonight. Things were definitely on the up for him.

Carla was equally as smiley. So far she and Will had been to the cinema, the theatre and had two dinner dates. No, they hadn't slept together, she had told a giddy Theresa over coffee, they were both enjoying taking things very slowly. Carla was as skippy as a teenager and the news that lovely Leni had won an award for the Teashop on the Corner was the cherry on today's cake. Even if it was an award issued by the *Daily Trumpet*, the most inept newspaper known to man. She half-expected them not to turn up here at eleven because they had gone to a café in Rotherham.

Leni was delighted to see Molly and gave her a huge hug when she entered with Pavitar and Carla.

'It's so good to be back,' said Molly with a happy sigh. 'Harvey loved it here.'

'I had so many arguments still to have with him,' Pavitar nodded regretfully.

Leni busied herself making tea and coffee, glad of the opportunity to be doing something that took her mind away from the awful task she needed to do that day. She had phoned social services once that morning but put the phone down as soon as it connected. She was too preoccupied to realise that Molly and Pavitar were looking out of the window a lot and Carla was sitting in the tearoom long after she had finished her coffee. She didn't even notice when her three customers started to grin like loons and nudge each other. Leni had no idea what was happening when the teashop door opened and a bunch of strangers bearing recording equipment strode in.

'Leonora Merryman?' asked a woman with a microphone, walking up to her. 'Hi, I'm Ailsa Shaw from Trumpet FM.'

A photographer at Ailsa's shoulder levelled his camera at Leni and there was a flash.

'Congratulations, Leonora Merryman of the Coffee Shop in the Corner of Spring Hill Square. You have won the *Daily Trumpet* Most Welcoming Café in South Yorkshire award. Now, folks, this is a big surprise for Leonora who doesn't know anything about it. What are your immediate thoughts, Leonora?'

Leni's face seemed to drain of colour before Carla's eyes. She didn't look wholly comfortable with all this attention.

'I'm … I'm …' was all Leni managed.

The photographer was adjusting his camera and setting up a remote flash on the counter.

'Absolutely gobsmacked,' reported a delighted Ailsa. 'Now how long has the Coffee Shop on the Corner been here?'

Clearly annoyed by the inaccuracy, Pavitar stepped forward. 'Excuse me, it's the Teashop on the Corner,' he said.

'Sorry, sorry,' gushed Ailsa. 'The Teashop on the Corner, folks. We're on live broadcast so remember it's the Teashop not the . . . whatever I said before.'

Leni's totally frozen voice was no good for a live broadcast, so Ailsa turned back to Pavitar.

'We're going to have a word with one of the teashop's satisfied customers. And your name, sir?'

'Pavitar Singh,' he replied proudly. 'And this is the best café in the world, never mind South Yorkshire. Leni Merryman makes the most delicious tea and cakes on the planet.'

Ailsa let loose a tinkly laugh. 'Leonora is clearly in a state of delighted shock, folks. Remember to buy the *Daily Trumpet* on Thursday and see for yourself where we are today in our new supplement. Those cakes look fantastic. Are they home-made, Leonora?'

'Yes,' Leni replied, the word flat.

There is something wrong here, thought Carla. Leni was beyond uncomfortable. No one else seemed to notice how startled Leni appeared by the camera lens. It was the first time that Carla had seen her without a smile on her face. Leni looked totally bewildered, like an animal used to cover which had been suddenly exposed. Then Shaun walked in and Carla could tell immediately that he saw Leni's trauma too.

The photographer started taking pictures of Leni as Ailsa walked around the teashop and began to report what was in the cabinets to the listeners of Trumpet FM. Pavitar and Molly were chatting to her, pointing out the gifts, and then they moved on to the wall of postcards from Anne.

Carla watched Leni trying to pose for photographs, her great big mud-coloured eyes reflecting the worst kind of discomfort and felt awash with guilt that she had been complicit in all this. She wanted to bundle her friend out of the door and rescue her but she was trapped within a cage of strangers.

The photographer was asking Leni to cut a slice of cake. He took a picture of her handing it over to Ailsa, then snapped one of the spaghetti-thin reporter eating it with an orgasmic look on her face.

Another girl with a pad was trailing behind Ailsa taking notes.

'Thank you so much for showing us around your gorgeous literary café,' said Ailsa into the mike. 'I think we should present you with your prize.' Notepad girl unrolled a huge cheque and thrust it into Leni's hand whilst holding the other end straight. *Leonora Merryman, the sum of five hundred pounds.*

More photos.

'Have you any ideas what you'd like to do with the money?'

'God, give her a chance to get her breath,' mumbled Shaun.

'I, er ... I'll probably give it to the Guide Dog charity,' said Leni, struggling to appear coherent.

'I hear you support them,' said Ailsa. 'You save all the stamps from the postcards that your daughter Anne sends you from her far-flung adventures, I've been told.'

'Yes, that's right,' said Leni, her voice a dry quiet croak.

'This is Ailsa Shaw reporting from the award-winning Teashop on the Corner café on Spring Hill, Barnsley. Back to Roger in the studio.'

Ailsa let loose a relieved 'Whoof. That was brill, folks.' She rubbed Leni's arm. 'Sorry to spring it on you like that, if you'll excuse the pun. I've never seen anyone so shocked. We have a certificate for you as well but I'm going to have to get it altered because some stupid chuff put "the Coffee Shop on the Corner" on it. I'll have it sent on.'

The photographer was packing up his kit and notepad girl was rolling up the cheque.

'This is wipe clean,' she explained. 'We re-use it. I'll give you your real cheque in a minute.'

'Gorge place you have here. Can I take the rest of that slice of cake with me? Haven't had time for any breakfast,' said Ailsa.

'Yes, of course,' replied Leni. Her hands weren't steady as she wrapped it up in a serviette.

'God, you really are knocked for six,' laughed Ailsa watching her.

'Here's your proper cheque,' said notepad girl, putting it on the counter.

'Thank you.'

'Cheers,' said Ailsa, as Leni handed over the cake. 'Check out the supplement on Thursday. You'll be on the cover and take up the whole of the centre.'

The girl with the notepad was tapping her watch.

'We need to go now, Ailsa.'

Ailsa tutted and trilled. 'Deadlines.' And she breezed out of the teashop with the same efficient energy as she had entered it.

'Are you all right?' Carla asked Leni.

'Yes, yes,' Leni forced out a smile. 'It was all such a shock.'

'Oh, wasn't that exciting. I'm so happy for you, Leni,' said Molly. 'You deserve more customers. The Teashop on the Corner is a wonderful place. Everyone should know about it.'

'I nominated you,' said Pavitar, proudly. 'We wanted you to win so much.'

'Thank you, everyone,' said Leni. 'That was so kind of you all.'

And it was too, she knew that. To be held in such affection that these dear people would do this for her. If only they'd known what they'd done.

Pavitar and Molly left soon after that with beaming smiles on their faces. Carla went back to the florist shop after Leni had convinced her that she was fine, but had never had any media attention before and had been stunned by it. Carla bought it. Only Shaun remained certain that there was more to what he had just witnessed than met the eye. He recognised true fear when he saw it. He'd seen too much of it in his life not to.

Chapter 115

Leni opened the door and saw the bump of Ryan sleeping underneath his new quilt cover, Mr Bingley at his feet, both of them snoring softly. With all the events of the day, Leni hadn't rung the authorities, but it didn't matter. They'd come of their own accord soon enough. Ryan apparently knew also that she had been nominated for the award and had wanted to know all the details. Now he was safely asleep, she could drop the act of trying to hold up that rictus smile. She closed the door softly, tears dripping off her long dark brown eyelashes and down her pale cheeks.

It was over. Her little safe world was punctured and her dreams were going to bleed out and taint everything. And the irony was that kindness and affection had been the weapons of her destruction.

Chapter 116

The next day started ordinarily enough. Ryan went off to school happy that he only had three more days of term left and Leni got ready for work. She faced herself in the mirror and wondered how she was going to cancel out all the dark shadows under her eyes that were evidence of little sleep. She applied her mascara and hoped that no one she knew had heard the live transmission yesterday – Trumpet FM was hardly Radio 1, after all. She squeezed her eyes shut and pleaded: *Please, please God – don't take it all away from me. Not yet. I'm not ready.*

She tipped her head back so that the tears threatening to come and ruin her make-up would sink back to their waiting place. No doubt they would be called for soon.

She walked into the tearoom and saw a vision of the photographers and that woman with the notepad, following Pavitar and Molly, pausing by Anne's postcards and she felt physically sick.

She would work in the back and not open up the shop. She couldn't serve anyone with a smile. She didn't have one to give today.

Chapter 117

As promised, Pavitar arrived at Molly's house with three copies of the *Daily Trumpet* early on Thursday morning. They had arranged to read it together and then go over to the teashop with a copy for Leni in case she hadn't seen it.

'What's wrong?' asked Molly, seeing the grim cast of his features as he unfolded his copy.

'Oh Molly,' he said, he looked almost tearful. 'Poor Leni. What have we done?'

*

Shaun went against his own grain and bought a *Daily Trumpet* on the way to work. He never bought that trash, but today he made an exception. He picked up the folded copy on the stand, paid for it, bypassed the lure of the headline about a fantasist and turned straight to the middle colour supplement, but there was no mention of the Teashop on the Corner or Leni. He shook his head, bloody typical. All bells and whistles and no substance. He threw it down on the passenger seat and it was then he fully noticed the front page headline.

MY EX-WIFE, THE SAD FANTASIST

And underneath it was a photograph of Leni, smiling and holding a piece of cake.

*

The recent winner of the Daily Trumpet *Most Welcoming Café in South Yorkshire award was yesterday revealed as a sad fantasist by her ex-husband Rick Merryman.*

'I couldn't believe it when I heard the radio broadcast declaring her the winner and what was going on,' said Mr Merryman, 45. Originally from Bradford, taxi-driver Mr Merryman happened to be transporting a customer to Penistone when he heard the live broadcast on the radio. 'I heard some people talking about all the postcards she had received from our daughter Anne and I nearly crashed. Anne died over a year ago just before she was due to fly out and spend the summer working in Greece after her A-level results.'

Tragically eighteen-year-old Anne Merryman died of SADS, Sudden Arrhythmia Death Syndrome, sometimes referred to as Adult Cot Death.

'We had been divorced for many years. Alas, I hadn't seen my daughter since she was five, but I thought about her every day,' said Mr Merryman. 'Leni refused to accept that she had passed on. She didn't even go to the funeral and has never visited her grave. Leni grew up in care and Anne was her world. Anne's death made her go mental. I thought she'd be in a loony bin by now. She should be if she is writing postcards to herself pretending they are from Anne.'

'I can't read any more,' said Molly. 'Poor darling Leni. We should go and see her, Pavitar, and show our support.'

Pavitar screwed up the newspaper in disgust. 'They

shouldn't report something as tragic as this,' he said. 'I'll drive you, Molly.'

*

Will only nipped out for five minutes to buy a *Daily Trumpet* but by the time he had returned, there were four cars in the Spring Hill car park and two more pulling in behind him.

'What's going on?' he asked Carla.

'I'm hoping it's people visiting the teashop,' replied Carla excitedly, holding out her hands for the newspaper. 'Come on, I'm dying to see it.'

Will wasn't convinced that the *Daily Trumpet* could have that much influence. Something felt wrong. He stared out of the window and watched people getting out of the cars and heading across the square towards Leni's shop.

'There's a news team from TV,' he said to Carla who was frantically flicking through the supplement.

'I can't find it. They haven't put her in.'

'There's two cars with *Daily Trumpet* written all over them. What are they doing back so soon?'

Then Carla saw it. Plastered all over the front page of the main newspaper. She scanned the words and some of them stuck like barbs in her brain. 'Sad fantasist. Ex-wife. Leni. Mental. Anne. Died.'

*

Shaun crossed over to the group of people clustered outside the Teashop on the Corner. He recognised Ailsa, the woman who had been carrying the microphone when they awarded Leni the prize just a couple of days ago. There were two men with cameras, another woman talking into a voice recorder. He had to stop himself from charging at them like a bull and scattering them.

'Is she in?' Ailsa asked Shaun. 'The shop says closed and the door is locked but I'm sure I've seen someone moving about.'

'Wouldn't that indicate that she didn't want to talk to you then?' growled Shaun. 'Haven't you done enough damage?'

'Who are you?' asked a woman, holding a voice recorder out to capture what he said.

'Never you mind who I am, just get lost the lot of you. There's no more stories here. Have some respect for a grieving mother. You've got all you are getting, you bunch of emotional leeches.'

'It's local news and of interest to the public,' said Ailsa, a cocky glint in her young eyes.

Shaun's quiet voice brooked no alternative. 'I said go away and I meant it. Ms Merryman won't be answering your questions today or any other day. It might be in the interests of your crappy little newspaper, but unless you want to find yourself the subject of a harassment order, trust me – you better leave.'

There was something about the man that made Ailsa Shaw back right down. Maybe it was the clipped tone of his Irish accent, or the sub-zero look in his eyes, but she did believe that with him on sentry duty, she wasn't going to get any more of a story. Plus her boss had told her to forget it if there was any trouble. He didn't need any more heat. He was in the process of being sued by a Doctor David Thompson after the *Daily Trumpet* had reported him incorrectly as being a paedophile rather than a paediatrician.

She shrugged confidently so the team with her didn't suspect she was cowed by this man.

'Oh, we've stopped the cheque,' she threw behind her as she walked off on her heels.

'I'm sure Ms Merryman will be absolutely gutted,' Shaun batted back and turned to the others. 'Please go. Leave her in peace.'

Surprisingly they did. He'd expected to have more of a battle, verbally or physically, and he would have given it to them, but they surrendered their interest.

Shaun waited until they had all gone before he knocked on the teashop door.

'Leni, let me in because I don't have a skeleton key on me and I'm likely to break the door down any moment,' he called. 'And you know that I will.'

Through the glass he saw her emerge from the back room and cross slowly to the door. She lifted the catch and he stepped in and the sight of her hunched and red-eyed and so desperately lost wounded him and he knew then why she had slipped past all his defences. She was of his world. She was damaged and broken and still bleeding from the trauma of her daughter's death and a part of him had recognised her distress signal and responded to it. His arms closed around her, crushable and fragrant and shaking and he pressed his lips into her lemon-scented hair and she felt every bit as wonderful as he had imagined.

'Oh Leni, you poor wee thing. What pain you must be in.'

He felt tear drops soak through his shirt.

'What a mess,' she said. 'I'm so sorry. I've lied to you all.'

'Let me just say this. You are the nicest, kindest, gentlest person I have ever met. Your friends adore you, Ryan adores you. Those bastards don't mean a thing.'

Carla and Will appeared in the doorway and saw the big Irishman holding her.

'Oh God, Leni. Don't be upset,' said Carla coming up behind her and stroking her hair. 'You must not worry about anything. It's all tomorrow's chip paper, as my mum used to say.'

Shaun pulled her to arm's length but daren't let go because he thought she might crumble to the floor. He bent down so he could look her straight in the eyes.

'You'll be all right, Leni. We'll all make sure you're all right.'

Then Pavitar and Molly rushed into the teashop and took her out of Shaun's arms and into their own.

*

'I found her,' said Leni, after taking a sip of the tea which Carla had made for her. 'She had her case packed and the passport was on her dressing table and she was leaving for Athens with her friends early that morning. And I went to wake her at four o'clock because they all had a taxi booked for five to take them to the airport, and she was in bed, snuggled in her quilt, her head on the pillow and she was so cold.'

Tears dropped slowly down her cheeks.

'I didn't want to believe she was gone. Rick tried to make me face up to it, but I wouldn't. He said I needed to go to the funeral and I'd accept that she'd ... but I didn't want to. Instead, I wrote postcards to myself and I pretended that she was still alive, doing what she had planned to do before she went to Cambridge. She had her whole life in front of her. She was fit, she was healthy, she looked after herself, she didn't take drugs – there was no reason for her to die. There was no explanation why she didn't wake up. They couldn't find a cause.'

Leni dropped her head and her shoulders started shaking uncontrollably. Molly's eyes drifted to Pavitar, for help, for enlightenment, but he shook his head, unable to think of anything he could say that would be of comfort.

'I think anyone with a heart would understand,' said Carla as Will held her hand.

'I'm sorry,' said Leni. 'I've deceived you.'

'Bollocks,' said Carla. 'I'm sure that none of us are even thinking that. We're concerned about you, not about a wall of bloody postcards.'

'You should go home, Leni,' said Molly softly. 'You aren't in any fit state to be here. Let this whole thing blow over. Horrible people. They're the ones who should be ashamed.'

'I'll drive you,' said Shaun, his voice more gentle than Leni could have thought possible.

'Thank you,' said Leni. 'Thank you all for your friendship.'

Carla smiled at her. 'You have become one of my dearest friends, Leni. I should be thanking you for all the support and kindness you've given me. Sod what narrow-minded ignorant people think. They mean nothing.'

'Go and get your handbag and Mr B,' commanded Shaun as Pavitar, Molly, Will and Carla filed out of the Teashop on the Corner after hugging her and telling her to take care. Leni went into the back room for her bag and coat. She was struggling to put it on when Shaun came up behind her to help. He wanted to wrap her in cotton wool so no one would ever harm her again. He picked up Mr Bingley's cat carrier in one hand and put the other around her shoulder and steered her out to his car, locking up the Teashop on the Corner behind him. Had she always been so small? She seemed to have shrunk in the past twenty-four hours, as if all the joy and smiles had been sucked out of her.

He drove her to the cottage and walked in with her. He noticed the framed certificate on the wall and the scrolled lettering underneath – *Three Years Running*.

'Don't worry about the boy,' he said. 'We'll sort it.'

She had been in care too, he had read in the newspaper. She had buried her sadnesses deep under her smiles whilst he had buried his under work.

'Thank you, Shaun. Thank you for all your kindness.'

She took off her coat and slumped to her sofa. She looked totally drained of everything but pain and shame. He sat down on the chair next to her and took her small hand in his. She was frozen.

'I was in care too,' he said. 'I know what it's like. I understand. I was one of the unlucky ones, never finding a family to settle with.'

'Me neither,' replied Leni.

'Surely not.' He thought of Leni as the young girl she must have been and couldn't believe that a family wouldn't have been blessed to have her.

'I was very different back then. Bit of a handful. I don't think I knew how to love until I had Anne,' she said. 'I wasn't sure I ever had the capacity.'

'You?' he said. 'I find that hard to believe.'

'Learning to love opens you up to all sorts of pain,' she replied. 'But I wouldn't have missed having her for the world.'

Learning to love. Is that what he was doing now? No one had managed to make Shaun McCarthy feel like he was feeling now. It was killing him seeing this woman in front of him suffering so much.

'Shall I stay with you?' he asked.

'I want to be on my own for a bit,' she said, forcing out a tired smile.

He rested his hands on her shoulders and looked unblinkingly into her eyes.

'If any one of those journalists turns up, you ring me straightaway, do you hear?'

'I will,' she said.

He kissed her head. His lips didn't want to leave her.

'Ring me, if you need me,' he said. He would drive past her house later, to check that all was okay. 'Remember, you don't worry about anything. Ryan O'Gowan. I'll sort it. I'll sort everything.'

And he walked slowly and reluctantly out and Leni, with no more tears left inside her, closed her eyes and savoured her memories of Anne. Before she began the process of letting her go.

*

Ryan had bought a newspaper on the way home from school and read it on the bus. When he rushed into Thorn Cottage, Leni was putting his tea on the table. He threw his arms around her waist and squeezed her with all his might.

'I love you. You're like the best mum in the world,' he said.

And that was all he needed to say on the matter.

Chapter 118

There was nothing further mentioned in the newspaper. Leni didn't open up the Teashop on the Corner on Friday morning, but by the afternoon Carla noticed her outside watering the pots of plants. She threw together a bunch of frilly pink flowers and ran over to her.

'I'm not staying, I'm just giving you these and then I'm off,' she said, leaning over and kissing Leni on her cheek as she pushed the blooms into her arms. The card read, 'We love you.'

Shaun saw Carla leave the teashop and he couldn't believe that Leni had opened up. He strode over and in through the door, nearly knocking her flying as she was standing behind it. She was in the process of unpinning the postcards and dropping them into a carrier bag, destined for the bin.

'Sorry,' he said.

She laughed. She was pale and tired looking but she was wearing a smile, even if it wasn't as wide as the one her lips usually carried.

'I'm still alive,' she said.

'How are you feeling?'

'Better than yesterday,' she answered him. 'Trying to

think what to do with Ryan in the holidays, if the authorities let me keep him. I rang them this morning and explained why he was in my care. I can't do anything else, can I?'

'The boy loves you. He won't want to live anywhere else than with you. I'll make sure that happens. Somehow.'

She didn't doubt it for a moment. Shaun McCarthy was ridiculously rude, rough, emotionally scarred, a man of paradoxes and yet she understood him completely. He was treading through life as if it were covered in snow that was disguising deep pits, just as she was. They were going the same way. Forwards, but slowly. Company on the journey would be good.

'Here, let me help you,' he said, reaching the postcards that were too high for her. 'Then you can serve me some of that award-winning cake and coffee.'

'That I didn't get an award for in the end,' added Leni.

'Oh and they stopped your cheque. Doesn't matter anyway, because I noticed they'd made it out to Leonora Merryfield. I'll write you a cheque for the five hundred pounds myself. Bastards,' he snarled. Then, as he smiled down at the face of the loveliest woman in the world, words sister Rose-Maria had once said came again to him as clearly as if she were standing at his shoulder: *we are at our most vulnerable when we trust, but if we cannot trust we cannot find joy or love. Open your heart, Shaun. And give.*

Chapter 119

They began to come three days later. The first postcard had a picture of Leeds Town Hall on the front.

Dear Ms Merryman,
I read your story on the internet and I felt compelled to write to you. My name is Daniel Fellowes and I'm eighteen and will be going to Oxford in September. I'm about to go off to the Greek Islands with friends for the summer to work before I settle down and be a good boy.
 I read your story with much sadness - for you. My mum died two years ago - breast cancer. She would have loved to hear that I had a place at Oxford to read medicine. I intend to become a specialist in breast cancer and crack the code of that bloody awful disease. I would give anything to have written postcards to her to tell her where I was and what I was doing this summer.
 With your permission, I would like to send you a postcard or two - the ones which I am sure

your daughter Anne would have sent to you, and
I hope you receive them with the same joy that
my mother would have.
  Very kindest regards
  Daniel Fellowes.

Leni read it with tears raining down her cheeks. *Of course
you can write to me*, she said. *For your mother, for Anne.* She
pinned it on the empty board by the door where it was
joined, the following day, by three more.

Dear Leonora
I'm on a gap year in Spain. I shall be going to
Durham University to study English next
year. I was orphaned at seven and grew up in
care and I so wish that I could have written
postcards to my parents to tell them that
I'm doing fine.
  I was deeply moved by the story I read on
the internet about you and your daughter. I
cried for you both and decided that I should
brave a postcard to you from here in
Seville, as your lovely Anne might have done.
I don't hope to fill the hole she left in your
heart, but it would be a pleasure for me
and I hope you might enjoy receiving it.
  My best wishes
  Maria Matthews.

Dear Mrs Merryman
May I write to you. My mum passed away . . .

Dear Ms Merryman
I read your story on the internet and it touched my
heart so much because I wish I send postcards to
my mother. She died last year and I miss her so
much . . .

Dear Anne's mum
Please accept this postcard from
someone who wishes you well. I lost my
mother three years ago . . .

A week later there were thirty postcards from all over the
world as Leni's story went viral on the internet. Many more
followed from students who just wanted to send a postcard
to 'Dear Mum' but, for whatever reason, they couldn't.

Anne's wall was full within four weeks.

Epilogue

I

Five weeks later

'Look at this one,' raved Pavitar. 'It's from Venice. If you tilt it, the gondola moves. Ryan, you need to remind Leni to buy more drawing pins. You have only a few left in the box.'

'We need another wall,' grinned Ryan, well aware that another giant pinboard was on order.

'There are some very kind people in the world,' said Molly, lifting the cup of tea to her smiling lips. 'Such lovely postcards from these dear young people.' She was going to Venice herself at the weekend – with Harvey. His final journey. At least in this world.

'I'll send you loads when I'm on a gap year and going around America,' said Ryan, carrying two buttered scones over to Molly and Pavitar's table.

'Oh, and who is going to be paying for all that, I wonder?' laughed Leni, her hands coming to her waist. 'You better get some serious washing up done, my lad.'

'Mr Mac will stump up a bit, I bet,' said Ryan, winking at Leni. He was under no illusion whatsoever that something special was blossoming between the woman he thought of as mum but daren't quite say it to her face yet, and the once-scary Irishman who looked at Leni with the same deep affection that Ryan reserved for his Kindle. And Mr Bingley.

Ryan had had a meeting with social workers and the speech he had delivered to them about how happy he was with Leni was worthy of Rumpole of the Bailey. He cried with relief when they said that he could stay with her, subject to periodic review. But he wasn't afraid that he'd be moved. Mr Mac had said he would stay with Leni, and what Mr Mac said seemed to happen.

'Made the *Daily Trumpet* eat their words, too,' said Molly. Much kinder stories had been written in the *Barnsley Chronicle* and the magazine *Woman's World* and others had followed suit. Leni hadn't enjoyed being interviewed for them, but had been encouraged to do so by her friends, to redress the balance of the *Trumpet*'s cruel reportage. And now she had a wall of wonderful postcards to show off and would soon have another. Local people were even popping in to deliver bags of stamps for the Guide Dog collection and then stayed for tea and bought things from the cabinets. Business was booming.

The teashop door opened and Shaun's head appeared around the edge of it.

'You ready?' he asked.

'As I'll ever be,' said Leni.

'Here you go,' said Carla, leaning over to kiss her cheek before placing the pink and cream flowers in her arms. 'We'll lock up for you and take Ryan home.'

'Time to say goodbye,' nodded Leni and followed Shaun out of the Teashop on the Corner.

II

'Her favourite colours,' said Leni, straightening up after placing the flowers on her daughter's grave. 'She had a thing about pink and cream. Every birthday I used to make her a pink cake with cream icing. She would have eaten the whole thing at one sitting if only I'd let her.'

'Want me to leave you alone for a wee bit?' asked Shaun.

'No.' Leni shook her head. 'I want her to see you. She'd approve, I think.' Anne would be happy that her mother had found a man to love as much as he loved her. They fitted each other exactly, Leni and Shaun. Both damaged creatures, but not quite broken. And they would heal with each other, for each other.

'Well, I'll do my best, Anne, to make your mother happy. You have my promise on that,' said Shaun, directing the words towards the pink-marble headstone.

ANNE MERRYMAN, BELOVED DAUGHTER
AGED 18
ALWAYS LOVING, ALWAYS LOVED

'Goodbye my darling,' said Leni and blew a kiss up into the air. 'Until we meet again.'

She felt Shaun's large hand come around her shoulder and his warmth sink through her coat and into her skin.

Together she and Shaun began to walk back to the car. These two people whom life had kindly nudged together. Against any odds that even Harvey Hoyland would have risked, big Shaun McCarthy's heart had opened and Leni Merryman and her cakes and her stationery and her big ginger cat and the O'Gowan boy who read books had strode in, kicked off their shoes, switched on the light and lit the fire. And he had walked into hers and found home.

It's never too late to have a happy ending

HARVEY HOYLAND

Acknowledgements

Writers couldn't do this job alone – so many people are involved in getting a book into your hands and I would like to say thank you to a whole host of them.

To my family at Simon & Schuster, because that's what you feel like: God (or Ian Chapman as he's better known), Suzanne Baboneau, Clare Hey, Alice Murphy-Pyle, Gill Richardson, Jo Dickinson, Carla Josephson, James Horobin, Nico Poilblanc, Sara-Jade Virtue, Ally Grant and also Rik Ubhi for helping me with Mr Singh's details. Sorry I had to ask daft questions like, 'Are Sikhs allowed to eat chocolate?' Thanks also to Sally Partington for her superb copyediting. I only wish I had her eyes!

To my wonderful agent – and friend – Lizzy Kremer and all at David Higham. You're mint, as my sons would say.

Thanks to Nigel Stoneman – for being simply smashing.

To Karen Brookes, solicitor extraordinaire from Wosskow Brown for her advice.

To Gail Lawrence Evans at Flowers of Distinction for her flowery tips.

To the Literary Gift Company (www.theliterarygiftcompany.com) for giving me lots of inspiration and supplying me with must-have author stationery.

To the press for their fabulous continued support – Andrew Harrod and Steph Daley at the *Barnsley Chronicle*, Jo Davison at the *Sheffield Star*, Liz Smith at *My Weekly*, Natasha Harding at the *Sun*, Sadie Nicholas and the gang at Radio Sheffield.

Special thanks to the girls and manager at WH Smiths in Barnsley and Mike Bowkett at Gardner's for being such great support.

To the people I love most in the world – my mum and dad, Uncle John, Tez, George and Pete without whom I wouldn't have written a single word.

And to Molly and Harvey Clemit who wanted to be immortalised in book form. I only wish you were here to hold this book in your hand, darling Molly. You're so very dearly missed.

And last, but definitely not least, to those wonderful teachers who gave me a love of learning and fun and made me realise I just might catch the stars if I aimed for them: Miss Kate Taylor, Miss Mary Walker, Mrs Sykes, Mr Fewster, Mrs Fairclough, Mrs Crockett, Mrs Stuart, Mr Jerome, Mr Nelson, Mrs Gunsen. You made my schooldays a joy.

**SIMON &
SCHUSTER**

Milly Johnson
A Spring Affair

When Lou Winter picks up a dog-eared magazine in the
dentist's waiting room and spots an article about clearing
clutter, she little realises how it will change her life. What
begins as an earnest spring clean soon spirals out of
control. Before long Lou is hiring skips in which to dump
the copious amounts of junk she never knew she had.

Lou's loved ones grow disgruntled. Why is clearing out
cupboards suddenly more important than making his
breakfast, her husband Phil wonders? The truth is, the
more rubbish Lou lets go of, the more light and air can get
to those painful, closed-up places at the centre of her heart:
the love waiting for a baby she would never have, the
empty space her best friend Deb once occupied, and
the gaping wound left by her husband's affair.

Even lovely Tom Broom, the man who delivers Lou's
skips, starts to grow concerned about his sweetest
customer. But Lou is a woman on a mission, and
not even she knows where it will end . . .

**Paperback ISBN 978-1-84739-282-4
Ebook ISBN 978-1-84739-866-6**

SIMON &
SCHUSTER

Milly Johnson
A Summer Fling

When dynamic Christie blows in like a warm wind to take
over their department, five very different women find
themselves thrown together.

Anna, 39, is reeling from the loss of her fiancé, who ran off with
a much younger woman. Her pride in tatters, these days Anna
finds it difficult to leave the house. So when a handsome,
mysterious stranger takes an interest in her, she's
not sure whether she can learn to trust again.

Then there's Grace, in her fifties, trapped in a loveless marriage
with a man she married because, unable to have children of her own,
she fell in love with his motherless brood. Grace worries that Dawn
is about to make the same mistake: orphaned as a child, engaged
to love-rat Calum, is Dawn more interested in the security
that comes with his tight-knit, boisterous family?

At 28, Raychel is the youngest member of their little gang. And with
a loving husband, Ben, and a cosy little nest for two, she would seem
to be the happiest. But what dark secrets are lurking behind this
perfect facade, that make sweet, pretty Raychel so guarded and
unwilling to open up? Under Christie's warm hand, the girls
soon realise they have some difficult choices to make.

Indeed, none of them quite realised how much they needed the
sense of fun, laughter, and loyalty that abounds when five
women become friends. It's one for all, and all for one!

Paperback ISBN 978-1-84739-283-1
Ebook ISBN 978-1-84983-102-4

**SIMON &
SCHUSTER**

Milly Johnson
An Autumn Crush

*In the heart of the windy season, four friends are about
to get swept off their feet . . .*

Newly single after a bruising divorce, Juliet Miller moves into
a place of her own and advertises for a flatmate, little believing
that, in her mid-thirties, she'll find anyone suitable. Then, just
as she's about to give up hope, along comes self-employed
copywriter Floz, and the two women hit it off straight away.

When Juliet's gentle giant of a twin brother, Guy, meets Floz,
he falls head over heels. But, as hard as he tries to charm her,
his foot seems to be permanently in his mouth. Meanwhile,
Guy's best friend Steve has always had a secret crush on
Juliet – one which could not be more unrequited if it tried . . .

As Floz and Juliet's friendship deepens, and Floz becomes
a part of the Miller family, can Guy turn her affection for them
into something more – into love for him? And what will happen
to Steve's heart when Juliet eventually catches the
eye of Piers – the man of her dreams?

As autumn falls, will love eventually bloom for them all?
Or will the secrets of the past turn the season's gold
to the chill of winter?

**Paperback ISBN 978-1-84983-203-8
Ebook ISBN 978-1-84983-204-5**

SIMON &
SCHUSTER

Milly Johnson
A Winter Flame

When Lou Winter picks up a dog-eared magazine in the
dentist's waiting room and spots an article about clearing
clutter, she little realises how it will change her life. What
begins as an earnest spring clean soon spirals out of
control. Before long Lou is hiring skips in which to dump
the copious amounts of junk she never knew she had.

Lou's loved ones grow disgruntled. Why is clearing out
cupboards suddenly more important than making his
breakfast, her husband Phil wonders? The truth is, the
more rubbish Lou lets go of, the more light and air can get
to those painful, closed-up places at the centre of her heart:
the love waiting for a baby she would never have, the
empty space her best friend Deb once occupied, and
the gaping wound left by her husband's affair.

Even lovely Tom Broom, the man who delivers Lou's
skips, starts to grow concerned about his sweetest
customer. But Lou is a woman on a mission, and
not even she knows where it will end . . .

Paperback ISBN 978-1-84739-282-4
Ebook ISBN 978-1-84739-866-6